Adopted from birth, Pam Weaver trained as a nursery nurse working in children's homes, premature baby units, day nurseries and at one time she was a Hyde Park nanny. A member of West Sussex Writers' Club since 1987, her first novel, *A Mother's Gift* (previously published as *There's Always Tomorrow*) was the winner in the Day for Writers' Novel Opening Competition and was bought by HarperCollins Avon. Pam's novels are set in Worthing during the war and the austerity years which followed. Her inspiration comes from her love of people and their stories and her passion for the town of Worthing. With the sea on one side and the Downs on the other, Worthing has a scattering of small villages within its urban sprawl and in some cases tightknit communities, making it an ideal setting for the modern saga.

THE
LOST
ORPHAN

PAM WEAVER

avon.

Published by AVON
A division of HarperCollins*Publishers*
1 London Bridge Street
London SE1 9GF

www.harpercollins.co.uk

HarperCollins*Publishers*
Macken House,
39/40 Mayor Street Upper,
Dublin 1
D01 C9W8A
Ireland

Paperback Original 2023
1
First published in Great Britain by HarperCollins*Publishers* 2023

A catalogue copy of this book is available from the British Library.

ISBN: 978-0-00-853839-2

Typeset in Sabon by Palimpsest Book Production Limited, Falkirk, Stirlingshire

Printed and bound in UK using 100% Renewable Electricity by CPI Group (UK) Ltd

MIX
Paper | Supporting
responsible forestry
FSC™ C007454

This book is produced from independently certified FSC™ paper to ensure
responsible forest management.

For more information visit: www.harpercollins.co.uk/green

For the members of St Flora's Road home group whose names are hidden between the pages of this book. Happy hunting guys!

December 1941

Amélie Osborne finished wrapping a bandage around the toy rabbit's head and put it beside the breakfast tray and the glass of milk. As a final thought she put a tiny portion of the marmalade sandwich into an egg cup and put it between the rabbit's feet. There, she would encourage Vera to 'feed' the rabbit and at the same time, get the little girl to eat herself. Amélie heard a movement behind her and spun around to see the ward sister staring at her.

'What on earth are you doing?'

Amélie flushed. 'I – I'm sorry. It's for Vera Douglas. Nurse said she hasn't had a mite to eat in days. I thought it might encourage her to have something. The rabbit is supposed to be like her. The bandage, I mean. I did the same sort of thing for my little sister once when she was upset.' Amélie chewed the side of her mouth anxiously. She was babbling. Talking rubbish.

Sister frowned.

Amélie ran her tongue over her lips and swallowed hard. What an idiot she'd been. It had worked for Linnet when they'd been evacuated to Worthing and she was desperate to go home but re-enacting it here on the hospital ward was a stupid, stupid idea. Besides, she wasn't supposed to use her initiative. 'You are not paid to think,' old Sister Patterson had told her when she'd been caught reading a story to Johnny Drake behind the closed screens. 'You're a ward assistant. It's your job to make toast or tea for the patients, clean the floors, wash the lockers and keep everything tidy . . .' she'd said, adding with emphasis, *'that's all.'*

Well, Sister Patterson had retired now and Sister Doughty had taken her place. Everyone said things would change and, to some extent, they had. The first thing Sister Doughty did was to change the rules about visiting. Sister Patterson had the view that having mothers on the ward was disruptive. 'As soon as the mother has to go home,' she declared, 'the child cries and that's bad for their recovery.'

For that reason, Sister Patterson only allowed visiting from two till four on Sunday. It seemed heartless and of course it was. For both mother and child the thought of parting hung over their time together and spoiled the occasion. Amélie would often see a distraught mother sitting on the bench outside, trying to compose herself before she caught the bus home because she'd left her child sobbing and it would be a whole week before they met again. Now the mums were allowed to see their children every day, even if it was the same day as their operation. But poor little Vera had no visitors. Her mother was in hospital with complications while she was having a little baby brother or sister so she wouldn't be coming at all. Vera had an older sister, but allowing an unaccompanied child under sixteen on the ward was against hospital rules. Lonely and miserable, the little girl had lost her appetite.

Putting the rabbit back on the table Amélie picked up the tray.

'No, no,' said Sister Doughty. 'Leave it there. It might work.'

Amélie allowed herself a small smile but then Sister added brusquely, 'But next time, ask me first.'

'Yes, Sister.'

'And after you've cleared up the kitchen, I want you to go to maternity,' said Sister Doughty. 'They're short-handed and need a ward maid.'

Amélie hesitated. 'Sorry Sister but I have the afternoon off. I'm to be a bridesmaid at a wedding. I have permission.'

Sister Doughty pursed her lips. 'You can help them out until one-thirty,' she said sweeping from the room.

Amélie was about to protest that the wedding was at two but what was the use? You spelled ward sister 'g-o-d'.

Twenty minutes later, Amélie was on her way back to the kitchen with the empty plate and glass, leaving Vera cuddling the poor bunny with the sore head. The idea had been a complete success. Vera had eaten all of her breakfast and Bunny's too; it was the first thing she had eaten for two days. And she'd downed the milk in one go.

As she put the dirty dishes in the sink, Amélie sighed. In lots of ways, Vera reminded her of her younger sister. The same big brown eyes, the same pouty mouth and under the huge bandage on Vera's head, Amélie could see the same kind of light blonde hair. It didn't take much to remind her of Linnet and bring back the familiar ache and longing. She could feel her bottom lip beginning to quiver and there was already a lump in her throat. Mireille, their older sister didn't seem to miss Linnet very much but then she hadn't seen her since before the war. Amélie missed her sister more each day.

'Oh Linnet,' she whispered into the void before she dashed off to maternity, 'I wish I knew where you were.'

Chapter 1

Pushing her light brown hair behind her ears then under her cap, the girl in the WAAF uniform took a deep breath and gave the door three sharp knocks. Buffing her shoes on the back of her leg, Mireille Ffox-Webster waited until a querulous voice said, 'Come.' Taking another deep breath, Mireille opened the door and marched smartly into Group Officer Dizzard's office. Standing to attention at the desk, she waited for her commander to finish whatever it was she was writing at her desk.

'76542 Ffox-Webster reporting, ma'am.'

Dizzy still didn't look up. Already wound up, Mireille could feel her sense of panic rising. *Come on, come on . . . If you make me hang around much longer, I'm going to miss the wedding altogether.* She stared at Dizzy-the-Lizard's head, willing her to look up but slowly the realisation dawned. She was doing this on purpose, wasn't she? Her little bit of power. Cow!

When Mireille had arrived at the airfield at Tangmere, Group Officer Dizzard's nickname sounded crass and cruel. She wasn't of the same opinion now. Ursula Dizzard seemed to take a great deal of pleasure in being spiteful and vindictive for no apparent reason. As Officer in Charge she would argue that she was only doing whatever was necessary for the discipline of the girls under her care but everyone knew that she took particular delight in handing out punishments. Every single girl in Mireille's hut had found themselves on jankers for the least misdemeanour. Not standing smartly enough to attention meant a week of cleaning toilets to a mirror shine; an untidy uniform, which was probably nothing more than a slightly dull button, meant having to sweep all around the outside of the Nissen huts, no matter what the weather or the time of day; one leaf fluttering over the concrete path during inspection could mean having to do it all over again. The officer's favourite punishment was tipping everything out of a girl's locker and dumping her stripped bedding on the top of the pile. After that, the victim would have to spend the next hour or so folding everything in neat piles and remaking her bed which was exactly what had happened to Mireille this morning.

Despite it being the beginning of December and the inadequate heating in their hut, Mireille had woken with a warm glow of pleasure. The weather outside was cold but it was one of those crisp winter mornings when the sun left a milky haze over the countryside, a day when you could almost forget there was a war on. With a forty-eight-hour pass, her overnight bag was packed but Mireille had come back from breakfast in the canteen to find a huge heap on the floor. It almost broke her heart. *Please . . . not today of all days . . .* It would take at least an hour to put everything back and then she would have to find Dizzy to ask her to inspect her things once more. Until all that was done, she was not allowed to begin her leave.

Mireille shifted her weight from one foot to the other. The only sound in the room was the high-pitched scratch, scratchy, scratch of the officer's fountain pen as she wrote.

Everybody had hoped the war would be over by Christmas but it was still raging more than two years later. The people of Britain had gone through the phoney war, so called because nothing happened, the Battle of Britain and now the Blitz. Since the summer, the war had become global and now British troops were fighting in far flung places nobody had ever heard of such as Tobruk in North Africa and the Western deserts of Egypt and Libya. On the home front, women were being called up for war work in unprecedented numbers. The response had been amazing. Housewives had joined volunteer groups while single women who had done little more than shop work and hair-dressing, had become mechanics, munition workers and drivers of ambulances and fire engines. Mireille had joined the WAAFs. She had done her training at No.2 WAAF Depot in Gloucester and then spent a brief period at Bishopbriggs, near Glasgow where she was part of the No. 18 Balloon Centre. With a wage of seven shillings a week, she was part of a team mending frayed ropes on the massive barrage balloons and sometimes the balloons themselves. Once repaired, they were hung in built up areas to stop enemy planes from flying low enough to drop their bombs. Tangmere was her first proper posting. It was quite good as postings go but she could have done without the likes of Dizzy-the-Lizard.

Still waiting for Dizzy to acknowledge her, Mireille glanced up at the clock. She had planned to travel back to Worthing the night before but as a favour, she had stood in for a girl who was desperate to see her fiancé who had been rushed to hospital after an accident. Iris was beside herself with worry. When she'd begged Mireille to swap duties, Ginger, one of the lads on the base, said he had to drive over to RAF Durrington with a message in the morning so he could give her a lift as far as the gate. 'Coming back the next day too, if that's any help,' he'd said cheerfully.

As Durrington was only a mile or so from Clifton Road in Worthing, everything would work out well and she could catch the bus from there.

The Lizard looked up. Her eyes were wide apart and the bridge of her nose was slightly flat which, along with her surname, had given rise to her nickname.

Mireille was so tense with anger she almost expected a long forked tongue to emerge from her lips. 'Reporting for inspection, ma'am.'

The Lizard let out an impatient sigh. 'I hope your bed is made properly now, Ffox-Webster,' she said sharply. 'Can't have you toffs thinking any old thing will do. No maids to tidy up behind you in the RAF you know.'

Mireille bristled. That remark was grossly unfair. For a start she was no toff. Her double-barrelled name had come from her step-father and given the choice, she would have kept her mother's name of Osborne had she not been given the impression by Jago Ffox-Webster that when he had married their mother, he had also adopted her and her two younger sisters.

The Lizard came around the desk and sailed past her out of the office. Mireille followed. By the time they reached the Nissen hut where Mireille was billeted with five other girls, she was a bag of nerves. The room looked perfect. While Mireille stood smartly to attention, the Lizard opened her locker and surveyed her neatly folded belongings. Then she ran her hand along the bed, paying special attention to the knife edged corners of the blanket and the folded back sheet. It looked perfect but there was one heart jarring moment when Mireille saw her tug at the edge of the bottom sheet by the pillow. At the same time, Dizzy sucked in her lips over her teeth. It wasn't unknown for the Officer in Charge to pull everything apart a second time, leaving the poor girl to remake her bed and tidy her space once again. Mireille took in a silent breath. If Dizzy stripped her bed again, there was no way she would make it to Rene's wedding. Ginger was probably long gone by now so timing was tight if she had to resort to catching the train from Chichester.

Officer Dizzard hesitated then, leaning over the edge of the bed, she pulled out Mireille's overnight bag. 'What's this doing here?' she said coldly.

'My bag, ma'am,' said Mireille. 'I have a forty-eight-hour pass which began at eight last night.'

The Lizard arched an eyebrow as if she had no idea.

'I'm going to a wedding.'

The Lizard made no comment. Mireille was dying to say more but she didn't dare trust herself. The woman knew about it anyway. She'd signed the paperwork herself. Turning back, she pulled the bottom sheet away from the bed. Now Mireille was wrestling with murderous intent. She was doing this on purpose. Tormenting her. Was she going to strip the whole bed and pull everything out of the locker again? A tear smarted her eye. The cow! The bitch. The bloody bitch!

The officer spoke with her back turned. 'Come closer, Ffox-Webster,' she said as she stretched the sheet then folded it back over the bed before tucking it under the mattress. 'You do your corners like this.'

'Yes ma'am,' said Mireille, her voice controlled despite the rage she felt inside.

The Lizard turned and faced her. 'Well, hurry up girl,' she said. 'You'd better get a move on if you want to get to that wedding.'

Mireille picked up her bag and headed for the door . . . not too quickly or the Lizard might call her back, but once outside the hut, she ran like the wind.

Just as she'd feared, Ginger was gone but when she arrived at the gate, Sergeant Berry pulled up in a jeep and offered her a lift. Mireille hesitated. Normally she wouldn't go near Berry with a bargepole. He had a terrible reputation which she had discovered for herself at the mess dance. He was far too free with his hands.

'I'm going as far as Ford,' he told her. 'Any help?'

'Thanks,' she said. 'I can catch a train from there but I can't hang about. I'm to be a bridesmaid at my aunt's wedding.'

'What time?' he asked.

'Twelve-thirty,' she lied coolly.

Actually, the wedding was at two o'clock but if she told Berry that, he'd want to stop along the way.

'Hop in then.'

The journey turned out to be much as expected. Every time he changed gear, she could feel his little finger running up her leg no matter how close she sat to the outer edge of her seat. He made small talk and asked her what time she was coming back to base but Mireille tried to keep everything as vague as possible. As they drew close to Ford station his attitude changed from smarmy to irritated.

'You still a virgin then?'

If only you knew, she thought but turning her head away from him to look over her left shoulder, she ignored his remark.

'I won't bite, you know,' he went on. 'We can take all the time you like.'

'The flowers are here.'

Norah Kirkwood let go of the bridal gown and it slipped effortlessly over her sister Rene's shoulders and down her body. Behind them, they heard Norah's mother-in-law,

Christine, gasp in appreciation. 'Oh Rene, love, you look as pretty as a picture.'

At the same time, Norah and Rene's mother, Elsie Carson, put her hand over her own mouth to suppress a small sob. 'Oh Rene . . .'

'Come on now, Mum,' Norah said teasingly. 'This is no time for tears.'

'You look so lovely,' Elsie said, her voice tight with emotion.

Rene smiled as she twisted and turned in front of the mirror.

Someone called 'Coo-ee,' by the back door and everybody except Norah froze anxiously. 'That'll be the florist with the bouquet,' she said.

'I'll go,' said Elsie and a moment later they heard the muffled sound of voices.

Rene arched her back and laid her hand across her completely flat tummy to admire her own reflection. 'This should make those nosey old biddies sit up and take notice,' she said. 'No sign of a baby there!'

'Take no notice of them,' said Norah. 'If they've got nothing better to do . . .' She checked herself before she spoiled the moment.

Elsie appeared in the doorway and held up the bridal bouquet.

'Oh Mum,' cried Rene, 'It's beautiful.'

It was too. Made up of hellebores, carnations and camellias, it might not have been as lavish as bouquets had been before the war when more materials were available but the florist had put her skills to good use with the flowers Norah had been nurturing in the lean-to by the kitchen.

It was twelve-thirty and the wedding was at two. It would take half an hour to walk to St Matthew's and considering it was a nice day, it went without saying that friends and neighbours would gather on the pavement or lean over their gates to wish Rene good luck.

Norah made her sister sit down so that she could take her curlers out. Unlike her own wildly curly hair, Rene's was straight. The plan was to pile it on top like the film star Betty Grable and thread some carnations in between the curls. After that, all Rene would need was a little make-up. Thankfully there was no need to put beetroot water on her lips today. Penny Draycot, now Penny Andrews, Norah's friend, had loaned her a lipstick called Red Velvet, a plush colour which suited Rene perfectly.

Norah hadn't been too keen to take Penny up on her offer at first. Her husband had been a POW since Dunkirk. Penny missed him dreadfully but she was gaining a reputation because she was a little too pally with some of the Canadians billeted in the town, one in particular. She and Norah had had words about it, not because Norah was being nasty, but because she knew how toxic gossip could be. However, when Penny heard about Rene's wedding, she had offered the lipstick by way of an olive branch so of course, Norah couldn't say no.

They heard a bump, the sound of a bicycle being leaned against the wall outside the kitchen and Amélie, Mireille's sister, back from the hospital where she was working as a ward orderly, called, 'Hello.' Special time off was as rare as hen's teeth but she'd managed to get a half day for the wedding, albeit grudgingly, from the ward sister. Looking hot and flushed, she hurried through the kitchen and into the bathroom, barely stopping long enough to tell the bride-to-be that she looked amazing.

Norah's husband, Jim, came back with the dogs and there was a moment of panic when everyone was afraid that Max and Sausage might jump up on Rene's dress before he had time to shut them away in the room downstairs. It had been suggested that they might spend the day at Norah's parents' house but it seemed unfair to leave them on their own for so long. In the end it was agreed that so long as they were kept away from the food, they could be let out when everybody came back from the service.

Rene glanced up at the clock anxiously. 'Mireille's late,' she remarked. 'I do hope nothing's happened.'

At Ford station, Mireille had to wait for twenty-five minutes for the train; twenty-five very long and anxious minutes. Thankfully, by the time she'd arrived at the ticket office, Sergeant Berry was keen to be at the aerodrome so he'd driven away pretty smartly. Mireille glanced up at the station clock. If all went well, she would make it but there would be no time to change into something pretty. Disappointed, she sighed. It wasn't unusual for women to wear their uniform to a wedding but given the opportunity, no girl wanted to pass up the chance of wearing something a little more feminine.

By the time Amélie came out of the bathroom, Elsie had made a fresh pot of tea.

'Your dress is hanging upstairs on the back of the bedroom door,' Norah said.

'I suggest you get dressed *after* you've had a cuppa,' Elsie suggested.

Amélie nodded and sat next to Rene.

'You look like the cat that got the cream,' Elsie remarked as she noted Amélie's smile.

'I held my first newborn baby today,' she said, releasing her light brown hair from the elastic band and letting it fall to her shoulders. 'I wasn't supposed to but the mother was fainting and Sister shoved him in my arms as she went to catch her before she fell off the bed.'

Norah smiled. 'Lucky you. Was the mother all right?'

Amélie nodded dreamily.

Norah patted Rene's hair for the last time. 'There. All done.'

As the women in the room clucked their approval, the two sisters gave each other a gentle hug. 'Thanks Norah,' Rene said.

Amélie hardly noticed them. She sipped her tea with a faraway smile. Her face always lit up as she talked about her experiences on the ward. She was only supposed to be a ward orderly in the hospital, but sometimes, like today, there was magic in the air. The fact that some of the ward sisters were real tartars didn't faze her in the slightest. She wanted to be a nurse. She had always wanted to be a nurse. She was determined to be a nurse. Jim used to joke that if they chopped her in half, the word 'nurse' would be wrapped around her insides like the inside of a stick of Worthing rock.

Today, Amélie and Mireille were to be bridesmaids for this wedding, Amélie in pale pink and her sister in blue. The pink dress had come from a jumble sale, a true 'make do and mend'. Once an over-blown party dress in a much larger size, Diana Marshall from the corner shop had skilfully removed all the frilly bits and changed it into a rather chic bridesmaid dress. The blue dress had been made from scratch with material from the market. It wasn't exactly the same pattern as the pink one but they complemented each other beautifully. Both girls would have a corsage.

Suddenly aware of her surroundings, Amélie glanced at the clock. 'What time is my sister coming?'

'She should have been here half an hour ago,' said Norah

as she patted her own hair in front of the mirror. She sighed. Whatever the occasion, Norah's hair always looked the same – like a bush. 'I hope she gets here soon or there won't be time to change.'

'There's probably some flap on,' Rene said matter-of-factly.

Mireille's journey to Worthing central was uneventful and took its usual twenty-two minutes although strangely enough, despite the fact that she was going back to the Lilacs for such a joyous occasion, she felt a little subdued. It would be lovely to see Norah and Jim again, and it felt wonderful to be included, but these gatherings only heightened the fact that she and Amélie were a fractured family. Their parents were dead and nothing could be done about that, but their younger sister Linnet was missing. Not missing in the sense that her life was in danger, but the two girls had no idea where she was or who was looking after her. As the older girl, it was probably down to her to try and find out where Linnet had been billeted, but where to start? Mireille shook herself. She had to stop thinking about this. That all too familiar ache was forming in her chest and what good did crying do? She sighed. This blasted war had caused more casualties than simply the physically wounded.

Once she arrived at the station, Mireille knew there was no time to go to the house and change so she headed straight for St Matthew's church and as luck would have it, she met up with the wedding party already on its way to the service.

'Mireille!' cried Rene, her bridal train looped over her arm. 'You made it. We were getting worried.'

'I'm so sorry I'm late.'

'Don't worry. You're here now.'

The two of them hugged and kissed each other and while Jim took charge of her overnight bag, Norah stuffed a corsage through Mireille's uniform lapel.

When they reached St Matthew's, Mireille glanced around as she stood in the church porch. They were all there. The people she loved most in the world. She and her sister Amélie weren't related to them in any way but they were family. Amélie and their younger sister, Linnet, had arrived with the evacuees in Worthing three years ago. The following year, 1940, Norah and Jim found Mireille and offered her a home as well. Sadly, their step-father refused to allow Linnet to stay which was why nobody knew where she was. Norah's parents, Elsie and Pete Carson had joined them in Worthing after being bombed out during the Blitz and Christine, Jim's mother, had just embarked on her second marriage to Ivan Steele. Both had been widowed but they had known each other since their school days.

Rene looked as lovely as a film star. Her dress, a shimmering creamy white, clung to her slim and pretty figure. Elsie Carson slipped inside the church with Christine and Ivan while Norah arranged the bride's train. As Mireille heard the organist strike up 'Here Comes the Bride', Amélie handed Rene the bouquet and taking her father's arm, the bride walked ahead of the two sisters. At the other end of the aisle, the bridegroom, Dan, and his best man rose to their feet and a precious moment of joyful happiness in the middle of the horrors of war began.

It was after eight o'clock before the last of the wedding guests had gone home. Most wanted to get back before the blackout or else they had to report back to their units by ten and needed plenty to time to get there. Public transport wasn't always reliable and a serving airman could easily be delayed by other troop movements – something which the guards on the gate didn't take into consideration if he was late.

Mireille and Amélie joined Norah in the kitchen at the Lilacs to help with the clearing up. Any leftovers were carefully stored either in the meat safe or the pantry which had a flag-stone floor that kept the atmosphere permanently cold. There wasn't a lot left anyway. To encourage everyone to enjoy themselves, Norah had joked that they should eat up or Jim would be forced to eat egg sandwiches until Christmas. Not that there was any real chance of that. Norah, Elsie and Christine had everything down to a 'T'. They had to. The wedding cake, such as it was, was cleverly decorated. Instead of white icing, Elsie had put rice paper around the top. Almond icing was still allowed although quite a few peanuts had found their way into the packet. Norah put the remains of the cake into a tin. When she got back from honeymoon, Rene could take the rest of it with her to her new home and decide what to do with it. Rationing made celebrations quite challenging and Christmas was just around the corner.

'There's a letter for you on the dresser,' Norah told Mireille as she wiped down the draining board. 'It looks official.'

Amélie had made a pot of tea so Mireille brought the letter with her into the sitting room. Jim and Ivan were already there glued to the radio. Elsie and Pete Carson, Norah's parents, had returned to Queens Street and the happy couple were honeymooning for two nights in Brighton.

As Amélie hovered over the table with the tray, Jim slammed his hand, palm down in the middle. 'They're in, Norah,' he cried.

'Who's in?' Norah said irritably. 'Jim, move your newspaper, will you? The girl can't put the tea tray down. And please turn that radio off. I'm sick to death of all that doom and gloom.'

'Sorry, sorry,' Jim murmured as he scrambled to clear a space.

Norah arranged the cups into saucers and began to pour the tea. 'Where's Christine?'

'Gone to fetch her slippers,' said Ivan.

'Didn't you hear what I said?' Jim complained. 'The Yanks have come into the war.'

'After Sunday's devastation of Pearl Harbor that's hardly surprising,' said Amélie.

'I thought I heard someone say they declared war on Japan the day after,' said Norah handing Ivan a cup of tea.

'They did,' said Christine, coming through the door.

'You don't understand,' Jim said, exasperated. He began to spell it out for them in a school-teacher voice. 'Japan is allied to Germany, so the Germans have declared war on America and America has declared war on Germany! We're all in it together now.'

There was a note of excitement in his voice. He didn't seem to notice the sombre atmosphere he'd created.

'So what you're saying is that the whole bloody world is at war now,' said Christine, slumping into her chair.

'Johnny come lately,' murmured Ivan. 'They turned up late last time.'

'Surely that means it'll be over a lot quicker now,' Amélie suggested, but it was obvious from the looks on their faces that nobody was convinced.

Mireille looked up from her letter. 'Well at least I've got one bit of good news,' she said lamely. 'This is from the National Registration Office. They say my name *is* Osborne and that my step-father never did adopt us. They've sent my new identity card at last.'

Everyone was thrilled. When Norah and Jim met Jago

18

Ffox-Webster, he was annoyed that the girls had reverted back to their French names. Although their mother was French, Jago had wanted his step-children to appear one hundred percent English. It wasn't until Amélie's identity card came back from boarding school that a question mark was raised about her surname. The card was registered in the name of Osborne, her natural father, and yet her older sister was registered as Mireille Ffox-Webster. From the moment she came to live with Jim and Norah, Mireille had been determined to jettison the name of the man she hated. In fact, she hated him so much that at one time there had even been some discussion around the idea that Norah and Jim might adopt the sisters so that they would be called Kirkwood rather than Ffox-Webster.

Norah gave Mireille a hug. The pair of them had spent a lot of time trying to find out the truth of the matter and now at last it seemed that the problem was resolved. Both girls would keep their birth surname of Osborne. Adoption was no longer necessary, although for official purposes Jim and Norah would be known as next-of-kin.

'What about Linnet?' Amélie asked. 'Did he adopt her?'

Mireille shook her head. 'Apparently not,' she said. Their younger sister was never far from their thoughts. Amélie hadn't seen her since Jago had sent them both to boarding school and it had been nearly six years since Mireille had clapped eyes on her. She sighed. 'I really dread the thought that he might turn up again.'

'We might be safe,' said Amélie, 'but Linnet is still a minor. He could come for her as soon as he gets out of prison.'

Norah was packing the used cups onto the tray to take them back out into the kitchen. 'Well he can't, can he?' she said absentmindedly. 'He's dead.'

When she looked up, everyone was staring at her in a stunned silence.

Chapter 2

'What do you mean, he's dead? When did he die?' Mireille's tone was measured but it was obvious that she was annoyed.

Norah hesitated, dropping her gaze at the same time. 'I didn't want to upset you,' she said lamely as she put another dirty cup onto the tray.

'Why would I be upset?' Mireille retorted. 'You knew how much I hated him.'

Norah looked over Mireille's shoulder to Jim standing behind her. He was bringing his empty cup to the tray she had just picked up to take to the kitchen. Mireille spun her head. 'Did you know about this?' she demanded.

Jim shook his head and raised a hand.

'Leave Jim out of it,' said Norah. 'He doesn't know anything. I didn't tell another living soul.'

Amélie leaned forward in her chair. 'So how long have you known he was dead, Auntie Norah?' she said softly.

'Two men came from London a couple of days after he was . . .' Norah hesitated again. 'After he died.'

'Two men?' said Christine. She turned to her husband. 'I don't remember two men, do you Ivan?' And looking back at Norah again she added, 'When was this?'

Norah felt suddenly cornered. 'Last January,' she said, turning to leave the room.

'January!' Mireille squeaked. 'So you've known about this for almost a year, and you've never thought to mention it?'

'I'm sorry,' said Norah.

'Well I think you bloody well ought to say something now,' Mireille snapped.

Norah stopped in her tracks and blinked at her. Mireille had never spoken to her like that before. Her mind was in a whirl. She'd never wanted the truth to come out this way. She'd planned a quiet talk perhaps when Amélie was twenty-one and certainly in a more convivial setting. Right now, everyone was tired after the wedding and it was obvious that Mireille already had a very short fuse.

'How come these men never spoke to the girls?' Christine chipped in. 'After all, he was *their* step-father.'

'I don't see any point in talking about it,' Norah said defensively. 'What's done is done. It won't change anything and I didn't want you girls upset any more than you already were.'

'Look Norah,' Mireille said tightly, 'I'm grateful for all that you've done for us, but that doesn't give you the right to treat us like children. I'm twenty years old for God's sake!'

'I don't understand why you're so angry with me,' Norah complained. 'I was only trying to help.'

Amélie rose from her chair and stood next to her sister. 'Auntie Norah, I know you mean well,' she said quietly. 'but whatever happened, we have a right to know. You must tell us. Please.'

'I think you'd better do as she says, Luv,' Jim said gently.

Norah put the tray back on the table and lowered herself into her chair. 'One of them was Detective Inspector

Havelock,' she said. She glanced at her husband. 'He was the man who questioned me the night Ffox-Webster got me arrested. The other one was called Rupert Bromley.'

'You mean the night you went to London to try and talk to Ffox-Webster about my suspension?' Jim asked.

Norah nodded. Her hands were trembling. She looked up at him helplessly. 'I only wanted to plead with him to call the dogs off, Jim. You love being a copper and it seemed so unfair that you were being suspended over something you didn't do.'

Jim squeezed her shoulder. 'Go on, Luv.'

'It just so happened that as I was about to ring Ffox-Webster's doorbell,' Norah continued, 'that the police came out with him in handcuffs. I just stood there like a lemon while they bundled him into the car. I don't know what he told them but the next minute, the car drove off and they arrested me.'

'You're not saying they turned up here to arrest you again, are you?' said Christine.

Norah turned to her mother-in-law and shook her head. 'No, they came to tell me that Ffox-Webster was dead.'

Amélie frowned. 'But I thought he was in prison awaiting trial.'

'So there must have already been a court case,' said Ivan, 'but I don't remember reading anything about him in my paper.'

'He did have a trial,' Norah admitted, 'but it was what they call *in camera*.'

'What does that mean?' Christine said.

'It means that it was held in secret, Mother,' Jim murmured.

'But why?'

Norah shrugged.

'And he died in prison?' Christine asked.

Norah sucked in her lips.

'What?' said Mireille.

'He was found guilty of being a traitor,' Norah said cautiously, 'and he was hung.'

The room had gone very quiet.

'Dear God,' said Christine, as she put her hand over her mouth.

'So that's that then,' Mireille said bitterly. 'What about Linnet? Did he say anything about our sister?'

Norah rose eagerly. 'He did send something . . . well, DI Havelock did really.' She turned to leave the room. 'Wait here. I'll get it for you.'

She took the stairs two at a time but when she reached the drawer where she'd hidden the letter, Norah hesitated again. She pulled the envelope from beneath her underwear and lifted the flap. There were four things inside: two rings belonging to the girls' mother, a newspaper cutting and the letter written by Ffox-Webster himself on the eve of his execution. With a trembling hand, Norah unfolded the pages and re-read the traitor's last message. Several words leapt off the page. *'I have no regrets . . .' 'The girls were charming. I enjoyed my time with them . . .' 'you shall not have Lillian . . .'*

With a cry of contempt, Norah screwed up the letter and threw it in the wastepaper basket.

'What are you doing?'

Norah jumped. She hadn't realised Jim had followed her upstairs to the bedroom. As she turned towards him, her face heated with embarrassment. 'Nothing, nothing.'

Her husband strode to the bin and bent to pick up the letter.

'No Jim,' she cried desperately. 'Don't, please don't. It's horrible. I should have destroyed it long ago.'

Jim shook his head. 'Whatever it says, it's not yours to destroy, darling. Those girls have a right to know.'

Norah's eyes were filling with tears. 'But he was a monster,' she choked. 'You know he was.'

'That's as it may be,' Jim said gently, 'but right now they won't settle for anything other than the truth. Whatever he's written, you can't keep it from them any longer.' He bent his head and kissed her cheek. 'I know you meant well, but no more secrets, okay?'

'But it will destroy them,' she said, her voice choking.

'Those girls are tougher than you think,' he said.

When they entered the sitting room once more, every eye was on Norah's hand and the envelope. 'I have a confession to make,' she began. 'Your step-father was hung. The truth of the matter is he was a spy. They actually saw him passing secrets to the Germans. That was one of the reasons why he came down here to Worthing. He thought he was meeting a contact but the man turned out to be someone from MI5.'

Mireille scowled and Amélie stared at her open-mouthed.

'The day they came,' Norah continued, 'Havelock and Bromley gave me this. And before you get cross again, it was addressed to *me*.' She turned to look directly at Mireille. 'I couldn't bring myself to open it for almost a week. I just couldn't.' She tipped the envelope up. 'He'd put your mother's rings in it,' she said, letting them roll onto the table.

Amélie picked up the engagement ring and held it to admire the opal and diamonds. Mireille looked at them but made no move to touch them. She searched Norah's face, her expression angry and dark.

'He wrote a letter,' Norah began again.

'Our letter,' Mireille said in a harsh tone.

'No,' said Norah. 'Like I told you, he wrote to me. It was horrible. That's why I didn't want to show you. Now I wish that I'd put it straight onto the fire.'

She held it towards Mireille who stiffened, but didn't take it.

'Do you want someone to read it out?' asked Jim.

Mireille nodded.

'I'll do it,' said Christine reaching for her reading glasses. There was a short pause then she said, '*Dear Mrs Kirkwood, By the time you read this I shall be dead. I have no regrets for what I have done. I sincerely believe that—*'

Christine looked up with a puzzled expression. 'Some of the words have been crossed out.'

'It's been censored,' said Norah.

Her mother-in-law took a deep breath and began again. '*When I married Natalie Osborne it was for one reason and one reason only. The cause.*'

'Bloody Nazi,' Ivan murmured.

'*Her money and her position helped us enormously,*' Christine continued, '*but she was expendable.*'

Amélie began to cry softly.

'Do you want me to go on?' Christine asked anxiously.

'Yes, yes,' said Mireille her eyes blazing with anger and her expression hard.

Christine looked down at the page again. '*The girls were charming. I enjoyed my time with them very much and I have some delicious memories.*'

Norah turned away and blew her nose.

'*You meant well,*' Christine continued, her voice tight, '*I can see that now, but I shall not allow you to have my little Lillian. You can rest assured that she is perfectly safe but far out of your reach. I give you no forwarding address. Lillian is an obedient child so she will not be contacting you or her sisters. She has been told they both died in an air raid in London. I think it better if she has a clean break and a completely new start in life.*'

Christine looked up. 'And it's signed Jago Ffox-Webster.'

'I'm so sorry,' Norah said helplessly. 'I didn't mean to . . .'

'What's that other bit of paper?' Mireille said coldly.

'A newspaper cutting,' said Norah. 'I've thought a lot about it. I don't think Ffox-Webster put it with the letter. The edges have been cut with sharp scissors and I don't imagine he would have been allowed to have scissors in the condemned cell. I get the feeling that it was DI Havelock who put it in the envelope.'

Mireille snatched it from her. It was an advertisement.

'Parents. Are you worried about the safety of your children? Why not consider sending them to the safety of the British dominions, with guaranteed safe passage to Canada, South Africa and Australia, and escorts arranged for the voyage. Once there, your child will be placed in a respectable family with impeccable references. With the chance to be educated in the very best schools, this is an opportunity not to be missed.'

Mireille handed the cutting to Amélie.

'I think Havelock was trying to let us know that your sister has been sent abroad for the duration,' said Norah, doing her best to appease them.

'So you've known the whereabouts of our sister all this time and you've never once thought to tell us?' Mireille spat.

'No,' cried Norah. 'I have no idea where she is. It's just an educated guess.'

'You should have told us, Auntie Norah,' said Amélie, dabbing her eyes.

'I know. I realise that now,' said Norah. 'I was just trying to protect you.'

Mireille threw her hands into the air and let out an exasperated gasp.

'I'm sure Norah meant it for the best,' said Christine.

'But it was not her decision to make!' cried Mireille as

she rounded on her. 'Linnet is *our* sister. She's nothing to do with you. Any of you!'

'Let's all try to stay calm, shall we?' Jim said.

'I don't want to be calm,' Mireille shouted. 'You just heard it read out to you! That man used my poor mother. I've got nothing of hers; nothing.' She was crying hot and angry tears now. 'And after he'd finished with her . . .' Her voice trailed and she choked back a sob. Norah reached out her hand to comfort her but Mireille batted it away.

'And now we find out that he's lied to our younger sister. He's told her we're dead and he's sent her to God knows where. And you say be calm? What's there to be calm about? Go on, Jim,' she cried rounding on him, 'You tell me!'

Norah reached for the rings but Mireille got there first. Grabbing them up, she flung them across the room. 'And you can keep those,' she cried angrily. 'They may be my mother's but *he* put them on her finger and I want nothing that man touched. Do you hear me? Nothing!' And with that she flounced out of the room, slamming the door so loudly that the dogs sat up and barked.

Norah looked around the room helplessly. What a terrible end to a lovely day. Amélie was sobbing in Christine's arms, and the old lady herself had tears on her cheeks. Ivan sat staring into the fire with a blank expression. Jim picked up the rings and laid them on the table.

'Oh Jim,' Norah blurted out, her voice thick with emotion. 'I'm sorry. I never meant for this . . .'

But her husband couldn't look at her. He was shaking his head in disbelief. Unable to bear it, Norah let out a sob and made a dash for her bedroom.

Chapter 3

Norah woke up with a splitting headache. As soon as she'd washed and dressed, she reached for a glass of water and a couple of Aspros. It was quiet in the kitchen. She let the dogs out and tucked her untidy hair under a turban. It wasn't very pleasant looking at her reflection in her mirror in the bathroom. She had dark circles under her eyes and her complexion was sallow. At first glance she looked ten years older than she was. She sighed miserably. What an awful end to what had been a lovely day.

She couldn't stop thinking about that ghastly moment when Christine had read Ffox-Webster's letter aloud. *'The girls were charming. I enjoyed my time with them . . .'* She could almost hear his smarmy voice as the words swirled round and round in her head. How that must have hurt them and he was still controlling them even from the grave. *'You shall not have Lillian . . .'*

When they spoke about her, the girls preferred to use their sister's French name rather than the English name picked out for her by Jago. Norah could only imagine how devastated they were feeling right now. There was no guarantee that they would ever manage to trace Linnet, leaving a very real possibility that three sisters might never ever meet again. And even if they did begin a search, where on earth would they start? There were so many obstacles in the way, not to mention the war itself and the huge distances between Britain and her dominions. All this was compounded by their change of name and the fact that Linnet had been told that her sisters had been killed in an air raid. How cruel to give the poor child such grief.

Norah made herself a cup of tea and sat at the table with her head in her hands. Everyone else was still asleep (it was only twenty past six) but it wouldn't be long before they were up. What should she do? What *could* she do? Being a fixer, she tried to work out how she could repair the relationship between them all. Amélie had found comfort in Christine's arms but Mireille was simply too angry. Mireille had shut herself in her bedroom and refused to answer the door no matter how many times Norah had knocked. Perhaps after sleeping on it, she might be more amenable but there wasn't a lot Norah could do except perhaps apologise again and hope that the girl would accept her olive branch.

She heard a movement. Jim was standing in the doorway. 'You all right, Luv?'

Norah nodded dully.

'I'm just off to the bathroom,' he said.

She frowned. 'I thought you weren't going in until later.'

'No such luck. Earlies today,' he said. 'Seven o'clock start and I'm already late.'

'Oh Jim, I'm sorry. I don't know what I was thinking of.' She reached for the frying pan. 'It won't take me a minute to get you some breakfast.'

'Don't worry, Luv,' he said. 'I'll get something in the canteen. If I'm lucky Ma might even rustle me up a fried

29

egg sandwich.' Ma was the nickname the men had given to the cook in the police canteen.

'Are you sure?' said Norah.

'Well, a dried egg sandwich more like,' he quipped. 'And you stop worrying.' He leaned over and kissed her forehead. 'It'll be all right. Just give them time.'

Norah swallowed the lump forming in her throat. ''Course,' she said but without conviction.

As soon as Jim had set off on his bike, Norah let out a long sad sigh and sat down again with the fresh pot of tea she'd made for him when he'd come out of the bathroom. What a fool she had been to keep that damned letter. Given the choice, she wished she'd had the opportunity to plan what she was going to say before telling Mireille and Amélie about Linnet. She could have softened the blow and she certainly would never have shown them that letter. On the other hand, Mireille was right. Being that much older, she should have been told straight away but even as the thought crossed her mind, Norah knew she would have moved heaven and earth to protect her from Ffox-Webster's cruel and venomous words. It was going to take a while before their relationship was back to normal. A thought struck her; she could ask Mireille out to lunch somewhere for a treat. The gas man had come last week so she had a small collection of shillings left from when he'd emptied the meter box, enough to buy a half decent lunch in the town. Mitchell's near the new town hall, a firm favourite of the family, had been bombed out but the Sunnyside Café was still standing.

She could hear voices and people moving about. It wouldn't be long before the whole family came into the kitchen. Norah stood to her feet and began to lay the table. There wasn't a lot in the larder. Nearly all their coupons had gone on the wedding breakfast.

She reached for her home-made recipe book where she kept all her Ministry of Food leaflets. A quick thumb through brought her to leaflet No. 11 and she decided that eggs in a nest would do. They still had half a tin of reconstituted egg.

By the time the rest of the family appeared, she had mixed the dried egg with water and made a hole in the centre of five slices of bread with a pastry cutter. After dipping the slices into water for a couple of seconds, she fried them on one side with some dripping. When she turned the slices over, she poured some egg mixture into the hole and cooked it until the underside of the bread was brown. Everything needed to be dished up straight away and while they were eating their portion, Norah toasted the leftover bread circles and put a pot of home-made jam onto the table.

When she turned around from the cooker, apart from her own, there was still one vacant chair. 'Where's Mireille?'

'Having a lie-in, I suspect,' said Christine.

'She did say she was very tired last night,' said Amélie.

'She ain't having a lie-in,' said Ivan, banging the bottom of the HP sauce bottle to get the last drop out. 'She'm gone.'

'Gone?' Norah gasped.

'I heard someone come down the stair just afore six,' he continued, 'and when I looks out of the winder I seen her going through the gate, bags and all.'

'Without even saying goodbye?' squeaked Christine.

Ivan shrugged. 'Looks like it.' He looked up. 'Got any more tea in that pot, Norah?'

Amélie leapt up from the table and they heard her running upstairs. Scarcely able to breathe, unshed tears pricked her eyes as Norah busied herself with the tea pot.

A few minutes later Amélie was back. 'He's right,' she said. 'The bed's made and everything. She left me this note.

"Sorry darling. Had to go. Duty calls. Will write. Love M."' Amélie sat down heavily, disappointment written all over her face. 'And I've got a half day off,' she said brokenly. 'I was hoping we could spend some time together.'

Christine squeezed her hand and they shared a sympathetic smile.

Norah put Ivan's cup of tea down in front of him.

'How's she'm going to get back then?' he said. 'There's no trains. It's Sunday.'

'Maybe she's arranged for someone to pick her up,' his wife said, but everyone seemed sceptical.

Norah sat down to eat her breakfast. In the silence that followed, she forced herself to swallow her egg nest but it tasted like sawdust.

Mireille had quite forgotten it was Sunday when she'd set out from Clifton Road. Her temper had cooled but she had no wish to begin the inquest into what had happened and why. She hated the fact that that man – she would never use his name again – still had power over her beyond the grave. *'Charming, enjoyable . . .'* Those words swirled in her brain and made her sick to her stomach. She pushed them out of her mind again and concentrated on where she was going.

Of course, now she realised that, being Sunday, there were no trains except for essential troop movement and she was hardly likely to be allowed to hop aboard one of them. Anyway, the gates at the entrance of Worthing station were firmly shut. Buses were few and far between because they only operated a limited Sunday service. Once the penny had dropped, Mireille couldn't bring herself to go back to Clifton Road, but what was she to do?

It was still dark and it was very cold but then she remembered Ginger had said that he was going back to Tangmere today. Thank goodness! She would walk to RAF Durrington and cadge a lift. It was only about two and a half miles and although she was carrying her overnight bag, it wasn't that heavy.

Forty minutes later she had reached the complex which was set in the middle of some muddy fields. The whole place was surrounded by barbed wire and all the buildings appeared to be without windows. The entrance was guarded by a soldier from the Black Watch. He checked her papers then told her to wait while he verified her story. A few moments later, Ginger came to the gate house and Mireille was invited in to join him for breakfast.

'You made it to the wedding all right then?' he said as they made their way to the mess. He was a pleasant-looking fellow, short and beefy with a shock of red hair – hence his nickname.

'I was a bit late,' she confessed, 'but I got there in the end.'

'I hung around as long as I could,' he said. 'I wondered where you'd got to.'

Mireille was looking around for a runway but she couldn't see it. 'What is this place?'

'Can't tell you much,' said Ginger. 'Top secret but it's what they call a ground-controlled interception station.'

Mireille pulled a face, none the wiser.

The mess was teeming with people, a hubbub of sound. Every eye turned in her direction as she walked in the door and from what she could see, she was the only female in the room. They made a great fuss of her, pulling out a chair and offering to get her some tea. After that, Mireille enjoyed a hearty breakfast of bacon, egg and fried bread with as much tea as she could drink.

Ginger had to collect some airmen and deliver them to Tangmere. 'They're all frogs,' he said matter-of-factly. 'Part of De Gaulle's Free French.'

Mireille pricked up her ears. 'What are they doing at Tangmere?' But Ginger only shrugged.

She was told to wait by the car while he went to the office to fetch some papers. When he came back about twenty minutes later, he was with three other men. Once they all got in, the car was packed. Mireille sat in the front next to Ginger while the others were all squashed in the back. Ginger was chatty but the three Frenchmen said very little. Ginger introduced them as Albert, Henri and Toussaint. Albert was dark haired with a small pencil moustache and a wide smile that revealed his top gums. He looked about thirty. By contrast, Henri was much younger, clean shaven with an almost downy faced, boyish look. He had sad dark eyes and a rather enigmatic smile. Toussaint was very different. His hair was fair and his slanted close set eyes were on a lean, almost frail-looking face. It struck Mireille that this man had a great sadness in his life. As they headed towards Chichester, Mireille turned slightly and, facing Toussaint, she tried a little French. 'Which part of France do you come from?'

Toussaint stared at her, his eyes popping. 'You speak French,' he gasped in English. The other two, who were dozing, sat up.

Mireille chuckled. 'I am half French,' she said in French. 'My father was English but my mother was French.'

'I didn't know you could speak the lingo,' Ginger piped up.

'I used to,' Mireille said reverting back to English, 'but it's years since I spoke it. I'm a bit rusty.'

'Not at all,' said the Frenchman. 'You are word perfect.'

'Have you lived in France?' It was Henri's turn to speak and he used his own tongue.

'I did until I was ten,' she replied. 'That's when my father died.'

34

'I am so sorry,' Henri said, shaking his head sadly.

'What's he on about?' Ginger chipped in.

'He was asking me if I'd lived in France and I told him I had.'

'Well, blow me down with a feather,' said Ginger. 'Always knew you were a cut above the rest.'

'Hardly,' Mireille laughed.

Ginger gave her an admiring glance. 'Exotic, that's what you are,' and despite herself, Mireille blushed to her roots.

They had reached the periphery of the airfield and everybody settled back until they reached the guard at the gate.

'Mademoiselle,' said Henri as they parted, 'you must come to the house to meet the rest of us.'

'House?' she queried.

All at once it was obvious that Toussaint was annoyed with Henri. Speaking very quickly in a hushed whisper, the tone of his voice was harsh. Henri replied but Mireille couldn't quite grasp what was being said.

'Looks like he's having a ticking off,' said Ginger, taking Mireille's bag from the boot of the car.

'But why?'

'What did he say to you?'

'He invited me to the house sometime, that's all.'

'That's why then,' said Ginger. 'He shouldn't have done that. Everybody knows about it, but we're not supposed to talk about it.' Then he added in a plummy voice, 'Top secret, all very hush, hush you know.'

Intrigued, Mireille said nothing.

Ginger came closer. 'If you keep it under your hat, I'll tell you,' he grinned.

'No thank you,' Mireille said stiffly. 'If it's a secret I'd rather not know.' She turned to go.

'Just as you like,' Ginger said, clearly offended.

Instantly regretting upsetting him, Mireille called over

her shoulder. 'Sorry, I didn't mean to be rude but I don't like secrets. They have a way of coming back to bite you on the bottom.'

When she reached her hut, she looked back; he was still standing by the car. She waved her hand. 'Bye, and thanks for the lift.'

'You're welcome,' he said, returning her gesture.

Chapter 4

Christmas turned out to be a rather subdued affair. Jim was working and so was Amélie. Mireille hadn't replied to Norah's invitation. Pete and Elsie Carson, Norah's parents, came and of course Christine and Ivan were there too. Norah had also invited Penny Andrews, Mrs Draycot and little Victor to join them and because Victor was a toddler, the Lilacs took on a bit of a party atmosphere. The one person who was sorely missed was Penny's husband Ted. He had been captured the previous year and was still a POW somewhere in Germany. The saddest thing was that he'd never even seen his baby son.

'Ooh Norah,' cried Penny as Norah ushered her and the baby into the sitting room. 'You've made everything look lovely.'

The room was festooned with ivy and holly branches which Norah had dipped in a strong solution of Epsom salts. She'd read the tip in *Woman* magazine. 'It will look beautifully frosted when it's dry,' the article said, and so it did. In fact it looked just like snow. The tree Jim bought way back in 1938 had been dug up again, put into a bigger pot and brought indoors. Victor was fascinated by the tinsel and the baubles hanging from the branches and leaned forward to touch them.

'I think this will probably be the last time we can get that old tree in here,' said Norah, looking at the Christmas angel tied to the top branch. It leaned drunkenly against the ceiling at a forty-five-degree angle. 'It hardly fits in the corner now.' As well as the few old decorations which had survived over the years, Norah and Christine had decorated the room with home-made garlands such as paper chains and knitted angels from a pattern given to them by Anne Ward, the vicar's wife. Their Christmas presents to each other were laid carefully around the bottom of the tub. Victor wriggled free from his mother's arms to play with the dogs.

Their dinner was a far cry from what they'd been used to but everyone had pooled their coupons to make the best of it. The government played its part. A week before Christmas, the tea ration had been doubled and the sugar ration had increased to twelve ounces, so they could enjoy a few extras such as fairy cakes and soda biscuits. Their main meal was roast pork with apple sauce, carrots, Brussel sprouts, roast potatoes and parsnips.

Penny fed Victor strapped in his pram because Norah didn't have a highchair and his grandmother was afraid that he might slip off a normal sized chair. It made no difference to the little boy and although he made a bit of a mess with his fingers, nobody minded.

'Nothing a damp flannel won't cure,' Christine said stoutly.

After Victor had had his dinner, he was left in his pram in the alcove to have a rest while everybody else settled down to eat their meal.

Norah put a plate of food aside for Jim and another for Amélie.

'This looks wonderful,' Mrs Draycot sighed as they all passed the serving dishes around.

Christine had made Christmas hats out of newspaper which everyone put on before they started eating and Penny raised her glass of home-made elderberry wine to propose a toast. 'To absent friends,' she said, her eyes a little teary.

Everybody else raised their glass of water, beer or wine to join in. 'Absent friends,' Norah said with a heartfelt longing to see Mireille again.

'Let's hope it'll all be over by next year,' said Christine as she put her glass back on the table.

'I must say I feel a bit more optimistic these days,' remarked Mrs Draycot, 'especially now that the Americans have joined in.'

'At least we've got the Luftwaffe off our backs,' Pete agreed, 'now that damned fool Hitler has turned his attention towards Russia.'

'He'm spread himself too thin,' Ivan remarked soberly.

'Right,' Norah said firmly. 'From now on, I'm banning all talk of the war. This is supposed to be a happy time, okay?'

There was a collective nod from around the table and everybody tucked in.

The meal itself had been a joint effort. Elsie had made one of her legendary Christmas puddings and Christine had managed to get some Camp coffee on the market. Mrs Draycot had brought a small Christmas cake and some nuts she'd been given by the Canadian soldiers who frequented the café where Penny worked. Making good use of the extra rations the government allowed over the Christmas period, they also had luncheon meat and a tin of salmon for tea time sandwiches.

After dinner, everybody helped with the washing up and

clearing up the kitchen while Norah fed the dogs. Once the jobs were done, they went into the sitting room where they drank coffee and listened to the King's speech on the wireless.

That done, as if on cue, Victor woke up and after Penny sat him on his potty, they set about opening their presents. Most gifts were of a practical nature. A new trowel for Ivan, a thriller for Mrs Draycot, a pile of second-hand gardening magazines for Norah and some bottling jars for Elsie. Pete had a new cap, Penny had a bar of toilet soap which everyone agreed smelled lovely and Christine had some knitting wool. Of course, Victor had the lion's share of presents. Christine had knitted him a jumper, while Norah had knitted him a scarf and matching gloves. His grandmother had given him a rabbit with long floppy ears, Ivan had squirrelled away some chocolate over the past few weeks to give him and Pete produced a toy train. Someone had left it on the bus several months ago and when he handed it in to the Lost Property Office, he'd asked if he could have first refusal should it be unclaimed.

Norah passed around some home-made ginger wine and they all relaxed. Although Penny had to keep dragging Victor away from the tree, it was an opportunity for the pair of them to catch up.

'Have you heard from your Ted?' Norah whispered. The Olds were dozing and she didn't want to disturb them.

'A postcard,' Penny said bitterly, 'and half of that was censored.'

'Oh, I'm so sorry, Pen.'

'I won't lie to you,' Penny admitted. 'The whole bloody business is getting me down.'

Norah nodded sympathetically. Christine's head drooped forward and she began making little puffing noises in her sleep. Mrs Draycot's paper hat had fallen over one eye. Penny giggled.

'Let's go out in the kitchen,' Norah whispered. 'You can help me make the sandwiches for tea.'

Victor was delighted to see the dogs again and they seemed equally pleased to see him. They put him on the floor with his new train and Norah gave him a couple of saucepans and a wooden spoon, a tin filled with dried rice to shake and an old tin tea pot and enamel mug. It wasn't long before he was happily banging, shaking and pouring out his pretend tea.

In between drinking gallons of 'ten tea' from the mug, Penny and Norah set about making sandwiches. 'Have you heard from Mireille?' Penny asked.

Norah put a precious egg into some water to boil while Penny opened the tin of spam. Norah shook her head.

'What, nothing at all?'

Norah shook her head again.

'The little cow,' Penny muttered disgustedly.

'Oh don't say that, Pen,' said Norah. 'I hurt her quite deeply.'

'What about what she's done to you?' Penny exclaimed. 'You bent over backwards to help those girls and now the ungrateful little so and so tosses you to one side like some old dish cloth.'

'It's not quite like that,' Norah protested mildly. 'She was right. I never should have kept Ffox-Webster's death from her.'

'You were trying to protect her,' Penny insisted.

Norah pursed her lips together. Penny was right but Mireille didn't see it like that. In the first letter she had written to Mireille after she'd walked out, Norah had apologised for not telling her the whole truth about Jago Ffox-Webster. '*I realise now how foolish I was treating you like a child,*' she'd written. '*You had every right to know, even though it was unpalatable. Please forgive me.*' But Mireille never did. Since then, the thought had crossed Norah's mind more than once that something might have happened to Mireille. In these uncertain days of war, it was becoming more and more common to hear of people being killed in air raids or in action overseas. Jim had lost two of his ex-policemen and the son of the man who ran the garage in Teville Gate had been killed in Egypt. Christine and Ivan had lost a mutual friend in an air raid while she was on a visit to her daughter near Birmingham but life carried on. People learned to cope with their grief without show; after all, everyone was in the same boat. Norah's letters to Mireille weren't returned to her, so eventually she reasoned that they must have reached their destination. Besides, as far as Norah knew, Amélie hadn't had a telegram with bad news so her sister must be still alive and well. Norah could only hope that one day Mireille would understand that she had meant well, but until then, she was doing her best to keep the lines of communication open. She always spent her Sunday evenings writing letters, so top of the list was a letter to Mireille even though the girl had never once replied. There had been no Christmas card either.

'What does Amélie think of it?' Penny asked as Norah stood up to fetch the egg.

'She doesn't say much,' Norah admitted.

Amélie's attitude towards Norah seemed unchanged although it was obvious that she had been deeply hurt by the revelations about her step-father as well.

Victor accidentally hit himself with the wooden spoon and cried. Penny got up from her chair to comfort him, although Sausage was already licking the little boy's tears away. Coming back to the table to mash the egg with a little salad cream to make it go further, Norah's mind drifted back to the time when Amélie and her younger sister, Linnet, first arrived in Worthing. Right from the start it was obvious to her and Jim that the older girl was keeping something secret from them but it wasn't until much later that they found out the truth. It had taken a long time before Amélie had been able to talk about what had happened to them and Christine had been her confidante. Perhaps that was why she wasn't so condemning of Norah's misguided intentions to hide unpleasant things.

Penny was back at the table and the two friends carried on making sandwiches.

'What happened about you and Jim adopting a baby?' Penny asked. 'At the beginning of this year you were full of it, but now you hardly mention it at all.'

'I'm not sure it's going to happen,' said Norah cutting the egg sandwiches into four. 'We found out that Ffox-Webster put a black mark against us and it's proving almost impossible to get it taken off.'

'Why did he do that?'

'Spite, I guess.'

'Oh Norah, I'm sorry,' said Penny. 'Can't you go for a private adoption?'

'I wish it were that easy,' Norah sighed. 'If we can't adopt, we may foster instead.'

'What time does Jim get back?' Penny asked, changing the subject.

Norah glanced up at the clock. 'He'll be back at six-thirty-ish and Amélie will be back just after seven.'

'How does she like the hospital?'

'Loves it,' said Norah with a smile. 'In fact she'll be moving there in January.'

'Moving? Why?'

'It's a condition of their training,' said Norah. 'She has to live in the nurses' home in Park Road. Personally I think it's only an excuse; a crafty way to make sure they've got them close at hand if there's some sort of emergency.'

'You might be right there,' Penny chuckled. She looked around for Victor who was pushing his train along the edge of the room. The dogs stood beside him with cocked ears and curious expressions as he made a 'chuffa, chuff-chuff,' sound.

Norah sighed. 'I hope Mireille writes before she goes otherwise the two of them might lose touch.'

'I shouldn't think there's much danger of that, is there?' said Penny, picking up her son and swinging him onto her hip.

'I remember Mireille saying she was going to be posted somewhere else shortly,' said Norah, tipping the bread board, knife and eggy plate into the sink.

'Then she'll write to the hospital, won't she?' said Penny. She was washing Victor's hands with a flannel. 'All the nurses have their own pigeon holes with a number.'

Norah froze. So that was why Amélie hadn't had a Christmas card at the Lilacs. She felt a pang in her chest. The rift between them must be much worse than she'd first thought. Mireille had cut her out. She was still in contact with her sister, which of course was a good thing, but she and Jim didn't mean anything to her anymore.

'I'm just going to take Victor to the bathroom,' said Penny, reaching under the bottom of the pram for his potty.

Norah kept her face towards the glass in the window over the sink. Her eyes were tingling as she battled her huge sense of loss. She couldn't cry. She mustn't cry. It was Christmas day. She heard a bump as Jim leaned his bicycle against the wall outside. And at the same time, the kitchen door creaked open and Christine came in. 'Now that Jim's home, shall I make a cup of tea?' she asked.

'You know I was just thinking the same thing,' Norah

said cheerfully as she sniffed back her tears. 'As soon as I've washed up these things, we'll call everybody for tea. Amélie won't be far behind him.'

The family came into the kitchen protesting that they weren't hungry but they still managed to put away a plate full of egg and salad cream sandwiches as well as some salmon sandwiches and a couple of the spam sandwiches. Jim and Amélie ate their warmed up Christmas dinners and once the tea table was cleared for the second time, they opened their presents. Jim had a couple of National Savings Certificates, a pair of socks, some new slippers from Norah and a 6d bar of chocolate. Amélie had mostly scented soaps, a pair of nylons from Norah and Jim and some handkerchiefs. Victor had a whale of a time playing with the few bits of unusable wrapping paper although the rest of it was smoothed out and neatly folded to use another time. In these desperate times, nothing was wasted.

Soon after they'd tucked into the Christmas cake, Mrs Draycot, Penny and Victor had to leave. Victor was getting tired and niggly. Besides, there were no buses and it was a tidy walk to Broadwater.

'Thanks for a lovely day, Norah,' said Mrs Draycot as she pushed her grandson's pram through the gate and onto Clifton Road. 'We've so enjoyed ourselves.'

'You're welcome,' Norah called.

'After all your hard work today,' said Penny, 'make sure you put your feet up tomorrow.'

'Fat chance of that,' Norah said with a chuckle. 'Rene and Dan are coming.' She turned to give Penny a hug. 'Better times just around the corner,' she whispered encouragingly.

'I hope so,' Penny said dully. 'And don't you go worrying about Mireille. She'll come round. She won't want to lose you as a friend.'

'I'm sure you're right,' said Norah but as she waved them goodbye, in her heart of hearts, Norah wasn't so sure. Would Mireille come round? Maybe, maybe not. *And even if she did*, Norah thought acidly, *after the way she's treated me, would I really want her as a friend?* Immediately, she checked herself. Of course she did. She hated all this bad feeling. Oh dear, dear, what was she to do?

Chapter 5

Amélie was in trouble. When she'd applied to train as a nurse, she hadn't realised that she was required to pay so much money up front. Even though her pay as a ward orderly was small, she had saved a little money but it was nowhere near enough. What on earth could she do? She didn't like to ask Norah and Jim for help. They'd done more than enough for her and Mrs Steele, Mémé, as she called her, was only a pensioner. Sister Tutor said the money should be paid by the end of December and if she couldn't make up the shortfall, it looked as if she would have to wait another year before she could apply to the school of nursing.

Just after Christmas, Amélie and her sister arranged to meet at the pictures in Littlehampton. Alfred Hitchcock's *Suspicion* was showing at the Regent which was opposite the railway station so neither girl had far to go. Almost as soon as Mireille saw her, she knew Amélie was troubled about something but it took a little while to tease it out of her.

'Nurse's school starts on January the eighth,' Amélie

said dolefully. 'They've given me a day of grace, but got to find twenty pounds by January the fifth.'

They were sitting in the cinema waiting for the main lm to start. 'Twenty pounds?' Mireille gasped. 'Whatever for?'

'My uniform and textbooks,' said Amélie. 'I've saved seven pounds fifteen shillings but there's no way I can get that kind of money in such a short space of time. I can't ask Norah and Jim, I just can't.'

The lights began to dim. Mireille leaned towards her. 'Don't worry. I'll give you the rest,' she whispered. 'I'll send you a postal order tomorrow.'

Tears sprang to Amélie's eyes. 'Oh but . . .'

'But nothing,' Mireille whispered. 'That's what sisters are for.'

Just then a woman behind them poked Mireille viciously in the back and told them to 'Shh,' so the two girls couldn't say any more but Amélie reached for her sister's hand and gave it a tight squeeze.

The film was brilliant. When Joan Fontaine, a rich woman, married the delicious Cary Grant, a penniless gambler, she was very much in love but as time went on, she began to suspect that he was trying to kill her. 'Real edge-of-the-seat stuff,' Amélie remarked as they crossed the road to have a cup of tea in the railway café before they parted.

'Mireille,' she began, as her sister brought their cups of tea to the table, 'about Norah . . .'

'I don't want to talk about it,' Mireille snapped.

'I think you should know,' Amélie began again cautiously. 'She gave me our mother's rings. As the eldest, are you sure you don't want them?'

'I want nothing that man has touched,' Mireille snapped. 'Nothing.'

Amélie stared into her cup. 'I feel a bit awkward about

them as well,' she said, 'but they belonged to Mama and we don't have anything else of hers.'

'You do what you like with them,' said Mireille, her tone softening. 'Keep them if you want to but if you don't, sell them and use the money for your nursing.' She paused for a moment then, giving Amélie's hand a squeeze, she added, 'Mama was a good person. She would have wanted you to follow your heart.'

Embarrassed, Amélie kept her head down as she reached for some sugar. 'Well if you're sure . . .'

'I am.'

They drank their tea and made small talk until it was time to go. The two girls linked arms and crossed the road to walk towards the station.

'I wish we could find Linnet,' Amélie sighed. 'It doesn't seem right the two of us being together without her.'

'I keep thinking that too,' said Mireille. 'The trouble is we haven't even a clue where to start looking.' She squeezed her sister's arm a little tighter. 'I mean we've no proof she's gone abroad. I wouldn't put it past him to put that cutting inside the envelope just to upset us.'

'But Norah said she thought Havelock put it in the envelope,' Amélie reminded her. 'The business about the scissors, remember?'

They'd reached the station and Mireille was putting tuppence in the machine for a platform ticket.

'I want to have a go at finding out about those organisations that sent kids abroad,' said Amélie. She frowned. 'Why did you just buy a platform ticket? You've got your train ticket, haven't you?'

Mireille stared at the platform ticket and laughed. 'I've no idea. I must be going dippy in my old age.' They sauntered onto the platform. 'Anyway, how are you going to find out about all those organisations?'

Amélie shrugged. 'Contact the newspaper?'

'Darling, we don't even know what paper it came from.'

Mireille saw her face fall. 'We'll both try,' she said encouragingly. 'You look for the organisation and I'll think of something else.'

Amélie's train came in and the sisters hugged each other on the platform as it pulled in.

'Take care of yourself,' Mireille said.

'And you,' said Amélie as she climbed aboard. After closing the door, she pulled the strap and let the window down. 'Thanks for offering to help me out and if I don't sell the rings, I promise I'll pay you back.'

'No hurry,' said Mireille. 'And don't worry about Norah. I'll get it sorted.'

The train juddered and moved slowly on its way. Mireille waved until her sister disappeared from the window and sat down. She had tried to give Amélie the impression that she was going to catch the train to Chichester but Ginger would be waiting for her on the corner of Terminus Road. She hurried to meet him. He'd spent the afternoon with the Royal Artillery Coast regiment at their battery which was cleverly disguised as a bungalow but she knew better than to ask him what he was doing there. She was just happy that he'd offered to meet her and give her a lift back to Tangmere.

'Nice day?' he asked as she jumped aboard the jeep.

'Very,' she said, giving him a grin.

He smiled and started the engine. He would have loved to kiss her but he'd learned over time that Mireille was very sparing with her kisses. He'd managed it once or twice but if she saw one coming, somehow it didn't happen. When he lay on his bed at night and thought of her, it crossed his mind to wonder if she batted for the other team but in the end he decided she was just an innocent.

He would have done anything for her and she knew it, but she never really took advantage of his good nature.

'What about you?' she asked. 'Successful day?'

'Yes,' he said. 'I think so.'

They drove on in silence until they came to the hairpin road blocks on the Arundel Road. Having shown their passes, and made their way through them, Ginger put his foot down.

'There's a dance at Climping village hall on Saturday,' he said tentatively. 'Fancy coming?'

Mireille shook her head. 'Sorry,' she said. 'I've had an invitation to the French house.'

Ginger frowned. 'Are you sure that's wise?' No sooner were the words out of his mouth than he felt her tense beside him. 'Sorry, sorry, none of my business.'

'I'm not your . . .' she began.

'I know,' he said, at the same time thinking to himself, *more's the pity*. 'It's just that I care about you and you will be one girl in a room full of foreigners.'

'Allies, not enemies,' she said.

'Point taken.'

He stared at the road ahead. If only she knew. It tore him to pieces to think of her with those men. Supposing one of them sweet-talked her into doing something she didn't want to. But even as the thought went through his mind he knew perfectly well that Mireille wasn't the sort of woman to be sweet-talked into anything. She was not only the most beautiful creature on God's earth but she was also strong-willed and determined. If he was honest with himself, that's why he admired her so much. He sighed inwardly. Ever since he'd first met her, he knew that if she was to be his girl, he'd have to play the waiting game. She wouldn't be rushed and he was scared of frightening her off. He'd been courting her for a few weeks now but she didn't even seem to realise. He turned his head and glanced at her. She smiled and his heart leapt. *Oh God*, he thought as he turned his eyes towards the road again. *If only you knew how I feel about you, Mireille Osborne. If only you knew.*

Chapter 6

It was five-thirty on a cold winter's morning when Jim and seven other police officers crept around the back of a row of terraced houses in Newlands Road. At the end of the street, a lorry containing several army personnel drew up and waited. After a few minutes, a captain from the Royal Army Ordnance Corps and a corporal walked towards them, the metal studs on the corporal's army boots making far too much noise on the brick passageway for Jim's liking. When they reached him, the captain tapped the front of his cap with his silver-topped swagger stick as the corporal snapped to attention beside him. 'Good morning, Inspector,' the captain said all too loudly.

Jim winced. 'Good morning, sir,' he said in a much more measured tone. 'I would appreciate it if we could be as quiet as possible.'

'Yes, yes of course,' he said, his plummy voice now matching Jim's cautious whisper. 'Captain Carruthers.' He held out his gloved hand.

As Jim shook hands, the captain's ring finger and little finger failed to connect with the rest of his hand and Jim realised that part of the glove was empty. The fingers were missing. Captain Carruthers gave Jim a sheepish grin. 'Dunkirk,' and Jim gave him a sympathetic nod.

Captain Carruthers had once been a handsome man but now an ugly scar disfigured his face. The skin under his left eye was pulled down to reveal the red fleshy underneath and the scar ended near his chin. With a damaged hand and injured face, Jim guessed he must have been shot at some point.

'So,' said Carruthers deliberately ignoring his discomfort, 'are we all ready?'

'We're ready,' said Jim. 'Two of my men are at the front of the house, three at the back and I've placed a constable at each end of the alleyway.'

'Virtually the whole contingent of the Worthing police force in one place then, eh?' the captain added with a snort.

'Not everyone, sir, but enough.' Jim wondered vaguely if he was being funny, facetious or was it sarcasm? He knew the high-ups and pen-pushers regarded the men who policed the town as mere country yokels, but Jim was proud of them. These days the Worthing police force was mostly made up of more mature men. The lower ranks had been called up, so men of forty-five or more, stayed on beyond their retirement date. Although there was some talk of amalgamating with the County and Borough forces of East Sussex, Worthing managed to keep ahead of the criminal fraternity by using its share of reserve officers, special constables and even some women officers. Not every man liked the idea of using women police officers but to Jim every person was necessary. Not only were his men (and women) required to keep the peace, to catch criminals, to make sure traffic flowed freely and check that licensing laws were being observed, but now they had a whole raft of new regulations to enforce; which was why this morning they were to be part of an operation which would never have happened before 1939, namely pursuing some army deserters.

The captain pulled up his sleeve to look at his watch. His wrist was bare. 'Oh blast it,' he muttered. 'Keep forgetting I've lost the damn thing. Is it time yet?'

Jim nodded. Right on the dot of their pre-arranged time, he hammered loudly on the front door. 'Open up, open up, this is the police.'

As his men forced it open, they could hear a dog barking ferociously somewhere inside. They could also hear scuffling and panicky cries. As the door frame gave way, Jim and his men rushed in. Fortunately the dog wasn't as brave as its bark so three of the army deserters were quickly arrested but a fourth man was nowhere to be seen. The dog stood at the top of the stairs letting out a few worried yips while the soldiers rounded up their quarry and everybody else searched the rest of the house. It turned out to be a good day. In the pantry they found a large quantity of stolen cigarettes, the sitting room was littered with ration books, presumably forgeries, and in the kitchen they found several army-issue tins of jam and marmalade, all bound for the black market Jim supposed. That being the case, he arrested the homeowner, a well-known ne'er do well who had seen the inside of His Majesty's prisons more often than Jim could remember.

As the soldiers clambered back outside empty-handed, Jim turned to his prisoner. 'If you tell us where the other man is, Snowy, I'll see to it that the court knows you co-operated.'

'You know me better than that, Sergeant Kirkwood,' said Snowy, using Jim's former rank. 'I'm no grass.'

Jim nodded to one of his constables.

'Make sure somebody looks after me dog, Sergeant Kirkwood,' Snowy called out as he was led away.

'Wish we could have caught the other blighter,' said the captain. 'Damned nuisance that he's still at large.'

The dog was still at the top of the stairs. Jim began to make his way towards it, when he paused halfway up. Captain Carruthers came up behind him. 'What is it?' he said cautiously.

Jim frowned. 'When they were looking for the contraband,' he began, 'your men scattered food all over the kitchen floor.'

'So?' said Carruthers.

'So why is this dog up here? I've got dogs and my dogs would have been down there like a shot to make the most of an opportunity to gobble up free food.'

'Perhaps it's too scared,' Carruthers suggested. 'You know, strangers in the house and all that.'

'Then, why not make a dash for it through the open door?' said Jim. A distant memory was stirring in Jim's mind and grasping the captain's sleeve, he said, 'Did your men look in that roof space?'

Carruthers nodded. 'No joy up there, I'm afraid. It was nothing more than a glorified dumping ground, filled with old boxes and bits of old rolled up carpet.'

'You do realise that the roof space goes right along the length of this terrace,' said Jim. 'I lived in a house just like this as a kid. Given half the chance, we used to get up there and dodge our mums for hours on end.'

Captain Carruthers' eyes grew wide. He made to go past Jim but Jim shook his head. The captain gave him a puzzled look until Jim jerked his head towards the dog. It had sat up and was whining softly as it stared at the loft hatch.

'He's still up there, isn't he?' whispered Carruthers.

'I reckon he is,' said Jim.

'I'll get my men to go up there.'

'You do that,' said Jim, 'but let's you and me go to the other end of the road.'

'I don't understand,' said Carruthers.

'You soon will,' said Jim, beckoning.

With a couple of corporals already putting the loft ladder underneath the hatch, Jim took the captain outside.

'Which way?' gasped Carruthers and he looked up and down the street.

'Too much activity this end,' said Jim. 'If he wants to make a getaway he'll come down from the loft by number two.'

With a constable repositioned by the house next door as a precaution, the two men hurried to the other end of the terrace. When they arrived, they could hear whistling. Someone was making an early morning delivery and just off the street, they spotted a coal lorry parked in the alleyway.

As they reached the back gate of number two, a grubby-looking man came out of the back door.

'Just the coalman,' Carruthers sighed.

They watched as the man stopped by the tail gate of the lorry, turned and pulled a sack towards him to put it onto his back.

'I think the game's up now, lad, don't you?' Jim said.

At the same time, the real coalman came out of the house with an empty sack. 'Oi,' he shouted. 'What d'you fink you're doin'?'

The man by the lorry let go of the sack of coal and made a feeble effort to run but two constables were upon him in a flash. There was a small scuffle and he was arrested.

'How did you know it was him?' Captain Carruthers gasped as the deserter was led away by his men.

'His hands,' Jim said coolly. He smiled at the captain's puzzled expression. 'When was the last time you saw a coalman with lily-white hands?'

SPRING 1942

Chapter 7

On her next day off, Amélie took the opportunity to talk to Christine about Linnet. In fact it was Christine herself who initiated the conversation when she brought up the subject of their mother's rings.

'Mireille says she doesn't care what I do with them,' Amélie told her, 'but I feel a bit awkward about it.'

'Your sister is angry,' Christine began. 'Those rings belong to all three of you girls. Linnet isn't here and Mireille has washed her hands of them, so you should feel free to make a decision.'

They were sitting in the kitchen enjoying a moment or two of peace and quiet before the rest of the family came home. Jim was at work, Norah had gone to post a letter to her sister Rene and was on her way to take some gooseberries to the WI in Broadwater who were hosting a 'Preserve your own fruit' afternoon for young mums. Ivan had taken the dogs for a walk. Amélie had been studying hard all morning so when Christine suggested a cup of tea, she welcomed a little relaxation. She and a few of the other nurses had been invited to a party in the evening. It wouldn't be a lavish affair, but Amélie was glad to be invited.

'So do you think it would be right to sell my mother's rings?'

'Why not if you need the money for your course,' said Christine, handing her a cup and saucer. 'Look, whatever you get, divide it into three. Mireille may say she doesn't want it right now, but she may change her mind one day then you can give her her share. I'll hold on to Linnet's share if you like.'

Amélie nodded uncertainly. 'I wish we could find a way of finding out where Linnet is,' she said sadly. 'Have you ever heard of an organisation that took British children abroad?'

'There was a group who set up a helpline in 1939,' Christine began. 'CORB they were called, if I remember rightly. I think that's Children's Overseas Repatriation Board or something like that. Lots of children went but then a ship called *The City of Benares* was torpedoed and it was all stopped.'

Amélie gasped.

'Oh I don't think for one minute that your sister would have been aboard that one,' Christine added quickly. 'That happened in September 1940. She would have still been at boarding school back then.'

Amélie nodded. 'But you said all the sailings were stopped.'

'There have been private arrangements with others since then,' said Christine. 'I know that because one of the ladies in church said her granddaughter went to Canada at the very end of 1940.'

Amélie looked thoughtful. 'So how can I find out?'

'Can't help you there, dear,' said Christine. 'I suppose you could ask in the library, or maybe the post office?'

After a great deal of thought, Amélie decided that she would take their mother's rings to a jeweller. She plumped for A.R. Whibley's on the corner of Warwick Street, a family-run business which had been in Worthing more than sixty years. Inside the shop there were small tables dotted around a large open area and it smelled of furniture polish. A smartly dressed assistant invited her to sit down.

'Someone left me her rings,' Amélie began. 'I don't wear jewellery so I'm thinking of selling them.' She took them from her bag and laid them on the table.

The assistant picked up the wedding ring first then the engagement ring and looked at each one through his loupe. 'Umm, a nice little ring,' he said putting the engagement ring down. 'The wedding ring would probably fetch around twenty pounds but I shall have to ask our senior jeweller to give a more in-depth valuation for the engagement ring. Having said that, it should be in the region of around one hundred pounds.'

Amélie took in a breath. One hundred and twenty pounds? That was a fortune. She had no idea they would be worth that much. The assistant muttered something about going to the workshop and left her at the table. What was she going to do? She was sure Mireille had no idea of their worth and it didn't seem right to simply sell them and keep the money. For all her irritation, the rings belonged to the both of them; well, the three of them actually. The assistant came back to the table.

'My senior agrees with my guesstimate,' he said, lowering himself into the chair opposite her. 'We would be interested in buying it although we could have offered you more if it weren't for the inscription.'

'Inscription?' Amélie said blankly. 'What inscription?'

When the assistant pointed to the inside of the engagement ring, Amélie could see some letters but she couldn't make it out. She frowned.

'It's French,' said the assistant. 'My schoolboy French is a bit rusty, but I'm fairly sure it says something like, "True love is eternal".'

Amélie was slightly surprised. It was a lovely sentiment so why wouldn't someone want it inside the band. 'So why does that devalue the ring?'

'That bit doesn't,' the assistant said apologetically, 'but the previous owner has had their initials engraved on either side, see?'

Amélie leaned forward and looked through the huge magnifying glass he was holding. She gasped and put her hand to her mouth. 'Oh my goodness,' she cried when she saw it. 'Then I can't. I can't possibly sell them.'

'Walk, Nurse, walk.'

Sister Dunn's voice boomed out like a foghorn as Amélie dashed along the corridor. 'Have you seen a fire?'

Amélie juddered to a halt. 'No Sister.'

'Is your patient bleeding to death?'

'No Sister.'

Sister Dunn sniffed. 'The only time you run in this hospital is if there's a fire or your patient is having a haemorrhage.'

Amélie did her best to look suitably chastened. 'Yes Sister, sorry Sister.' She resumed her walk at a brisk pace towards the ward. As she pushed open the swing doors, the ward sister was already giving the night staff her report.

'. . . give her an enema before she goes to theatre in the morning,' she was saying.

Amélie slid inconspicuously beside the other nurses standing around the desk, but the woman had the eyes of a hawk. Without a pause for breath, she interrupted her discourse with, 'You are late, Nurse,' then continued once more. 'Mrs Mercedes managed to walk along the corridor to the bathroom this afternoon. Doctor Charters has changed her medication . . .'

Still in her probationary period, Amélie was expected to

listen to the nursing report as the shift changed but even though she had been doing her after-school duties since January, she knew she wouldn't be allowed to do very much on the ward. In general terms, probationers were treated as general dogsbodies. She wasn't permitted to do anything technical but she was expected to take the initiative to make herself useful. She could help in the ward kitchen, which meant she could make a patient a sandwich or a cup of tea if needed; she could take temperatures and if the doctors were doing their rounds, she was allowed to hand the patient's chart to the consultant but little else.

For the past six weeks, Amélie and the other eight probationers in her set had been studying hard in the Preliminary Training School. Every Friday they were tested on their work but all that was about to change. Last week she had taken her National Nursing Examination and now the nail-biting experience of waiting for her results was over. Instead of coming immediately to the ward after classes were finished, Amélie had dashed to the nurses' home to collect her post. There were two letters in her cubby hole. One was from Mireille and the other (the one she was expecting) was in a brown envelope marked NNE. The letter had come this morning but this was the first opportunity Amélie had had to collect it and another from the same source marked J. Hawke. Now that the brown envelope was in her hands, she really couldn't wait until she finished her duty at seven-thirty to know if she had passed her exam. She had to know as soon as possible. It was unbearable enough to have to wait until class was over, but to wait another three hours until she came off duty, seemed like a lifetime. Would she be able to stay in the hospital or would she be leaving next week? If she passed, as a student nurse, Amélie could work on the wards full-time. If she failed . . . well, it didn't bear thinking about. She heard the hall clock strike six. There was no time to look now. She should be on the ward straight away which was why, wrapping her cloak right around her body, Amélie had set off at a pace.

The ward sister finished her report and each girl was assigned a particular duty. Amélie and Probationer Hawke were assigned to stripping the bed of a patient who had been discharged during the afternoon and making it up ready for the next patient. There was a knack to getting the sheets and covers exactly as Sister required them to be and the two of them worked well as a team.

'Did you get it?' June said out of the corner of her mouth. Amélie nodded.

As June pulled the screens around the bed, Amélie drew the two brown envelopes from her apron pocket and handed one to her friend. While June ripped open her envelope, Amélie busied herself by pulling the dirty sheets off the bed and stuffing them into the laundry bag. 'I'm in!' June squealed in an almost inaudible whisper. They both knew if Sister caught them they'd both be in trouble.

'Congratulations,' Amélie whispered as loudly as she dared. Her heart went into her mouth. Now it was her turn to open her envelope. She was well aware that only forty percent of the girls who went into the Preliminary Training School went on to become student nurses. This was not only because it was challenging but also because the hospital and Matron in particular were so strict. Already three of their number had been dismissed for insubordination or disobeying the rules; a couple of others had left because they couldn't keep up with the lessons and failed the end of the week examinations; and one girl had got herself pregnant.

Turning her back to the screens, Amélie tore open the envelope.

Dear Miss Osborne,
I am pleased to inform you that . . .

'How are you two girls getting on?' Staff Nurse Taylor's voice right behind the curtain made Amélie jump but she had the presence of mind to stuff the paper into her pocket before she grabbed a cleaning cloth from the washing bowl and joined June who was by now rubbing the mattress rubber with vigour.

'Fine, Staff Nurse, thank you,' June said airily.

A second later, the staff nurse snatched the screen back and surveyed the scene. 'Make sure you give that locker a good going over,' she said curtly, 'and if the patient has left any belongings behind, don't forget to put them in a bag and take them to the porter's office.'

Without stopping what they were doing, the two girls nodded their assent. After hovering for a while, the staff nurse turned to go. 'Oh and Nurse Osborne,' she said with just a hint of a smile tugging the corners of her mouth, 'you'd better be quick about taking a look at that letter of acceptance before Sister gets back from her break.'

Back in the nurses' home, Amélie discovered that of the girls who began the course, only eight of them had achieved a mark which permitted them to progress to the wards. Their excitement was palpable but it was also tempered by the sense of loss for those who hadn't made it. A couple of girls had already left in tears; one girl was relieved ('now me and Harry can get married straight away'), and another girl declared stoutly she'd much prefer to join the WRENS anyway.

It was supper time before Amélie got around to opening Mireille's letter. Most of it was pretty mundane. She mentioned going to a dance with Ginger and taking part in some of the fund-raising initiatives going on in the area but near the end, Amélie had quite a surprise. *'You'll never believe this,'* her sister wrote, *'but I've discovered some of our old countrymen are based here. I can't tell you much about them, but it's been wonderful to meet them. I've always felt a little out of place in England but now I know where my roots lie. Vive la France! By the way, did you find out about that organisation?'*

When she'd finished reading, Amélie looked up and gazed somewhere in the distance. Yes, she had found out about CORB. Worthing library had come up trumps for her. Christine hadn't got it quite right. It was Children's Overseas Reception Board and she'd written to them about Linnet. Everything was such a muddle. If Linnet had gone to Australia or South Africa or some such place thousands of miles away, would that mean she would become a citizen of that country? Amélie sighed. And if Mireille felt her roots lay in France, where were her own roots? Surely this was her home. Worthing, Lancing, Littlehampton . . . they were all part of beautiful Sussex. Yes, it was scarred by war at the moment with bomb craters, blown up buildings and great gouges in the fields where enemy and RAF planes had come down, but it was still home. How did she feel about France? She'd been a small child when they'd left and she hardly even remembered it now. She was half French, half English, but in this moment, if someone asked her, Amélie, for all her lovely French name, would say her home was England now. Clearly her sister didn't feel the same. She looked down at her sister's writing. Even though Mireille had only put words onto paper, Amélie could feel her passion coming off the page.

Chapter 8

The cottage Henri had talked about was really a fairly large house with a Virginia creeper covering the walls not far from the airfield itself. She had planned to go much earlier in the year but so many things got in the way, chiefly the training the men were doing. Mireille knew she shouldn't be there but was unable to resist his invitation. More than anything in the world she was longing to use her native tongue again and what better way than with her own countrymen.

Henri showed her into a rather basic sitting room. Clearly male territory, it lacked a woman's touch. No embroidered cushion covers and no homely acquisitions, instead home-made shelves lined the walls either side of the open fireplace, which already being late spring, was unlit. Several leather armchairs were positioned around the fireplace. An outdated copy of *The Times* had been discarded on the arm rest of one chair and above the mantelpiece a row of empty beer bottles stood either side of a wall clock. To her absolute delight, Henri spoke to her only in French.

'You see, this is where we wait.'

'To be sent into France?'

He nodded and motioned for her to sit down. 'You speak French very well.'

'I was born in England but my mother was French and my father worked in France.'

'What did he do?'

'It sounds pretty ridicules, but I don't quite know,' she began. 'I was only ten when we left France, younger than that when he died, and you don't really take much notice of what adults do for a living when you're that age, do you?'

'Ridiculous,' he said. Puzzled, Mireille frowned. 'You said ridicules,' he continued. 'The word is ridiculous.'

'Yes of course,' Mireille said, blushing slightly.

'Do you have brothers and sisters?'

'Two sisters, both younger than me.' She paused, well aware that she shouldn't ask more pertinent questions and even if she did, any Free Frenchman worth his salt wouldn't answer anyway. People like him were fiercely loyal. The Free French Forces was made up of men from the French military and other militia groups who had fought alongside the Allies before the occupation. Most had come to Britain after Dunkirk but they aligned themselves with General Charles de Gaulle rather than the British armed forces.

'If you don't mind me asking, how did you come to be in England?'

'I was at Dunkerque,' he said, his expression clouding. She understood his reticence to say more. It was well known that whereas the little ships had snatched more than three hundred thousand men from the beaches, it also marked the fall of France, something which clearly had affected him deeply.

'Where are the others?' she said, looking around. 'I thought Albert and Toussaint would be here too.'

He perched himself onto the arm rest of her chair and

leaned over her with his arm on the back of the chair. 'I thought it would be nice . . .' His voice had become low and husky. 'Just the two of us together. We can get to know each other . . . you know.'

'No I don't know,' she said haughtily, waving her arm to make him move back.

He sat back up as if stung.

'I don't know what sort of a girl you think I am,' she said tetchily, 'but I came here to talk about France.'

He got up and helped himself to a cigarette from the box on the table, without offering her one, and moved into the chair opposite.

Mireille turned her head away. This was all so disappointing. What on earth had she done that would make him think she would welcome some sort of intimate tête-à-tête? Blinkin' men. Why did everything centre on what was in their trousers?

'Tell me about your mother,' he said, breaking into her angry thoughts.

'She died,' said Mireille.

'My condolences,' said Henri. 'I am alone too. My parents were killed when the Germans came.'

Mireille had been about to get up and flounce out until he said that but now she relaxed. 'No brothers or sisters?' she said, softening.

Henri shook his head.

'I am so sorry.' She paused. 'Like I said, I have two sisters. One is training to be a nurse. The other one was sent to one of the British dominions but I'm not sure where. I have to find her.'

'Everything I have is in France,' he said.

'But you will go back one day,' she said encouragingly.

He nodded. 'The General has said so.'

'General De Gaulle?' she said, relaxing a little more.

'I heard him on the radio in 1940. A good man and a strong leader. I remember he said you either follow the path of abandonment and despair like Pétain or you walk the path of hope.'

'Honour and hope,' Henri corrected. 'This is why I fight. I will fight and die for my country.'

'Me too,' Mireille said heartily.

'For England?' said Henri.

'For France,' said Mireille.

Norah had taken some produce to the house in Canterbury Road where the wives of some of the Worthing Worthies, such as Mrs Strange, Mrs Thornycroft and Mrs Wenban-Smith, housed some refugees. Her heart went out to them. They were well looked after but they had lost everything and some of their families were in Hitler's concentration camps. Afterwards, Norah took the first of her lettuces to the café in Broadwater where Penny worked. Apart from their occasional evening out at the pictures, she hadn't seen her for a while and Norah welcomed the opportunity to have a bike ride and a chat. Her uncle Fred who employed Penny in the café, gave them a few minutes to themselves so the two girls went out to the back room.

'Have you heard from Ted?' Norah asked because she'd noticed her friend seemed more relaxed, happier, chirpy even.

'Not for a couple of months,' said Penny as she busied herself with making them coffee in a chipped mug, one of the ones she and her uncle used. 'I'm getting used to it now.'

Norah frowned. So why was she so chipper? 'How's Victor?'

'Fine,' said Penny. 'He and Mum have quite a bond. Sometimes I feel a bit left out.' She laughed. 'No, not really but I'm really glad they get on so well. It helps me earn a few bob and it's good to get out of the house.' She handed Norah a steaming mug and sat opposite her. 'What about you? How's Amélie liking her training? Have you heard from Mireille yet?'

Norah shook her head. 'Not a dickie bird.'

'I shouldn't beat yourself up any more about that girl,' Penny said firmly. 'You did your best and if that's not enough, tell her to sling her hook.'

Norah didn't respond. They'd had this conversation time and again. Nothing had changed and she still didn't feel any better about it. 'Amélie seems to love being at the hospital.'

'I always thought she'd be good at nursing,' said Penny. 'She's such a caring girl.'

'You're right,' said Norah. 'They work jolly hard but she sometimes comes to see me on her day off.'

'What about you and Jim?'

'Oh we plod along you know,' Norah said cheerily. 'Ivan helps out in the nursery and now that the warmer weather is coming, he and Christine are going to start up the market stall shortly. Which reminds me, are you going to do your allotment this year? You're a bit late starting.'

As the person in charge of the Clifton Road allotments, it was Norah's job to make sure that they were all being used. The government had encouraged the digging up of waste ground, parks and gardens as part of the Dig for Victory initiative to feed the nation.

Penny looked a little sheepish. 'I meant to tell you about that. I don't think I'm going to have the time, what with the café and Victor and all and then I have to get the bike out to come over. Quite frankly I can't fit it all in.'

Norah nodded. Penny had never been a dedicated gardener but at one time she'd been grateful for the home-grown produce. When he was declared a POW, Ted's pay had still gone into his bank account but that account was in his name only so Penny had none of it. After filling in a load of forms and having to send her marriage certificate and proof of identity, the army had eventually sorted it out and she was able to access his pay. This meant that life was a lot easier for both Penny and Mrs Draycot so the allotment was surplus to requirements.

'That's fine,' said Norah although she wished her friend had mentioned it before. Now that it was already the first week in May, whoever took the allotment over would struggle to get everything done for the growing season. She sipped her Camp coffee.

'Did you know that the WI have a canning machine now?' Penny's comment brought Norah back to the present. 'Mum says that anyone who has too much produce in their back garden can go to their meetings and get it canned.'

'That sounds like a brilliant idea,' cried Norah. 'Can you take anything at all?'

'Not vegetables,' Penny said. 'Apparently that needs a much higher temperature.'

'I might take her up on that with my raspberries,' said Norah. 'I do use Kilner jars but it's getting harder and harder to get hold of them. Sometimes things taste a lot better from a can.'

'I'll have a word,' Penny promised.

The door creaked and Uncle Fred called out, 'You going to do any work today?' He sounded a bit peeved.

'I'd better go,' said Penny. 'It's getting close to lunch time anyway.'

Norah stood to her feet. 'Fancy coming to the pictures on Saturday?'

'I can't,' said Penny. 'I promised one of the boys I'd go to a concert with him.'

Norah was puzzled. 'What, one of the Canadians?'

Penny nodded. 'It's at the assembly rooms. They're raising funds for Spitfire Week and some big-wig is coming down from London. He got a couple of tickets and invited me.'

Norah didn't know what to say. A married woman going out with a Canadian soldier? Didn't she realise the gossips would have a field day?

'And don't look at me like that,' Penny added. 'It's only a concert.'

Norah felt herself blushing. 'Yes of course,' she said quickly. 'I hope you have a nice time.'

As she biked back home, Norah couldn't help worrying. She was sure Penny's invitation was innocent enough, but if tongues started to wag, it might get back to Ted, then who knew what might happen when he came home?

Amélie was on lates when she discovered that her favourite patient, Mr Swinnerton had died just before the shift change. This was her first real encounter with death and Amélie struggled to remain totally professional about it. As she dabbed her eyes behind the screens pulled around his bed, she heard Sister asking the staff nurse to show Amélie how to do the last offices.

'What's that?' she mouthed to the nurse standing next to her.

'You've got to lay him out.'

Immediately thrown into a panic, Amélie was battling the urge to cry again. She had spent quite a lot of time with Mr Swinnerton. He was a lovely old man and reminded her in lots of ways of Ivan. It wasn't an easy moment when she went behind the curtain and saw him for the first time. She'd never even seen a dead body before, except perhaps for a hedgehog which had been run over by a car. Luckily for her, Staff Nurse was both efficient and understanding.

'We'll wash his body first,' she said gently. 'Then we'll give him a clean gown and brush his hair.'

Amélie's hands were a little shaky but listening to Staff Nurse quietly talking to Mr Swinnerton as she worked on him made it more of an act of kindness than a perfunctory duty. Having washed him all over, they took off his wrist watch and a ring he wore on the little finger of his right hand. Staff Nurse wrote what she'd done in the buff folder and put the jewellery in a paper bag marked with the patient's name on the side. After that she put a name tag onto his left wrist and the big toe of his right foot. Eventually they were ready to cover his face with the sheet.

Somewhere in the ward an emergency bell was ringing.

'I'd better answer that,' said Staff Nurse as she pulled off her rubber apron and hastily washed her hands at the sink. 'You stay here until the porter comes in with the trolley. Then you can go with him to the mortuary. Don't forget to take the buff folder with you.' She straightened her apron and smiled. 'You've done very well.'

She had no sooner gone when the big mortuary trolley came rumbling into the ward and a second or two later, the porter pushed it between the curtains which hung around Mr Swinnerton's bed.

The porter was a lot younger than she'd expected, probably not much more than twenty-one. Not only that, but she couldn't help noticing that he was breath-takingly handsome with thick, slicked back, light brown hair and large brown eyes. He seemed so strong and muscular that she wondered, vaguely, why he wasn't in uniform.

The trolley was made to look like an ordinary trolley with a false mattress on the top. Amélie and the porter slid Mr Swinnerton underneath in such a way that the long sheet over the mattress hid him from view. Any patient or visitor seeing the trolley would have no idea that there was a dead body underneath. Not that there was any risk that his fellow patients on the ward would see him leave anyway. Amélie stuck her head out from behind the screens to give one of the other nurses a nod, then the screens were pulled around every bed in the ward.

Amélie laid the buff-coloured folder on the top of the trolley and the two of them set off.

'Is this your first death?' the porter asked as they walked along the corridor.

Amélie nodded. Was it so obvious that she was still struggling not to give way to tears?

He smiled sympathetically. 'The first time is always tough,' he said in a rich plummy voice. 'I suggest you tell yourself he's at rest now. You did all you could and he's out of pain.'

It sounded like good advice so Amélie nodded again.

The morgue was outside the main building and it was raining. It didn't help her mood to have to take the trolley across the courtyard in the dark. The wind whipped her cloak up and at one point, Amélie had to grab her cap before it was ripped from her hair. When they reached the big green double doors, the porter backed into it and pulled the trolley into the room. Amélie managed to report to the attendant, a much older man with round glasses and a moustache, in a semi-professional way but then she burst into tears.

'This is the young lady's first one,' said the porter by way of explanation.

'Take her into my office and make her a cup of tea,' said the mortuary attendant.

The porter guided Amélie into a small room which had a sink and table and two chairs. He motioned Amélie to sit down and busied himself by filling the kettle. There were a couple of cups on the draining board which he washed in cold water.

Amélie did her best to pull herself together. 'Sorry,' she sniffed.

'That's quite all right,' said the porter, his posh accent so out of place for his position. 'Please don't worry about it. If you don't mind me asking, what's your name?'

'Amélie Osborne.'

'Amélie. That's a pretty name.'

'That's what poor Mr Swinnerton always said,' Amélie sniffed.

The porter put two mugs onto the table and sat opposite her. 'I'm Bob,' he said. 'Bob Kane.' He held out his hand. 'I'm pleased to meet you, Amélie.'

Chapter 9

The next day, Amélie was called into Sister's office. As she waited by the desk, she could tell by her expression that something was seriously wrong. She racked her brains to work out what she'd done. The door opened and Staff Nurse walked in. Amélie sucked in her lips anxiously.

Sister opened the buff-coloured folder on her desk. 'We have received a complaint,' she began. 'When you prepared Mr Swinnerton for the morgue, it says here that he had a ring and wrist watch.'

'Yes Sister,' said Staff Nurse. 'I put them in an envelope to go into the locked cupboard here in your office.'

Sister rose majestically to her feet and taking her key from on top of the desk, she opened the cupboard. It was empty. Staff Nurse gasped. 'Oh Lor . . .' Her face coloured. 'But I'm sure . . .' she began again.

'Did you see what happened to the watch and ring, Nurse?' Sister directed her question to Amélie.

'Yes, Sister,' said Amélie. 'I saw Staff put it in a brown envelope and then she put it on the top of the locker.'

'That's right!' Staff Nurse exclaimed. 'Then somebody rang the emergency bell and I had to leave the room.'

They were both looking at Amélie now. 'Well I didn't touch it,' she said quickly.

Sister pressed a buzzer on her desk and shortly afterwards a ward orderly appeared in the doorway. 'Phyllis, would you look on the floor next to bed five for a brown envelope.' The girl turned to go. 'And perhaps you could look in the locker as well.'

The girl was back in a few minutes. 'Nothing there, Sister.' Sister waved her away.

'I definitely put it on the locker,' Staff Nurse said doggedly.

'Well, it's not there now,' Sister snapped. 'So where is it? At best this looks like carelessness, at worse it smacks of theft.'

Amélie took in her breath, her hand automatically going to her mouth.

Staff Nurse turned towards her. 'Did you take it with you to the morgue?'

Amélie shook her head. 'No, Staff . . . at least I don't think I did. I . . . I don't remember.'

Sister's mouth was set in a hard line. 'I'm afraid the matter doesn't end there. We cannot have the reputation of the hospital sullied by an incident like this. The board of governors take a very dim view when patients' property goes missing and I don't have to remind both of you that theft is a sackable offence.'

Outside in the corridor, Staff Nurse glared at Amélie. 'You stupid girl,' she spat. 'I'm telling you now, I'm not going to get the push because of something you did.'

'But I didn't touch it, Staff. I promise. It was on the locker when we took the body . . .'

'I want you to go outside now and scour that pathway with a fine-tooth comb,' she said. 'Talk to the mortician and the porter and if you come back here without that

80

watch and ring I'll sack you myself.' With that she sailed off leaving Amélie to blink back her tears.

One of the refugees in Canterbury Road had just had a baby. When Norah arrived with some radishes, spring cabbage and some purple sprouting broccoli, the baby was in the back garden in a rather dilapidated pram which had been donated by someone. It was crying piteously. After she'd parked her bike, Norah laid her hand gently on the top of the mound of blankets and spoke softly. 'There, there, little one. You want your mummy, don't you? That's quite a pong you've made.'

Someone came out of the kitchen. 'Oh hello, Luv,' said Cook.

'I've brought you some veg,' said Norah, 'and I think this little chap needs changing.'

Cook pushed open the kitchen door and shouted, 'Molly, call Mrs Stein, will you? The baby needs changing.'

By the time the two women had unloaded the box Norah had put in the basket on the front of her bicycle, Mrs Stein had appeared in the doorway. Norah realised then that she'd seen the girl a couple of times before: a sad-faced young woman with tired, sunken eyes and stringy black hair. At this moment in time, she looked far from healthy but with some good food and plenty of rest, in just a few months she'd have every chance to look a lot better. As the pair of them smiled at each other, Norah's heart went out to her. Right now, the poor girl would have mixed feelings. Stuck here in a strange country with a different language, she would be relieved to be safe and the birth of her baby had brought some joy but it could also exacerbate the grief that, in all probability, her husband would never see his newborn child.

As his mother lifted the child from his pram, Norah could see that he was dressed in a child's jumper, three sizes too big. It was then that she decided to go up into the loft at the earliest opportunity.

It didn't take long to find the small suitcase. She carried it downstairs and took it into her bedroom. Laying the case onto her bed, Norah opened the lid and immediately her throat tightened. It had been almost two years since she'd seen Eric's layette. Way back in 1940 she had been promised a baby to adopt. The lady from the Welfare, Miss Bundy, had told her his name was Eric, a name Norah wasn't too keen on, but once he became their baby, Miss Bundy assured them they could call him what they liked. But, thanks to Jago Ffox-Webster's meddling, Eric had been given to another couple. Over the months, she and Jim had tried to adopt another baby but it seemed that Ffox-Webster's powerful friends still had plenty of clout. It didn't take long to find out that their names were black-listed.

Norah ran her fingers over the exquisitely knitted jackets, vests and booties. How much love had been put into every stitch. Underneath she found the embroidered shawl, three white nightdresses and the beautifully made romper suits. She sighed. It seemed such a waste to leave them here when a little baby just a few streets away had absolutely nothing. She sat down beside the suitcase. Was she giving up hope of ever having a baby of her own? No. She was simply giving Eric's things away. She wondered what he was like. He'd be coming up for two now; a little boy scampering around his garden, playing with his toys, discovering the petals on buttercups, blowing dandelion clocks for the first time . . . Norah felt moisture on her cheeks.

'Have a happy life darling. May God bless you, my Eric.'

She closed the case and glanced up at the clock on the chest of drawers. Three-thirty. There was just enough time to nip back to Canterbury Road before she had to get Jim's tea.

The man in the mortuary wasn't the one Amélie had seen last evening. This one was a little man, balding and dressed in shabby clothes under his brown overall. He was quite sniffy when Amélie told him why she'd come. He had been sweeping the floor with a heavy broom and as she finished telling him why she was here, his eyes narrowed.

'I 'ope you're not suggestin' that anyone in this mortuary 'ave been thieving,' he snapped.

Amélie sighed inwardly. She had tried to explain what had happened as tactfully as she could, but now *he* was annoyed with her too. 'I'm not suggesting anything,' she said quickly. 'The point is a watch and a ring are unaccounted for and Sister has sent me to try and find them.'

He leaned his broom against the wall and reached in the top pocket of his overall for his pipe. She had noticed that he smelled of pipe tobacco and that his fingers were heavily stained.

'No personal effects come down 'ere,' the man said. 'Any valuables goes straight to Sister's office.'

'Yes, I know that,' Amélie said meekly, 'but the point is, they didn't and now Sister thinks I've taken them.'

'That's your look out, Nurse,' he said unsympathetically. 'Nothing to do wi' me. I'm sick of people comin' in here and implying I've taken the patients' stuff.'

'Oh, please,' Amélie cried, 'I wasn't suggesting . . .'

The man knocked his pipe out against his broom handle. 'I've had the coppers down here three times and I don't mind telling you, I'm ruddy sick of it.' He frowned crossly. 'And I'm telling you now, if it carries on for much longer, I shall give in my notice, you see if I don't.'

Reluctantly, Amélie turned away. What was she going

to do? If she didn't find the items it looked as if she would say goodbye to her nursing career before it had even started. She was trembling now. One the way back to the ward, she kept her head down, her eyes searching every corner of the grounds outside and the corridors inside, hoping against hope that she might come across it but, of course, there was no trace of a brown envelope.

'Hello Amélie,' said a familiar voice. 'You look a bit upset. Is everything all right?'

She looked up into a pair of dark brown eyes. 'Bob!' she cried. 'Oh Bob.'

'My dear girl,' he said. 'Whatever's the matter?'

Amélie began to explain, her words tumbling over one another as she told him about Mr Swinnerton's ring and watch. As she spoke, he laid his hand comfortingly on her shoulder.

'I remember that envelope,' he said, frowning slightly as he was thinking back. 'I feel sure that Sister had it in her hand.'

'But now it's gone,' she said, her eyes filling with tears, 'and I've looked absolutely everywhere.'

'Outside?'

'Yes.'

Bob looked thoughtful. 'You know, as I recall it was very windy that night.'

'But it's not there,' she insisted. 'I've looked.'

'Well two pairs of eyes are better than one,' he said with a smile. 'I think we should look again. Come on. I'll help you.'

'It's no good,' she mumbled, but he took her by the arm and before she knew it, Amélie was on her way back outside.

'You look in that flowerbed,' he instructed as he wandered along on the opposite side of the path. They pushed the vegetation with their feet and searched under a wooden bench.

'Well, I'll be dashed!' cried Bob. 'Look what I've found.' He was holding up a brown envelope.

'You found it!' she cried. 'Where was it?'

'Right there under the rose bush.' He wiped the envelope with his hand. 'It's a bit mucky but it's all there.'

Amélie looked inside and sure enough Mr Swinnerton's ring and watch were there. She was so relieved her knees almost buckled.

'Oh please, don't start crying again,' he chuckled.

'Oh Bob I can't tell you how grateful I am,' she began. 'Sister threatened me with the sack. You're my hero.'

He gave her a mock salute. 'One hero happy to be of service,' he said and Amélie laughed.

He walked with her towards the ward. As they came to the public toilets, Amélie excused herself and nipped inside to wash her face and tidy up. When she'd dried her hands, she took the envelope out of her pocket. It was quite dry but there was still a little bit of earth on one side. The envelope itself looked as if it had come unstuck. It had rained quite hard during the night but the rose bush must have protected it from the wet. Thank God the ring and watch were both safe and sound.

When she came out, Bob was still waiting. 'If you need back-up,' he said, 'just gave me a shout and I'll come running.'

'Thank you, Bob,' she whispered. 'I don't know how to thank you enough.'

He saluted her and turned to go. 'Actually,' he said turning back. 'There is one way you can thank me.'

Amélie gave him a blank stare.

He raised his eyebrows and said cautiously, 'How would you feel about coming with me to the dance on Saturday week?' He shook his head apologetically then added, 'I'd ask you to come this Saturday but I've already arranged to go and see my mother.'

Amélie's mind was in an absolute whirl. He was so good-looking and he sounded really posh. She gave him a shy smile. 'All right Bob,' she said. 'Yes. I'd like that. I'd like that a lot.'

The people at the refugee house were very touched by Norah's kind gesture, especially the baby's mother. She wept when she saw Eric's layette.

'So kind,' she kept saying, 'so kind.' Norah was treated to a cup of tea laced with a little brandy and a few moments later, the baby, protesting loudly, was laid in her arms dressed in his new romper suit.

As she biked back home, Norah felt strangely contented and she couldn't help smiling. When she reached the crossing the gates were down which was a bit annoying because at this time of day it meant she would have to wait for at least three trains to go by. Several people stood in front of her and to her surprise and delight Norah spotted Penny on the other side of the gates. She was about to wave and call her friend's name but as she opened her mouth, the tall, good-looking Canadian soldier in uniform who was standing just behind Penny put his hand on her shoulder. Penny turned and looked up at him and as the first train hurtled by, Norah, staring through the speeding carriage windows, saw them kissing passionately.

She held her breath. What should she do? It would be too embarrassing to come face to face with Penny now but when the gates opened she couldn't simply bike past with her nose in the air as if nothing had happened. That would be even worse.

In the distance she could hear the scream of aircraft

engines coming closer. As the second train rumbled by someone cried out, 'It's a bloody Jerry. Get under cover.' It was then that Norah heard the machine gun fire. The pilot had obviously seen the people standing around and the train coming into West Worthing station. Dropping her bike on the ground she rushed, with others, towards the open doors of the shops close by. She only just had time to fling herself into the butcher's before bullets ripped along the wall. Picking herself up from the doorway, Norah hurled herself to the back of the shop where several other people huddled together on the sawdust covered floor. A little girl was crying and her mother was trying to comfort her. Shivering and shaking herself, Norah covered her head with her hands, the only protection she had, and waited for it to pass. There was a loud bang as the glass window of the hairdresser's next door exploded. They could hear the sound of falling glass. Now the child was hysterical.

The sound of the aircraft faded but everyone stayed where they were for a few seconds. Norah rose to her feet to go but then the butcher said, 'Stay down, Mrs. The bugger's coming back.'

And to her horror, Norah heard the sound of machine gun bullets hitting walls on the other side of the road but thankfully there was no one on the street now. Everyone stayed down until they were sure the plane wasn't coming back. Norah stood to her feet and brushed the sawdust from her clothing. Following the crowd, Norah joined them as they filed out of the shop, each person thanking the butcher as they went.

An ARP had arrived. 'Anyone hurt?'

Outside in the street, the hairdresser was already sweeping up the broken glass, but there were no injuries. Norah picked up her bike and rather shakily set off over the crossing and headed for home. Penny was nowhere to be seen.

Chapter 10

His mother's care home was in an unspoiled area on the outskirts of Ruislip. It was a big house, a bit run-down but set in its own grounds. Bob Kane felt a little awkward walking up the gravel path and he couldn't stop himself from looking over his shoulder as if he shouldn't be there. When he reached the door, he checked the address on his letter once again. Yes, he'd got the right place. The Corner House, Ruislip Lane.

It had taken him several months to find the place where his mother was living. The people who looked after him in the children's home where he'd grown up gave little away but he had known that once upon a time his father had lived in London, in some posh house near Marble Arch. He couldn't remember who had told him that or when they'd said it, but all his life that fact had stuck in his brain as if it was glued there. That was why he'd practised talking with a posh accent. If he came from such a salubrious area, he'd better sound the part. He'd save up enough money to have tea in a hotel foyer or a drink in the bar and listen to the way people spoke until he had it off to a 'T'. He never did manage to find the posh house and at first the people living in the area looked down their noses at him, but once he'd perfected his new speaking voice, they did their best to help but it was all needle in the haystack stuff.

His parents had been separated because his mother had been taken ill. No one said what was wrong with her but after his fruitless search for his father, he'd discovered that she'd been put in a nursing home near Battersea Park. When Hitler bombed London, many of the big institutions were moved out of the city and the place where his mother lived was one of them.

'I've come to see Mrs Kane,' he told the woman who opened the door after he'd rung the bell. 'I'm her son.'

They took him to the matron's office first. She was a rat-faced woman with thinning hair and a tufty-looking cyst on her top lip. He couldn't stop himself staring at the grey hairs growing out of it as she spoke. She checked his identity and his story and after a few minutes he was allowed to see his mother. She was smaller than he remembered, grey hair and thin, a nervy woman who sat bolt upright with her hands in her lap.

Matron slid her arm along his mother's shoulders and leaning down she said gently, 'Ivy, dear, this is Robert. Your son.'

Bob Kane's mother looked up with rheumy eyes but no hint of recognition. But then why should she know him? They hadn't seen each other since 1926 when he was eight. He sat beside her and reached for her hand. 'Hello Mother,' he said stiffly. 'How are you?'

Jim was surprised to see a familiar face coming through the door of the police station. 'Captain Carruthers!' he cried. 'Long time, no see. Have you been on Monty's manoeuvres?'

'Not me,' Carruthers chuckled. 'Only having half a hand does have its advantages you know.'

For the past few days, the whole town had been disrupted by what was being called a 'super austerity endurance test'. As part of a plan devised by Lt General Montgomery who had a punishing reputation for the physical fitness of his men, it involved a great 'battle' involving British and Canadian troops. What with armoured cars permanently parked in Sompting Avenue, convoys of tanks meandering along the country roads and war games taking place on every bit of public ground from Broadwater Green to the Territorial barracks on the Upper Brighton Road, the people of Worthing were grumbling that the whole town was beginning to resemble the siege of Leningrad.

The two men shook hands warmly. 'So what does bring you back here? Not searching out more blokes absent without leave I hope.'

'No, no,' said the captain. He put a wrapped bottle onto the desk. 'I was so grateful for your help, I wanted to give you a rather belated thank you.'

Jim raised an eyebrow. 'That's very civil of you, sir, but I'm afraid I shall have to refuse. It could look like a bribe,' he said teasingly.

The captain sighed. 'That certainly wasn't my intention,' he said taking off his gloves revealing his damaged hand for the first time. 'It's just that . . .'

'I know, I know,' Jim cut in.

'I don't know how you do it,' Captain Carruthers went on. 'We spend hours and hours chasing bloody AWOLs. On top of that, we're losing an awful lot of petrol. Black market of course but I can't for the life of me, pin down how they're doing it. The top-brass want to keep it all under wraps. Not good for morale they say but it sticks in my throat. The country can't afford to let these blighters get away with it and quite frankly, neither can I.'

Jim nodded. 'Tell me about it,' he said. 'Right now, we're after some low life who's passing forged ration cards in the town. I'm told this sort of thing is getting so serious in some places that the government is considering cancelling whole batches.'

'And they call it *petty* larceny,' Carruthers said adding quickly, 'anyway, I'm sure you'll track them down. Jim, I was so impressed with your reasoning when we caught Hughes.'

Jim was modestly flattered. 'A little local knowledge goes a long way, sir,' he said with a shrug of his shoulders.

'Call me Lennard,' Carruthers interrupted.

'Lennard,' Jim said. He picked up the wrapped bottle. 'Now about this bribe . . .'

'It wasn't intended . . .' Lennard began again.

'A good wine needs to be drunk with good food,' said Jim. 'My wife is a pretty darned good cook. Perhaps you might like to bring that bottle around to my home some evening and join us in a meal.'

Lennard Carruthers smiled. 'You know what? I could do with a bit of good home cooking.'

'That's all settled then,' said Jim. 'Saturday week?'

'Saturday week it is then.'

Bob met Amélie on the corner of Park Road the following week. They had planned to go to the dance but she couldn't get the time off on Saturday so he'd suggested the pictures instead.

It was a lovely evening and she had taken a great deal of care with her appearance. She was wearing a summer dress made of a rayon and cotton mix with a fitted bodice and gathered skirt. The pattern on the material was made up of small blue and pink circles, each with a flower in the centre. Although it was quite warm at the moment, she'd brought along her pink cardigan for when the evening cooled. Bob smiled when he saw her.

They strolled along Lyndhurst Road towards the town and he took her to the Rivoli cinema for tea and a bun in the tea rooms in the vestibule above the entrance. The cinema was popular with young lovers in the town especially in the summer months when on hot days they would open the roof, and what could be more romantic than cuddling your girlfriend (or boyfriend) under the stars?

As they talked it didn't take Bob long to find out that Amélie had a sister and that she'd come to live in Worthing in 1939. She told him about Norah and Jim leaving him with the impression that they were in some way related. She briefly mentioned her mother but she didn't say much about her step-father except to say that he had died at the end of 1940.

As for Bob, when it was his turn, he told her that he had two brothers, one of whom had died in a bombing raid.

'Oh I'm so sorry,' said Amélie. For a moment or two he looked quite teary. Her heart went out to him. She held his hand as Bob shrugged bravely on, telling her that his other brother was somewhere in North Africa. His parents, he said, lived in Ruislip.

'Where's that?' Amélie asked.

'Just outside London,' he said. 'It's a village on the River Pinn.'

'It sounds a lovely place,' she said tucking into her iced bun.

'It is,' he said with a condescending smile.

'Do you have a picture?' she mused.

'Sadly no, but it's a hobby of mine to collect postcards of the places where I've been. I have one of Ruislip. I'll show you one sometime.' He paused and added with a sad expression, 'I wanted one of Worthing to show my mother but since the war you can only get ones with flowers on or jokey ones.'

'Oh, I've got one you can have,' Amélie blurted out. 'I was going to send it to my little sister but I never got around to it.'

'Thank you.' He smiled and Amélie blushed.

'Excuse me, but you've got some icing on your mouth. May I . . . ?' He reached over and gently wiped the corner of her mouth with his thumb leaving Amélie with a feeling far more delicious than cake.

'Haven't you been called up yet?' she asked.

'I have,' he admitted, 'but I'm not going. I'm what's called a conscientious objector.'

Amélie frowned. 'What does that mean?'

Bob brushed his lapels with his fingers. 'It means that I don't believe in picking fights.'

'Is that because you're religious?'

'No,' he said, 'but I have very strong beliefs.'

'But surely,' she began, 'we have to stop people like Hitler. We can't allow him to carry on bombing us and killing innocent people.'

'That may well be the case,' said Bob sniffily, 'but don't ask me to pick up a rifle and kill some poor German who didn't want to fight either.'

When he put it like that Amélie thought he had a point but surely, the thought of Hitler and Mussolini settling their differences with Churchill over tea and buns was the stuff of fairy tales.

'I've heard that people like you are sent to prison,' she said cautiously.

'That may well happen,' he said defiantly. 'I've been summoned to a tribunal but I'm hoping I get an exemption because I'm already working in the hospital.'

Their tea finished, Bob looked at his watch, a rather splendid-looking one with French writing on the face. She caught his wrist to get a better look and read aloud the words, *'ancre 15 rubis antimagnétique'*. She was impressed. 'That means Anchored 15 rubies. Antimagnetic. It's Swiss, isn't it?'

'A twenty-first birthday present from my father,' he said. He opened his mouth to explain but thought the better of it. Best not to complicate things this early in a relationship.

Amélie was smiling. 'It's lovely.'

He took his arm back and pulled down the sleeve of his jumper. 'The film starts in ten minutes. Are you ready?'

Outside the tea rooms, she took his arm and he led her in. The film was called *Next of Kin* a thriller starring Ft. Lt. Mervyn Johns and 2nd Lt. Jack Hawkins. It was a cautionary tale showing how a few careless words, lackadaisical actions or sharing something seemingly innocuous could cost lives. Amélie would have preferred something lighter but it didn't matter. It was just wonderful being with someone like Bob.

He had paid for her too, two seats in the one and nines, and halfway through the film, he held her hand.

They walked to Park Road after the film and at the gate of the nurses' quarters he stood in front of her with his hands on her upper arms. 'Thank you for a wonderful evening, Amélie.'

'No, *thank you*,' Amélie said with feeling.

He traced the outline of her face with his finger. 'May I kiss you goodnight?'

Amélie closed her eyes and a moment later she felt his lips brush her cheek. It was a little disappointing that he hadn't kissed her on the lips but at the same time, she was glad that he was so respectful.

'Thank you Amélie,' he said again, 'and goodnight.'

Chapter 11

On her day off, Amélie hurried across the railway lines and headed along South Street towards the centre of town. She and Mireille were meeting in Chichester known affectionately as Chi by the locals. She wasn't late but every moment was precious. Even here there was war damage. Basin Street had suffered a hit in the previous year and although the rubble had been cleared, the scars remained.

The street narrowed and a few moments later she saw her sister waiting near the ancient Market Cross. Considering how old it was, she had expected it to be heavily protected by sandbags but surprisingly, for a city so close to the battle of Britain airfields, it wasn't. Mireille was gazing into the window or Stead and Simpson's shoe shop on the corner.

'Coo-ee,' Amélie called.

Mireille turned and as soon as she saw her, waved. A moment or two later the two of them were giving each other a big hug.

'It's good to see you.'

'It's good to see you too.'

Mireille held her younger sister at arm's length. 'How are you? Train journey all right?'

'No problem. How did you get here?'

'I cadged a lift from Ginger,' said Mireille.

Amélie raised an eyebrow and gave her a knowing look. 'Umm, Ginger. You told me he gave you a lift the day after Rene's wedding, I seem to remember.'

Mireille cuffed her playfully on the arm. 'Behave yourself, will you,' she said. 'There's nothing in it.'

Then laughing, the two of them linked arms as they turned towards West Street. 'Cup of tea first I think,' said Mireille.

The Cathedral View café was right opposite the building itself and next to Morant's department store. They found a window seat and made themselves comfortable. Mireille ordered a pot of tea for two.

'So how are you enjoying your nursing?' she began.

Amélie nodded. 'Love it. Thanks for helping me out with the money. I'd've been completely stuck without you. I'll pay you back as soon as I can.'

'Don't worry about it,' Mireille said with a wave of her hand. 'Like I said, that's what sisters are for.'

All the same, Amélie knew she would be eternally grateful. She had managed to send her sister six shillings and sixpence out of her wage in February and she hoped to be able to keep it up until the money was paid back. What she didn't know was that when Mireille had come to the rescue with her own savings, she'd also had to borrow from friends, including Ginger. Her sister knew it would be easier for her to pay back her loans but Amélie would struggle. While it was true that as a student she didn't have to pay for her board and lodging, nurses only earned eighteen pounds a year.

When the tea arrived, Mireille set about arranging the cups and pouring. 'I half expected you to turn up in uniform,' she remarked with a chuckle. 'I haven't even seen you in it yet.'

'And you won't unless you're in hospital,' said Amélie. 'We're not allowed to wear it outside the wards.'

Mireille expressed her disappointment by pulling the corners of her mouth down.

'It's all to do with hygiene,' said Amélie. 'They're very strict.'

Her sister pushed a cup of tea in front of her. 'So tell me, what's it like?'

'It's hard work but I don't mind. It's the long hours that make it so difficult,' Amélie began. 'I start at seven-thirty. We have to be on the ward in time for the night sister's report and then we line up for inspection.'

'Inspection?' Mireille repeated as she spooned some sugar into her cup.

'Sister checks that our uniform is clean and we have to hold our hands out like this so she can look at our nails.'

'Crumbs,' Mireille exclaimed. 'So what's your first job?'

'Helping the patients to wash and clean their teeth,' Amélie began again. 'After breakfast, we give the really sick ones a blanket bath, and then we make the beds. At the moment most of my day seems to be taken up with dishing out bed pans but everything runs like a well-oiled machine and you have to be very careful to do everything properly.'

Mireille pulled a face. 'Smelly bed pans, ugh.'

'You get used to it.' She hesitated for a second or two. 'There's something I have to tell you.'

'Go on.'

'I want you to promise me you won't get cross until I tell you everything.'

Mireille pulled a face. 'All right,' she said uncertainly. 'What is it? You're not getting married, are you?'

'No, nothing like that,' said Amélie. 'It's about those rings.'

She saw her sister stiffen.

'You promised not to be annoyed, remember?' Amélie continued. 'I took them to a jeweller's. I was going to sell them, like you said, but then the jeweller pointed out an inscription inside the band. It said "Love is eternal" with the initials of the couple at each end. He explained that such a personal inscription devalued an item.'

'Shame,' said Mireille, sipping her tea.

'The point is,' Amélie went on, 'the initials were N D and D O.'

'So?' Mireille challenged.

'Don't you see? Our father must have given those rings to our mother,' said Amélie. 'Just to be sure, I wrote to Somerset House and got a copy of their marriage certificate. Natalie Delacroix and David Osborne.' She laid it on the table in front of them.

When Mireille looked up again, she had tears in her eyes. 'And did you sell them?'

'Of course not,' Amélie cried. 'How could I?'

'But I thought . . .' Mireille began.

'I know you did,' said Amélie, 'and so did I.'

By now both girls were dabbing their eyes.

'I've left the rings at the Lilacs,' said Amélie. 'They're safer there than in the hospital.'

Mireille nodded her approval. 'I'm sorry I was so hasty.'

'It's fine,' said Amélie. 'Whenever I go back home, I keep looking at them. It's good to have something tangible to remember them by. I did think I might bring them today, but I was too scared of losing them.'

They paused as a group of Canadian soldiers marched past the window, their arms swinging in unison, their faces facing front except for one man who risked the wrath of his sergeant by turning his head slightly and giving them a wink. As he marched on, the two girls giggled.

'Cheeky sod,' Mireille murmured.

'Are you going out with Ginger?' her sister asked.

'I do sometimes,' Mireille admitted with a nonchalant air. 'He's handy for a lift or to get me home from a dance late at night, but don't go reading anything into it.'

'Why's that?'

'You know perfectly well why,' said Mireille. She'd lowered her voice and Amélie could hear the bitterness. 'I'm not letting anyone do that to me again. Not ever.'

Amélie looked down and fiddled with the edge of the tablecloth. 'Not all men are like him.'

Mireille looked up sharply. 'Have you met someone then?'

'I have,' said Amélie, looking up to meet her sister's eye.

Mireille smiled. 'So come on. Spill the beans.'

Amélie took a deep breath. 'His name is Bob Kane and he works at the hospital.'

Mireille looked impressed. 'So what is he? A doctor, in administration, an ambulance driver?'

'He works as a hospital porter,' Amélie began cautiously, 'but he sounds really posh. I'm sure that given the chance he could get a really good job. Actually . . .' She hesitated, then deliberately avoiding her sister's eye she added, 'he's a conscientious objector.'

Mireille choked on her tea. 'Well, that's a turn up for the books.'

'Oh please don't be like that,' Amélie said. 'He's not a coward or anything but he does have a deep-seated belief that we shouldn't kill anybody.'

Mireille took a breath. 'That sounds very commendable but what happens if he gets his call-up papers?'

'He says he will refuse to go with a gun,' Amélie added with a passion that wasn't entirely her own, 'but he's perfectly willing to drive an ambulance in the war zone and pick up casualties or something like that.'

'That's big of him.'

Her sarcasm wasn't wasted on Amélie. 'Oh Mireille, he's a lovely man. He really is.'

Her sister smiled. 'You really like him, don't you?'

Amélie nodded shyly.

'Then that's good enough for me.' Mireille began pouring herself another cup of tea. 'So how long have you been going out?'

'Actually we've only been out a couple of times, just to the pictures,' Amélie admitted, 'but we have lovely chats in the canteen.'

'In that case, good luck to you.'

Amélie glanced up at her sister, a tad unsure of what she meant but she said no more. They sat quietly for a few minutes looking out of the window and then Mireille said, 'I've never been in that cathedral, have you?'

Amélie shook her head.

'Shall we give it a go then?'

Passing the campanile, the only free-standing bell tower in the country, the two sisters entered the cathedral. If the green tiled roof and imposing spire were breath-taking, the inside was even more so. At the far end of the church, eighteen boys, choristers from the Prebendal choir school adjacent to the precinct, had filed into the choir stalls, their high-pitched clear voices echoing around the stone walls. Mireille and Amélie slid into a pew about halfway up the aisle and sat silently listening. Mireille would never have thought of herself as religious but as she'd walked towards the high altar in this place, she'd had goose-bumps all over.

Amélie knelt as the Dean rose to offer the collect for the day while the scattered congregation said the Lord's prayer in unison. Mireille gazed at the beautiful stained-glass windows. She couldn't stop thinking about all the people who had worshipped in this very place for at least a thousand years. Hadn't they faced conflicts and tyranny, plague and civil war, the threat of invasion and even been part of the war to end all wars? And yet the British people, as a nation, had survived. Once again, the country had her back to the wall but across the channel, the land of her birth had already lost her freedom.

Mireille had only a hazy memory of her life in France. She had been no more than ten when she'd come to England with her family but she recalled the flower seller's stall next to Glaces Maison where they bought ice creams on the way to the park. She remembered Mama wearing a big summer hat with a bright yellow scarf around the brim as she lay on the grass next to her gramophone playing records. And before Linnet was born, when she and Amélie were much younger, she remembered a day out when she'd sat in a seat on the back of her mother's bicycle while Amélie rode on her father's cross-bar. She had been happy then, when Mama and Père were alive. She swallowed the lump that had formed in her throat.

The choir boys finished their hymn and began to walk in procession once again. Amélie sat back onto the pew and the sisters exchanged a smile.

'Mireille, why won't you forgive Norah?'

Amélie's question brought her up with a jolt. 'I have,' she flustered.

'You still haven't written to her.'

'I will, I will. I'm just not ready to do it yet, that's all.'

Amélie reached out to squeeze her sister's hand. 'She didn't mean to upset you,' she said. 'Norah is a good person.'

Mireille sucked in her lips. 'I know. And I'm sorry.'

'Then why?' There was a pause. 'She's written to you nearly every week.'

'I was going to reply, really I was,' Mireille protested,

'but then the weeks became months and I felt awkward about it.'

Amélie put her head on one side.

Mireille looked away. 'Yes, you're right. I admit I was very angry when I realised that she'd been keeping stuff from us. She had no right . . .'

'She knows that,' Amélie interrupted, 'and she did apologise if you remember.'

'Okay, okay,' Mireille hissed. 'I just needed a bit of time to sort myself out.'

Amélie slid out of the pew. 'Come on,' she said, deliberately lightening the moment. 'Let's have a look around.'

'There's something I want to tell you first,' said Mireille.

Amélie sat back down.

'You remember I told you a few months ago that I'd met some French airmen,' she began. 'Well, they've invited me a few times to join them in a house near the airfield.' She heard her sister take in a breath. 'It's not what you think,' she added quickly. 'Just listen.'

Amélie nodded.

'They're part of the Free French,' Mireille continued. 'They don't have much to do with the RAF because General De Gaulle doesn't like it, but they use Tangmere for their operations.'

'What operations?'

Mireille pulled a face.

'Sorry, sorry,' said Amélie raising a hand in mock surrender. 'You can't tell me.'

'When I'm with them,' Mireille continued, 'we don't talk about things like that. We talk about France. They are so brave, so determined to set her free.'

Amélie raised an eyebrow. 'You're not thinking of joining them, are you?'

'I can't,' Mireille said simply. 'I'm in the WAAFs.'

Her sister seemed confused. 'So what's your point?'

'My point is,' Mireille said deliberately, 'I've even been speaking to them in French and I love it. It's helped me to connect with our past; our home; our country.'

'But surely, after all this time, this is our country,' Amélie protested mildly.

'Up to a point,' said Mireille, 'but then so is France.'

Chapter 12

The two sisters remained in their seats, each lost in her own thoughts. It wasn't until Amélie turned her head as a noisy party of girls in the Land Army walked by that the spell was broken. Their green sweaters and brown corduroy breeches, a familiar sight in the country, seemed a little out of place here in the cathedral. Somehow they should be clearing ditches and planting seed and driving tractors for forty-five bob a week, rather than wandering around in a place like this.

'The thing is,' Mireille went on, 'I read this advertisement in the paper asking for anyone who had personal experience of being in France and spoke the language to come to an office in London. You had to write to the Ministry of Economic Warfare, so that's what I did.'

Amélie's eyes nearly popped out of her head. 'The Ministry of Eco . . . I've never heard of it.'

'Economic Warfare,' Mireille repeated. 'Not many people have, but it's real enough. Anyway, I've been asked to report for an interview. I have no idea where this is leading but it's possible that I could get a job where I have to translate documents, or help with interviewing aliens, or something like that.'

'Sounds interesting,' said Amélie. 'When you get back, you must tell me all about it.'

Mireille gave her a sheepish look. 'That's why I'm telling you now,' she said. 'When I know what this is all about, it may be totally hush-hush. I might not be able to share anything and if they post me to God knows where, I might not even be able to write to you.'

'Oh.' Amélie frowned and let out a tired sigh.

Mireille reached for her hand. 'I'm sorry, darling.'

'You must do what you think is right,' said Amélie. 'I shall miss you but I want you to be happy and if this is what you really want . . .'

They stared at each other for a second then the two sisters threw their arms around each other. 'One day . . .' Mireille whispered urgently into Amélie's hair, 'God willing, one day we shall *all* be together again; all three of us. Linnet too, and there will be peace.'

They pulled apart, smiling bravely. 'If you can't actually say where you are,' said Amélie, 'but want to keep in touch, we should have a code word or something so that I know you're all right.'

'Bit *Boy's Own* comic, isn't it?' Mireille chuckled.

'I'm serious,' said Amélie. 'And if you're in trouble, you should let me know.'

'But even if I am, what would you be able to do about it?' said Mireille.

'I'd still want to know,' Amélie said doggedly.

'I'm not planning to go to the front, darling. You mustn't worry. They never send women into places that are too dangerous. I'll be a French speaking secretary in London or,' she shrugged helplessly, 'I don't know, translating some sort of secret documents or something, that's all.'

Amélie relaxed and nodded. 'Okay,' she said quietly.

Mireille took a deep breath. 'Now, let's have a look

105

around this place then go and find somewhere for a late lunch, shall we?'

Norah reached the post box just as the postman arrived for the three-thirty collection. She felt quite chuffed with herself. It had been a bit of a rush but now Rene would get her letter first thing in the morning. Norah always enjoyed her sister's letters. Rene still sounded blissfully happy although she was a little impatient that she hadn't fallen pregnant yet.

'You've only been married five minutes,' Norah had written. 'Give the poor man a chance.'

Although the words were true, Norah understood perfectly well how Rene felt. She'd felt that same heartache for years and still there were no babies for her and Jim. Now she hoped against hope that it wasn't a case of history repeating itself.

Rene and Dan lived near Tangmere now. They had three rooms upstairs in a cottage in the village, one of the few houses that hadn't been requisitioned or pulled down by the RAF. She still worked in the parachute hangar and Dan was part of the ground crew on the airfield. Norah handed Rene's letter to the postman and headed towards the cinema.

Penny wasn't outside the Odeon for their usual late afternoon at the pictures once a fortnight. For a moment, Norah was almost relieved. She'd spent nearly a week wondering what she would say to her friend when they met. Ever since she'd seen Penny's hungry kiss with that Canadian soldier, the consequences if she'd been caught had bounced in and out of her mind every single day. Should she confront her or keep quiet? Perhaps Penny thought her secret was safe but Norah couldn't be sure if she'd been seen dashing into the butcher's shop when the Jerry machine gunned the street or if Penny had spotted her on her bike when the gates went up again. On the day itself, Norah had fluctuated between anger, disappointment and sadness but she felt a little ridiculous about it now. After all it was none of her business, but Ted Andrews, Penny's husband, was her friend as well. What would he say if he came home to find his wife had had an affair with some other chap while he'd been away? Norah shook her head crossly. No, that wasn't likely to happen. Ted was still a POW and wouldn't be home until the war ended and the way things were going, that could be a lifetime away. If the war went on much longer, anything could happen. That sinking feeling was creeping back. Norah wished she had someone to talk to but she hadn't discussed it with anyone, not even Jim.

She paced up and down outside the Odeon and glanced at her watch. The film looked good – *How Green Was My Valley*, a story about a Welsh mining village. It would be a nice bit of escapism and Lord knows she could do with a bit of that. All at once Norah made up her mind. She would go in on her own. Right now she needed a little time to herself.

Mireille and Amélie found a small café along Chapel Street and ordered fish pie, mashed potato and peas. For once, the portions were generous and they enjoyed their meal.

Once they'd done a little window shopping, it was time for Amélie to catch the train back to Worthing.

'So when am I going to meet this Bob?' Mireille asked as they made their way along Southgate.

'Soon, I hope,' said Amélie before adding cautiously, 'you will give him a chance, won't you?'

'Of course I will, you ninny,' said Mireille. 'Any friend of my sister's is a friend of mine.'

They had reached the station. Mireille bought a platform ticket.

107

'What time is Ginger coming for you?' Amélie asked.

Mireille glanced up at the station clock. 'In about half an hour. We're going to the pictures.'

The station gates were slowly closing and when they looked down the line, they could see the train coming in the distance.

'He obviously thinks a lot of you,' Amélie said but her sister ignored the remark. She suddenly shivered. 'Take care of yourself and don't forget to write.'

'I won't.'

They held on to each other until the train juddered to a halt. One of the station staff beside them shouted 'Chichester, this is Chichester,' then Amélie opened the carriage door. Once inside, she slammed the door and tugged the leather strap to let the window down.

'Good luck with Bob,' said Mireille.

The train began to move. 'And you give poor old Ginger a chance,' Amélie called out of the window. 'God bless.'

They waved until they were both out of sight then Mireille stuffed her hands into her pockets and headed back into the city centre. In these troubled times it was always scary saying goodbye to someone you loved. Thank goodness she'd always kept Ginger at arm's length. He was a nice enough bloke but she didn't want to be reliant on anybody. You never knew if you would see them again or if they'd ever come back home. Home. Where was home? Clearly Amélie felt it was with Norah and Jim but Mireille knew she didn't have that same tug at her heart strings. Home? The only time she'd ever felt at home was a long, long time ago in France.

Bob Kane was visiting his mother again. He'd managed to see her twice before and he was beginning to feel that she trusted him. His first visit had been overshadowed by the

108

matron sitting in with them. He'd asked after his mother's health and then talked of the few memories he had as a child. They didn't amount to much. Playing mud pies with the boys next door and getting into trouble for dropping dirt on the kitchen floor.

'Your father was very fussy,' she'd interrupted. 'He liked things to be kept clean.'

'Quite right too,' he'd laughed. What she'd said had triggered another memory but he didn't voice it, not with the old witch in the same room. He remembered that his father was a bit too free and easy with his leather belt and he'd been given a real walloping for leaving a mess on the floor.

On his second visit, his mother had been in the lounge. Once again, his being there was not private so he'd been forced to make small talk until it was time for her tea. Then he'd kissed her leathery cheek and said his goodbyes.

This time, she was in her room. There was nobody about so he cut to the chase.

'We once lived near Park Lane, didn't we?'

His mother looked up sharply. 'How do you know about that?'

'I was told that we lived in a posh house.'

His mother looked down at her hands. 'You didn't. Your father did.'

Bob had moved closer. 'Tell me about my father.'

Her expression was stony.

'Where did you meet him?'

She settled back in her chair and relaxed. 'At the rally.'

'Rally?' he repeated.

'With Oswald Mosley. Your father was a Blackshirt.'

Bob ran his tongue over his lips eagerly. His father a Blackshirt? His mind was suddenly filled with pictures he'd seen at the cinema: pictures of smart young men marching through the streets of the east end of London; of the Royal

Albert Hall filled with flags and banners and Mosley delivering a speech as fiery as Hitler himself.

'He was one of the high-ups,' she said, her eyes becoming sleepy.

'What was he like, Mother?'

There was a wisp of a smile on her face as she told her son about moonlit walks and kisses by the Thames.

'No, no,' Bob said. 'I'm not interested in all that crap. What was he really like? Tell me about him.'

But she was too tired. He watched her helplessly as she drifted into a doze. As soon as he was sure she was asleep, he stood up and moved silently towards her chest of drawers and opened the top one. It was full of faded brassieres and knickers so old they were grey. He rummaged underneath but nothing was hidden there. It was the same with the other two drawers. Nothing. He lifted the lid of a trinket box on the top but only found a few Kirby grips and a couple of cheap brooches. He glanced back at her and noticed for the first time that there was a photograph in a silver frame next to her bed. It looked good quality. He could get a few quid for that.

The photograph was of two men in Blackshirt uniforms. The one on the left looked every inch the toff: smart suit, expensive watch . . . He grinned. It was the one he'd taken from her handbag the last time he was here. He'd told Amélie his father had given it to him for his twenty-first birthday and looking at this picture, there was an element of truth in that.

His mother stirred and opened her eyes. 'Your father,' she said with a smile.

Bob looked at the photograph with renewed interest. 'I can see that,' he said, staring at the good-looking man. 'He looks just like me.'

Chapter 13

The letter from the Ministry of Economic Warfare told Mireille to report to the Inter-Services Bureau in London. She had to apply for a pass and Dizzy was her usual awkward self until she saw the official paperwork. It was very satisfying to watch her pinched expression as she reluctantly signed the pass to let her go.

After a long train trip and mastering the complexities of the London Underground, it came as a bit of a disappointment to find the offices behind a rather grubby-looking door hidden away at the side of a rather dilapidated building. For a second or two it crossed her mind that she might be the victim of some sort of hoax, but with a mindset of nothing ventured, nothing gained, she knocked on the door. A moment or two later a man in RAF uniform opened the door and asked to see her papers. He gave her letter a quick scan then stepped aside to let her in. She followed him down a dingy passageway until they reached a row of uncomfortable-looking chairs standing against the roughly painted walls where she was asked to wait.

The RAF chap left and Mireille looked around. There wasn't much to see. Here and there, a few government posters covered the peeling paint. '*In an air raid open your door to strangers. They need shelter too.*' '*Donate rags for salvage.*' There was also one Mireille hadn't seen before. '*Planted crops for garden wealth assure the family's winter health.*' Mireille smiled to herself. Norah would like that one. Immediately she started to feel uncomfortable. Why did it always happen when she thought of Norah? Mireille felt her neck heating up. Despite her solemn promise to Amélie, she still hadn't got around to writing to her.

A door opened and an attractive, smartly dressed woman in a donkey-brown suit came out into the corridor. As she leaned in again to close the door she said, '*Au revoir Monsieur, merci,*' to whoever was inside, and a man's voice replied curtly, '*Envoyez le prochain, s'il vous plaît.*'

The woman nodded at Mireille and the two of them exchanged a shy smile as Mireille stood to her feet. Although she had heard what the man said, Mireille knocked before she entered the room.

It was sparsely furnished with a cluttered desk and a chair on either side. A tall filing cabinet stood next to the desk and although the day was slightly chilly, the one bar electric fire wasn't on.

'You can call me Parker,' the man said in French, barely giving her a second glance as they shook hands. His French was perfect. 'Please take a seat and we shall converse the whole time in French, is that all right with you?'

Mireille nodded. He had a pleasant face, dark hair slicked back and deep-set brown eyes. He was clean shaven with a rather enigmatic smile. He reminded her vaguely of Dana Andrews the Hollywood film star.

'First of all, may I ask you why you've come here,' he said. 'That is to say why did you write to this office?'

'As you can see, sir,' Mireille began. 'I am in the WAAFs but I am partly French. I've been in this country since I was ten years old but I still love the country of my mother's birth. I have been talking to some of De Gaulle's Free French airmen and it has rekindled a strong desire to do more to help liberate my country.'

'Are you in love with one of these men?' he asked. 'You are very young. Are you sure this is not simply a romantic notion?'

'Absolutely not, sir!' cried Mireille, so emphatic in her denial that she saw just the ghost of a smile forming on his mouth.

Leaning back in his chair and lacing his fingers together, Parker nodded. 'Now I want you to tell me all about yourself,' he began. 'Take your time and try to remember as much as you can. If you've had any . . . er, awkward moments in your life, I shall want to hear about them too. It's important that we have no secrets from each other, no matter how unpleasant they may be.'

Something told Mireille not to hold back. She had planned to avoid the subject of Jago Ffox-Webster but judging by the intense look in his eye, she had a strange feeling that Parker (so obviously not his name) knew all about him anyway. Of course he did. They would have made checks, wouldn't they? Even her change of name was on her service record. If she was going to be part of this, whatever it was, she had to be utterly frank. So she began at the beginning.

It took some time but by the end of the afternoon she'd told him about the death of her father, her mother's second marriage and her subsequent death. She'd told him how she and her sisters had come to Britain and how her step-father had wanted them to become completely Anglicised to the point of even changing their names. Having been unable to contact her sisters for some time, through meeting Norah, she discovered that they had once lived in Worthing and because of the generosity of the family who had taken her sisters in, she had been able to join her middle sister in the same house. The whereabouts of her youngest sister, Linnet remained a mystery. Then came the discovery that her step-father was in fact a German spy. Mireille didn't stint on her revelations but the more she spoke about it, the more angry she became. Finally, when she'd finished, she was surprised to discover that her cheeks were wet. All this time, Parker had listened impassively. Now the room was silent.

Mireille blinked and fished into her pocket for a handkerchief. Keeping her head down as she dabbed her cheeks, she cursed herself for being such an idiot. If Parker was looking for someone to do something a little out of the ordinary, she should have shown him that she was tough instead of behaving like some blubbering schoolgirl.

'Well thank you, Miss Osborne,' he said at length. 'I think that will be all for today. I appreciate the fact that you have been so honest. I do hope you haven't been too distressed.'

'No, sir,' she said quietly. She squeezed the end of her nose with her handkerchief and leaned forward as if to rise.

'If you want to continue with this process,' he said, shuffling some papers on his desk, 'we should be happy to see you again.'

'Oh.' Mireille couldn't hide her surprise. She'd thought she'd blown it.

Parker didn't react to her outburst but looking up at her he said impassively, 'A letter will come in due course. Good afternoon.'

Back out on the street, Mireille took a deep breath. It

114

was only then that she realised that she still didn't know what it was all about. Her knowledge of French was imperative and as far as she knew, she'd spoken well but what were they recruiting for? Translation work? Interviewing refugees?

Suddenly drained and tired, she crossed the road and went into a café. Ordering a sandwich and a pot of tea, she tried to collect her thoughts. Parker hadn't seemed fazed by her revelations about Ffox-Webster; in fact, the more she pondered on the matter, the more she had a funny feeling that her first hunch had been correct. He already knew about him being a traitor. All that stuff he'd said at the beginning about 'awkward moments' and 'no secrets no matter how unpleasant'; of course he knew. But she hadn't told him everything. There was one thing that was too painful to speak about. She took a breath. Well, if Parker wanted to see her again, she couldn't have blotted her copy book too badly, could she? She poured herself another cup of tea and stirred in half a spoon of sugar. It was taking ages to cut it out altogether. Tea without a little sweetness was bitter and unpleasant. She wondered how people could drink it and yet most of the folks she knew had either given up smoking or sugary drinks. Mireille had never liked smoking and only done it for a very short while to look fashionable so that was easy to give up but sugar in tea? No. Norah had suggested making the amount on the spoon smaller and smaller until you didn't need it at all. Mireille had got it down to half a spoon but there it stayed.

Across the road, two women embraced each other affectionately. Mireille frowned to herself. Norah was hardly ever out of her thoughts these days and the churning in her stomach when she did think of her always left her feeling sick. It was no good burying her head in the sand any longer. The next time she got leave, she would go to Worthing to see her. She could take a bunch of flowers or, better still, a few goodies. Norah would like that and it would be good to see Mrs Steele and Jim again. She wondered vaguely if Ivan still did the market stall. The waitress came with the bill and Mireille stood to leave. She felt a little better now that she had decided to bury the hatchet.

Norah felt as if she was chasing her own tail. The dogs seemed to be under her feet all the time and there was so much to do. This morning her mother-in-law and Ivan had loaded the handcart and taken it to the open-air market in the centre of Worthing. After three years of war, people were used to rationing and shortages but they welcomed the opportunity to buy fresh food. If previous weeks were anything to go by, the stall would do well. There were benefits all round. Christine and Ivan had made many new friends among the other stall holders and their customers. Norah smiled to herself as she remembered the prickly bad-tempered woman who had foisted herself on the Lilacs way back in 1939 and the woman Christine was now. Ivan had made such a difference to her. Of course, it worked both ways. Ivan had lost his way after his beloved Ada died until she and Jim had rescued him, a down and out, living under the railway bridge by Worthing station.

Today, Norah not only had to make sure the market garden was up to scratch, serve the customers who popped in and do a bit of housework, but she also had to get a meal ready for tonight. Jim was bringing an army officer friend back home for tea. With a little bit of careful planning, Norah had managed to get a nice rabbit from the butcher's. She had plenty of vegetables in the garden and

116

she would use the last of the apple and blackberries she'd stored in Kilner jars last autumn to make a crumble. She glanced at her watch. There was no time to lose.

The sound of a bicycle being leaned against the outside wall was the last thing she wanted to hear. There was no time for tea and chat today, not if she was going to have everything ready and the house spic and span for Jim's friend.

'Coo-ee, it's only me,' called a voice.

'Penny!' cried Norah. The dogs rushed outside and danced around her feet. 'Come in, come in. I've just put the kettle on.'

Chapter 14

When she came through the door, Penny looked different. For a start she had a new hairstyle. Always one for fashion, she now had two victory rolls either side of her head. She'd lost weight as well. Her trim figure was back to pre-Victor size and she wore make-up, all very tastefully done. Norah almost envied her powdered face, blusher and lipstick, and blurted out, 'You look fantastic!'

Penny did a mock curtsy. 'Why thank you ma'am.'

Turning her back, Norah filled the kettle. Should she tell Penny she'd seen her with that soldier? With the tea made, she apologised that she had to get on so while Penny sat at the table she busied herself with making the rabbit stew.

They made small talk. 'How's Victor? How's your Mum?' Norah couldn't bring herself to say, *I saw you . . .*

'Have you heard from Mireille yet? Is Jim keeping well? Have you heard from Rene since she got married? So, what have you been doing?'

Ignoring the elephant in the room, Norah brought her up-to-date with all her news, such as it was. The weather was glorious. Hot summer days, a glut of gooseberries and strawberries, loganberries and peas coming along nicely and all the allotments being kept up to scratch. The world news was a little more encouraging. In North Africa, the British and American troops were making good progress and the BBC said eleven thousand Italian troops had surrendered on the island of Pantelleria. Nobody had ever heard of it, but it sounded good anyway. On a personal level, life at the Lilacs carried on much the same in a rather uneventful way. Jim was busy, too busy. Christine and Ivan more or less lived their own lives. Apart from meal times when they all got together, they were on the market stall, at a whist drive in the church hall to help raise funds for a Spitfire for the war effort or in the Richard Cobden. Sometimes they took a bus ride to Brighton or Chichester or their favourite place, Arundel.

'Sounds like they've got a better social life than you have,' Penny joked. That remark was a little too close to the truth but Norah chose to ignore it. 'What about Rene?'

'She's as happy as Larry,' said Norah. 'No sign of a baby yet and she's still in the WAAFs. She's been learning to drive and there's talk that she might be transferred up to Scotland.'

'Oh dear,' said Penny. 'Dan won't like that.'

'He's already up there,' said Norah. She slid the casserole dish into the oven already on a low heat and bumped the door closed with her hip. 'Not working today?' she asked, anxious to change the subject because she would miss Rene dreadfully, but she didn't want to mention the incident by the station.

Penny shook her head. 'Uncle Fred gave me the sack.'

Piling the vegetable peeler, knives and chopping board into the sink, Norah gave her friend a shocked look. 'The sack? Whatever for?'

Penny rose to her feet and picked up the tea towel while Norah started the washing up. 'He said I was being too riendly with the Canadians.' She looked up sharply. 'It's not true of course. I was only being nice because they're customers. I mean you've got to, haven't you? You won't keep them as customers for long if you don't smile and chat. The trouble with Uncle Fred is that he's got a dirty mind.'

Norah bit her lip. She had a feeling the rift between them was a little more than Penny was admitting. Had Uncle Fred found out she was seeing a Canadian? Norah cast her mind back to the time she'd popped into the café to see Penny a few months ago. Uncle Fred had seemed a bit tetchy even then.

Norah decided to keep mum. 'Oh I'm sorry, love. What will you do now?'

Penny shrugged. 'I've got to find something,' she said. 'If I don't they'll be wanting me to do war work and I'd hate being stuck in a factory all the time. Besides, I'd have to catch the bus over to Lancing or Shoreham every day.' She hesitated. 'I don't suppose you know of anybody within biking distance – someone who wants someone part-time?'

'I'm afraid I don't,' said Norah, 'but I'll keep an eye out for you.'

'What about the police canteen?'

Norah pulled the corners of her mouth down and shook her head. 'I can ask.'

The kitchen was clean and tidy. Norah put the kettle on again. 'Been to any more concerts with that chap?' she asked trying to make her remark sound as innocent as she could.

'I may have done,' Penny said in a tone of voice which told Norah it was a no-go area. Her friend seemed edgy now. She glanced up at the clock. 'Anyway I'd better go,' she said. 'I don't want to leave Mum on her own with Victor for too long. He's such a live wire these days.'

'Fancy the pictures sometime soon?' Norah asked.

Penny looked thoughtful. 'Why not?' she said. 'The chaps are on manoeuvres the next few days so I'll be at a loose end.'

Norah looked away quickly.

'Oh sorry,' said Penny. 'I didn't mean it like that. It came out all wrong. Yes, I'd love to come to the pictures. Friday?'

Norah nodded and bent to check on the stew in the oven. Thankfully, when she stood to her feet again, Penny had gone. Good job she hadn't seen the emotion in her eyes. *Pull yourself together*, she told herself crossly. She took off her apron and glancing at the clock, she realised she had just enough time to have a quick bath and change into something more presentable.

Ivan and Christine were first through the door. They had set off early in the morning for a bus ride to Portsmouth. When they came in they looked tired and sunburned.

'Ooh, you look nice,' said Christine.

'Thank you,' said Norah, pulling on a clean apron. After her bath, she had changed into an ice-blue cotton and rayon button-through dress, with a darker blue piping down the front. It had short sleeves, a nipped-in waist and a tie belt. When she saw it in the window of Smith and Strange, Norah couldn't resist it. It had cost her seven coupons but she told herself she didn't care. She hadn't had a new frock since 1939. 'Nice day?' she asked.

'Lovely,' said Christine. 'Just let me have a wash and then I'll help you.'

'No rush,' Norah said cheerfully. 'It's all in hand.'

Captain Carruthers and Jim were not far behind them. When Jim introduced him by his title, the captain interrupted him. 'Lennard, please. Your husband said you were a good cook but he forgot to mention how pretty you are.'

His remark could have sounded cheesy but as he said it,

Lennard had a mischievous twinkle in his eye. 'Oh and forgive the paw,' he said as she shook his hand. 'I tell people I'm getting to heaven on the instalment plan. Already got two fingers waiting for me at the gate.'

No one could resist chuckling at his joke.

Lennard had brought a bottle of wine so Christine went into the sitting room to fetch some glasses from the cabinet. Everyone sat down and Norah got the casserole dish from the oven. As soon as she took off the lid, a delicious smell filled the kitchen.

'Oh my,' said Lennard appreciatively, 'that smells wonderful.'

'Certainly got my juices goin',' Ivan quipped.

Their table conversation was centred round getting to know each other but inevitably it was peppered with thoughts of war.

'I've never seen so many tanks,' Christine said after she'd told them about their trip to Portsmouth. 'They're along the coastline almost all the way. We could see that they've been building slipways out to sea as well.'

'Sounds like something's about to happen,' Norah remarked.

'The bus conductor reckons some US tank general has come over here,' said Ivan.

Lennard nodded. 'Eisenhower.'

'There's talk of a big push,' said Christine but Lennard wouldn't be drawn.

'Do you have family, Captain . . . er Lennard?' said Norah deliberately changing the subject.

'A brother,' he said. 'He's been a bit of a scally-wag, I'm afraid, but since he's been called up, he seems to have settled down.'

Ivan snorted and Christine gave him a nudge.

The meal finished, Ivan and Christine retired to their

room. Norah stayed in the kitchen to do the clearing up, leaving the sitting room free for Jim and the captain to chat. When she brought in the coffee, the two men were clearly enjoying each other's company.

'What did you do before the war?' asked Norah as she handed their guest a cup.

'I worked in pictures,' said Lennard. 'Not acting, you understand. I was on the other side of the camera.'

'How marvellous,' said Norah. 'What sort of films did you make?'

'A cousin of mine, Selwyn Jepson, wrote a short story called *Sailing Away* and they made it into a film. It starred Jessie Matthews.'

'Oh I like her,' said Norah, sitting beside Jim. 'I'm sorry; Selwyn who?'

'Selwyn Jepson,' said Lennard. 'You won't have heard of him. Nobody ever remembers the writer.' He gestured towards the photo frame on the mantelpiece. 'I may not be in the business anymore but I still have an eye for a photogenic face. Who are they?'

'Mireille and Amélie,' said Norah. 'They're sisters. Amélie lived with us for a while as an evacuee. Mireille came along later.'

'Pretty girls,' Lennard said, peering closer.

'When all this is over, will you go back to it? Filming I mean?' Jim asked.

Lennard held up his hand. 'Perhaps not, old boy.' It was a slightly awkward moment until Lennard gave them a mischievous chuckle. 'Anyway, my cousin packed it up. He's something hush-hush in the war office now.'

'Damned war,' Jim muttered.

Just before nine-thirty, Lennard glanced at his watch. 'Well, I'd better be off,' he said. 'This has been the most delightful evening.'

'The pleasure was all ours,' said Norah.

They stood by the door as he put on his coat. 'I can't cook you a meal but I'd be delighted if you would both allow me to take you out one night.'

'I'm sure we'd love that,' said Jim, glancing at Norah.

'Good, then that's settled,' said Lennard. He waited a moment or two until Norah had switched off the hall light then he opened the blackout curtain and finally the door. ''Night all,' he said cheerfully. 'And thanks again.'

Jim closed the door and drew the curtain.

'What a nice man,' said Norah.

Her husband caught her by her waist and pulled her close to him. 'He certainly cheered you up,' he said. 'I've been worried about you, darling. You haven't been yourself lately.'

'Oh, I felt a bit blue for a while,' she admitted, 'but I'm all right now.'

'If you want to talk about it, I'm listening.'

'Talking won't change anything,' she said bitterly. 'Best just to get on with it.'

He kissed her hair line. 'The baby?' he whispered.

She tried to pull away but he wouldn't let her. 'Yes Jim, the baby.'

'Sweetheart.' His voice was tender. When he cupped her face and kissed her she could already feel the lump in her throat.

'Well it's over now,' she choked. 'I gave all Eric's baby clothes to the refugees.'

For a split second, she felt him stiffen and it occurred to her, perhaps for the first time, how much all of this had affected him too. Poor Jim. He'd wanted Eric as much as she had done. She put her arms around his neck. 'I'm sorry, Jim. I should have asked you first.'

'No, no,' he said. 'I'm sure it was the right thing to do.

Better that some baby is warm and well wrapped up rather than everything getting damp and mouldy up in the loft.'

They stood for a moment just holding one another.

'I haven't given up,' she suddenly said defensively. 'I still want a baby . . . don't you?'

'Of course I do, my darling.' She lifted her face and he kissed her again. 'We should go and see Miss Bundy again.'

'Oh Jim, you know her hands are tied,' said Norah. 'Somebody high up has put the kybosh on it all and I'm sure it was that Jago Ffox-Webster. It was his way of punishing us for having the girls. He's made damned sure we can never adopt a child of our own.'

'Maybe,' said Jim, 'but that doesn't make it right.'

'But what can we do?' Norah cried.

Jim shook his head. 'You tied my hands, Norah. You don't want anybody to know what he's done, but look at you. It's breaking your heart, darling. We have to speak out, don't you see?'

'Just leave it, Jim,' she said doggedly. 'There's nothing we can do.'

Jim sighed. 'Oh Norah, all I want is for you to be happy.'

Chapter 15

It just so happened that the day Bob was due to stand before the tribunal, Amélie had a morning off. She didn't have to be on duty until two o'clock. He met her outside the nurses' home and they strolled hand in hand to the Old Town Hall together. His appointment was for ten-thirty and she could tell he was nervous.

'I've brought you a little present,' she said.

He seemed surprised.

'I thought it might cheer you up,' she said, handing him an envelope.

Bob's face lit up when he opened the envelope and saw the picture postcard. It was of Worthing seafront and the pier as it was in 1938. Holidaymakers strolled along the promenade and the sun shone. The postcard had been touched up, so the colours were vividly beautiful but the back hadn't been written on. 'Thank you,' he said giving her a peck on her cheek. 'That's perfect for my collection.'

'I'm sure everything will be fine,' she said encouragingly as they parted by the sandbags on the town hall steps. 'How long do you think you'll be?'

'Twenty minutes, half an hour,' he said.

'In that case, I might have a wander around the shops,' she said.

As it was market day, she knew Christine (or Mémé as she had taken to calling her) and Ivan would be manning their stall in Montague Street. It would be a chance to have a quick catch up. Besides, she couldn't wait to tell Mémé that she'd at last had a letter from CORB.

Their stall was very busy. Amélie waved to let Mémé know she was there. As soon as she'd finished with her customer, Mémé apologised to the next person in the queue and came around the cart to embrace Amélie. 'How lovely to see you, dear.'

'I can see you are busy and I can't stop anyway,' Amélie said quickly. 'I just wanted to give you this. Show Norah and Jim but I want it back because I have to show it to Mireille. It's about Linnet.'

'Good news?' Christine asked.

Amélie shook her head.

'Oh sweetheart, I'm sorry,' said Christine. 'But don't give up hope.'

Amélie could feel her chin quivering. 'I won't. I promise.' The two of them hugged once more.

'Is it your day off?' Christine asked.

'I'm on duty at two,' Amélie said. 'I'll come and see you next week. I'm off on Thursday.'

'Lovely.' Christine smiled and a moment or two later Amélie heard her calling out, 'Right, now who's next?'

As she walked back towards the town hall, there was a bit of kerfuffle by Woolworths and Amélie was drawn towards it. People often queued for ages outside a shop without having a clue what they were queuing for.

'What's happening?' she asked the girl in front of her.

'There's a rumour they've had an assignment of lipsticks,' she said. 'You're only allowed one so there's a good chance there might be some left.'

Lipsticks! Amélie held her breath. She couldn't remember the last time she'd seen an affordable lipstick in the shops. Hubbard's had a few on their counters but she would have to part with almost three weeks' wages to buy one of them! Fishing in her handbag she found her purse and ration book. This was too good an opportunity to miss. There were only three left by the time she got to the cosmetic counter, all of them dusty pink. Amélie would have preferred something a little more colourful but, as she told the assistant, 'beggars can't be choosers,' and she parted with her two and eleven pence halfpenny. Once the lipstick was hers, she asked to use the store's mirror and put some on. It was subtle but quite a pretty colour. Best of all, it made her feel more attractive.

'It really suits you,' said the assistant.

Amélie smiled. She'd never be allowed to wear make-up on duty but at least she could look good for Bob. She glanced up at the clock on the wall. Crumbs, he'd be out by now, maybe even waiting on the steps. She set off at once, running all the way.

When she arrived back at the town hall, he was nowhere to be seen. For a few panicky seconds she worried that he might have already gone but as she walked past the big tank which was parked in front of the town hall, the door opened and Bob came down the steps. She could tell at once that things hadn't gone well. He glowered at her and his cheeks were flushed.

'How . . . ?' she began.

'Don't ask,' he growled. 'The whole thing was a bloody sham.'

He strode towards the shoreline, his shoulders hunched and his hands in his pockets. Amélie was almost running to keep up with him. She'd never seen him so angry. When they reached Marine Parade he turned and headed towards the Dome Café. Without a word he went inside. Amélie followed him to a table.

'Two teas,' he snapped at the waitress as she came up to them.

Amélie chewed her bottom lip. The teas, the colour of paint stripper, arrived and the waitress made a point of banging the cups onto the table. Some of Amélie's tea slopped into the saucer.

Bob reached for the sugar. 'Bloody morons,' he grumbled. 'They'd already made up their minds. "Are you doing this on religious grounds?"' he added in a sing-song voice by way of an impersonation, 'and when I said no, one of the panel looked down his nose and said, "We all have to do our bit, you know."'

'Didn't you tell them you were already working in the hospital?'

'Of course I did! I just don't believe that warfare should be a means of settling international disputes.' He banged the table with his fist. 'This country signed the Paris Agreement in 1928, so I have every right to refuse to take up arms. I told them I would be quite happy to work in the Non-Combatant Corps. I said I'd work with the army medics or do farm work. I told them I wouldn't go down a mine or something like that, but they wouldn't have any of it.'

'So you've got to go?' Amélie said in a small voice.

'I shall refuse the medical,' he said determinedly. 'You can't go into the army without a medical examination.'

'But can't you go to prison for that?' asked Amélie.

'Of course you can, you silly moo,' he hissed, turning on her, 'but I don't care.' He looked up as if seeing her for the first time and his face clouded. 'What's that filthy muck you've got on your face?'

Amélie was stung. 'Lipstick. I . . . I thought you'd like it.'
'Wipe it off now.'

She could feel her eyes tingling and her throat growing tight as she reached for her handkerchief to wipe the lipstick away. He watched her do it, his angry expression never changing.

'A waste of money,' he snarled. 'You look like a bloody tart.'

The manager who had been polishing glasses behind the counter came over to them. 'Listen pal,' he said. 'Two of my customers have already left because of you. Keep your voice down and your mouth civil to the lady.'

Bob looked as if he was going to burst a blood vessel. 'Come on,' he said, standing up so forcefully he knocked his chair to the floor. 'We're going.'

Outside in the street he suddenly turned towards her, his expression softening. 'Listen Amélie, I liked you because you looked natural,' he said, taking her hand. 'You're pure like a woman should be. An English rose. I don't want a girl who looks like a tart.'

'It was only a little bit of lipstick,' she protested mildly.

He said nothing more but she saw something flicker in his eye. Something rather unsettling.

Mireille was spending her first afternoon in the Ops room. WAAFs had to be jacks-of-all-trades and so with that in mind the powers-that-be had made sure she'd been trained up to work on the plotting table. Wearing a blue tin helmet, it was her responsibility, along with others, to move the counters around a giant map. On the wall above the table, was a plotting clock divided into red, yellow and blue triangles, each representing a two-and-a-half-minute period. Along with the other plotters, Mireille's head phones were continuously connected to a cluster of observation posts.

Her newfound skill lay in moving the counters along the map references in the direction in which the raid was taking place, thus giving the controller and other big-wigs an accurate idea of the battle progress.

As the last of the aircraft made it back home, the controller congratulated everybody on a job well done. As he left the room, nobody spoke. They were all absorbed with his or her own thoughts. Mireille found herself fighting back her tears. A job well done, yes, but her beloved France was still in the grip of Nazi Germany.

Chapter 16

Ginger drew up just short of the base. Mireille turned a sleepy head towards him and frowned. 'Why have we stopped?'

'I want to talk to you.'

She felt herself tense. *Oh here we go again*, she thought acidly. The big 'come-on'. She waited for him to make his move but he turned off the engine and sat still. They'd had a wonderful evening. Usually he took her to the local dances in the village halls around Tangmere – Yapton, Clymping, the Empire Hall at Grafham and occasionally Littlehampton. Tonight he had suggested something a little more special so they'd gone to the Lavant Memorial Hall just outside Chichester where rumour had it that they had a pretty decent band. They had not been disappointed. It had been wild. The place was heaving and the band was terrific. They'd enjoyed everything from the waltz to swing-time. There were so many servicemen in the area and organisers were keen to attract girls, so she'd got in free. In fact, the only snag as far as Ginger was concerned, was that the bar only served teas but Mireille didn't give a fig. Usually if there was booze it led to fights which could be ugly, frightening and sometimes dangerous. In fact she'd heard on the grapevine that even sleepy old Worthing had become a hotspot for drunk and disorderly conduct.

Mireille turned to look at him. 'What do you want to talk about?'

'Us.'

'What about us?'

Ginger turned his head towards her. 'You must know how I feel about you by now, Mireille,' he said cautiously. 'I've done everything by the book because I want more than just a fling. I want you to be my girl.'

'Listen Ginger,' she began.

'I'm not asking you to do anything you wouldn't want to,' he interrupted. 'I'm willing to wait until we get married but I need to know where I stand.'

Even in the half light, Mireille could see the earnestness on his face. Her stomach was beginning to twist into a knot. She liked Ginger. She liked him a lot but she couldn't bear to think about all that. She squeezed her eyes to shut out the unwelcome memory of all that humping and heavy breathing in her ear; the weight of him on top of her; and afterwards the feeling of being used and then discarded.

'I'm not ready,' she said, her voice small.

He touched her shoulder and as she pulled away, he snatched back his hand as if he'd been scalded. A troubled silence descended into the car until he said, 'Don't you even like me a little bit, Mireille?'

Now she felt bad. His touch hadn't been demanding. Ginger was always gentle. She didn't want to lose him as a friend but she had an awful feeling that if she didn't give in, he would leave her. She didn't want him to leave but equally she didn't want him. Not in that way.

'Mireille,' he said quietly, 'talk to me. Please?'

She turned her head away. How could she explain? She

wasn't the girl he thought she was. 'I can't,' she whispered. 'I'm sorry Ginger, but I can't.'

He stared at her helplessly then she opened the car door and ran.

Jim and Lennard decided to organise a football match. It had been a bit of a struggle for Jim to find enough manpower for the police team but he'd included a young lad whom he had been trying to help. Charlie Evans had been caught red-handed shoplifting but rather than march him off to face a custodial sentence, Jim gave the lad a good talking to. It was obvious that the boy was easily led and that he had a difficult family life but Jim could see something redeemable about his character. A day or so after the incident, Jim took Charlie back to the shop to apologise. The boy was terrified of the shopkeeper's reaction, but unbeknown to him, Jim had already had a word with him and they had both decided to try and turn Charlie's life around.

He'd got the idea from Lennard. 'When this damned war is over,' his friend had told him, 'I plan to get myself some training. There has to be a better way than locking these boys up with hardened criminals who then teach them all sorts of other mischief.' The idea made sense to Jim and he was pleased with Charlie's reaction.

The football match was between the armed forces and the police, the Tommys and Bobbys, with a sprinkling of bus drivers and conductors (thanks to his father-in-law) alongside Charlie and his younger brother. Norah, Elsie and Christine were put down to organise the refreshments.

When the bus pulled up at the bus stop opposite the football field, quite a few relatives and friends of the players got off.

'Coo-ee,' cried a familiar voice.

Norah looked up to see Rene and Dan hurrying across

the field towards them. She hadn't seen her sister since she'd got married so Norah ran to meet her and the two of them spun together in a happy circle as they hugged each other.

'What a lovely surprise!' It seemed that Elsie had known they were coming but had kept it to herself for that very reason.

Dan was immediately co-opted onto the field because the referee hadn't turned up, while Rene borrowed an apron to help her mother and Norah. In a breathless twenty minutes, Rene babbled like a brook as she told them what a brilliant husband Dan had turned out to be and about the new decorations she'd done in the house. 'I'm a bit bored with blue but that was the only other colour they had apart from donkey brown,' and, 'I've embroidered the pillowcases and I made cushion covers out of that old curtain you gave me, Mum, and you'll never guess what . . .'

Elsie was laughing. 'Slow down, slow down,' she cried, 'I can't keep up with you,' but everyone could see the laughter in her eyes. Rene's excitement made everybody happy.

It had proved impossible to play football on Broadwater Green, the preferred ground, because it was still being used for exercises with the surrounding leafy streets being used as a tank park so Jim found a patch of reasonable waste ground belonging to a smallholder called Keith Varney just north of Durrington-on-sea station. One policeman had managed to borrow a trestle table from his church for the teas and Norah had packed as many cups and mugs as she could find into a box. They had two primus stoves and a large tea pot. People brought picnic blankets or folding chairs and the occasion took on the atmosphere of a relaxed afternoon out. Even the weather was kind.

Christine was delighted when Amélie turned up with her young man. They'd all heard so much about him that it was nice to meet him at last. Good-looking and polite, the women were soon captivated by his charms. Everybody said they made a lovely couple. Amélie was dressed in a pretty pink frock with a nipped-in waist and a tie bow on the front but she wore no make-up. Bob was quickly pressed into joining Lennard's team who were short of one man. Amélie sat demurely on a picnic blanket until Bob went onto the field with the rest of the team. After that she came up to the trestle table to help Norah and Christine set up the teas.

'You all right, Luv?' Christine said after she'd given Amélie a hug.

'Yes, fine.'

'Your Bob seems a very nice young man,' Norah remarked. 'Why don't you both come and sit with us?'

Amélie unwrapped the egg sandwiches to put them on a plate. 'Bob prefers me to be alone with him,' she said and behind her back, Norah and her sister exchanged a quizzical look.

'So, did you get your birth certificate to send off to CORB?' Norah said anxious to change the subject in a rather awkward moment.

'Yes.'

'And Mireille's?'

There was a shout from the field. Paul Critchley had scored a goal. Distracted, Amélie looked up but the referee ruled it off side. Everything was held up for a few moments then Dan blew his whistle and play resumed. Amélie turned back to Norah and Christine. 'What were we saying?'

'I asked you if Mireille had sent you a copy of her birth certificate,' said Norah. They were busy unwrapping the newspaper and putting cups onto saucers.

'Yes, but Bob thinks I should wait until the war is over before sending it off. He says everybody's too busy to deal with it right now and I might be disappointed.'

Christine frowned. 'But she's *your* sister, Amélie. You must do what *you* think best,' she said, emphasising the personal aspect of the matter.

Amélie blinked.

'Mémé is right,' said Norah adding her weight to the argument. 'You've both waited a long time for this.'

Amélie looked distraught. 'Oh now I don't know what to do. I don't want to upset Bob.'

Norah was concerned. Amélie had always been such a determined girl. Look how she'd moved heaven and earth to start her training in the hospital. She'd always seemed such a tough person, full of ambition and drive. It was hard to recognise this indecisive weakling as the same person.

Most of the cups and saucers were out on the table now.

'What does Mireille think?' Norah asked cautiously.

'I haven't told her yet,' said Amélie.

'But Linnet is her sister too,' Christine pointed out.

Amélie turned her head towards the field as Norah and Christine glanced at each other with worried expressions. This was more than simple devotion. Bob had some kind of hold over her.

'I'd better go back and sit down,' she said and the two women guessed that she was worried that Bob might see her talking to them.

'All right, Luv,' said Christine and once Amélie was out of ear shot she added, 'I'm not sure that boy's good for her.'

'She does seem to be under his thumb,' Norah agreed.

'You should tell her,' Rene said.

'We've tried,' said Norah. 'She won't listen.'

At half time, everybody congregated around the tea table and the three women were kept busy. The two primus stoves were on the go all the time boiling the water they'd brought in large containers for tea and the players tucked into the sandwiches.

'I never expected all this,' said Lennard as Christine handed him a cup of tea. 'You've all gone to so much trouble.'

'It's our pleasure, Captain,' said Christine.

'Tell me,' said Lennard looking Amélie's way. 'I recognise that girl from Norah's photograph in the sitting room. Which one is she?'

'Amélie,' said Christine, quickly adding, 'and that's her young man.'

Lennard clicked his fingers with a frown. 'Oh drat. All the best ones get snapped up.' He grinned. 'I was even too late for you.'

'Oh, be off with you,' Christine said, her face colouring.

'Flirting with my mother?' said Jim, coming up behind him. 'I'll have the law on you.' The two men enjoyed a little light banter. Jim picked up a couple of sandwiches and called, 'Got one in the pot for me, Luv?'

Norah filled his cup then went off to serve some of the others.

'You've got a real gem there, Jim,' said Lennard. He stared after Norah with an admiring smile before turning back to his friend and adding, 'Lucky dog.'

The spectators had brought their own refreshments, although Norah did notice that Amélie wasn't eating. As the players went back for the second half, she took a cup of tea and the remaining sandwiches over to her.

'You should have come to the table,' Norah said, sitting down beside her.

'Bob says I work so hard in the hospital he prefers me to sit and look pretty,' she said with an embarrassed chuckle.

It sounded thoughtful but Norah was wary. During the break, Bob had been very attentive towards Amélie. She'd noticed him re-tying the bow on Amélie's dress but while he had a box full of sandwiches, he offered her nothing.

That was no way to treat a girl. He could at least have brought her a cup of tea!

At the end of the day, everybody said their goodbyes. Norah waited at the bus stop with Rene and Dan for one last hug before they left.

'Thanks for a lovely day,' said Norah.

'No, thank you,' said Rene.

'It was lovely to see you all,' said Dan, kissing her cheek as the bus came. 'Well, almost everyone.'

Norah waved them goodbye then went back to finish the clearing up. She sighed. It seemed that not one member of the family liked Bob.

Chapter 17

Mireille found herself back in the same dingy office in London for the third time. Her second interview had been much the same as the first although it seemed a lot more serious. By now she was aware that she was talking about SOE, the Special Operations Executive. She had no real idea of what they did except to send people into occupied France. Parker had asked her about her family ties and obligations and seemed satisfied when she'd told him that although she'd kept in touch with her sister, there was nobody else in her life and she was footloose and fancy free.

'No young men courting you then?' he'd asked.

Mireille thought of Ginger and shook her head. She had still been seeing him since that rather awkward moment in the car that night but thankfully he seemed content to stay just friends. That's when Parker had told her that the work he was offering could be dangerous.

'I have to warn you that there is a very real possibility that you may find yourself in a position where nobody can help you,' he'd said, his expression grave. 'In fact, not to put too fine a point on it, you could be killed.'

With this dire warning ringing in her ears, he had sent

her on her way. 'I shall send you another appointment in a few weeks,' he'd said. 'In the meantime I want you to think very carefully about what has been said. Get all those romantic notions out of your head for a start. This is deadly serious.'

Mireille had nodded. Parker rose to his feet and walked to the door but before he opened it for her, he'd added, 'And I must also warn you not to speak of this to anyone else, not even your family. If you do decide to come back for the third interview, I shall ask you to sign the Official Secrets Act.'

Well, now she was back. She hadn't told another living soul but she had done a lot of thinking. Her passion for France was sacrosanct and although she loved Amélie, her sister had embarked on her own career. She had Bob in her life and she still spent time with Norah and Jim. In Mireille's eyes, Amélie was settled and happy. Although at her sister's request, Mireille had sent a copy of her birth certificate and other relevant papers to prove her identity for CORB, quite frankly she didn't hold out much hope that they would be reunited with Linnet before the war ended anyway. With this in mind, Mireille reasoned that the more she could do to help the war effort the better. She'd never got around to seeing Norah again and she did feel a bit guilty about that but somehow it was always going to be tomorrow, next week or next month, and now it was too late. Once she'd signed the Official Secrets Act she'd have no time to patch up old relationships.

Parker opened the door to the office and invited her in. This time there were two other people, civil servants she supposed, in the room with him. Mireille took a deep breath as she signed the relevant papers. There was no going back now. Parker shook her hand warmly and the other two men left.

'You are now part of F section,' he told her. 'As such, you are not a spy but our job is to actively support and encourage the French people to resist the Germans.'

Mireille frowned, puzzled. 'I thought there was already a French resistance movement.'

'There is,' said Parker. 'A bloody good one and we support them.'

Mireille felt a frisson of excitement. The French resistance – they were legendary. 'When do I start?'

'First,' he began, 'we shall inform your commander that you will be leaving at the end of the month. From September, you'll embark on a period of training which encompasses several disciplines. Over the next few months you must expect to go for Preliminary training, that's Group C, Guerrilla training, Group A and Finishing school which is known as Group B. We shall start your training near Guildford.'

'How long shall I be there?' Mireille asked.

'In Guildford, two weeks,' said Parker, sifting through a sheaf of papers on his desk. 'The other courses are longer and in different parts of the country.' He looked up and smiled as he handed her a card. 'I suggest you take this voucher and get yourself a meal. There are a couple of other girls outside. You can go with them. Make sure you're back here at fourteen hundred hours on Tuesday September first and then we'll transport you to Wanborough Manor.'

Mireille stood, saluted smartly and turned to go. As she walked out of the room she had mixed feelings. Excitement, nervousness and the feeling that she was walking into the unknown.

The Canadian army was charged with the safe keeping of the whole of the south coast from Newhaven to Worthing and beyond. They used much of the South Downs as a training camp; properties were requisitioned and farming was restricted. There were check points at every major road and country crossroads. Even the training gallops had been taken over. People put up with these irritations (what else could they do? There was a war on), but it was well known that the troops were restless. Drunken and disorderly conduct was coming between the army and their hosts and tempers were short. The soldiers were keen to fight but they were overlooked – or so they thought. All that was about to change. The month of August became a hive of activity. Manoeuvres seemed to take on a life of their own and rumour had it that a raid was imminent.

When Jim came home and told the family that two houses in Lyndhurst Road had been badly damaged by a German plane which had crashed into them, Norah's face paled. 'Is the hospital all right? Have you heard from Amélie?'

'As far as I know she's fine,' said Jim. 'There's no other damage.'

'Was anyone killed?' Christine asked.

'Nine of them,' said Jim. 'The five-man German crew and four Canadians who were billeted next door.'

'Poor souls,' Norah mused quietly. 'Fancy coming all this way to be killed by a falling plane.'

Ivan shook his head sadly.

Worthing was having its 618th air raid warning. Everyone at the Lilacs knew that because Christine was still counting.

'Why do they always do it just as we're starting a meal?' Norah grumbled.

They knew they should go to the air raid shelter but nobody had the heart or the will so although nothing was said, they carried on with their tea.

'Ooh, I keep forgetting to tell you,' said Christine, getting up from the table. 'Amélie has heard from CORB. She gave me a letter to show you.' She went to her coat hanging on the hook and fiddled around until she found an envelope.

'Has she found Linnet?' Norah asked.

'No,' said Christine unfolding the paper inside. 'Here, I'll read it to you. *"Dear Miss Osborne, Thank you for your letter which has received our careful attention. I regret to inform you that I am unable to give you information as to the whereabouts of Lillian Ffox-Webster. Her father told us he was dying of cancer and that Miss Ffox-Webster has no living relatives. This was the reason why she was sent to the dominions for a completely new start in life. If she is as you say, your sister, we should need proof in the form of a sworn affidavit as well as the copies of your birth certificates which we already have. As far as we are concerned, Miss Ffox-Webster has no living relatives. I do hope you understand our caution. You will be pleased to know that all our children are well and happy in their new environment. Yours sincerely, Janet Gates, secretary to The Right Honourable Lord Snell (Chairman of C.O.R.B)"'*

'That man was a pathological liar,' Norah hissed. 'Dying from cancer indeed.'

'I suggested that she and Mireille should both send sworn affidavits to prove their identity,' said Christine. 'That way if one can't get to Linnet, the other could.'

'In these uncertain times,' Jim remarked, 'it sounds like a good idea.'

A moment later, the all-clear sounded. They'd got away with it and feeling deliciously naughty, they all grinned at each other.

Even in the days leading up to August the nineteenth, there had been a lot of activity at Tangmere. A big joint operation had been taking place off the French coast. For the first time since 1940, the RAF were going to be sent across the channel to act as air support for ground troops. Mireille was thrilled that at last the Allies were

144

actually going to fight on French soil and although she would not witness the action first-hand, she was going to be part of the liberation of her country. She had been very busy in the Ops room. As a WAAF she'd been trained up to work on the plotting table. Right from the start, it became obvious that the Dieppe Raid was not going to plan. The Canadians soon realised that the element of surprise was lost and the Germans had got wind that they were coming. Then it turned out that the fortifications were much more than everyone had been led to believe. Allied air reconnaissance was woefully inadequate and as a result, tanks bogged down on the shingle beach became sitting ducks for the massive anti-tank guns dug into the cliffs. The few tanks which did make it over the sea wall to land were ground to a halt by concrete road blocks. Men coming up the beach behind them were slaughtered by machine guns hidden in those same cliffs. By the time the order to withdraw came, it was obvious that there had been a great loss of life. As the last of the aircraft made it back home, the BBC was announcing that the Dieppe raid had been a success, but in reality it was a failure. France was still firmly in the grip of Nazi Germany.

'I'm afraid your mother has caught a bit of a chill.'

Bob was back in Ruislip visiting his mother in the home once more. He frowned anxiously. 'But she's going to be all right?'

'Oh yes,' said Matron. 'She's in her room. You know the way but we would be grateful if you make this a short visit. She needs to rest.'

Ever the dutiful son, he nodded. He visited her quite often now. He'd usually find some worthwhile pickings in her handbag or in her room when he came and nobody challenged him. After all, she was his mother. As for Mrs Kane herself, luckily for Bob, she didn't seem to know whether it was Monday or Easter.

The room itself was hot, stuffy and smelled of Vick's vapour rub. His mother lay under the covers, her normally neat grey hair tumbled all over the pillow like a cloud. As he drew closer, she opened her red rimmed eyes and smiled up at him.

'How are you, Mother?'

'Not too bad, son. Mustn't grumble.'

He picked up the photograph of his father on the table beside the bed. 'You were going to tell me about him. He looks very smart.'

'Oh he was,' she said. 'Everybody admired him. If Mosley had been elected, he would have been in government. They always said he was made for high office.'

Bob could feel his chest expanding.

'I was there, you know,' she said quietly. 'In 1934, when Mosley spoke at Olympia. "The soul of the Empire is alive, and England again dares to be great."'

'Can I have this picture of my father?'

'No, son,' she said. 'That picture is all I have of him.'

Bob put it back onto the table. He wished he hadn't bothered to ask now.

'I'm sorry, darling.' Jim slipped his arm around Norah's shoulder and spoke directly into her ear. The pub was packed and noisy and she struggled to hear what he was saying.

They'd had a very enjoyable day. It was their wedding anniversary and when he'd come home, Jim had taken Norah to the Stanhoe Hotel for a slap-up meal. It had been a long time since Norah had been spoiled like that and she'd loved every minute. The meal over, they'd strolled

146

back to the Richard Cobden and popped in for a quiet drink. Fat chance of that because unbeknown to them, a local soldier was home on leave and there was a party underway. Before they'd hardly got through the door, they were swept up with the celebration. Christine was hammering out popular songs on the piano and Ivan was playing the spoons. 'Roll Out the Barrel,' 'The White Cliffs of Dover' and 'Pack up Your Troubles'; everybody sang at the tops of their voices which was why Jim was having such a hard time telling Norah what he wanted to say.

'What have you got to be sorry about?'

'I've been neglecting you.'

'No you haven't.'

'Yes I have. Lennard is right. I've got a gem of a wife and sometimes I take you for granted.'

'Oh don't be daft, Jim.' She cuffed him playfully on the top of his arm. The music grew louder. He said something else but she didn't hear. 'What?'

All at once, Christine stopped playing and at the same time, Jim yelled, 'I love you.'

Every head turned in their direction. Jim went scarlet and Norah put her hand over her mouth to hide her smile. Then a deep, male, rather boozy voice somewhere near the bar called out, 'And I love you too darling,' just before the whole pub erupted into laughter.

Chapter 18

'. . . *happy birthday dear Amélie*
Happy birthday to you.'

Her face pink with pleasure, Amélie blew out the single
and much used candle on the top of the small Victoria
sponge.

The family were sitting at the table in the Lilacs, their
faces aglow with pleasure as they celebrated Amélie's seven-
teenth birthday. In the middle of the table, a small pile of
presents waited for her attention. She couldn't stay long. It
was early afternoon and she was back on duty in just over
an hour but Amélie had promised Norah she would come
for tea and cake on the actual day. While Amélie tackled
her presents, Norah cut slices of cake for the birthday girl,
herself, Ivan and Christine, Elsie and Pete. Jim was still at
work and apparently Mireille had written to tell her sister
she couldn't make it. Hearing the sound of paper being
unwrapped, the dogs waited expectantly close to the table.

'Ooh lovely,' Amélie cried as she unwrapped a bottle of
scent from Elsie and Pete. She lifted the cap and sprayed
a little onto her wrist. A delicious flowery perfume filled
the air.

Norah's present next. She and Jim had bought her a fob watch, something she had been wanting for ages. All the other nurses had one pinned onto their aprons. It was so useful when taking the patients' pulse rates but Amélie had to rely on an old wrist watch she kept in her pocket. It was obvious from her expression that Amélie loved it.

Christine and Ivan's gift was a lot larger. Amélie was thrilled when she pulled back the brown paper and a cherry-red crepe dress fell onto the table. She shook it and held it out for everyone to see. It was knee-length and had three-quarter-length sleeves. The bust was gathered onto the yoke at the neck and shirring elastic running through the dropped waist gave it a clingy, attractive shape. The skirt itself was loosely pleated. A peep hole at the front was topped by a large bow in the same material.

'Did you make this, Mémé?' Amélie cried delightedly. 'It's amazing.'

'Glad you like it, dear,' said Christine as Amélie planted a loud kiss on her cheek.

'Ah, hem . . .' Ivan was pointing to his cheek so Amélie obliged him with a kiss as well. She held the dress out to admire it. 'Mireille has sent me a pretty bracelet which would go perfectly with this dress.'

'The flowers on the table are from Lennard,' said Jim.

Amélie seemed surprised. 'Lennard?'

Christine nodded. The bouquet, all pastel colours, pinks, pale yellow, mauve and white had obviously come from a florist. 'He had hoped to be here but he couldn't get leave.'

'They're very beautiful,' said Amélie, 'but I hardly know him.'

'He really admired your and Mireille's photograph,' said Jim. 'Perhaps he's trying to get into your good books.'

Amélie smiled to herself as she fingered one of the petals. 'Gosh I've been so lucky,' she sighed. 'You've given me so many lovely things. Thank you. And,' she added dreamily, 'Bob has promised to take me out tonight.'

'You're still going out with him then?' said Norah.

'Oh yes,' said Amélie.

'Is he taking you somewhere nice for your birthday?' Elsie wanted to know.

'There's a lecture in the Labour Hall in Lyndhurst Road he wants to go to,' she said.

'A lecture?' Christine squeaked.

'It was very hard to get tickets,' Amélie said defensively.

'A lecture,' Christine repeated.

'It's about the new world order after the war,' Amélie went on. 'Bob says it will be a good education for me.'

'I bet it will,' Elsie said dryly.

'I shall wear my new dress,' Amélie said happily. 'My bracelet and my lovely perfume.'

'Let's hope Bob likes them,' said Pete.

'He will,' Amélie said. 'He's always very complimentary.' She chuckled as she added, 'He only wants the best for his perfect angel.'

Mrs Draycot was busy in the kitchen when Norah put her bike against the wall outside an hour or so later. She gave her a little wave through the window. 'I've come to see Penny,' Norah said as she opened the door.

Victor, a long candlestick of mucus hanging from his nose, came over to her. 'Hello sweetheart,' said Norah. 'How are you?'

'My tar,' he said, holding up a battered-looking sports car with one missing tyre. Norah went down on her haunches as he demonstrated how it moved.

'I love it,' Norah enthused. Mrs Draycot had turned back to the washing up in the sink so Norah pulled her own handkerchief from her pocket and wiped the little boy's nose. She stood to her feet. 'Where's Penny? She asked me to look out for a job for her and I've got some good news.'

'She could do with that,' Mrs Draycot said in a flat tone. 'She's upstairs.'

Norah hesitated. 'Can I go up?'

Mrs Draycot nodded. 'Be sure to shut the kitchen door or Victor will follow you.'

Norah nodded. Mrs Draycot carried on washing up the plates and cutlery. She didn't look at her again. Norah wondered what to do. She was behaving very oddly. Had something happened? Her immediate thought was Ted. Heavens above, don't say something had happened to poor Ted. She took the stairs two at a time while Victor wailed behind the closed kitchen door.

Penny was in her bedroom. She was lying on her back staring at the ceiling. 'Pen?' Norah said gently as she hung around by the door. 'You all right?'

Her friend sat up. 'Oh Norah,' she said brokenly, 'he's dead.'

Shocked and stunned, Norah perched herself on the edge of the bed. 'Oh Lord, Penny, I'm so sorry. What happened?'

Penny burst into tears.

Norah put her arm around her shoulder. 'How do you know he's dead?' she asked. 'Did the Red Cross write and tell you?'

Penny frowned. 'No, of course not. His mates told me.'

'I don't understand. So, Ted was back over here? When did they release him?'

'I'm not talking about Ted,' Penny said irritably. 'Who cares about him? I'm talking about Waldo. Waldo Yates.'

'I'm sorry,' said Norah. 'You've lost me.'

'Waldo went on that raid to Dieppe. He was killed on the beach.'

151

Norah was speechless, so Penny added, 'You may as well know, Waldo was my Canadian.'

'*Your* Canadian?' said Norah.

'Yes,' Penny said defiantly. 'I don't care who knows it. He was a wonderful, wonderful man and he didn't deserve for this to happen.' She began to cry again.

Norah put her arm around her friend's shoulders. 'I saw him once,' she said quietly.

Penny blew her nose and gave Norah a puzzled frown. 'When?'

'It was the day the Jerry machine-gunned the gates by West Worthing station. I saw you kissing a soldier.'

Penny's eyes filled with tears again. 'Where were you then?'

'I was the other side of the gates,' said Norah, 'waiting to go through. When Jerry came back, we all had to dive into the shops. I went into the butcher's.'

Penny looked down at the sodden handkerchief in her hand. 'We ran into the station buildings,' she said quietly. 'We stayed there for quite a while.'

'Is he the one who took you to the show?'

Penny nodded dully.

Norah took a deep breath. What could she say? It was wrong but the poor man was dead. 'I'm so sorry,' Norah repeated. 'You were obviously very close.'

Penny heaved a great sigh. 'That's not the worst of it,' she said eventually, lifting her head to look Norah in the eye. 'I haven't even told Mum yet. I'm pregnant.'

Norah's eyes grew wide. 'Oh Penny,' she said softly. 'What are you going to do?'

'Well Mum can't cope with two of them and I know Ted won't want to raise another man's kid,' Penny said. Her voice had an edge to it. 'I'll have to get rid of it.'

'But it's illegal,' Norah said.

'Of course it is,' Penny snapped. 'But what other choice do I have?'

'You could be risking your own life,' Norah protested.

'Don't you think I know that?' Penny hissed. She blew her nose then stared at Norah with a challenging look on her face. 'Come on then clever dick. Tell me what you would do.' They heard a noise on the stairs and Penny's face paled. 'Don't say anything in front of Mum,' she whispered.

'Only if you promise me you won't do something stupid.'

Amélie hurried down the stairs of the nurses' home and signed herself out. In all the excitement of her birthday she'd forgotten to ask for a late pass so she didn't have much time. She glanced up at the clock. Seven-thirty already. That meant she only had just over a couple of hours with Bob. Oh dear, if only she'd remembered to ask Sister she could have stayed out until ten-forty-five.

As she reached the front door a man cycled by and she heard a wolf whistle. A nurse coming in the opposite direction said, 'Wow. You look fantastic. I've not seen that dress before.'

Amélie held out the skirt and did a twirl. 'Brand new today. It was a birthday present.'

'Oh happy birthday,' said the girl. 'It really suits you. Makes you look like a film star. Your boyfriend will love it.'

Laughing aloud, Amélie swung her bag onto her shoulder. 'I hope so.'

Bob was waiting at the end of the street. As she hurried towards him, she saw his face cloud. She expected him to say happy birthday or to give her a peck on the cheek but he didn't do either.

'Hello Bob,' she said but he didn't answer. As she slipped her arm through his, she wondered what she had done wrong.

They walked quickly towards the Labour Hall but a few

yards from the entrance, he pulled her into a twitten. Amélie was expecting a birthday kiss but far from it. Looking around to make sure no one was watching, he reached for his handkerchief.

'Cover yourself up,' he whispered angrily.

'What?'

He waved the handkerchief in front of her. 'Put this inside that hole on your dress,' he said.

'But it's meant to be there,' she protested mildly. 'It's quite high up. You can't see anything.'

'It's indecent.'

Shocked, Amélie frowned. Indecent? What did he mean? All you could see was a little of her chest just below her shoulder blades. She wasn't showing any cleavage; not that she had much anyway. 'Oh Bob . . .'

'Just do it,' he hissed.

He turned his head as she obediently looped his handkerchief inside her dress just beneath the bow. She couldn't see what it looked like but she felt ridiculously silly. It was bound to spoil the whole look.

He turned back and was satisfied. 'Don't ever wear that thing again when you come out with me,' he said, snatching her hand. 'Now come on and hurry up. We're already late.'

Back home, Norah had an anxious wait until she and Jim were alone in the house. After their evening meal, Jim walked the dogs. Luckily Christine and Ivan were off to the church hall whist drive tonight, where they were raising funds for the Worthing Spitfire Appeal. As soon as they'd gone Norah joined her husband in the sitting room. He looked tired.

'Busy day?' she asked as she put a cup of tea in front of him.

He nodded. 'Short staffed.'

'Then let's hope they don't send *you* any call-up papers,' Norah quipped. 'There'd be nobody left.'

Jim gave her a tired smile. She sat on the arm of his chair. 'I went to see Penny Andrews today.'

'Oh yeah,' Jim said vaguely.

'I never told you but I saw her with some Canadian chap,' Norah went on.

'You what?' Jim gasped.

'The thing is she's very upset,' Norah continued. 'He was in that raid on Dieppe. He's been killed.'

Jim relaxed back into the chair. 'Oh I'm very sorry to hear that although it sounds like poetic justice if he was messing around with Penny.'

'Oh Jim,' Norah scolded. She chewed her lip anxiously. 'Penny is going to have his baby.'

'Good God!' Jim exclaimed.

Norah took a deep breath. 'She says her mother can't cope with two little ones and she's in such a pickle she's talking about getting rid of it.'

'Norah, don't tell me that,' said Jim sitting up straight. 'I'm a policeman. Abortion is against the law. What I don't know I can't do anything about.'

'I know and that's why I've been thinking,' she went on. 'Why don't we offer to adopt it? We know Penny. She's a bit flighty but she's a good mum to her Victor. Jim, we've waited for so long for Miss Bundy to get everything sorted but it just doesn't happen. Supposing we make a private arrangement with Penny. We can still do that can't we?'

'Now hang on a minute . . .' said Jim.

But Norah was too excited to stop. 'I mean Penny would know we'd look after her baby. We'd be good parents, wouldn't we? Don't you see? We could arrange for Penny to go into a nursing home and have the baby then I could bring . . .'

'Norah, stop,' Jim cried. He took her hands in his. 'Just think about this. Wouldn't it be a bit awkward to have the real mother of our baby living only a stone's throw away?'

'But she says Ted would never accept another man's child,' Norah protested.

Jim looked thoughtful. 'I don't know . . .' He sighed, shaking his head at the same time.

Norah was chewing her bottom lip again. 'Can't I just talk to her about it?' she pleaded. 'I'm sure we could work something out.'

Jim looked up at her anxious face. 'I just don't want to you to be disappointed and upset.'

'I won't be,' Norah insisted. 'I promise but please Jim, please.'

'All right,' he said. 'If you think she might be amenable to the idea, invite Penny over one evening and we'll talk it through.'

Norah flung her arms around her husband's neck and kissed him.

Chapter 19

Most of the lecture went over Amélie's head. The speaker was Sir John Hope Simpson, a man who had once been a Liberal member of parliament but was now sought after for his expertise on refugees. A balding man with round rimmed spectacles, he was softly spoken but authoritatively. Amélie may have looked as if she was taking everything in but as the meeting started she was already fighting the desire to give in to her tears. As time went on she felt less emotional but she was still mulling over what Bob had said. Did he really think she dressed in an indecent manner? What was wrong with this frock anyway? Mémé had spent hours and hours making it for her and now she was forbidden to wear it ever again. It wasn't fair. For a moment she was distracted from her own thoughts when Sir John said that after the war a new League of Nations should be formed with an international army to safeguard smaller nations from aggressors. That suggestion was greeted by thunderous applause and Bob was on his feet, clapping and shouting out, 'Here, here!'

As the meeting ended, the chairman stood to thank Sir John for his timely remarks.

'It's obvious,' the chairman continued, 'that steps must be taken to re-educate the German nation.' There was more applause. 'We must also grasp the nettle as far as morals and conduct are concerned and we must re-educate the female of the species to take back their God given role – that of wife and mother.'

There wasn't quite so much applause for that remark but Bob was still on his feet clapping enthusiastically.

For the first time, Amélie felt uncomfortable. Where was all this leading? Women had found a new impetus during the war. They had discovered that they were just as good as the men, given half a chance. Was this man saying that once the war was over, women had to go back to the kitchen and stay there? And why was Bob so enthusiastic? She thought back to the way he'd behaved over her new dress. Was he trying to re-educate her thinking?

Amélie glanced at him as he sat back down beside her. His eyes were lit up and there was a half-smile on his mouth. Clearly Bob was enthralled. She'd better start paying attention. As difficult as it was, she was beginning to realise that she was going to have to submit to a whole new way of life if she was going to follow the man she loved to the ends of the earth.

Most women destined for SOE trained in other places but Mireille and her two fellow recruits were driven to Wanborough Manor near Guildford. It turned out to be a beautiful Elizabethan house with red roofs set in stunning countryside on the Hogs Back. Mireille had never seen such a beautiful place. Inside it was a tad Spartan, probably because it was no longer a private residence and had been requisitioned by the military. She and her two companions were billeted in the same room. They had travelled together from London in the same car but Mireille knew very little about them except that they were obviously upper crust. Belinda said she was the daughter of a Rhodesian tobacco grower and Harriet told them she'd been working as a journalist. 'It does annoy me that because I'm a woman, they only give me the garden fetes and WVS stuff,' she complained in her high-pitched plummy voice, 'Half the men on the paper are chain-smoking drunks but they get all the best assignments.' Mireille changed the subject when they asked her about her parents. There was no way she wanted to talk about her past again. She understood the need to tell Parker everything in detail but she'd made a vow to herself that she would never repeat the story to another living soul. There was no need for her to explain what she did for a living. Her WAAF uniform said it all.

When they were shown to their room, their cases were already there waiting for them. They were given a little time to unpack their belongings into the two chests of drawers, one built-in cupboard and two tallboys before going downstairs. Belinda had stacks of clothes but Harriet and Mireille didn't have nearly as much.

Their commander, Major de Wesselow was waiting for them in the communal sitting room, a fairly large but cosy space. He was a smart man with an obvious military bearing so it was hardly surprising when in his opening introduction he told them that he was an officer in the Coldstream Guards. Mireille was impressed to meet someone from a regiment whose principal duty was the protection of the King. She tried to imagine the Major in his tall Busby marching or even riding a horse beside the royal family on ceremonial occasions. Dressed in a less formal uniform, he welcomed them warmly and having invited them to sit on one of the armchairs or the sofas, he told them that this period of training would probably be the most difficult of their lifetime.

'It's our purpose to find out if you are suited to the work,' he told them, 'and for that reason it will be tough. In all honesty we shall be looking for an opportunity to tell you to leave rather than encouraging you to stay. You will also have to be very fit. From now on, you will speak only French. I want you to learn to think in French as well.'

Rising to the challenge, Mireille smiled to herself.

'Parker probably told you that you would be here for a couple of weeks,' he continued in French, 'but we believe three to four weeks would be more beneficial.'

'What exactly are we going to do?' Harriet asked.

'Speak in French if you please, Miss Crossley,' de Wesselow reminded her. 'We aim to get you to a high level of physical fitness and train you in all the skills you will need to be an undercover agent.'

They were each given a small folder which contained details of what was expected of them and the punishing routine they would have to follow week by week. Most alarmingly, they were expected to be ready for physical exercise at six the next morning and it seemed that their day wouldn't end until late at night. Major de Wesselow excused himself as they read their folders and left the room.

'Bloody hell,' Belinda murmured in English, 'this is worse than prison camp.'

'Speak in French if you please, Miss Crossley,' Harriet said, mimicking the major to a tee. Belinda glared at her.

Mireille tried to take it all in. Yes, it was going to be hard but she was excited to see that once she had completed her time here in the Guildford countryside, she could be expected to move on somewhere else for further intensive training which might include the use of weapons and explosives and becoming proficient in the use of short wave radio. Parker had told her to discard her romantic notions but it was proving to be very difficult. She had no romantic notions about men but right now she felt every inch an enthusiastic partisan who would do her best to set the French people free from Nazi tyranny.

Norah had done a lot of thinking. At first, everything seemed so simple. Get Penny to agree to go into a nursing home and have the baby and then she could bring him or her back to the Lilacs as her own. But the more she thought about it, the more complications she found. If Penny stayed in Worthing long enough for her pregnancy to show, her reputation would be seriously damaged. She could just imagine how the tongues would wag. People would shun her, or worse still, expose her. Some well-meaning busy-body might even decide to write to Ted. The scandal would not only affect Penny, it might mean her child growing up with the stigma of being called a bastard. That didn't bear thinking about. And now that Uncle Fred had sacked her, Penny needed another job, but who would employ a pregnant woman – especially one who had broken her marriage vows and had a fling with a foreigner? Everything whirled around and around her head but in the morning she woke up thinking about Mrs Harrison. Of course! They'd struck up a friendship after Norah and Jim had looked after her two little girls when they'd been evacuated in 1939. Gwen had written more than once to tell her that if she ever needed help, she knew where to come. Right now, Gwen could be the answer to all her prayers.

As soon as everybody was out of the house, Norah reached for the telephone.

A woman's voice answered. 'Stanmore 253.'

'Hello Gwen? It's Norah. I wondered if we could have a little chat . . .'

*

161

The alarm went off at five-thirty. Belinda groaned and turned over in her bed. Harriet and Mireille rolled out of bed at the same time. Grabbing her wash bag, Mireille headed to the bathroom while Harriet made her bed. As soon as Mireille was washed and in her gym kit and Harriet had taken her place in the bathroom, Belinda was sitting on the edge of her bed scratching her head.

'Better hurry up, Bel,' said Mireille. 'It's nearly six-twenty.'

'Whoever invented this time of the morning wants shooting,' Belinda grumbled.

At six-thirty, Mireille and Harriet were already doing star jumps and running on the spot. Because she had been in the WAAFs, Mireille was used to early morning exercise but this was on a much higher level. It didn't take long for her muscles to protest.

'If you're going to out-run the Boches,' their unsympathetic instructor told them, 'you're going to have to be super-fit.'

By the time Belinda showed up, they were doing press-ups, squats and sit-ups. The exercise was hard and all three girls could only manage a small number at a time but their instructor promised them that they would soon reach a decent level of fitness.

Breakfast was wonderful: an egg each, bacon and sausage with a hunk of fried bread to mop everything up. Mireille had worked up an appetite which was not disappointed.

'Reminds me of breakfasts on the farm,' Belinda sighed, although she only picked at her meal.

During the day, the girls were taught how to use a weapon and strip it down. After that it was target practice. There was also training which included learning codes interspersed with cross-country runs and unarmed combat.

'Just look at the state of my nails!' Belinda exclaimed at the end of their first week.

They were allowed to write letters but of course everything was read and censored. They could say they were on exercise but not where they were or anything about the place. Mireille wrote a couple of postcards to Amélie. The picture on the front of the first one was of a British Tommy in WW1 battle dress. He was on sentry duty and startled by a rabbit, he was firing a gun into the air. The second was of a strait-laced spinster watching a chicken risking her life running across a busy road as the cockerel chased her. The caption underneath said, 'That's right little hen, rather death than dishonour.' As her message on the cards had to be very brief, Mireille reasoned that at least they would make her sister smile. She told her she hoped that Amélie was doing well in her studies to be a nurse and not to worry about her because she was doing fine. How she wished she could send something to Linnet.

After a lot of thought, during the third week, Mireille sent Ginger a card. It was just a picture of some people dancing. The message on the other side said, 'Hope you're still having a good time. Keep safe,' but somehow or other, she never got round to posting that one.

There was little time to think of home, although Mireille did miss Ginger . . . a bit.

Chapter 20

At the end of October, everyone in the town was asked to donate non-ferrous metal for the war effort once again. Christine and Ivan made themselves available to collect items as soon as the loudspeaker van went past. Apparently a depot had been set up in an empty shop at the end of Montague Street so the pair pushed their cart along the road collecting stuff on the way. By the time they reached the shop, they had a variety of things including fire screens, fenders, plant bowls, old sporting trophies and coffee pots. Some items looked quite new but despite war-weariness, people happily parted with anything that might be useful to do their bit.

Norah had already started collecting all sorts of things. In the pantry she had boxes and jars for just about everything from milk bottle tops to wastepaper and cardboard, to pig food and even a jam jar for cheese rind which was grated up and given to the hens. They were getting used to eating grey bread (grey because the flour contained the whole of the wheat grain, including the husks). For the past year everybody had been told that their baths must have no more than five inches of water and there were fire bricks in the hearth to save on fuel. Life could be tough. It wasn't unusual to go to bed hungry.

'I dreamt I went to Mitchell's last night,' Ivan told them one breakfast time. (Mitchell's had been bombed to the ground in 1940.) 'I was the only customer in there,' he continued, 'so I asked for a piece of fruit cake. They gave me a plate with what looked like your wellington boots on top.' Everybody chuckled.

'I hope they were tasty,' Norah quipped.

She was feeling a lot happier since Jim had agreed to talk to Penny. They were going round there tonight, not for a meal but because Mrs Draycot went to the Methodist Church Bible study on a Thursday so it meant they could talk to Penny privately.

Norah was busy working in the nursery when she heard the gate go and the dogs started barking. She looked up to see a young man walking towards the house. He was quite short, five foot five or six but he had broad shoulders and was obviously very fit. He was dressed in RAF uniform war service dress, so she knew he was ground crew, a cap perched on top of his bright red hair.

'Can I help you?'

'I hope so,' he replied. 'I'm a friend of Mireille and I wondered if you have any news of her.'

Norah frowned. It was a while since she'd heard Mireille's name mentioned in her own home. She'd spent the first couple of months of the year trying to rekindle their relationship by writing letter after letter but it was obvious by her silence that Mireille was having none of it. She'd explained; she'd asked for forgiveness; she'd written chatty letters with no mention of their differences, so many that it became embarrassing and all to no avail. Norah's own feeling swung between irritation and frustration, anxiety and hurt. It was a roller-coaster. She would always enquire about her when Amélie came home but after a while she could see she was embarrassing the girl. Although it was painful for Norah, she realised that she had to let it go. Mireille didn't want her friendship anymore and there was nothing she could do about it. As she looked up into the eyes of this earnest young man, she could see the same sort of pain there. 'No,' she said gently, 'I'm afraid I don't. I'm sorry.'

The dogs seemed delighted to see him even though they had never met him before. He petted them as he spoke. 'She once told me that she and her sister used to live here,' he went on.

'She did,' said Norah, putting her trowel down and taking off her gardening gloves, 'but we haven't seen Mireille since before last Christmas.'

He looked crestfallen.

'What did you say your name was?'

'I didn't but it's Hugh Slater,' he said, adding, 'but everybody calls me Ginger. You must be Norah?' She nodded and they shook hands.

'Well Ginger,' said Norah, 'would you like to come in for a cup of tea?'

He seemed pleased with the invitation and with the dogs bouncing around their ankles, he came in. Norah sat him at the kitchen table while she washed her hands and got the cups out. 'Are you by any chance Mireille's boyfriend?'

'I should like to be,' he said. 'We do go out quite a lot but she's reluctant to commit to anything serious.' He looked a little embarrassed then added quickly, 'I don't mind. I'm willing to wait.'

As she filled the kettle, Norah smiled to herself. He was in love with her. It was as obvious as September follows August. 'I'm sure she'd appreciate that.'

'Only she's gone,' said Ginger, 'and I don't know where she is.'

'I'm so sorry I can't help you,' said Norah. 'Like I said we haven't seen her since last Christmas. I know she's been seeing her sister but as I expect you already know, she and I had a bit of a falling out and well . . . there it is.'

'She told me,' said Ginger. Norah's head shot up. 'She never told me what it was all about,' he added, 'but I know she felt bad about it.'

'She did?' Norah squeaked.

'She said you were a good person and that you'd helped her and her sister a lot.' Max had his head in Ginger's lap and Sausage was lying across his foot. 'I think she was angry with herself for causing the argument, whatever it was, but somehow or other she's never really got round to sorting it out. I know she means to, so I wondered if this time she may have come back to put things right with you.'

Norah felt quite emotional as she poured the tea.

'Do you know anything about her family?' he went on. 'Mireille never told me much but I'm guessing she must have had a hard time as a child.'

'I'm afraid I can't discuss that with you,' said Norah, putting the cosy over the pot, 'not without her permission.'

He nodded resignedly. 'You're right. You mustn't betray a confidence.'

They sat opposite each other sipping their teas. 'What about her sister,' he asked. 'Can you tell me when she'll be home?'

'Amélie doesn't live here,' said Norah.

'Oh.' He seemed disappointed. Max whined so Ginger fondled his ear.

'When did you last see Mireille?' Norah wanted to know.

'About four weeks ago,' he said. 'She was on her way to London for some sort of an interview. I don't know what for but I got the impression it was something pretty hush-hush.'

Norah frowned again. 'I don't understand. She's in the WAAFs.'

'I know,' said Ginger. 'That's where I met her but just lately she's been talking a lot about France. I've got a funny feeling it has something to do with that.'

Norah's eyes grew wide. 'You're not trying to tell me she's going to France?'

'I don't know what to think,' he said sadly, 'but I'm worried sick about her.'

That was obvious. Norah's heart went out to him. 'Look,' she said, 'why don't I give you pen and paper and you can write a note to Amélie. I'll make sure she gets it the next time she comes. I'm sure if she knows anything she'll tell you.'

Ginger nodded grimly. 'That's very kind of you. I'd like that. Thank you, Norah.'

'Take your time,' she added as she gave him her Basildon Bond. 'And when you've finished it, perhaps you would like to stay for tea. My husband comes home in about half an hour.'

Ginger smiled. 'If you're sure . . .'

After Jim arrived home, they all had a pleasant meal together and Norah invited Ginger to pop round anytime he felt like a few home comforts. Ivan and Christine took to him straight away as did Norah's husband.

'The dogs have made a real pal of you,' said Ivan as he watched Max's tail wagging.

'I don't think I've ever known the pair of them to be so friendly with a stranger,' Christine remarked.

They discovered that he came from a large family with three sisters and two brothers. His parents had a farm in Yorkshire and he spoke warmly of them all as well as the Dales and the beauty of the countryside.

'Have you seen much action?' Jim asked.

'Not unless you call driving nobs and big-wigs around the country, no,' he said dryly. 'For some reason I've become nothing more than a glorified taxi driver.'

Everybody laughed.

When it was time to go, he gave Norah and Jim a lift up to Broadwater, dropping them off right outside Penny's door.

'If we hear anything,' Norah promised as she got out of the jeep, 'we'll let you know and don't forget to pop by whenever you feel like it.'

He gave them a cheery wave and then he was gone. Norah and Jim took a deep breath and walked up Penny's driveway to the front door. When she opened it, Penny still looked a mess. Her face was grey and she had bags under her eyes. More than that, she was listless and miserable. While Jim made for the sitting room to play with Victor before Penny put him to bed, Norah gave her a hug.

'Oh Norah,' she said. 'I can't do this. I just want to die. My chest hurts so much.'

'I know, I know.' She didn't, but Norah had no idea what to say. She couldn't imagine how horrible it would be to lose Jim.

With Victor in his cot and a cup of tea in their hands, the three of them settled down to talk about Penny's baby.

'Have you told your mother yet?'

Penny shook her head. 'But I think she's guessed. I'm quite sick in the mornings now.' She sighed then whimpered, 'I'm not sure I can do this.'

Jim put his policeman's hat on. 'Penny, I have to remind you that I'm a copper. I understand the need to be frank, but please don't talk about anything that's against the law.'

She looked at him and nodded dully. 'I understand.'

He leaned forward. 'I think you know that Norah and

I would very much like a child of our own.' He paused, allowing the thought to sink in. 'How would you feel if we agreed to adopt your baby?'

Norah's heart was pounding so hard she could hardly draw breath. Her whole future rested upon Penny's answer to this question. There was a long silence. All they could hear was the sound of the clock on the mantelpiece ticking. Tick, tock, tick, tock. Penny had her head down. Still staring at her own lap, she pulled her handkerchief from her sleeve and blew her nose. Tick, tock, tick tock. Norah opened her mouth but as she glanced at Jim, she saw him shake his head. Tick, tock, tick tock.

Penny looked up. 'What about Mum? The gossips would have a field day. She won't want me waddling around Worthing for all to see. I know her. She'll be devastated by the shame of it.' Penny blew her nose again. 'She'd probably kick me and Victor out. What would I do then?'

Now it was Norah's turn. 'You might not have to stay in Worthing,' she began.

'What and go to one of those awful mother and baby homes?' Penny squeaked helplessly. She began screwing and unscrewing her handkerchief. 'Oh I couldn't, I couldn't.'

'You wouldn't have to,' Norah said. 'Look, you may think this is a bit cheeky of me, but I think I may have the solution.'

Penny blinked.

'You remember Gwen Harrison?' said Norah.

'What, the mother of those two little girls you had as evacuees?'

Norah nodded. 'We've kept in touch ever since the girls went back,' Norah continued. 'Her husband is in the RAF and he's based at Stanmore in Middlesex.'

Penny leaned back in her chair, listening intently.

'The thing is, she's very active in the war effort. I've

telephoned her. I didn't tell her it was you, but she'd welcome a live-in help for the girls. It does mean you'd have to look after three children but she says if you could manage to work up until the last two months, she'd look after you then. What do you say?'

Penny frowned. 'Three children?'

'Her two girls,' said Norah, 'and Victor.'

'She'd let me take Victor?'

Norah nodded.

For the first time since they'd arrived, Penny smiled. 'That's amazing!' Her expression suddenly became more sceptical. 'There's a catch, isn't there? What's the catch?'

Norah chewed her bottom lip. 'Not much pay. She says she'll give you and Victor bed and board but you'll have no more than pocket money.'

They heard someone put the key into the front door. Penny sat bolt upright. 'Don't say anything to Mum, okay?' she whispered urgently.

'So what do you say?' Norah said, anxious for an answer.

'I'll think about it,' said Penny.

Chapter 21

Christine and Ivan had had a good day at the market. The weather had been a bit mixed but by three-thirty most of their produce had sold. What was left wasn't the best quality but still eatable so they let it go at a bargain price. Over the months they had come to know the people who were on very small incomes so when they came to the stall, they'd knock off a penny or two here or a sixpence there. Nothing was wasted. Any bruised items were cut up for stews or soup and the outer leaves of the cabbages or the odd squashed tomato or battered apple that had rolled onto the ground was used to feed the pigs. Like many others in the town, the residents of Clifton Road shared some pigs which were kept on a smallholding in South Farm Road. When the time came for them to be killed, the government had one half of each animal and the rest was shared out among them all.

The pair were weary by the time Ivan had finished washing down the cart and Christine had cut up any edible stuff and put the rest in the pig bin. They were just getting ready to come indoors when Norah came out of the house looking nervously back over her shoulder.

'Everything all right, gal?' said Ivan.

Norah put her finger over her lips and pulled them away from the back door. 'Amélie is engaged,' she whispered.

Christine took in a noisy and excited breath. 'Engaged!'

'Shh,' Norah cautioned.

'Not to that Bob, I hope,' said Ivan.

Norah nodded and Christine's face paled.

'He wants her to give up nursing.'

Christine looked aghast. 'But she can't,' she protested. 'Give it up just to get married? Why can't she wait?'

'Never liked the chap meself,' Ivan murmured.

'Didn't you talk to her, Norah?' Christine demanded.

'It's not her,' said Norah, 'it's him.'

Christine sniffed and drew herself up to her full height. 'Where is she?' Without waiting for an answer, Norah's mother-in-law strode through the back door and into the kitchen.

Amélie was sitting at the kitchen table gazing into the face of her fiancé. She looked very attractive in a pretty floral cotton dress and the blue cardigan Christine had knitted her last Christmas. Bob was rearranging a curl which had flopped onto Amélie's forehead. 'There, that's better,' he said. 'Much tidier.'

'Thank you,' Amélie said, holding her head stiffly for fear of it falling out of place again.

The two dogs were sharing Max's bed in the corner of the kitchen. Max looked up at Christine as she walked in and made a throaty complaint. The sound made Amélie turn her head. 'Ah there you are Mémé. Did Norah tell you my news? Would you like to see my ring?'

Slightly disarmed, Christine walked towards the proffered hand to admire the magnificent opal set in between pink diamond chips. 'Umm, very nice, dear,' she said in a noncommittal way. Where would a mere hospital porter get the wherewithal to buy a ring of that quality?

173

'It was my grandmother's,' said Bob as if reading her mind. He said it with conviction but for some strange reason, Christine didn't believe a word of it.

Norah had invited them to stay for tea. Ivan and Christine took turns in the bathroom and came back to the table changed and smelling sweeter about twenty minutes later. Jim had arrived home a little before them. Although they had already met a couple of times, this was the first time they'd all had a meal with Bob. They weren't very keen on him but they could all see that Amélie was besotted with him. Norah dished up and Bob took his share first before putting Amélie's food on her plate for her. It seemed that she wasn't allowed to do a thing for herself. Irritated, Christine was tempted to ask him if he'd like to put a bib on her and feed her with a spoon.

'Have you got brothers and sisters?' Norah asked as she reached for the vegetable dish.

'No.'

Christine thought she saw a look of surprise on Amélie's face.

'Where were you brought up?'

'Shropshire.'

'What brought you to Worthing?' Christine wanted to know.

'My job.' It seemed all Bob's answers were going to be monosyllabic.

'You know, I still have Rene's wedding dress upstairs,' Norah said, anxious to defuse the awkward moment. 'Would you like me to write to her and ask if you could use it for your wedding?'

'There won't be time, I'm afraid,' Bob said.

Norah blinked.

'So,' said Jim, 'when do you two plan to get married then?'

'This coming Saturday,' Amélie said breathily.

Now the whole family was in shock. 'But that's only three days away,' Christine cried. 'That gives us very little time to get everything ready. Have you told Mireille?'

Amélie shook her head and glancing at her fiancé for approval she added, 'Bob and I want a quiet wedding.'

Christine was horrified. 'But she's your sister,' she protested. 'You can't not ask your own sister to your wedding.'

'Why the rush?' asked Norah.

'We want it that way,' said Bob. 'There's no need for a fuss.'

'But you only do this once in a lifetime, sweetheart,' said Christine, her voice mellowing. 'Of course we have to make a bit of a family celebration.'

Bob turned to her with a determined expression on his face. 'But you're not, are you?'

Christine bristled. 'What do you mean?'

'*You* are not her family.'

Sensing by the tone of his voice that something was wrong, Max stood up and barked. Sausage followed suit with a series of short yips.

'What Amélie and I do,' Bob said coldly, 'is none of your concern.'

Norah's face flushed angrily. 'How dare you!'

Max barked again. Ivan reprimanded him sharply.

Amélie suddenly looked embarrassed and uncomfortable. 'He didn't mean it like that, Norah. I know you mean well, but really we don't mind. You see as soon as we're married, we have to travel up to Liverpool.'

'What's in Liverpool?' said Jim.

Amélie looked back at Bob and laid her hand on his. 'Bob's taking me away from all this grief and sadness. I won't have to stay here and risk being bombed or killed when the Germans come. We're sailing next Tuesday. We're going to live in Canada.'

'Canada!' Christine gasped.

The room fell silent while the family tried to digest what she'd just said.

'I take it that your appeal against conscription failed then,' said Ivan.

His sarcasm wasn't wasted on Bob. 'Maybe it has, maybe it hasn't,' he said. 'Like I say it's got nothing to do with you.' Rising to his feet he turned to Amélie, 'Come on, girl. We're going.'

Jim stood up as well. 'Hang on a minute, Pal,' he began. 'You have to be twenty-one to marry without your parents' permission. Amélie is a minor.'

'And her parents are dead,' Bob snapped angrily.

'But perhaps she forgot to tell you that she and her sister appointed me as her legal guardian,' Jim said, 'so strictly speaking you should have come to me first to ask permission to marry her.'

Bob seemed confused and turning to Amélie he said, 'Is this right?'

She nodded.

'You should have told me,' he said petulantly. 'You should tell me everything.'

Norah put her hand to her mouth. What was it with this man? It was as if he wanted total control over the girl. Was Amélie really so blind that she couldn't see that?

Amélie looked up helplessly. 'I'm sorry,' she said, her eyes filling with tears. 'I didn't think it would matter.'

'Look Bob,' said Jim, his voice calm and relaxed, 'why don't you and I go into the sitting room and have a quiet chat about all this. After all, we both want the same thing, don't we? Amélie's future happiness.'

'Anything you have to say, you can say here and now and then we'll be going,' Bob said doggedly.

'All right,' said Jim as he sat back down. 'So what's in Canada? Do you have a job; somewhere to live?'

Bob said nothing but his face coloured.

'Having a wife is a big responsibility,' said Jim. 'And as soon as you marry, you have to think of the babies which will come along too. They'll need a home and food on the table.'

'We'll cross that bridge when we come to it,' said Bob.

Ivan let out a snort of disapproval. Bob glared at him.

'Not good enough,' said Jim. 'I suggest you go to Canada if you will. Find yourself a job, save a little money and get a proper house, then you can send for Amélie. By that time she will have finished her nurse's training which will mean you'll both have another string to your bow.' He paused. 'What do you say to that?'

Bob squared his shoulders. 'Come on Amélie,' he said with a sniff. 'We're going.'

'Oh, Amélie,' Norah whispered, but she rose obediently from her chair and bent to kiss Christine's cheek.

'Please don't do this, Luv,' Christine whispered into her hair.

'If you are thinking about doing a runner to avoid conscription,' Jim said picking up his knife and fork to tackle his now cold dinner, 'you'd better watch out for the military police.'

With a sad look on her face, Amélie took Bob's hand and they hurried out of the back door to the sound of Max's barking.

As soon as they heard the front gate click shut again, Christine burst into tears. 'Oh Jim, what can we do?'

'Not a lot,' said Jim. 'If he's telling us they're going from

177

Liverpool, I wouldn't mind betting my next week's pay that they're sailing from somewhere else, and I'm not so sure they'll be going to Canada either.'

The two men ate their meals and the dogs calmed down. Norah and Christine wept silently. They had both completely lost their appetites.

Amélie's stomach was all churned up. She and Bob walked for quite a while in silence. It seemed so unfair that she was being made to choose between them. She loved Bob and she loved Christine as if she was her own grandmother. If they went to Canada that awkward meal was probably the last time she would ever see her. And what about Mireille? It was bad enough that Linnet was halfway across the world but now she would be separated from her other sister as well. Why did love always come with such a terrible cost? She slipped her hand through Bob's arm and fought back her tears.

Eventually Bob was the one who started the conversation again. 'You do understand why we have to do this, don't you?'

Amélie nodded dully. 'I suppose so.'

'I only want the best for you my darling,' he said, his voice soft and tender, 'and Canada is the place to be. This country is finished. By the time the war ends it'll be bankrupt.' When she didn't answer he looked down at her. 'You do understand don't you?' he pressed.

'Yes Bob.'

'And as for Jim being your legal guardian, you shouldn't have kept that secret from me, Amélie. It could have spoiled everything.'

'I'm sorry.'

'Never mind,' he said. 'He can't do anything about it anyway.'

'But if we go to the registry office to get married on Saturday,' she protested mildly, 'he'll be waiting for us.'

'Let him,' Bob said. He grinned. 'By that time it'll be far too late.'

Amélie frowned, puzzled.

'Oh, didn't I mention it? Our wedding is tomorrow and we leave Worthing tomorrow night.'

'Tomorrow?' Amélie gasped. 'But you said . . .'

'I know,' said Bob, 'but I'm clever, see? I knew he'd want to stop us being happy so I let him think it was Saturday.'

'But I'm working tomorrow,' Amélie reminded him.

'Yes but you're off duty between ten and twelve,' he said. 'We'll do it then. It's all booked.'

'How did you know?' she asked. 'About my off duty, I mean?'

'I told you,' he preened. 'I'm clever. I checked the duty roster at the beginning of the month. Three weeks ago tomorrow.'

An uncomfortable feeling settled in the pit of Amélie's stomach. It was both exciting and very scary at the same time.

Dusk was falling and they'd reached Homefield Park. 'We mustn't have secrets from one another,' he told her as they went through the kissing gate.

She wondered if she should remind him that he'd already kept a lot of things from her but in the end she thought the better of it as he led her to a secluded bench and they sat down. He wasn't a demonstrative man, they'd never even kissed, but Bob sat close to her and put his arm on the backrest behind her. 'So, if you've got any more secrets . . .' he began.

'I don't.'

'Tell me how you came to live with Norah and Jim?'

The question was simple enough but for Amélie it was loaded. 'I already told you. I was evacuated.'

'With your sister.'

'Yes.' She was beginning to tremble.

'Then your step-father sent you to boarding school.'

'Yes.'

'So where is your step-father now? And if you already have him as a relative, why did Jim become your legal guardian?'

Amélie stared down at her fingers trembling in her lap. 'Some things are better left unsaid,' she said as firmly as she could. 'I don't want to talk about it.'

He sat up straighter and sniffed. 'If we are to be married, my angel, we shouldn't keep things from one another.'

Amélie reached for her handkerchief.

'Sweetheart, please. You can trust me with anything. All I want is to love and cherish you.' He tucked a stray curl back behind her ear and ran his finger down her cheek with a sigh. 'You are so perfect.'

'But I'm not.' The tears pooled in her eyes as Amélie took a shuddering breath. 'My step-father wasn't a good man,' she said softly. 'When my mother died, he wanted me to take her place.'

Bob seemed puzzled. 'Take her place . . . ?' he repeated.

'He said it was my duty,' Amélie whispered, 'that any little girl should do it for the person she loved . . .'

He stared at her in silence. 'So you . . . ?' he began. 'You and he . . . ?'

Amélie nodded miserably. Then with a loud cry, Bob jumped to his feet and the world went dark.

Chapter 22

With the rain trickling down the back of her neck, Mireille shivered. Honestly, they couldn't have picked a worse time for this. It was pitch black, cold and the wind was blowing half a gale. They were miles from anywhere and now she was getting soaking wet. Although there were five of them on the team, it was she who had worked out the co-ordinates and found the river. Not easy when they were stumbling around unfamiliar territory and doing their best to avoid road blocks and game keepers. Finding the boat was a little more problematic. The undergrowth near the water's edge was uneven and boggy. Mireille had already slipped a couple of times and she had mud on her trousers up as far as her thighs. It took every ounce of her concentration not to cry out as she fell because she knew the sound of a voice carried for miles at night.

There had been differences of opinion. When they'd started out, Jacques had assumed command simply because he was the only man but it quickly became apparent that he was no leader. Belinda was more concerned about the cold rather than what she was supposed to be doing and the other girl, Connie, a townie, spent all her time spooked up by the night time sounds of the countryside. 'What's that?' she'd say spinning round in an absolute panic when an owl hooted in the darkness.

It didn't take long for the group to decide that Mireille would make a much better leader. Having taken control, she made Sue Butler second in command because she was the only other sensible person among them. This might be their first night exercise but Mireille was determined to make it a success.

'Your brief is to find Hammond Farm,' their instructor told them as they'd set out, 'and collect the German guns we have left in the grey barn. When you find the river, load everything into the boat you will find hidden nearby and row to the bridge. When you reach it, go cross country to the railway line and plant your dummy device.' It sounded reasonably simple until he added, 'Because this is a field exercise, you must do it without the use of torches and in complete silence.' Not easy in the pitch black.

Sue discovered the boat. It was almost completely hidden behind the foliage of a large tree, probably a weeping willow. They stowed everything inside and then climbed in themselves. As they were about to push off, they heard the sound of someone splashing about in the water. Mireille knew the instructors used local poachers as the enemy, so she knew they had to get away before the man caught up with them. Motioning to Jacques, she sent him into the undergrowth to 'eliminate the opposition'. There was a short struggle while Jacques quickly overpowered the man giving the girls a chance to make their getaway. They made it to the bridge and across country but were 'captured' before they could sabotage the rail line.

Exhausted and soaking wet, they were bundled into an army truck and returned to base where, justifiably Mireille thought, Major de Wesselow was unequivocal in his reproach.

'You made several classic mistakes,' he told them. 'To begin with, your leadership was shoddy, in some cases your commitment was non-existent, you lacked concentration and you left one of your party behind.'

Jacques immediately sprang to argue his own defence but everyone else hung their heads. The major held up his hand for silence. 'If this exercise was real, Jacques, you would be facing your torturers right now.'

It was a sobering thought.

'Go and clean yourselves up and get some sleep,' said the major. 'This has been a hard night for all of you. We shall discuss the merits and failures tomorrow. Just remember that, in the field, failure means death.'

The dejected group shuffled past him, Mireille last. As she walked through the door he whispered for her ears only, 'You'll do.'

Downstairs, the telephone was ringing. Jim rolled over in bed and groaned. The clock on the bedside cabinet said four o'clock. As he descended the stairs he could hear Ivan saying, 'Yes. Hang on a mo, he's just coming.'

Jim took the receiver and Ivan shuffled back towards his bedroom.

'Inspector Kirkwood?' said a voice he didn't recognise. 'Sergeant Wilson here. We've had a report of a victim of an assault. Apparently she's in a pretty bad way. Found in the local park by a dog walker. The St John Ambulance has just carted her off to Worthing hospital.'

Jim yawned silently. An assault in the park? Probably some prostitute who'd got into a dispute with a punter. There had been trouble in the town before with some of the Canadians who didn't want to pay up once they'd sampled the goods. Why on earth would Wilson bother to contact him about something as simple as that? True, it was a traumatic situation for some poor woman, but hardly the sort of thing that necessitated waking a man of his rank in the wee small hours. He scratched his head willing his brain to function. 'So?'

'I regret to inform you, sir,' the sergeant went on, 'that the young woman in question is your ward, Amélie Osborne.'

Jim froze. 'What?'

'She's been badly beaten up, sir,' Sergeant Smith went on. 'Left for dead, I imagine. It hasn't helped matters that she's probably been there all night. They were saying she has hypothermia. It rained overnight if you recall.'

'Hell's bells man!' Jim exclaimed. 'What ward is she on?'

'Women's medical.'

Jim slammed the phone down. Ivan was hovering in the doorway of his bedroom.

'Amélie's been attacked,' he said as he headed for the stairs.

'Attacked?' said Ivan clearly stunned. 'Attacked by who?'

'I don't know,' Jim called out as he took the stairs two at a time, 'but I'm willing to bet my next pay cheque it was that bloody man!'

Bob looked around his room. Everything was neat and tidy, just as he liked it. He glanced in the mirror over the mantelpiece and smoothed down his hair with his hand. He looked as smart as any toff. His father would be proud. Neatly brushed suit, creaseless and beautifully ironed shirt, Windsor knot tie. He carefully pulled on his Trilby hat and set it at a jaunty angle. What a night!

When he'd arrived home, he was a mess. His shoes were covered in mud; his trousers were splattered with her blood (dirty bitch) and the knuckles of his right hand were bruised and sore. He was breathing heavily and he'd worked up a sweat running all the way home. The red mist was gone but he'd had to sit on the wooden chair for a minute or two to collect his thoughts. Why did it always turn out this way? It upset him when he had to be the hand of judgement and the rod of correction for these women, but much as he hated it, he'd done his duty. He sat forward with his head in his hands. How could she have deceived him like that? Slept with her own step-father indeed! God, it didn't bear thinking about. Filthy whore. And she'd never breathed a word about it before. When the red mist came down he'd covered his ears and shuddered rather than hear the filth she was talking about. He'd thought she was pure, clean, an angel even, but when she'd shown her true colours, she was just the same as all the rest. Nothing but a Jezebel. He snorted. She deserved the same end as her namesake. He hoped that hungry dogs would find her body. He sat up and smiled, even better if no one ever found her and she lay unburied.

It was time to make plans. He'd have to leave Worthing. If he stayed they'd probably accuse him of something he hadn't done. People were too soft. They'd probably find it hard to believe the bitch had it coming to her.

He'd spent the rest of the night cleaning his room to perfection and packing his case. He was relieved that he hadn't told Jezebel's household where he was going. Inspector Kirkwood would go to Liverpool to look for him but he had been clever. Yes, he was going to leave the country but he was going from Fishguard in Wales. The ferry ticket was for Saturday but he could lie low somewhere close by until it was time for the sailing. Once he was in Ireland he could travel to Dublin and from there he'd sail to Toronto. Easy.

He rested from three until five-thirty and then washed and dressed. He would catch the early train to Portsmouth.

If by any chance they had found her body, they'd be looking for a ne'er-do-well. No one would give a smart well-dressed gent a second thought. He patted his coat pocket and smiled. His money and his postcard collection were in his wallet. He left his rent money in an envelope on the table and took one last look round. Perfect.

The sight that greeted Norah and Jim at the hospital was very upsetting. As the nurse pulled back the screens, they hardly recognised the person in the bed. Amélie's right eye was so swollen, it was completely closed. A livid bruise was forming over her mouth, and her bottom lip was split. As Norah lowered herself into the chair beside the bed, she leaned over to stroke her hair. Her hand hovered and to her horror, Norah could see that Amélie had a bald patch where some of her hair had been pulled out by the roots. As Norah stared, Amélie opened her left eye and flinched.

'Don't let him hit me again,' she whimpered pathetically. 'Please. Tell him I'm sorry. I'm sorry.'

Norah immediately regretted her action and drew her hand back. 'It's all right darling,' she said softly. 'He's not here. Bob's gone.' At the same time, she heard Jim who was standing behind her, murmur, 'I knew it. I bloody knew it.'

Amélie stirred and Norah grasped her hand. 'Don't worry. You're safe now.'

Jim leaned towards Norah and whispered in her ear. 'I'll be back in a minute. I've just got a call to make.'

She may have looked calm but Norah was in bits. Fighting the urge to cry, she sat very still, just watching the rise and fall of Amélie's chest. None of the family had liked Bob but equally it never crossed her mind that he was capable of doing such a thing. It had to be Bob's doing, didn't it? He was so possessive of her that if someone else had done this, she couldn't imagine him walking off and leaving her to make her own way home. Norah wished that Amélie had never met Bob. The poor girl didn't deserve this. Hadn't she suffered enough already? Norah found her thoughts drifting back over the past four years. When they first came to live with her, Linnet had been so young. Too young to understand what sort of a man her step-father was. Wherever she was now, she probably still thought of him as her hero. Mireille was the strong one but she was bitter and unforgiving while Amélie, gentle caring Amélie, had been the best of the lot. Always thinking of others; always looking for ways to be kind; thoughtful, loving, loyal. What on earth had motivated Bob to do something as dreadful as this?

Jim came back in the room and squeezed Norah's shoulder. She gave him a sad smile as Jim drew up a chair to sit beside her. Shortly after, a doctor poked his head around the screens and asked to talk to them.

'She's taken quite a beating,' he said quietly, as they sat in two chairs outside in the corridor, 'but she's tough. She has a broken arm and two of her ribs are fractured. She also has some nasty bite marks.'

'Bite marks!' Norah exclaimed in horror and disgust. She turned to Jim. His face had paled.

The doctor nodded. 'Fortunately, her body temperature has come up now and she's fighting.'

'So she will recover,' Norah said faintly.

The doctor nodded again. 'Her physical wounds will heal reasonably quickly,' he said cautiously, 'but of course, her mental scars may go a lot deeper.'

Outside in the pale morning sunshine, Bob clicked the gate shut and took one last look up at the place where he'd lived for the past year. He'd liked Worthing. Sleepy, old fashioned and respectable, it was his ideal seaside resort. He sighed. With the right girl, he could have made a home here, a home with children. He'd be the perfect husband and he'd bring his children up properly of course. Like his wife they would be obedient and respectful; he'd see to that. He turned and set off towards the station. Across the street, an army lorry waited its engine running. Three men with rifles climbed out of the back. The passenger door opened and a captain alighted onto the pavement. Bob shuddered when he saw him. The officer carried a rather ugly war wound; a scar running down the side of his face. He touched his cap with his swagger stick and Bob gave him a polite nod before looking away. How he hated imperfection.

'Robert Kane,' said the captain.

Bob turned to him with a puzzled expression. 'Yes,' he said uncertainly. 'How the Dickens do you know my name?' He became aware that another man, a police inspector was watching them from across the road. Bob felt a wave of heated anger. It was Jim, Amélie's guardian.

'Robert Kane,' the captain said, interrupting his thoughts. He was waving a piece of paper. 'You should have reported for duty at Aldershot thirty days ago but you failed to do so, I'm therefore arresting you for desertion.'

Chapter 23

The night air was pleasant and the scents in the garden were quite beautiful. Soon late autumn would bleed into winter and it would be months before the flowers bloomed again. Mireille was quite alone. Lost in her own thoughts, she had been looking up at the moon. What was that old song? *Please let the light that shines on me, shine on the one I love.* She thought of a little baby boy and sighed. It was at times like this that she found her mind drifting back to the past. Not all her memories were pleasant. When Jago Ffox-Webster married her mother, it seemed as if everything would be better after the awful trauma of her beloved father's death. She had quite liked Jago back then but when her mother died, she'd discovered what a monster he was. She was only eleven when it started.

'He stole my innocence,' she'd told Parker in one of her interviews. 'He abused me for nearly four years and when I had his baby, he packed me off to an approved school as a wayward delinquent.'

Her stomach churned as Mireille sat on a bench with her head in her hands. The thing that chewed her up the most wasn't just losing her baby for ever (and that was bad enough) but that as soon as she was sent away, Jago had done exactly the same to Amélie and she hadn't been there to protect her. Thank God Amélie, her brave and beautiful sister, had the sense to stop him taking Linnet into his bed as well. Their little sister had no idea what awaited her but because of Amélie's courage, they'd found shelter with Norah and Jim.

Mireille leaned back and looked up at the sky. What she wouldn't give to be able to go to a dance with Ginger tonight. She hadn't realised just how hard it would be to give up all contact with the people who mattered in her life. She'd had a letter or two from Amélie but their correspondence was very one-sided. Her sister's letters were full of Bob although, funnily enough, in her last one she hadn't mentioned him. SOE passed the letters on to her, but of course she couldn't reply, not properly. She couldn't mention anything which might tell Amélie where she was or what she was doing and she knew that even if she did let something slip, her letters were read and censored before being posted. Not only that, but they didn't put them in the local post box either. Someone from the organisation was detailed to take them to different locations all over the country so that the postmark on the envelope meant nothing.

Ginger hadn't written at all, but then, come to think of it, she'd never given him her post box number. She'd sent a few postcards saying absolutely nothing but he couldn't reply without an address. Anyway, she told herself, he'd have forgotten her by now. But strangely enough, she couldn't forget him. She'd been offhand with him, never letting him too close but somehow or other he'd got under her skin. Whenever she thought of him, she ended up with a dull ache of longing in her chest.

'Ready for the off?' Major de Wesselow had come up behind her so quietly he made her jump.

190

'Yes sir.'

'No regrets?' he added.

Mireille sucked in her bottom lip. 'I'd be lying if I said I didn't have a few, but I really want to do this.'

He nodded. 'You'll find life in the wilds of Scotland very exacting after the Guildford countryside.'

'I know, sir.'

'How do you feel about working with explosives?'

'I've never used anything as an aggressor, sir, but I am keen to learn.'

Again he nodded. 'When you get to France, you may have to kill a man,' he said solemnly. 'Do you think you can handle that?'

'I don't know, sir,' she said, 'but I'll try.'

He regarded her for a few moments without saying anything, then turning away from her he added, 'A lot of very brave women have come to this place. They may look feminine but they are deadly when cornered. It takes a special kind of woman to be an SOE agent and I happen to think you're one of them.'

Mireille was glad of the dark. She could feel her face heating up as she said, 'Thank you, sir.'

'Goodnight.' The major waved his hand and was gone.

Jim had cleared a room at the station to lay out everything in the suitcase Bob Kane had been carrying when he was arrested. Among his clothes, they found watches, fountain pens, necklaces and other jewellery.

'Regular magpie, wasn't he?' the desk sergeant remarked.

They were checking the items against a list of missing or stolen goods from the hospital. Jim picked up an opal ring set with pink diamonds. It had no box. It was simply thrown haphazardly into the case. Hardly the way to treat a valuable ring. It seemed familiar and then he recalled

191

Amélie's ring. He'd been so shocked to hear of her engagement he'd hardly given it a second glance yet this could be the one she was wearing. Norah or his mother would be able to tell him.

'That ring was reported missing last year,' said the sergeant looking at a page from the buff-coloured folder. 'A Mrs Scott-Merritt. She went down for an X-ray but they couldn't find it in the cubicle after she'd had it done.'

Jim nodded.

'And that watch, the Swiss one with the Froggie writing that belonged to Captain Carruthers. He came into the hospital for a check-up about six months ago.'

'Our Captain Carruthers?' Jim murmured and when the sergeant nodded he added, 'Come to think of it, I vaguely remember that when we first met he said he'd lost his watch.'

By the end of the morning, the pair of them had bagged fifteen items which had been reported stolen from the hospital, three items taken or reported missing in the Buckingham public house and various other bits and pieces which were probably stolen but not reported. They also found two stethoscopes and a quantity of medicines.

'So who is this blighter?' the sergeant asked.

'Your guess is as good as mine,' said Jim. 'Amélie reckoned he told her he had a brother in North Africa and that his parents live in Ruislip, but he told my wife and my mother he was an only child and both his parents were dead.'

'But according to the hospital records,' the sergeant went on, 'he said he'd been brought up in a children's home near Horsham.'

'When I was a kid,' Jim mused, 'my mother always said a liar has to have a good memory. We'd better contact the home and see if we can find the truth,' said Jim.

The sergeant nodded. 'How's your girl getting on?' he asked. 'They tell me she was pretty roughed up when they found her.'

'She's still in hospital,' said Jim. 'My mother is with her now. They both get on very well. Mother's like a grand-mother to her.'

'That's good,' the sergeant said sagely. 'You need a friend at times like these.'

'The super sent Policewoman Warboys over to the hospital to get a statement.'

'Warboys!' the sergeant exclaimed. 'Blimey, that's like sending in the army dogs to round up the sheep. Good job the poor girl's got your mother there.'

As she stared at Amélie, WPC Warboys, notebook in hand, had a look of disapproval on her face.

'When we sat on the bench together,' Amélie began.

'In the park,' interrupted the policewoman. 'Alone. Late at night.'

'He was her fiancé,' Christine said waspishly.

'I felt safe with Bob,' Amélie said innocently. 'I was a bit worried about the time. I knew I mustn't be late or Home Sister would report me to Matron.'

The three of them were sitting together in the hospital chapel. It was only a small room but Christine had suggested going in there because it was peaceful and far away from the prying eyes of the other patients. With Amélie in a wheelchair, they sat facing a table with a beautifully embroi-dered cloth on the top. In the middle of the table stood a plain wooden cross. The only other decoration in the room was a framed picture of Holman Hunt's *Light of the World*.

WPC Warboys was a sour-faced spinster who would never see the right side of forty again, Jim had mentioned a couple of times at home because she had a reputation for her tenacious interviewing skills. She sat on the row behind them and Amélie made a whimpering sound as Christine grasped her hands encouragingly.

'Go on,' Warboys said impatiently.

'It crossed my mind that if we married the next day,' Amélie continued, her voice wobbling slightly, 'I would have to give up my nursing anyway.'

Christine frowned. 'Why?'

'Married women are not allowed to train as nurses,' said Amélie. 'Matron says nurses have to be totally dedicated to the care of their patients and a married woman has other commitments.'

Christine nodded. 'I can see that,' she said. 'Keeping house is not easy.'

For a split second Amélie looked shocked. 'But why can't we do both?'

'Perhaps you're right,' Christine said gently, 'but couldn't you have waited to get married until after you'd finished your training? You're very young. There's plenty of time for all that.'

'Can we get back to the point?' WPC Warboys snapped and Christine glared at her.

'You know I have always wanted to be a nurse, Mémé,' Amélie said, 'but Bob just wanted to make me happy.' She dabbed her eyes. 'He always had my best interests at heart. That's why I don't understand why it happened. I know you didn't like him much but you never had a chance to get to know him. He was so amazing.'

Christine glanced behind her. The WPC who was scribbling something in her notebook looked up and their eyes met. Best interests at heart? She wanted to say, Pah. Stuff and nonsense. What Bob wanted was to control her, more like.

'I never even knew I was wearing the wrong things until Bob taught me how to look respectable.'

'Can you tell us what happened in the park?' the WPC interrupted again.

'I told Bob about you-know-who.' Amélie chewed her lip anxiously.

'You-know-who,' Warboys repeated.

'Mémé knows how much I hate talking about my step-father.'

'What's your step-father got to do with it?' said Warboys.

'Does she have to tell you everything?' said Christine.

Policewoman Warboys glared it her. 'Yes she does,' she said, her words spaced out and deliberate.

Amélie blew her nose noisily. 'I thought I could trust him.'

'Who?' The officer was beginning to sound irritated.

'Bob.'

WPC Warboys seemed confused and crossed something out in her notebook.

'So I said,' Amélie went on, '"it's a long story," and he said—'

'Who said?' Warboys wanted to know.

'Bob. He said, "I'm a patient man, my love," so I told him.' Her voice had risen to a squeak. She took a deep breath.

'Told him what!'

'That when my mother died my step-father made me sleep with him. I didn't want to do it. I never wanted to do it but he made me.' She lowered her head and began to cry.

'Amélie was only a child of ten,' Christine explained but as she turned to the WPC she could already see the look of disgust on her face.

Then Warboys blew out her cheeks. 'Look, we seem to be going round and round in circles,' she said her voice becoming more authoritative. 'Just tell me what happened in the park!'

195

'Bob was so angry. He hit me,' Amélie cried, the words rushing from her mouth now. 'He punched me in the eye and called me a dirty whore and when I stood up, he slapped me so hard I fell over.' She gave Christine a helpless look. 'I've never seen him so mad. The ground was wet and I slipped when I tried to get up, but he just kept hitting me on the top of my head like this and this . . .'

Christine stared in horror as Amélie demonstrated the blows she had suffered.

All at once, Amélie stared at her left hand. 'My ring,' she cried in anguish. 'Oh Mémé, I've lost my lovely engagement ring.'

'And then what?' the WPC said dispassionately.

The two of them stared at her in disbelief.

'After he hit you,' she repeated, 'what happened then?'

'He called me names.'

'What names?'

'Horrible names. Jezebel, Tamar, prostitute, slut, take your pick,' Amélie said in between her tears. 'He said I'd tricked him. He said that I'd made out that I was pure and untouched – a virgin. But it wasn't my fault. I tried to tell him that I'd never given myself willingly but he wouldn't listen. And then when I was back on the ground, he kicked me and kicked me until I must have passed out.'

'Who is Jezebel?' said Warboys. 'And Tamar? Are they nurses?'

'They're both in the Bible,' said Christine. 'Jezebel was the most wicked queen ever and Tamar slept with her father-in-law.'

The curl of Warboys' lip grew more pronounced. 'Well, all I can say is that you brought it upon yourself,' she said, closing her notebook with a snap. 'No man worth his salt would want a woman who went to bed with her step-father.'

'Now just a minute,' Christine said, rising to her feet.

'I've just told you Amélie was only ten years old when that happened.'

'Doesn't alter the fact though, does it?' the policewoman sneered.

'How dare you!' Christine snapped angrily. 'What gives you the right to pass judgement! I shall be speaking to your superior about this.'

'Go ahead,' the policewoman said loftily. 'No one will take any notice. It's all in the family, isn't it?'

'And just what are you implying?' Christine retorted.

'I'm implying nothing,' said the woman turning to leave, 'but I know what's respectable and what's not. I don't condone what he did, but in my book, she had it coming.'

The door closed with a bang. As she held the sobbing girl in her arms Christine was furious. Police officers were supposed to be fair-minded and most of all neutral when conducting interviews, weren't they? That's what Jim always said. What hope did anyone have of getting justice when faced with such out and out prejudice? How on earth did the stupid woman think a ten-year-old child could fight off a grown man? Did Jim know about that awful woman's attitude?

Amélie juddered in her arms. Christine softened. How was she going to help her now, poor lamb? Bob had manipulated her thinking. If he came back into her life, Christine felt sure Amélie would quite happily take him back. Why wouldn't she, when she so clearly blamed herself for what had happened? And on top of everything else, she was upset because she'd lost her ring. Right now, Amélie needed time and space to recover from the terrible ordeal she'd just gone through. The healing of her mind was going to take a lot, lot longer.

Chapter 24

News from the front had been mixed so by the time December came around, everyone was feeling war-weary. It seemed as if the tide was turning but then news of something awful would filter through, like the massacre of Kalavryta for example. Nobody had even heard of Kalavryta, an area in Southern Greece until the newspapers reported what had happened there. Apparently it was triggered when the Greek resistance had executed seventy-eight German prisoners of war. In retaliation the Germans destroyed twenty-eight communities, looting and burning monasteries and a thousand homes as well as killing more than seven hundred men, women and children.

Norah and Christine wept for them and later that day they put their arms around each other to weep for someone closer to home. A local girl who worked in the bakery in Westcourt Road had been killed by an anti-aircraft shell which fell short in Pavilion Road.

'I was only in that shop yesterday,' said Christine. 'She served me. Such a pretty girl. Oh Norah, she was only fifteen.'

Norah dabbed her own eyes. Coupled with what had

happened to poor Amélie, it seemed at times that the burden of sadness was almost too much to bear.

Amélie had made a slow recovery. She was still registered as sick but Matron had said she could go back to the hospital in the New Year to resume her training. They'd tried to contact Mireille to no avail. Norah couldn't help feeling a bit cross about it. It didn't matter to her if Mireille was still angry with her but to cut herself off from her own sister was irresponsible and unkind.

Jim wanted to keep the fact that Bob had been arrested by the army from Amélie but Norah hated the idea of keeping secrets. 'You told me when Mireille was upset,' Norah reminded him, 'that no matter how much it distresses her, it's her life and she has the right to know.'

So they told her but it didn't matter what they said, Amélie still blamed herself for everything.

As soon as Jim suspected Bob Kane was the cause of Amélie's injuries, he had involved Lennard. He told Lennard that as yet he had no concrete evidence apart from Amélie's testimony, and that she might withdraw, but he was pretty sure Kane was the culprit.

'There's a part of me that doesn't want to put the poor girl through any more trauma,' he told Lennard over the telephone. 'I've already had to reprimand a female officer for her handling on the case.'

'What about the stuff you found in the case?' Lennard asked.

'I'm following it up,' said Jim. 'If he gets convicted, it'll only mean a slap on the wrist; a five- or ten-pound fine and maybe a month inside, that's all, but at least it's something. It sticks in my craw if he gets away with it.'

'Look,' Lennard had said, 'leave it with me. I'll take my time with the paperwork.'

Bob was eventually sent to a military court while Jim's

colleagues worked hard to put together a case for the civilian courts. The suitcase had indeed opened a can of worms when the police discovered that the contents linked Bob to other offences recorded by several different police forces, some going back several years. They followed the leads up and soon everyone knew that once the army had finished with him, Bob Kane would be going down.

'You look worried,' Norah told her husband one evening.

'I am,' he confessed. 'They tell me Kane is blaming Amélie for taking some of that stolen stuff he had in his case.'

Norah's eyes grew wide. 'What!'

'He reckons she took a ring and a watch from a dead patient. He says when he found out, he wanted her to give it back because she would have lost her job.'

'I don't believe it,' Norah said stoutly. 'The man's a bloody liar.'

Jim shook his head. 'But they have to pursue it,' he said, 'and Amélie will have to give her version of the story.'

Lennard still spent as many evenings as he could at the Lilacs so Jim tried to find out what he could about Bob first-hand.

'He's a smooth talker, that one,' said Lennard, 'the sort that can charm the birds off the tree. Sly too.'

Jim voiced his concerns about Amélie and the accusation left at her door.

'I shouldn't worry too much,' Lennard counselled. 'He may be sly but he's not as clever as he thinks he is.'

Jim handed him a beer. 'What's going to happen to him?'

'He'll probably get three months and then they'll allocate him to some sort of pacifist position,' said Lennard. 'He could end up in bomb disposal or in a parachute medical unit or maybe they'll let him work in some sort of civilian position such as the one he was doing in the hospital.'

'The man's a thief,' said Jim.

'Then you deal with him,' said Lennard. 'Dig deeper. I would.'

Jim grinned.

Lennard enjoyed being at the Lilacs. They didn't do anything exciting but he found a sense of peace and family life as they played games, did jigsaws or listened to the radio. He joined in with great gusto when someone suggested a sing-song. Amélie didn't say much to him but he taught her how to play backgammon. There was a nine-year gap between them, but the girl always seemed relaxed with Lennard.

As for Amélie herself, she made little reference to the incident in the park. She was a lot quieter than usual and she had lost some of her confidence. She found it hard to make decisions. Even making up her mind what to wear was troublesome and she continually worried that she'd made the wrong choice. She'd become shy, keeping her gaze in her lap whenever she saw a stranger. She still received the odd card from Mireille but she seemed untroubled that since she'd left Tangmere, her sister never sent her new address.

'She's obviously doing something hush-hush,' was all that she would say when people asked after Mireille.

The police came to interview her about the stolen goods, but of course she knew nothing about it. 'Yes a watch and ring did go missing,' she admitted. 'Sister sent me to the morgue to look for it and on the way back, Bob found it.'

'Found it?'

'Yes, it was in the bushes,' Amélie said.

'And how did it get there?' She could hear the scepticism in the officer's voice.

'I don't know,' Amélie admitted. 'I guess it must have blown there. It was lucky that Bob spotted it.'

Even though it was obvious the officer was sceptical, the

testimony from the ward sister and Matron, backed her story. Everything was written down and Amélie signed her statement.

Just before Christmas, Norah took Penny with her to Stanmore in Middlesex. It was a fairly long journey because they had to go right into London, then switch to the underground and get onto the Bakerloo line to get to Stanmore itself. It had been years since Norah had taken a trip up to town and this was Penny's first time. Norah thought it was remarkable that Penny's condition hardly showed but she didn't say anything. They stared silently out of the carriage windows at all the destruction along the way.

'It'll take years and years to repair all this lot,' Penny remarked gloomily.

Gwen Harrison was delighted to see them. She met them at the station and they endured another ride, this time by bus to reach her home but it was worth it. She lived in a large red brick semi-detached house in a salubrious and leafy street.

'We live very humbly here,' she told them as she pulled out a large brass table top and lowered it onto the criss-cross legs. Norah and Penny exchanged a slight smile behind her back. 'My husband is only just up the road. He's been at RAF Stanmore ever since he was called up.'

'Is it a fighter base?' Penny asked.

'He flies a desk,' Gwen said with a shake of her head. 'The base mainly deals with barrage balloons.'

'Can I do anything to help?' Norah asked as she disappeared into the kitchen.

'No, no. I'm fine.' She reappeared with a tea tray. 'They're pretty big.' She pulled down the corners of her mouth. 'The balloons I mean. I'd say sixty odd feet long and twenty-five feet in diameter. My husband says they can go up as far as five thousand feet.'

Both Norah and Penny had seen plenty of barrage balloons as they'd journeyed to Stanmore so they were familiar with their purpose which was to frustrate enemy bombers.

'So what exactly does he do,' asked Norah, adding quickly, 'if you're allowed to tell me, that is?'

'He's in charge of keeping the balloons in working order and training the personnel. Quite a responsibility really.'

Gwen had put their cups of tea onto the brass table in front of them. She glanced up at the clock. 'I don't want to hurry you,' she began, 'but the girls will be home from school shortly and I'd prefer that they didn't know the ins and outs of everything. As you know, children chatter so I want us to get our story straight before they come in.'

Norah nodded. 'I think you and Penny had better decide on that,' she said. 'I'm happy to go along with whatever suits you both.'

Twenty minutes later they had decided that Penny was an old friend of Norah (true) who had tragically lost her husband. Her home had been bombed so she had nowhere to live. Mrs Andrews, as she was to be known, was coming to live with the Harrisons to 'help Mummy'. Mrs Andrews' son Victor would be coming too and when she'd had her new baby, she would go back to Worthing to live in a new home which was being prepared for them all right now. As she listened to the plan, Norah was astonished how plausible the lie sounded. Gwen's children, Marjorie, nine in a week's time and Ruth ten (her birthday was in September so Penny would be long gone before she was eleven) would be allowed to play with the toddler, but they must call his mother, Mrs Andrews. Victor and Mrs Andrews would have their own room at the top of the house but the girls would only go there at her invitation. Gwen would give Penny and Victor bed and board plus a small remuneration. They agreed on thirty bob a week. As soon as the baby was born, as far as the girls were concerned, Norah would come to take 'Mrs Andrews' back to her new home. The baby would be exchanged on the journey back to Worthing.

Just as everything seemed amicably settled, Marjorie and Ruth bounded into the kitchen. They were overjoyed to see Auntie Norah and couldn't wait to hear all about Max and Sausage.

Chapter 25

'Are you really sure about this?'

Mireille's course leader Heather Varney was leaning over her anxiously. She was holding a seven-day pass all signed and sealed. Mireille's other companions had taken theirs with gratitude and were even now packing a few things together to head off in different directions for a well-earned Christmas break but to Heather's surprise, Mireille had refused hers.

'You deserve to have a change of scene,' said Heather. 'You've worked hard. I know the Beak is impressed by your dedication.'

The Beak was what they called Maurice Buckmaster the head of 'F' section SOE. He kept a weather eye on all recruits and even though he was snowed under with work, he still managed to maintain a personal interest in all his agents.

Mireille's eyes were pooling with tears. Heather frowned. 'Is it trouble with the family?' she asked, her voice softening.

Mireille shook her head. 'It's not that. It's me. I've managed to come this far and I'm afraid if I go back to Worthing I shall lose all my resolve.'

'Why? Do you think they'll pressurise you?'

Mireille hesitated. 'I . . . I . . .'

Rather than continuing to hover over her, Heather sat beside her. 'Look Luv, you've signed the Official Secrets Act. All you have to do is tell them you've got to keep mum. They'll understand.'

'It's you that doesn't understand,' Mireille said doggedly. 'I've spent most of this year keeping them at arm's length for one reason and one reason only. I can't afford to have any baggage when I go over to France. As far as I know, they're all getting on with their lives quite well without me. My sister should be engaged, maybe even married by now. I don't like the chap but that's neither here nor there. I had words with the woman who rescued my sisters and somehow or other I've never got around to making it up. Now it's too embarrassing. Everything is best left as it is.'

Heather leaned back in her chair and breathed in. 'Well, if that's the way you want it . . .' she said uncertainly.

'It is.'

Heather stood to leave.

'You can stay here if you want,' she said, her air of authority restored. 'There'll be a skeleton staff around to keep an eye on the place but there won't be much in the way of Christmas festivities though.'

'I don't mind,' Mireille said stubbornly. 'I do it for France.'

With a sympathetic smile, Heather left, taking the seven-day pass with her.

Mireille went to her sink and poured herself a glass of water. There, she'd done it. When she'd woken up this morning, every part of her wanted to see Amélie. Just the same as the other recruits, she had looked forward to being back among friends and family. She'd dreamed of playing a game of whist with Christine and Ivan, she'd rehearsed her apology to Norah and Jim over and over again, and she'd imagined fondling the dogs and going for long walks with them. She would buy presents and wrap them. On Christmas Day she would go with them to St Matthew's and sing carols. It all seemed so cosy. But that was the problem. She knew herself well enough to know she wouldn't want to come back. How could she leave such a warm family setting to swap it for a muddy ditch somewhere in France? The past few months had been exceptionally hard. From the wilds of Scotland and learning about guerrilla warfare, she'd come here to Thame Park in Oxfordshire to learn about codes and how to be a wireless operator. Mireille didn't have a mathematical cell in her body, so she'd struggled with Morse. She still hadn't got her speed up to the required twenty-two words a minute and until she did, she would be refused a posting. Understanding the composition of her wireless set was just as difficult. Oscillation, skip, dead spots and jamming was a foreign language when she'd arrived and learning how to find a fault using makeshift materials wasn't easy for the best of them but for Mireille it was hell.

She splashed her face with water and dried it on a towel. Get this next year over and then she'd go home for Christmas, she told herself in the mirror above the sink. Running her fingers through her hair, she ignored the statistic that nagged her right now. 'Most SOE operatives don't last more than six weeks in the field.'

1943 brought a kind of new start for everybody. Penny and Victor went to live in Stanmore. A few of her neighbours tut-tutted that she'd left her mother on her own, but the whole business was a nine-day wonder and before long there were other things to talk about. Norah did her best

207

to contain her excitement but when they were on their own at the Lilacs, she and Christine started knitting another baby's layette. Whenever anyone else was around they carried on knitting thick jumpers for the men on convoy duty in the North Sea. Neither of them knew what it was like to be idle.

Amélie returned to work in the hospital in January. Matron gave her a stiff talking to, advising her to be more careful with her choice of friends and warning her that she would not get another chance to re-start her training. It seemed rather unfair considering none of the events were her fault, but Amélie accepted the reprimand without protest. Alone in her room, she told herself she had no plans to have another boyfriend, not ever, so long as she lived. She had hoped that Mireille would turn up at Christmas but she didn't. Amélie was disappointed but at the same time, she was sure Mireille had her reasons. Her gentleman friend Ginger turned up on Boxing Day but apart from one of those postcards saying absolutely nothing at all, he hadn't heard from her either. The two of them didn't talk about it but Amélie felt there was a mutual empathy between them.

Bob, she discovered had been sentenced to three months in the glasshouse by the army so he wasn't around either. On a good day she was relieved but every now and then she was overwhelmed with guilt. He'd had such high hopes of her and she'd let him down . . . badly. Somewhere in the very back of her mind, she sort of knew it wasn't her fault but he didn't feel that way. She recalled some of the things he'd said to her that night and they weren't pretty. In some ways he had been right. If she were half the girl he'd thought she was, she wouldn't have let her step-father do it. She would have been his perfect English rose. Oh Bob . . . Bob. She cried less but the pain was still there. Then to top it all, the request to CORB for contact with Linnet seemed to have stalled as well so Amélie made up her mind to concentrate on nothing else but her training.

The first letter came in the middle of the month. As expected it was short and full of vitriol. Amélie read it then tore it up. The second one came a couple of days later. It took her two days to pluck up the courage to open it and when she saw what it said, she finally broke down in tears.

Rene rang with some really good news. 'I'm three and a half months pregnant.'

Norah's eyes lit up. 'Oh Rene, that's fantastic!'

And it was. It meant her sister's baby would be born in late July when her own baby would be four months old. How wonderful. The little cousins could grow up together. By the time she'd replaced the receiver, Norah's head reeled with plans.

Next morning, Norah decided to make an early start. She had a bit of shopping to do, nothing major, but the family first aid kit was out of Aspro and bandages and Christine needed some corn pads so her first port of call was the chemist. From there she would buy a card for Rene and Dan and perhaps something small for the baby. She was biking down Salisbury Road towards Boots when she heard the scream of engines behind her. Glancing upwards, to her horror, she saw an enemy plane heading in her direction. There was no cover so Norah leapt off her bike and threw herself over the low wall of somebody's garden. The next thing she heard was the sound of machine gun bullets ripping along the houses in the street. Crouching behind the wall, she covered her head with her hands and prayed like billy-o. The plane headed off over the sea and after waiting a couple of seconds, Norah stood to her feet. A moment later there was an almighty bang and part of a house on the opposite side of the road, blew up. She ducked down again.

By now she was trembling like a leaf. The street was silent, but as she stood to her feet a second time, she realised that the gunner's main target must have been the Catholic primary school. A sick feeling in her stomach made her shiver. The children! How many had been hit? She knew that all the little ones had been taught to run for cover or lay down on the floor if they heard an aircraft coming towards them. If they'd been in the playground, and it was highly likely that they were, the children would have been totally exposed to the bullets.

Norah hurried to the entrance and ran into the school grounds. Several other people had thought the same. It was a huge relief for all of them to be faced by a huge empty space.

'Where are they?' an anxious voice said behind her.

Norah shrugged but then they saw a little boy emerge from the air raid shelter. He was carrying a clipboard, the pencil dangling from a piece of string tied onto its side. He seemed slightly surprised by the gathering crowd.

'You all right, Luv?' Norah called.

He nodded.

Norah walked towards him. 'Where are the other children?'

'In the shelter,' he said. His tone of voice was that of someone who couldn't imagine them being anywhere else. 'I'm the shelter monitor.'

'And you got them all in there by yourself?' Norah gasped.

'Yes.'

'Well done, lad,' a man said as he ruffled the boy's hair and everyone admired his quiet composure.

Teachers began to tumble from the building. A few had cuts from flying glass but by now other help in the form of the Home Guard and some nurses from the Central Clinic just across the road was arriving. Norah stayed to help a couple of children cross the road for medical assistance but all in all, everyone had had a lucky escape.

'I was supposed to go to the dentist this afternoon,' a little girl with bright yellow ribbons in her hair told her.

'Don't worry, dear. I'm sure you can still make it,' Norah said encouragingly.

'No need to,' said the girl, showing her a gappy smile. 'They're all knocked out now.'

It was peaceful in the New Forest. Mireille could hardly believe it but she was on the last leg of her training. It had taken months to get here but a parachute jump into France was nearer than ever. She had mixed feelings. It was terrifying and yet exhilarating as well. She'd completed all parts of the course and was ready to go. Somewhere in the wilds of Scotland she'd learned how to make explosives and the differences between British, German and American guns. In Oxfordshire she'd finally mastered a decent speed in her Morse code and everything concerning the wireless operator. After that, she'd been posted to Manchester where she'd learned the skill and then practised parachute jumping at Ringway airport. After a few practice drops in an aircraft hangar, the whole team, men and women alike, had gone up in a plane. The girls had noticed how some of the men held back, keen to be one of the last to go but it was Mireille's idea to tease them and now the men always were the first through the open plane door. Thanks to her courses, she'd also learned some unexpected skills like forging documents and picking locks.

'I shall make a first-class villain when I get out of the

WAAFs,' she'd quipped as her instructor showed her how to crack a safe.

Here at Beaulieu, Mireille was being taught how to recognise the ranks of the French police and the address of Gestapo headquarters. She also had time to catch her breath and enjoy the peace and quiet of the Hampshire countryside which was why her final test came as such a shock.

She was woken up by several men in her room. They were all shouting and in the half-light of an early morning, she'd felt herself being yanked unceremoniously out of her bed. For a few terrible seconds, all the horrors inflicted on her by Jago Ffox-Webster came flooding back, but then she realised that these men were in Gestapo uniform. Was this real or was she dreaming? Befuddled by sleep, Mireille was frog-marched to a small room and made to stand on a narrow stool. A bright light, so bright that it hurt her eyes, was shone directly into her face and one of the men began barking quick fire questions at her in French.

'Who are you? Where do you come from? What is your name? Tell me about Jacques. What is your job? Who is your mother? What is your name . . . ?' Any unlikely answer resulted in a slap which was none too gentle either.

They told her they knew all about her, that they'd been watching her every move and that she should tell them where the wireless was. Mireille hardly had time to catch her breath and it took all her concentration to answer the questions. She knew she had to stick to the same story or she would be doomed. Finally after what seemed like forever, the light was switched off and the curtains drawn back. The 'Gestapo', whom she now recognised as men from SOE, left the room. She was invited to sit on the chair and someone came with a mug of strong sweet tea laced with whisky.

Exhausted and relieved, she was told she could go back

to bed for a little rest and then she had to report to the course instructor who would go over the exercise point by point.

Later that afternoon, Mireille learned she had passed with flying colours.

Chapter 26

It was Rene's last day at Tangmere. The girls had given her a bit of a 'do' in the mess. To the sound of much laughter, she'd been given a ball and chain and lots of baby gifts. The canteen cook had baked a cake. They had drunk her health and wished her luck. She would miss being here and being a part of what was going on but now that her uniform skirt was beginning to stretch over her four-month bump, she was glad to be going. The rules were such that pregnant women were not allowed to work on the base. With still five months to go until July, she knew she couldn't sit at home and twiddle her thumbs. She would probably find another job but something away from the 'front line'.

The days and nights had been busy of late. Modern bombers from Tangmere and other stations were always in the skies overhead. Some went to the continent but others were sent further afield. Alongside the up-to-date fighters, for several months, Tangmere had been home to so called obsolete Lysanders which flew to France on a regular basis. Once considered a relic of the Great War, the Lysander had been modified for use with the French resistance. A fixed ladder had been built over the port side which enabled men or women to climb aboard the plane while it was taxiing and because they only flew at night, the planes had been painted matte black although a few were brown and green. Most operations took place when there was a full moon. That much Rene and her fellow WAAFs knew but not the detail.

There was a house by the perimeter of the airfield where they sometimes saw people moving about but they didn't talk about it. 'Careless talk costs lives' and all that. Well now she would never know what they got up to in there. Her stint in the WAAFs was over. She had done her bit and she would soon be a mother. It was with mixed feelings that Rene made her way to the office to report to her commanding officer for the last time.

'Ah,' said the CO when Rene knocked on the door and walked in. 'Nice time?'

Rene smiled. 'Yes thank you, ma'am.'

Her CO grinned and went back to her paperwork. 'You'll miss us, no doubt.'

'I will, ma'am,' Rene said with a sigh. She smoothed her rounded belly. 'I can't help wondering what sort of a world I'm bringing my baby into.'

'Don't,' the CO said firmly. She looked up over her silver-rimmed glasses with a stern expression. 'If you'll take my advice, you'll enjoy every moment as it comes. Believe you me, it all goes by so quickly. You'll be holding your baby in your arms one minute and taking him to school the next. Then before you know it, he'll be getting married.'

Rene chuckled. She knew that the CO's son had married last year, a few months after her own wedding.

'I'm sure you'll make a grand job of being a mother,' the CO said shuffling some more papers. 'People underrate how important it is. If Mrs bloody Hitler had done a better job, we wouldn't be in this mess would we?'

215

Rene blinked. It was a sobering thought.

Her CO rose to her feet, her hand extended. 'Well Wallace, all the best and good luck. Do your best for that baby.'

Rene suddenly felt rather emotional. 'I will. Thank you, ma'am.'

The CO sat back down. 'Oh, and Wallace, on your way off site, take this memo to the cottage, will you?' She handed Rene a buff-coloured envelope.

Rene stood to attention one last time. 'Yes, ma'am. Thank you, ma'am.'

Rene hurried across the field. Yes she would miss being here but she was glad to be going to a safer place. Not that anywhere was safe these days. As she neared the cottage, a group of what looked like French peasants milled around in the garden. Although the men had berets and wore working clothes and the women had head scarves and carried a coat over their arms, Rene guessed that they weren't French at all. They were agents – spies going to France on dangerous work.

As Rene hurried through the gate heading for the door, she accidentally bumped into a woman coming in the opposite direction. 'Oh sorry, Luv,' she said. 'Clumsy me.' As their eyes met. Rene took in a breath. 'Mireille!' she exclaimed.

Mireille snatched her arm and pulled her towards another part of the garden. Irritated, Rene yanked herself free from her grip. 'What are you doing?' she spat. 'Let go of me!'

'I'm sorry, I'm sorry,' said Mireille. 'Please . . . keep your voice down. I don't mean to be rude but I don't want the others to hear me.'

Rene glared at her. The cheek of the woman. She'd disappeared for over a year and here she was as bold as brass asking her to keep quiet. Rene rubbed the top of her arm where Mireille had grabbed her. 'What the hell are you doing here anyway?'

It was only then that Rene noticed what she was wearing. Mireille, who was always so smartly dressed, was now in a donkey brown coat which had definitely seen better days and she was wearing what Christine would have called 'sensible shoes'. Her head scarf completely covered her hair and she wore no make-up. What on earth had happened? Was she ill or something?

Mireille looked around nervously but once they'd reached the shelter of a couple of apple trees, she gave Rene a shy smile. Rene didn't respond. She was too angry. All she could think about was how much this woman had hurt her sister, but at the same time, she was puzzled.

'Please don't tell anyone you've seen me,' Mireille said. 'Especially not my sister . . . or Norah.'

'I don't understand,' said Rene. 'Why are you dressed like that? Where have you been? Everybody has been worried sick about you. I've written to you but you don't reply. You don't phone.'

'I didn't mean to upset anybody,' Mireille said. 'I thought it was for the best.'

'You thought it was for the best?' Rene squeaked incredulously. 'Well I think your behaviour has been pretty shabby. You must have known people would worry about you. You've put poor Amélie through hell.'

Mireille looked stricken. 'I'm sorry.' She closed her eyes. 'I just wanted to do this.' The tone of her voice was suddenly earnest. 'You must understand, I *have* to do this for my country.'

'Do what?' There was a moment of silence and then a light dawned somewhere inside Rene's head. 'You're an agent, aren't you? You're going to France tonight.'

Mireille nodded. 'I've signed the Official Secrets Act so I can't tell you more than that.'

'I understand that,' said Rene, 'but just to vanish off the face of the earth like you did, it's cruel.'

Mireille reached out to touch Rene's arm. 'I knew if I went back to Worthing to see Amélie I might not be brave enough to go through with this.'

The two women stared at each other.

'Oh, Mireille.'

'Promise me you won't say anything to Amélie.'

Rene took a breath as a rush of white-hot anger swept over her. Mireille obviously had no idea what she'd put her sister through. Heavens above, she probably had no idea about Bob Kane either. Should she tell her? She so wanted to tell her what a cow she'd been. She wanted to say, *you deserted your sister when she needed you most. When she was attacked, oh yes that rotter attacked her and left her for dead, she cried every night for you. Now she thinks that you must be dead. And as for poor Norah, she wrote to you for weeks and weeks and you never once bothered to reply. She and Jim gave you a home. They even offered you a place in their family and this is how you reward their kindness? For heaven's sake, you were a bridesmaid at my wedding!* Rene sniffed. That was what she wanted to say, but now that she was face to face with the girl, how could she? If Mireille was going into occupied France she had to have a clear head. If she was worried about family, she might put herself in danger. Rene chewed her lip.

'She is all right, isn't she?' Mireille asked anxiously. 'Amélie, I mean.'

Rene looked away. 'I guess so. I haven't seen her for a while.'

'She's still doing her training?'

'Yes.'

Mireille smiled. 'I'm glad. She'll make a good nurse.'

Rene felt heat flooding her face. For two pins she wanted to slap the woman. She turned away.

'Please don't be angry with me, Rene.'

'I'm not,' Rene said huffily. Holding up the buff-coloured envelope, she added, 'I have to deliver this memo, that's all.'

With that she walked away. Damn the woman. Mireille had put her in an awkward position. What was she going to say if the family started speculating about what had happened to her? Should she leave them with the same terrible uncertainty? And if she told them that Mireille was in occupied France, wouldn't that be ten times worse? She could hear Mireille following behind her, her shoes swishing the long grass but Rene was too angry to turn around.

Walking into the house, Rene handed the envelope to the man in charge. On her way out, she passed Mireille in the doorway.

'Goodbye,' Mireille whispered.

Rene didn't answer but by the time she'd reached the gate she was already feeling guilty. As she turned to close it behind her, Mireille was still standing in the doorway so fighting down her own personal feelings of betrayal, Rene said stiffly, 'Good luck.'

Gwen sounded breathless when Norah picked up the telephone. 'Norah? Ah, there you are. I've already rung twice this morning.'

'I've been working in the greenhouse,' said Norah. 'Is everything all right?'

'It's started,' said Gwen.

Norah frowned. 'What's started?'

'The baby,' said Gwen. 'Penny is in the ambulance on her way to hospital right now. She's in labour.'

Norah froze.

'Norah?' Gwen said tetchily.

Norah's mind was in a whirl. April, Penny had told her. The baby was due in the beginning of April. Today was only March 24th. 'But it's too early,' she blurted out.

'We can't do anything about that,' Gwen snapped. 'She went into labour this morning. I've got Victor but I've got several important dos this week. You'll have to come up and help me. I can't manage everything on my own.'

Norah looked around wildly. What just drop everything and go to London? She'd got everything planned for April. 'But I can't . . .' she began feebly.

'Norah, you have to,' Gwen snapped. 'This is your baby we're talking about. If you're going to be a mother, it's a full-time job. You can't just do it when you feel like it.'

'Yes, yes of course,' said Norah, her senses finally kicking in. 'I'll come as quickly as I can.'

The next hour rushed by like a whirlwind. Seconds after she put the receiver down, Norah was telling Jim what had happened.

'I thought you said the baby would be born early April.'

'That's what Penny told me but I guess she got the dates muddled up,' said Norah. 'When her man-friend died, she didn't know if it was Tuesday or Christmas.'

'When will you go up on the train?'

'Today,' said Norah.

'Be careful,' he said.

'Don't worry about me,' she said. 'Oh Jim, I'm going to fetch our baby. Isn't it wonderful?'

Next she biked over to Queens Street to ask her mum if she would get Jim's tea for when he came home. Christine would be too worn out by the time they'd pushed the barrow home from the market. From there she biked down to the market to tell Christine and Ivan. At this time of year they were selling mainly seedlings on the stall but they were doing a brisk trade.

'The adoption people have a baby for Jim and me,' she told them. 'I have to go up to London now.'

If Christine and Ivan had any suspicions they didn't show it. Less than an hour later, Norah was on the train with their good luck wishes ringing in her ears.

Chapter 27

Norah had been directed to the Stanmore Cottage Hospital on Old Church Lane, which, Gwen explained in her call, was just off Honeypot Lane. It sounded delightful but instead of finding a leafy country road flanked by open fields, she found herself in the middle of a large industrial area. The hospital itself was small but attractive: a two-storey red brick building with a semi-circular arched doorway under an attractive bow window. There were three chimneys. Norah rang a bell by the doorway and waited.

'Visiting hours don't begin until six,' said the nurse as she opened the door.

'I've come from Worthing,' Norah said lamely. 'I'm here to collect a baby for adoption. My name is Mrs Kirkwood.'

The nurse stepped back to let her in. She was shown to a chair and told to wait. A few minutes later the matron, a rather overweight woman with her hair in a bun, came to see her. Norah was invited into her office. Once they'd sat down, the matron looked at her with a sympathetic expression.

'I'm sorry, Mrs Kirkwood, but I cannot let you take baby at the moment.'

Norah's heart sank. 'Is the baby all right?' she asked anxiously, adding, 'And Mrs Andrews? Is she okay?'

'Both mother and baby are fine,' said Matron, giving Norah a reassuring smile. 'Mrs Andrews can go home in ten days' time but baby Andrews is a little small.'

'But healthy,' Norah interjected.

'At the moment, very healthy,' said Matron, 'but he only weighs four pounds eight ounces. For that reason, he's not here. We've sent him to the baby unit in the Central Middlesex Hospital.'

'A boy? She had a boy?'

Matron nodded.

Norah's heart rate quickened. A son. How wonderful. Jim would be over the moon. She frowned, suddenly anxious. The baby was in another hospital. She wasn't going to lose him, was she? Oh please God let him live.

'There's no need for alarm,' Matron said. 'It's merely a precaution and to make sure he gets specialist care. Premature babies are quite tough little things you know.'

Norah nodded. 'And Mrs Andrews? Can I see her?'

'Visiting hours are from six,' said Matron repeating the edict given to her by the nurse who opened the door, 'but on this one occasion, I'm prepared to allow you to see her.' She rose to her feet. 'It will have to be short, I'm afraid because the nurses are about to do their rounds.'

She led the way towards a small four-bed ward where Norah could hear the sound of babies crying. Penny was in the far corner surrounded by screens. Matron pulled the screen open to allow Norah in. Penny, who was facing the wall, didn't move.

'Mrs Andrews,' said Matron. 'Your friend is here. I've allowed her a short visit.'

Penny rolled over to face Norah. She looked terrible with dark circles under her red and swollen eyes and her hair framing her face in greasy clumps. As she saw Norah her eyes welled with tears. 'Oh Norah . . .' she croaked.

Matron slipped past her as Norah went to the bedside and grasped Penny's hand. Her friend began to sob. Norah hardly knew what to say. She felt dreadful but Penny's pain was her joy. She stood in silence with her arms around Penny's shoulders until the sobbing stopped. Penny pulled herself up and reached for a handkerchief in her handbag on the locker.

Norah chewed on her bottom lip, then took a deep breath. 'If you want to change your mind . . .' she began although it took every ounce of her courage to say it.

Penny was blowing her nose. 'No,' she said stoutly. 'I have no other choice. I know Ted won't accept him and I can't bring up two children on my own.' It was a well-known fact that children of servicemen had government help but if you had an illegitimate child you were on your own. You had nothing. Ted had been a POW for more than two years so there was no way that Penny's baby could be his.

'Your mother . . .' Norah began again. They were talking in whispers in case any of the other patients were eavesdropping.

'She still thinks I'm up here for a better paid job,' said Penny. 'I'm supposed to be saving up for when Ted comes home. I haven't said a thing.' She caught her breath. 'You haven't told her, have you?'

'Of course not,' said Norah.

'She never liked me going out with the Canadians,' said Penny. 'I reckon if it ever got out . . .' She began to cry again, 'she wouldn't think twice about chucking me out on the street.'

Penny blew her nose. 'Have you seen him?'

'They've sent the baby to another hospital,' said Norah.

Penny searched her locker for another handkerchief. Norah gave her hers. 'They said they were going to,' said Penny. 'I hadn't realised he'd gone already.'

'So what happens now?'

'Apparently we have to wait until he's gained weight,' said Penny regaining some of her composure. 'Might be a couple or three weeks, then we'll arrange for you to collect him.'

Norah's jaw clamped shut as she did her best to contain her disappointment.

'What about Victor?'

'Gwen says he can stay with her until I'm allowed out,' said Penny, 'and then I'll go home.'

A nurse came around the screens. 'I'm afraid . . .' she began.

Norah stood to her feet. 'Yes, yes I'm going.' She and Penny embraced then her friend lowered herself back onto the pillows.

'What will you tell your mother about the money?'

Penny gave her a puzzled look.

'The extra money you're supposed to be earning for when Ted comes home.'

Penny shrugged. 'I suppose I'll have to be the victim of a pick-pocket on the train, I suppose.'

Norah smiled. Good old Penny. Got every base covered. 'Keep your chin up,' she said. 'See you soon.'

It was only as Norah sat on the train back to Worthing that she realised how totally unprepared she had been. What a chump. She'd gone all that way to fetch her baby with nothing to carry him in, no baby clothes and not even a shawl to wrap him in. What a numpty. Perhaps it was just as well she would have to wait a week or two to bring him home.

*

Two weeks later, Jim and Norah had invited everybody, including her parents, for Sunday dinner. They didn't explain why but they were happy to discover that everybody managed to get time off or a pass. The meal was a joint affair with promises of butter, sugar and beer.

Even Ginger hadn't come empty-handed. As he climbed out of the RAF jeep, his arms were full. A bag of flour, half a pound of sugar, some sultanas and a couple of emergency ration tins. After dumping everything onto the kitchen table, Jim announced that he, Ivan and Norah's dad, Pete, were off to the pub for a drink. Lennard would meet them there. Norah wasted no time in shooing the men out of her kitchen saying she wanted to get the dinner ready.

As they went out of the back door, Ginger whispered in Ivan's ear. 'Why are we all here?'

'Search me, chum.'

Norah closed the door.

Elsie looked up from the sink where she was finishing a bit of washing up. 'Is Amélie coming?'

'In time for dinner,' said Norah.

'Good. She can do the rest of the washing up then,' Elsie quipped.

For just a while, as she, her mother and Christine pottered about, it almost felt like the Sundays before the war. The wireless was on as they laid the table and dragged in every chair they could find so they all sang along with Vera Lynn, Gracie Fields and Betty Driver. As they prepared the table to the sound of laughter, Norah held up her pinny as if it were her beau and danced around the table.

> '. . . And when two lovers woo
> They still say: "I love you"
> On that you can rely

226

No matter what the future brings
As time goes by . . .'

There was no leg of lamb to go in the oven but the small piece of brisket for which Norah had stood in the queue for forty minutes, made something of a substitute. She'd cooked it slowly with carrots, onions and some herbs from the garden. Christine had given them her last cupful of wine left over from Christmas and Norah had slopped it into the big casserole dish. It smelled all right but Norah was sure a purist might complain that the bottle had been opened for far too long. She'd roasted some potatoes (good job they were still in plentiful supply) and they had cabbage and parsnips on the side. For pudding she'd made a Brown Betty to use up the stale bread. The recipe called for a lemon but finding one of them was like asking for the moon. She had to trust that the apple, golden syrup, nutmeg and cinnamon would be enough to make it tasty. It certainly smelled good.

The men came back just before one o'clock and as they all squashed around the table, they heard Amélie's bicycle come round the back. Lennard moved from a chair to the piano stool as she walked through the door to cheery hello's, hugs and kisses. Norah dished up and soon everyone was tucking in, the war with all its horrors quite forgotten.

Once they'd all enjoyed some of the Brown Betty with a splash of evaporated milk, Norah said she'd put the kettle on for a cup of tea.

'Just a minute, Luv,' said Jim rising to his feet and giving her a grin. 'I have an announcement to make.'

Norah blushed a little as she sat back down. Now everyone was curious.

'We wanted you to be the first to know because you are the most important people in our lives,' Jim went on. 'We invited Rene and Dan but they've gone up to his parents for the weekend.'

Jim paused and glanced at his wife.

'Well, go on then,' Christine said impatiently.

Jim took a breath. 'Norah and I have been offered a baby.'

The table erupted with noisy cries of congratulations and good wishes.

'Boy or girl?'

'Boy.'

'When is he coming?'

'He's very small but we can collect him from hospital as soon as he weighs five and a half pounds.'

'What's his name?'

'Terence,' said Jim.

'John,' said Norah.

There was an embarrassed silence then the happy couple burst out laughing. 'Terence John Kirkwood,' said Norah. 'Terry.' And so it was decided.

With the table cleared and everybody in the sitting room talking about prams and baby food or dozing, Ginger and Amélie were at the sink doing the washing up. Lennard was busy moving all the chairs and the piano stool back to where they belonged.

'I've had a letter from Mireille,' Ginger said, leaning towards Amélie in a confidential manner as he picked up a plate to dry with the tea towel. Lennard had taken a chair out of the room. 'She's gone abroad.'

Amélie looked up. 'I know. She told me that too.'

Ginger sighed. 'Did she tell you where she's gone?'

Amélie shook her head. 'Not really, but I'm guessing it's France.'

'France.' His voice was barely above a whisper as he turned his head away.

'When the war came she always had a longing to do something for France,' said Amélie, swishing the dishcloth absentmindedly around a dinner plate. 'Our mother was French, you see.'

Lennard came back into the kitchen. Ginger and Amélie looked rather awkward. 'Everything all right?' he asked anxiously.

Amélie wiped her eye on her upper arm. 'Yes. Fine.'

Lennard frowned, uncertain. 'You sure?'

Ginger cleared his throat. 'I was just asking Amélie about her sister.'

Lennard hovered for a moment before picking up the piano stool and walking from the room.

'You've fallen in love with my sister, haven't you, Ginger?' said Amélie. Her voice was quiet.

Ginger nodded miserably. 'Fat lot of good it's done me.'

'In my letter,' Amélie began again, 'she told me she felt bad about the way she'd treated you. She asked me to keep in touch with you.'

Lennard was trying not to eavesdrop as he came back for another chair.

Ginger gave her a helpless look. 'Did she say when she's coming back?'

Amélie shook her head.

'It's not looking good, is it?' Ginger said brokenly.

Amélie shook her head again. 'I'm trying not to think about it.'

Ginger put his tea towel onto the draining board. 'Excuse me a minute.' He headed for the back door.

She watched as he sat with his back to her on the bench under the window. She could see his hands shaking as he rolled himself a cigarette and when he'd taken a long drag, he leaned forward, his head in his hands.

Lennard came back. Ginger had gone and Amélie was staring out of the window. 'Anything I can do to help?' he asked, coming closer.

Amélie looked at him for a second before her face crumpled. Instinctively his arm went around her and she leaned into him as she wept on his chest. He didn't say a word but he let her cry, her tears making a dark mark on the serge of his uniform. At last, her grief almost spent, she became aware of his thudding heart and pulled back. She lifted her head and they looked at each other for a few seconds. She didn't say a word but he was suddenly aware of his facial scar. He stepped back and fished into his pocket to hand her a neatly folded handkerchief. 'Do you want to talk about it?'

She took it gratefully and wiped her eyes.

He was cautious, afraid that if he said too much she might simply walk away and that if he said too little, she might think he didn't care. And he did care, he cared a lot.

She lowered herself onto a chair. 'Do you believe in reincarnation?'

The question caught him off balance. 'Reincarnation? No, I don't think so . . . why?'

'Because if it's true,' she went on, 'I must have been a very wicked person in a previous life.'

'Why on earth do you say that?'

'Because all the people I love the most, get taken away from me.'

The kitchen door suddenly banged against the wall making them jump. The dogs bounded in followed by Christine. 'Come on you lot. Haven't you finished that washing up yet? Your tea's getting cold.'

Amélie turned her head quickly and with her back to Christine, blew her nose. 'Sorry Mémé,' she said brightly. 'We're just coming.'

Chapter 28

It looked as if the afternoon would be spent in the sitting room until Lennard suggested a walk. Ivan and Christine opted to have a little snooze in their room and Norah said she would stay behind to get the tea ready. Elsie, excited at the thought of being a grandmother at last, stayed behind to chat to Norah.

'I can't wait to tell Rene and Dan,' she said.

'Oh Mum, please don't. When we found out they couldn't come today, Jim asked them over on Wednesday,' said Norah. 'We want to tell them then.'

'Yes, yes of course, darling,' said Elsie, looking a little crestfallen despite her bright smile.

'Tell you what, why don't you and Dad come too?'

Elsie patted her hand. 'We'd love to.'

The rest of them, Pete, Jim, Ginger, Lennard and Amélie set out with the dogs to walk down Clifton Road towards Gratwick Road and onto the seafront. On Marine Parade, they strolled as far as the old lifeboat station and then turned back up Crescent Road to head for home. The seafront still looked forlorn. Barbed wire and anti-tank devices littered the beach and black and white notices with a skull and crossbones warning of mines were dotted all over the place. There were no seats along the promenade and happy little children watching a Punch and Judy show was a thing of the past. Sometimes everyone accepted that's the way life was but, at other times, it made the war seem endless and everybody felt depressed.

They talked about the war, their jobs and how pleased they all were for Norah and Jim. Everybody was surprised that they weren't going to adopt a more local baby.

'Are you planning to bring him back by train?' Amélie asked Jim.

'I reckon I could drive you up to London and bring him back if it helps,' said Ginger.

'Will you be able to get a car?' Jim asked.

Ginger tapped his nose. ''Course I will.'

'Nothing illegal,' Jim cautioned.

'As if . . .' said Ginger and everyone laughed.

Lennard was itching to walk beside Amélie but some of the time she had her arm threaded through Jim's and at other times Ginger got in the way. It wasn't until they were on the home straight that he finally managed to fall in step with her.

'Are you feeling a bit better?' The question was lame but somehow he always felt tongue tied when he was near her. She nodded shyly.

'What you said to me in the kitchen,' he began. 'You really mustn't go through life believing you must have been a bad person.'

'My father died, my mother died, my little sister is somewhere across the seas and I might never see her again, my older sister has taken herself off to occupied France and my fiancé wrote to say he is in prison because of me,' she said bitterly.

Lennard blinked. 'I'm sorry.' He was feeling slightly

guilty. After all, he was responsible for putting Kane behind bars.

'He doesn't believe in war,' she said, 'so the army has locked him up.'

'You do seem to have had an awful lot of trouble,' he said cautiously. 'Can I ask, what do you mean when you say you might never see your little sister again?'

'My step-father sent her abroad,' she said. 'I've tried writing to CORB but they aren't very helpful.'

'CORB?' he questioned.

'Children's Overseas Reception Board,' she said. 'They sent British children abroad in 1939 and 40. My step-father told them he had cancer and that she had no living relatives. When I found out what he'd done, we – Mireille and me – told them she was our sister but they didn't believe us. They asked for a copy of my birth certificate and a sworn affidavit. I sent our birth certificates and sworn affidavits from us both but they still won't tell me anything.'

'Is your step-father still alive?' Lennard asked. 'Can you not approach him about this?'

'My step-father . . .' Amélie scoffed. 'The least said about him the better.'

'You're angry,' he remarked.

She tossed her head. 'Perhaps I am.'

They had reached the Lilacs. 'Listen Amélie,' he began cautiously, 'I can't promise anything but I should like to help you if I can.'

She laid her hand on his arm sending his pulse racing. 'You are a very kind man, Lennard, but I don't think you can. Everybody has tried. Uncle Jim, Mémé . . . but it's no use. Bob was right. There's an evil streak in me. I'm jinxed.'

'I don't believe that for one minute,' he said earnestly. 'And you mustn't think like that.'

Jim was holding the gate open for them. 'Ask Uncle Jim,' she said as she swept through. 'He'll tell you.'

'Tell me what?'

'About Jago,' said Amélie leaving Lennard with a puzzled expression on his face.

After another cup of tea and the offer of a few sandwiches, it was time to go home. Amélie wanted to get back to the hospital before it got dark, Ginger had to be back on base before ten and Lennard explained that he had to be on duty at five in the morning. Jim guessed that he had another AWOL to arrest.

'I need to talk to you sometime,' Lennard said as he and Jim said their goodbyes, 'in private.'

'Fancy a little fishing?' Jim asked. 'I've got a couple of days' leave coming up shortly.'

'Won't you need that for the baby?' Lennard teased.

'Maybe, maybe not,' said Jim. 'Got to grab my freedom while I can.'

The pair of them grinned at each other conspiratorially.

'I know a nice little spot near Pulborough,' said Lennard. 'You can get bream and perch there and if we're lucky we could land some pike as well.'

Jim licked his lips as if tasting them already. 'Champion.'

The two men shook hands vigorously as Lennard added, 'Phone me when you're free.'

Mireille was on French soil at last. Her jump from the plane had been textbook stuff. Not so for the agent jumping with her. The webbing of his parachute had somehow become entangled and hadn't opened properly. It had been a bit of a struggle on the way down, but he'd eventually managed to free it. The problem was he'd hit the ground really hard. Mireille had already released the mechanism on her parachute and was pulling it in ready to hide. Thomas

Barrington, code name Claude, rolled about on the ground for a few minutes then remained still. As soon as she was able, Mireille hurried to his side. 'Are you okay?'

'Twisted my bloody ankle,' he moaned. 'It hurts like hell.'

Mireille could see little in the shadowy moonlight but he was holding his lower leg and was about to undo his shoe. 'For God's sake don't do that,' she hissed in French. 'If it swells up you'll never get the shoe back on.'

'It bloody hurts.'

'What can I do?' she asked helplessly.

'Take the radio set and get the hell out of here,' he said wincing with pain.

'But I can't leave you,' she said desperately.

'Yes, you can,' he said. His face was white. 'You've got to. If the Germans find both of us, that'll be two agents down. Just make sure they don't find your chute.'

In the still night air, they could hear muffled voices coming closer. Mireille froze.

'That'll be the reception committee. Go on, go.'

The B2 transceiver suitcase which had fallen with them on another chute, weighed a ton. Capable of sending and receiving messages over long distances, the case contained spare parts as well. They had everything they would need to make emergency repairs but the problem was, it was all of thirty-two pounds of dead weight. Mireille buried all three parachutes in a nearby ditch and covered them with dead leaves and branches. As she hurried back to Claude he was surrounded by men in dark clothes. Two of them had slung their guns over their shoulders and were hauling him to his feet. She could see the beads of perspiration standing out on his face and he was so pale he looked as if he'd faint at any minute. Another man grabbed Mireille's arm and propelled her forward. 'Quickly, quickly.'

They hurried silently around the perimeter of the field, keeping as close to the shadows as they could. Mireille was relieved when one of the men had taken the suitcase from her. When they reached a crossroads, they explained that Claude was to go one way and she another.

'Where are you taking him?' she asked anxiously.

'We will find a doctor sympathetic to the Réseau,' said one man. 'Don't worry. We will see to him.'

Mireille glanced anxiously at Claude for confirmation, although what she could do, a woman alone against four armed men if he objected to the plan, was open to question.

'Get a message to Mother Hen as soon as possible,' Claude said through gritted teeth. Mother Hen was the code name for their contact back in Blighty.

'I will,' she promised.

The man who accompanied Mireille took her to a nearby farmhouse. Less than an hour after she had landed, she was already sending her first message from occupied France. *'CLAUDE HOPPING MAD. NO DANCING FOR HIM THIS WEEKEND.'*

When she'd finished, the radio receiver was stashed in a barn under the floorboards with several bales of hay pulled over the top. As for Mireille, code name Françoise, she was tucking into a cup of hearty vegetable soup. Her cover story was that she was a distant cousin of Yveline, the sister of Jules, the man who had escorted Mireille across the fields. Françoise had come to help with the animals because Yveline's brother-in-law had been killed at *la bataille de Dunkerque*. In fact, although he was on the beaches at Dunkirk, he was now safe in England and flying with De Gaulle's Free French. Yveline was a woman in her early thirties, dark-haired and, what the English would call plump. She was friendly and right from the start had treated Mireille as one of the family. In no time at all, the two women became firm friends.

Mireille's room was at the top of the house. It was sparsely furnished but spotlessly clean. There was no electricity so Yveline had given her an old-fashioned oil lamp. Its shadow danced along the wall as she walked towards the bedside table.

'Sleep well, chérie,' Yveline said as she closed the door, 'we have to be up early in the morning.'

There was a clean nightdress on the pillow. Mireille washed in the cold water taken from a jug standing on the washstand and put the nightdress on. Of necessity she had travelled with virtually nothing of her own. She wasn't allowed to take personal things on the plane. Apart from the fact that there was no room for anything but the bare essentials, there was always the risk that English labels and the English way of dressing might be a give-away if caught. There had been stories of agents captured and eventually shot because they'd accidentally left a London transport bus ticket in a top pocket which been discovered during a routine search.

As she laid her head on the pillow, Mireille's thoughts drifted back to England and the people she'd left behind. To her surprise, she felt a yawning chasm opening up inside her. She really thought that because she had cut herself off from them, it wouldn't matter but now she really, really missed them. Amélie, Norah and Jim, Ivan and Christine . . . and even Ginger. Her eyes smarted as she closed them to sleep the sleep which would obliterate them from her mind. The average survival of an agent was six weeks, so they said. She swallowed hard. Whatever she was asked to do on this side of the channel she would have to be very careful because now she knew for certain that she couldn't bear it if she couldn't see them one more time . . . especially Ginger.

Chapter 29

Jim and Lennard chose Greatham for their fishing trip. Getting off the bus, they walked over the medieval pack horse bridge which spanned the River Arun. It didn't take long to find a footpath which took them down to a fairly secluded spot, perfect for fishing. It was stunningly beautiful, miles from anywhere and very quiet. Both men would never have admitted it, but away from the rigours of the police station and the barracks, they looked forward to spending time in this rural idyll. The only sounds were the drilling of an occasional woodpecker and the cries of a few waterfowl. They set up their fishing rods in silence and then relaxed.

'Any news of the baby?'

Jim grinned. 'Norah's going up to fetch him next Thursday.'

'Better make the most of this then,' Lennard teased. 'You'll be confined to barracks from now on.'

Jim chuckled. 'I shan't mind. He's a grand little chap.' He pulled a flask from his rucksack and offered Lennard some tea.

'You said you wanted to talk to me,' Jim said eventually.

'Yes,' said Lennard. 'It's about Amélie. I'm worried

about her. She's got it into her head that she's jinxed. She says in another life she must have been a wicked person.'

'Tommy rot,' said Jim.

'I know it is but I don't know what to say to her,' said Lennard. 'She said you would tell me about her step-father. I'm guessing he has something to with the way she feels.'

'The man was an absolute bastard,' said Jim. 'Excuse my French.'

Lennard frowned. 'Why do you say that?'

'Let me ask you something first,' said Jim. 'Why the sudden interest in the girl? What are your intentions towards Amélie?'

Lennard chuckled. 'Bit old-fashioned aren't you, old man. You sound like my grandfather.'

'That's as maybe,' said Jim, 'but I mean it. She's a sweet girl and life has dealt her a bitter blow more than once. She's been hurt more than most. Norah and I would hate to see her hurt again.'

Lennard sat up a little straighter. 'If I had a real choice,' he said, 'I would ask her to be my girl.' He paused. 'Then if she'd have me, I'd ask her to marry me but that's not likely to happen, is it?'

'Why not?'

'Look at me, Jim,' he said bitterly. 'I'm hardly Ronald Coleman, am I? And I'm at least ten years older than her.'

'What difference does that make?'

Lennard looked confused.

'You're getting too sensitive about your face if you ask me. It's not that bad.' He paused. 'Besides, not all scars are visible.'

Lennard frowned. 'Excuse me?'

'That girl has scars too. She's told me to tell you about Jago Ffox-Webster, but are you sure you want to know? It doesn't make pleasant listening.'

Overhead a plane flew low over the trees, shattering the silence of the morning. The two men looked up expecting to see the smoke trail of an aircraft in trouble coming from one of the engines but there was nothing. The plane flew on. 'Go on,' Lennard said cautiously as they settled back down.

'When she came to us in 1939, Jago had been climbing into her bed for four years. It started when she was a kid of ten years old.' Jim let what he'd just said sink in. He half expected Lennard to jump to his feet or to start an angry protestation but the man said nothing. When he glanced over towards him, Lennard had been stunned into silence but the look on his face was one of pain rather than anger. 'You love her, don't you?' Jim said.

'Is it that obvious?'

Jim watched him lean forward and put his head in his hands. A second or two later, his shoulders trembled. Jim pulled a cigarette packet from his pocket and lit two. Giving Lennard a tap on his arm, he handed one to him. When his friend turned his head, his eyes were moist but Jim pretended not to notice. The two of them sat for a while drawing deeply on their cigarettes.

'I thought she was just upset about that Bob . . .' Lennard began again.

'She's scared,' said Jim. 'You know what some people are like; what they say about girls like her.'

'But it wasn't her fault, was it?' Lennard protested. 'Like you say, she was just a kid.'

'As for that Bob,' Jim went on. 'Another sod. He was looking for the perfect woman and when she didn't add up . . .' His voice trailed. 'That's why he beat her up. We never liked him anyway. Amélie is a very pretty girl but he wanted to control her.'

'Did she love him?' Lennard asked.

'Honestly?' said Jim. 'I don't know. All I know is that he made her life a constant misery by telling her she wasn't good enough. He persuaded her to give up all the people she loved the most. And what makes matters worse, I think she still believes some of the rubbish he told her.'

Lennard clenched his hand into a fist.

'From what I can gather,' Jim went on, 'Bob Kane never knew about Ffox-Webster until that night.'

'So who is Ffox-Webster?' Lennard interrupted.

'Her step-father. Kane persuaded her to tell him all and when she did, he couldn't handle it. The bugger beat her up. He went berserk. That's how she ended up with cracked ribs, half her hair pulled out by the roots, a black eye and bite marks.'

'Bite marks,' Lennard gasped, horrified. 'Good God, what sort of a man is he?'

'A very dangerous one,' said Jim. 'You boys have him banged up for desertion but we're making a case to have him arrested as he gets out. We've been digging around. He's done this sort of thing before. He thought he'd outwit us because he changes his name every time.'

'Then how did you find out?'

'Postcards,' said Jim, a note of triumph in his voice. 'All the places he's ever been, he's collected a postcard. We contacted the local police and guess what? We found a string of offences all over the country so it looks like we can charge him with grievous bodily harm on at least three other victims.'

'Does that mean that Amélie will have to testify in court?' Lennard asked anxiously.

'Not if I can help it,' said Jim. 'Kane's victims go way back. They're older women and more savvy and what's more, they actually want their day in court.'

Lennard's rod began to tremble and he reluctantly

responded. Between them they landed a pretty decent pike but neither man enthused about it. Somehow the joy of fishing wasn't there anymore.

After a while, Jim muttered, 'Fancy going for a pint?'

They found a small pub not too far away and ensconced themselves in a corner away from the bar.

'Amélie was telling me about her sister.'

'What, Mireille?'

'She's the one who's gone to France, isn't she? No, I meant the other one.'

'Little Linnet,' said Jim. 'Ffox-Webster had her sent abroad.'

'Why?'

'To keep the girls apart, I guess,' said Jim. 'He didn't want them comparing notes, did he?'

Lennard was horrified. 'You mean he's done it to all of them?'

'No, not Linnet,' said Jim. 'Amélie protected her from that. She was amazingly brave.'

Lennard sat back in his chair. 'So where is Ffox-Webster now? What happened to him?'

'He was hung,' said Jim. 'Not for what he'd done to those girls although in my book he should have been. No, they found out he was aiding and abetting the enemy.'

Lennard blinked. 'So he was also a traitor.'

'The man was a Nazi and passing secrets,' Jim said coldly. 'They topped him in 1940.'

'And you say he abused both girls?'

'Mireille and Amélie.' Jim nodded. 'As soon as they reached puberty he lost interest. Amélie did her best to keep him away from Linnet. She knew she was next.'

'Good God . . .' Lennard breathed. Jim noticed that his face was very pale.

'It gets worse,' said Jim. 'Mireille had his child.'

Lennard looked as if he was about to throw up. They drank in silence and then he said, 'Amélie is desperate to find her sister. Have you tried to help her?'

'We did,' said Jim, 'but we hit a brick wall. It seems the bastard told CORB that she was without relatives. She was sent abroad, that much we know, but nobody will say where she is now.' He sighed. 'Couldn't get her back anyway. Not with the war on.'

'I've got a few connections in high places,' said Lennard. 'Mind if I have a go?'

'Be my guest,' said Jim. 'If you can pull it off, Amélie will love you for it.'

Lennard gave him a ghost of a smile. A few minutes later, he stood to his feet. 'Another?'

Jim nodded. 'Thanks mate.'

Lennard negotiated the chair and then turned back. 'And don't you worry about Amélie, old man. I wouldn't do anything to hurt her.'

'I think I've got that now,' said Jim. 'And the next time you get disheartened by a look in the mirror, just remember, faint heart never won fair lady.'

Lennard grinned. 'Bloody philosopher now, are you?'

Norah couldn't stop looking at him. Terry was still quite small but already he could focus his eyes and right now he was regarding her with a puzzled expression.

'Hello sweetheart,' she said softly as she rearranged his shawl to allow him to wave his hands a little.

She had spent the past week close by the Central Middlesex Hospital so that she and Terry could get to know each other. Her digs were in a small guest house about a mile from the hospital and she tried to be on the ward for most of his feeds. The only time she wasn't allowed to be there was for the ten o'clock feed at night, the one at two in the morning and the early morning six o'clock feed. She spent the evenings in the call box down the road where she would ring Jim and tell him all about Terry.

'He smiled today,' she would say, or, 'The doctor took off his nappy to examine him and when he put the stethoscope on his chest, the doctor didn't notice that Terry was weeing up the sleeve of his house coat.'

'That's my boy,' Jim had chuckled.

Each day, Norah would arrive on the baby ward at around nine-thirty. The nurses were wonderful. They taught her how to bath him, change his nappy and feed him. They showed her how to make up the National Dried Milk formula and they encouraged her not to be shy but to talk to him so that they bonded.

'Baby will soon recognise your voice,' they said and it seemed that they were right. Norah smiled as Terry's mouth formed a 'coo' shape as if he was trying to reply.

Ginger, who had been putting her suitcase into the car boot, suddenly banged it shut. The baby started but didn't cry. Norah reached for his tiny hand and kissed his fingers. She was grateful to have a car ride home but she wished it could have been Jim at the wheel. Sadly he was in the middle of a huge black market fraud case which stretched as far as the home counties. Jim tried to reassure her but she always worried when he had to deal with some of these big gangs. They were invariably desperate and ruthless men who thought nothing of killing a policeman who got in their way. 'I'm safe enough Luv,' he said, 'and besides, we're very close to making arrests.'

Ginger climbed into the driver's seat and glanced behind him at Norah and her son on the back seat. 'All right?'

Norah nodded. 'I really appreciate this.'

'Don't be daft,' he said. 'That's what friends are for.'

244

Soon, without more ado, they were speeding through the Surrey then the Sussex countryside. Norah was bringing her baby home.

It was good to put on his own clothes again. There was no mirror of course, just a piece of polished tin screwed to the wall. Too risky to have one in prison, he supposed, even if he was on the way out.

Bob Kane had been unbelievably angry when he'd been sent here but it had been a godsend. HMP Winchester turned out to have plenty of undesirables of the Blackshirt variety and with them Bob found a kindred spirit. He was lucky to meet one man who had known his father personally.

'Great chap,' Sylvester had told him. 'Gave his whole life to the cause. Everyone said he was destined for greatness.'

It was here in the prison that Bob discovered some of his father's high ideals. Like Hitler, his father had championed the cause for the purity of the Aryan race, thus creating a people for future generations who were far superior. As Bob mulled it over as he lay on his bunk at night, it suddenly occurred to him that his father must have chosen Amélie's mother for a special reason. Although to the outsider it might have seemed unpalatable, what his father had done with Amélie herself, was all part of the master plan. Bob felt a frisson of excitement. It was his destiny to complete his father's work. Amélie had failed but there was still another sister, one young enough to be pure and virginal. It was his duty to uphold his father's values. All he had to do was find Linnet. Being so much younger than Amélie, there was a good chance that she was still untouched.

Until the light had dawned, he had thought that he

wouldn't go back to Worthing. He had planned to go to Bournemouth or maybe somewhere along the Devonshire coast, but now he was on a mission. He was supposed to report to the army when he got out and from there he would be assigned a position in a field hospital or some such, but that was impossible. A change of name, a clandestine meeting with Amélie and persuading her to ignore his previous suggestion to leave well alone and contact CORB for the address of her sister (the girl he now thought of as his wife-to-be) was much more to his liking. He slicked down his hair with a dollop of Brylcreem and combed a straight parting to the left. With one last look around his cell, Bob picked up his bag and headed for the door.

There were six of them leaving prison this morning. The prison guard escorted them to the big wooden doors and they waited by the small inner door as he fumbled with the keys. When the door opened Bob could smell something he hadn't smelled in three whole months: fresh air and freedom.

One by one, he and his fellow prisoners stepped over the high sill and onto the pavement. A scattering of relatives and friends greeted the other ex-prisoners but Bob looked up to see two policemen coming towards him. At first he was annoyed. They obviously didn't trust him to report for duty as stipulated by the court. Unbelievable! They had actually sent the buggers to fetch him. His nostrils flared and he clenched his fist. He was tempted to make a run for it but he knew it was hopeless.

'Robert Sidney Kane, alias Thomas Brymore, alias Edward Smith, I am arresting you on suspicion of robbery with violence, grievous bodily harm and theft . . .'

The copper droned on as his bag fell on the cobble stones and his colleague twisted Bob's hands behind his back to put on the handcuffs. Bob bristled with anger once more. This was all Amélie's fault. He never would have got caught if it hadn't been for her and her wretched family. Amélie and Jim and Norah – they were all as bad as one another. Damn them all, damn them all to hell.

Chapter 30

Things in France were not easy for Mireille and her fellow resistance workers. There was a feeling in the air that things were not good because the Germans had tightened their grip on the whole country. Even the town was ringed by the Boches and there were road blocks everywhere. As well as checking their papers, everyone had to have a special card stamped with the German eagle to get through.

After their drop behind enemy lines, Thomas Barrington, alias Claude, had been taken to a remote farmhouse about twenty miles away to recover from his twisted ankle. Once he could move freely, he began his assignment as a saboteur. Mireille spent her time working on the farm, making friends and relationships with the locals and sending messages back to London on the wireless. She had to change her location quite frequently to avoid the risk of being caught by those monitoring the air waves.

Claude, now recovered, had become quite a success, so she'd heard. He and his compatriots had blown up a railway track just before a troop train came by. The plan had been to do it in open country where the train would come off the tracks and roll down a steep embankment but Claude had persuaded the resistance leader to do the deed close to a railway bridge instead. It was a much more dangerous mission but as Claude pointed out, if they succeeded, it would be a double whammy against the Germans. They would leave both the railway beneath and the road above out of action.

Four days later, there was a terrible rail crash. A train was derailed and crashed into the side of a bridge killing five German soldiers. The bridge and the track were badly damaged, which meant that services were severely disrupted for several days. People shook their heads and agreed that the Boches were certainly having a run of bad luck, something which put a smile on everyone's face until the Germans decided to take reprisals. Fifteen men from the local area were rounded up and publicly hanged in the village square. It was meant to crush the French resistance but it only served to strengthen their resolve.

Mireille's part in the venture had been to send messages to London asking for more ammunition.

Flushed with success, the second mission followed a month later and once again Mireille passed a message on to Mother Hen. A week before the operation, the supplies were due to arrive. Mireille was asked to drive a van with a hidden compartment under the floor at the back. They had filled the van itself with some rather smelly compost which was supposedly destined for a local market garden. As instructed, she and Yveline parked under some trees close to the edge of the drop zone and waited. Every now and then they could just make out other members of the resistance, armed with Sten guns, waiting in the shadowy ditches surrounding the fields. Even though she had been told they would be reasonably safe in the van, Mireille's heart was in her mouth. So many things could go wrong. Supposing they had been betrayed; supposing the Germans saw the lights on the ground or worse still, the aircraft lights as it came in; supposing they heard the sound of aircraft engines and what if the RAF boys went off course and mistakenly dropped the guns in another field. Coupled with all that, she knew they had precious little time to grab 'the toys', as they were called, clear up the field and make their getaway, before the might of the German army descended on them. And it didn't end there. Even if all went smoothly, she still had to get her consignment to the secret hiding place without being caught.

'This is the worst bit,' Yveline remarked, 'the waiting.'

Resting her face on the cool window glass on the driver's seat door, Mireille's thoughts drifted back to the moment she had been dropped in France only a few weeks before. It seemed like a lifetime ago and just the thought of home created a familiar dull ache in her chest. Amélie . . . how was she? Were she and Bob married by now? Mireille sighed and almost hoped that she wasn't. She would love to have the opportunity to dance at her sister's wedding.

She could hear the hum of aircraft engines in the distance and three members of the team ran onto the field to position the lights. Yveline opened the passenger door and went to join them. A solitary plane appeared over the trees and a minute or two later five containers were on their way down to earth. They were obviously heavy because the parachutes hardly had time to open before they hit the ground. Mireille watched as more men emerged from the darkness and raced towards the boxes. The plane turned and the lights went out. In the silence that followed, Mireille could only hear the sound of her own panicky breath. A lorry which had been sheltering in the lane and covered with tree branches trundled towards her and seconds later, those same men were stowing guns and explosives in the back of it.

She heard the back door of her van open and someone

unbolted the secret compartment. Seconds later, she heard the scrape of metal against metal as the guns were being pushed along the length of the floor. The door closed, someone tapped twice on the side of the van and Yveline slid into the passenger seat beside her.

'Go, go,' she whispered urgently.

Mireille started the engine and moved at a sedate speed along the muddy and potholed lane. There was no other choice but it had been drummed into her not to drive too fast because that would draw attention to herself. The two women didn't speak as they motored through the darkness of the French countryside. Everything seemed perfect until they rounded a corner and immediately came face to face with a road block. There was no time to turn around or to back-track along another route.

'*Mon dieu*,' Yveline whispered as she crossed herself.

As they pulled up, a German soldier, his weapon slung over his shoulder, walked towards them. Mireille wound down the window and handed him her forged papers. He wrinkled his nose and said, 'You have smell,' in broken French.

'We are taking manure to a farm on the other side of the hill,' Mireille said with an apologetic smile.

'There is curfew,' said the German.

'The van broke down,' she said apologetically. 'We had to get water for the engine.'

His eyes narrowed.

'I'm sorry,' she said, lowering her eyes. 'We have to get home. My papa . . .'

The soldier looked at Yveline and grinned but by this time the other sentry had joined them. An older man, he seemed a little more sceptical. 'Open up,' he said brusquely. 'Out, out.'

Mireille opened the driver's door and got out. Her heart

was beating wildly but to all outward appearances, she seemed perfectly calm. At his behest, she opened the back door and a reeking stink seemed to flood around them. The younger man put his hand over his mouth and gasped. He stepped back while the older man fixed a bayonet onto his rifle and began to prod. Having checked that no one was hiding under the dung heap at the back of the van, he returned to the cab and pushing himself in front of Mireille, he knelt on the driver's seat and rolled up the metal curtain which separated the front and back of the van. As he lifted his bayoneted gun, Yveline let out an audible gasp. The soldier only glanced at her before he began spearing the dung heap again.

Eventually satisfied that no one was under the dung heap at this end of the van either, he stepped back into the road. 'Why are you *both* here?' The implication was that it didn't take two people to deliver a van load of animal dung.

Mireille hung her head. 'Monsieur, my papa says it is dangerous for young girls to be out at night . . .' She shrugged.

The soldier motioned her towards the driver's seat and she got back in. Handing her back her papers, he slammed the door with a disgruntled grunt. As she pulled away they heard him mumble, 'Stinking French.'

Mireille put half a mile between them before she and Yveline burst out laughing. 'It is dangerous for young girls to be out at night,' Yveline mimicked, 'and my papa . . .' They both roared again.

The guns were delivered without further hitch and rather than risk returning to that same road block, Mireille and Yveline hid in the barn. After a night of broken sleep, the two women returned to the farm early the next morning.

*

Amélie hurried along Worthing's Marine Parade. She was late. Even though it was her afternoon off, Home Sister had insisted she stay to clean the communal bathroom in the nurses' home before she could go. She and Lennard had arranged to meet in the Stanhoe Hotel in Augusta Place because, he wrote, '*I have news of your sister.*'

He was waiting by the entrance.

'I'm so sorry,' she said as she puffed her way towards him.

He smiled. 'It really doesn't matter but, if you don't mind me saying so, you look so hot I think a glass of lemonade might be in order.'

The hotel was just off the seafront. An attractive white building it had been around since Victorian times and before the war it had been popular with people who enjoyed meeting there to go bicycling around the Sussex countryside. There were tables and chairs in the small front garden so he ushered her to one. The weather was unseasonably warm for the time of year and for that Amélie was grateful.

'Has Norah come home with the baby yet?' he asked.

Amélie nodded. 'They came home at the weekend. I'm hoping to see him on my day off.'

'So Ginger got a car?'

'Of course,' Amélie chuckled. 'Norah had to change the day from Friday to Thursday but the hospital was happy to let her do that. Apparently some big-wig wanted to go to RAF Stanmore on the Thursday because he had to meet with some important American so Ginger wangled it that he'd have time enough to do a quick trip back home before taking the RAF chappie back to Tangmere.'

Lennard laughed aloud. 'I don't know how he does it.'

Amélie tapped the edge of her nose, Ginger fashion, and they both laughed again. She relaxed. She liked Lennard. He was a nice man.

The waiter, Malcolm according to his name tag, appeared with a large jug of lemonade and two glasses on a tray. As he left, Lennard poured her a glass and handed it to her. 'You look very pretty,' he said shyly.

Amélie blushed. 'Thank you.' She took a long drink from her glass. 'That was wonderful. Thank you.'

'You're welcome.' He was glad that she obviously felt comfortable and relaxed with him. He desperately wanted to hold her hand and tell her how he felt about her, but something told him that after her terrible experiences, she wouldn't want his advances – not just yet anyway. Their eyes met and he smiled. 'Shall I ask them to serve us lunch out here?'

'That would be rather nice,' she agreed.

The menu was sparse but the cottage pie with carrots and cabbage seemed acceptable so they both settled for that.

'I wanted to talk to you about your younger sister,' said Lennard snapping open his napkin and placing it on his lap.

'I told you, she was sent abroad.'

'She was actually sent to South Africa.'

Amélie's fork hung in mid-air. 'You know where she is?'

'Not exactly,' Lennard admitted, 'but I know where she was.' He had sought the help of his cousin Selwyn and this information was the culmination of three weeks of cajoling, persuading and a large whisky bill.

Amélie frowned. 'I don't understand.'

'Your sister was sent to a farm about thirty miles from Durban,' he continued, 'but it seems she's now left there and gone somewhere else.'

Amélie stared at him. 'To another country?'

'No, no. She's still somewhere in South Africa,' he went on. 'From what I can gather, it has something to do with her schooling. There had been some unrest in the area so they've changed her location. A cousin of mine is checking up on it for me.'

Amélie's eyes had filled. 'I can hardly believe it,' she said. 'I honestly thought I might never see her again.'

'Don't get too excited,' he cautioned. 'I wondered about telling you so soon. Maybe I should have waited until I had more positive news but I had the feeling you might like to know she's alive and from what I can gather, well.'

Amélie nodded. 'I am eternally grateful.'

Lennard waved her comment away. 'I'll let you know as soon as I have an address, okay?'

She nodded happily.

For dessert Lennard ordered them apple charlotte and they spent a pleasant hour or so together. Eventually Amélie glanced at her wrist watch. 'I have to go. I'm back on duty at four-thirty.'

'I'll give you a lift,' he said.

She smiled. 'You are very kind.'

Back in her room at the nurses' home, Amélie straightened her apron and put on her nurse's cap. Linnet was alive and well. How wonderful. Mireille would be so pleased. If only she could write and tell her.

It was only as she was walking towards the wards that a germ of an idea came to her.

Chapter 31

Bob Kane gripped the edge of the dock and stared straight ahead. His trial hearing had been postponed twice because of enemy action and it was May already. Months of his life had been on hold and he was itching to be back outside. The magistrate rustled his papers and everybody held their breath.

'In view of the fact that the defendant has pleaded not guilty to all offences,' he said without looking up, 'he shall be committed for trial at the next Lewes Assizes and because of the seriousness of the charges, I do not propose to grant bail . . .'

Furious, Bob lost his temper and shouted, 'This is a travesty of justice. I am innocent of all charges.'

'Accordingly,' the magistrate interrupted in a slightly raised voice, 'the prisoner will be held in custody in Lewes prison until a trial date is set. Take him down.'

'You can't do this,' Bob yelled as someone gripped his arm. He snatched it angrily away. 'This is a trumped up charge,' but the two officers manhandled him back down the stairs. 'They lied,' he yelled defiantly, 'It's all lies,' but nobody was listening.

Bundled into his cell, as soon as the door slammed shut behind him, Bob hit it with his fist and kicked out in a rage, but his protests fell on deaf ears. Hot and seized by a dizzy spell, he staggered backwards and sat down heavily on the bench.

Three charges: robbery with violence, that was the bitch in Southampton way back in 1938; grievous bodily harm, that was the silly old duffer who tried to stop him when he'd opened the door of the safe in Rye; and theft, that was Lady Dorothy's pearls. They weren't worth much anyway and the way she'd worked him to death in that huge garden of hers, he deserved a little consideration. Funnily enough, they'd not charged him with knocking Amélie about. He wondered why. She must have kept quiet about it – maybe she was dead? Nah, if she was dead that copper would have come after him. He'd move heaven and earth to get him banged up for something.

It took him several minutes to regain his composure and then a more sobering thought came to mind. If Amélie was dead, how would he find her sister? What was he going to do? Up until now he'd got it all sussed out. Who else would have avoided having the finger pointed at them for all this time? It wasn't fair. It wasn't right and now that he was thinking more clearly, it was all because of that French whore. If only she hadn't hoodwinked him into believing she was the perfect woman. His breathing was slower now but his mind was still whirling. If it was possible to kill someone with dark thoughts, she'd be frying in hell right now yet he needed to talk to her to find Linnet. He gripped the edge of the bench and began to rock himself. After a while, his mind cleared. He was beginning to put two and two together. Amélie wasn't the person he'd thought she was but he had to admit that his luck had changed when he'd met her. He'd gathered quite a haul from those patients, especially the dead ones. If it wasn't for her betrayal he could have stayed in the hospital doing what he was doing for years to come. It must be her fault that he was here. She was more than just a whore, she was poison. He stopped rocking and held his breath. 'And what do you do with poison?' he said out loud, his voice rising with each stanza. 'You cut it out . . . cut it out . . . cut it out!'

The slide on the cell door clattered open and a pair of eyes stared at him. He rose to his feet and rushed towards the door fully intending to stick his finger through the gap but the slide slammed shut just as he got there. Turning back to the bench he calmed himself again. He had to think. Think.

Ever since Terry had come home, Norah's days were radically altered. The baby came first with everything. She still worked hard in the market garden but now everything revolved around Terry's feeds and everything else that came with looking after a baby. Of course she wasn't without help. Elsie was just up the road so she popped in quite frequently and Christine was on hand to babysit if Norah had to go out. Jim spent every moment he could talking to the baby who kicked his legs and waved his hands excitedly whenever he heard his father's voice. As Terry grew older, Ivan dropped his teeth and blew raspberries to make the boy laugh and their frequent visitors, Ginger and Lennard never came to the house empty handed. Terry's toy box bulged with stuffed rabbits, teddy bears and rag books.

In the first few weeks Rene came over quite a lot. Compared to how small and well contained Penny had been even as late as Christmas, Rene already had a gently rounded belly and of course, unlike Penny, she stuck it out as she walked. In fact, she was already wearing maternity smocks.

Now that May had come around and Jim and Norah had signed the last of the adoption papers, Terry was theirs for ever. It was time to arrange a Christening and have a celebration party.

St Matthew's was booked for the afternoon and the family planned a small celebration at home. The war dragged on and the shortages were becoming more severe, but they knew they'd still have a good time. There was enough fruit in the nursery to make rhubarb crumble and gooseberry tarts, and Sharron Critchley's hens three doors down were laying nicely so she'd promised Norah some real egg sandwiches. Jim and Ivan had bought a beer barrel while Elsie and Christine baked cakes. The neighbours were invited to pop along anytime and Reverend Ward's wife, Anne, had lent Norah a baby dress for Terry. It wasn't a Christening robe but as good as and it had been the gown all three of her children had worn when they were christened.

They had asked Ginger, Lennard and Amélie to be godparents and each of them was more than happy to take on the roll. Ginger and Lennard had turned up in uniform but Amélie was looking as pretty as a picture in the dress Christine had made for her birthday last year. Her hair was piled up on her head in a riot of curls and she was wearing a very flattering lipstick.

'It's from Hubbard's,' she'd whispered to Norah as they'd got dressed. 'Lennard bought it for me.'

'It suits you,' said Norah. 'I've never seen you wearing lipstick before.'

Their eyes met and Norah wished she hadn't made the remark. For some reason unknown to her, it had touched a raw nerve.

'You look really lovely,' she added quickly.

They set off at two-thirty to walk to the church, Norah

pushing the pram and feeling every inch the proud mother. Ginger had already taken Rene and Dan down in the jeep he'd borrowed for the occasion to save her having to walk. Inside the cool church building, they gathered around the font for the familiar service, a service which had been repeated down the centuries for many thousands of babies before him.

When it came to the actual baptism itself, Norah placed Terry into the priest's arms and he recited the ancient words of the ceremony.

'I baptise thee, Terence John in the name of the Father and of the Son and of the Holy Ghost. Amen.'

As the cold water trickled over his head, Terry gave Reverend Ward a puzzled look but he didn't cry. When the man uttered the 'Amen', everyone was delighted to see Terry give him a wide smile. Norah had tears in her eyes as the priest handed her son back to her, but she still took on board the solemn promises she was making.

'Ye are to take care that Terence John be brought to the Bishop to be confirmed by him, as soon as he can say the Creed, the Lord's Prayer and the Ten Commandments in the vulgar Tongue, and be further instructed in the Church Catechism set forth for that purpose,' he said in a direct quote from the Church of England prayer book.

'Oh yes,' Norah said, and in her heart she repeated, '*I will, I will.*'

Bob Kane was still rocking a couple of hours later when the door opened and three officers came into the room. He was quieter now but no one was taking any chances. Handcuffed, he followed them outside where he was pushed into a prison van containing five other prisoners, all destined for Lewes. They sat on long forms running down the side of the van and as he lowered himself down, the men on his side shuffled themselves up. Two officers sat on the end and the doors were shut from the outside.

Nobody spoke as the van set off. For his part, Bob was wondering why he had been sent all the way to Lewes, which must be at least eighty miles away, instead of back to the much nearer prison at Winchester.

A young lad further up the bench started crying for his mother.

'Shuddup,' growled an older man. 'Whatever brought you 'ere, it's yer own fault.' And the angry look on his face was enough to encourage the boy to be silent.

Nobody actually saw what made the driver suddenly swerve. One minute they were motoring along nicely but the next there was an almighty bang and the van lurched wildly from side to side for several seconds. The men blasphemed in panic as everybody was thrown around and then tossed forward. There were no windows, so they couldn't see what was happening but all at once, it felt as if the van was travelling at speed down a steep embankment. A moment later, it came to a sudden and catastrophic stop.

At first there was the silence but as the uninjured pulled themselves away from the men underneath them, they could see that one guard had broken his leg. He was screaming in agony but nobody moved to help him. The other guard was unconscious.

'Get the keys,' one man hissed.

Another man searched the unconscious man's pockets but to no avail. The prisoners then turned to the injured guard. Despite his obvious pain, the guard put up some resistance but it was no use. The bunch of keys was ripped from his belt and passed around until everyone was free. There didn't appear to be any movement from the two guards in the cab so they set about kicking the doors open.

It was wonderful to spill out into the late afternoon air

a free man. The cab of the prison van had hit the archway of a railway bridge but nobody had the guts to look and see if the driver and his mate were still alive. It went unsaid, but it was every man for himself. Some ran along the railway line, some pulled themselves up the other embankment but Bob and one other man hauled themselves back up to the road. A large crater in the tarmac told them that an enemy plane must have jettisoned the last of its load and they had been hit by a bomb blast. The road itself was deserted. With a gesture of defiance, the two men went their separate ways.

It wasn't until he recognised the Brighton road that Bob knew where he was going.

Back home at the Lilacs, the tea was flowing and the sound of laughter filled the house once more. Terry had had his feed and Norah had put him upstairs in his cot where it was quieter. Downstairs was too crowded and noisy for him to sleep. Lennard had brought a couple of bottles of wine and was busy filling glasses. He and Amélie handed them around and then Jim called for silence.

'I feel very blessed today,' he began. 'This terrible war has taken so much from all of us but I have a beautiful wife and now a handsome son.' He turned towards his mother. 'I think having my mother here with me too, must make me the luckiest man in the world.'

Christine flushed and lowered her head.

'What about me?' Ivan cried out and everybody roared with laughter.

'Having you as well is the icing on the cake,' Jim called out. He raised his glass, 'I call on you now to drink to my son's health; to Terry.'

The assembled crowd raised their glasses and a wail from upstairs told them Terry was still awake. 'That's my boy,'

Jim quipped and everybody laughed. After that, the hub of conversation rose again as the sandwiches were passed around.

No one noticed Amélie and Lennard exchanging a shy smile.

Chapter 32

It didn't take long for Bob to realise that it would take all day to get to Worthing if he was forced to walk. The problem was he knew there was no way he could get a lift looking the way he did. Although the handcuffs were gone, his clothes were muddy, his jacket sleeve and his trousers were ripped and his shirt was splattered with someone else's blood. He also had a pain in his cheek, so there was every possibility that he had a bruise coming.

For the first mile or so he stuck to the country lanes and as luck would have it, he came across a remote cottage and spotted some washing on a line. In among the panties and petticoats he could see a pair of dungarees and two shirts. There didn't appear to be anyone about so very cautiously, he crept into the garden. A dog inside the house barked and for a moment he froze, but nobody came. The people were obviously out. Snatching the dungarees and a shirt from the clothes line he went around the back of the shed to change but before he put the clothes on, he washed his face and hands in some water in a watering can. He couldn't comb his hair but he did the best he could with his fingers.

Walking back into the lane, he decided to thumb a lift from the next passing car. He didn't have to wait long before a Ford 2 Tonne drop side lorry pulled up in front of him. The driver leaned out of the open window as he ran towards it. 'Where you goin'?'

'Worthing.'

'I'm going as far as Lancing.'

'That'll do.'

Bob was about to aim for the front passenger seat when he noticed that the driver's mate was already sitting there. 'Hop in the back,' said the driver.

The lorry was full of building material but once he was in the flat bed, it didn't take Bob long to make himself comfortable. The lorry lurched forward and he was on his way.

Terry was asleep in his cot and the neighbours had gathered for a few pints and a sing-song. Jim and Lennard pulled the piano out into the passageway and in an atmosphere of blue cigarette smoke, Ginger started the evening with a comic rendition of Stanley Holloway's monologue, King 'Arold. By the time he got to the last verse, *And after the battle were over, they found 'Arold so stately and grand, sitting there with an eye-full of arrow, on his 'orse with his 'awk in his 'and,'* everybody had joined in. Ginger took a bow to the sound of applause and laughter.

'You should be on the stage,' Ivan said as he pulled the piano stool out for his wife. Christine sat at the piano and they began to sing the old favourites like 'The White Cliffs of Dover', 'I'll Be Seeing You' and 'Pack Up Your Troubles'.

As the music died away, Amélie was sitting on the bottom stair so Lennard came to join her. 'I've been trying to talk to you all day.'

Her face lit up. 'Have you heard any more about my sister?'

'Not yet, but I'm working on it,' he said. It was obvious that she was disappointed so he squeezed her hand and said, 'Promise.' She nodded. 'You've got yours and your sister's birth certificates,' he went on, 'but have you thought of getting your parents' wedding certificate?'

'Why on earth would I want to do that?' cried Amélie.

'For a start,' said Lennard, 'your grandparents' names might be on it. They could possibly be dead now but with that information, you may be able to find other relatives – your uncle, an aunt or perhaps some cousins.'

Amélie stared at him in disbelief.

'I take it that they were married in this country?' he ventured.

'As far as I know,' she said. 'You know, I never thought of that. Thank you.'

As the sound of the people around them talking grew louder she leaned into him and laid her head on his shoulder making his pulse race. He reached for her hand and covered it with his own. 'Are you working tomorrow?' he said. 'If so I'll give you a lift back to the hospital tonight.'

She shook her head. 'Day off.'

For a few minutes, they sat in silence. One of Norah's neighbours pushed another glass of beer in Lennard's hand and it slopped all over his shoe. 'Whoops, sorry mate,' said the man. Lennard waved him away with a smile and so he said to Amélie, 'Can I get you anything, Luv?' His flat cigarette was stuck to his bottom lip and he had one eye closed to prevent the smoke from going in. Amélie held up her empty glass. 'A little more wine, perhaps?'

The man looked around wildly until Lennard said, 'It's on the kitchen table.'

'Cheers,' said the man and headed off.

Amélie giggled.

'Can I take you out tomorrow?' Lennard said cautiously.

'That would be nice.'

Lennard turned to look at her. She had a twinkle in her eye and Lennard guessed that she was slightly tipsy. All the same he felt over the moon.

'You'd better drink some of that beer. Your hand is shaking so much you'll spill it all over your uniform,' she said.

'In a minute,' he said and putting his hand through the banister rail, he put the glass onto the small table nearby. He turned his head slowly and looked at her. His kiss was gentle, undemanding and delicious. Amélie wasn't in the least bit afraid of him and it wasn't just because they were in a room full of people. She'd been with Lennard enough times to know by now that she could absolutely trust him.

Someone on the stairs trod on her skirt. 'Sorry.'

Amélie tucked her dress under her thigh and Lennard came a little closer. 'Okay?' he whispered.

She nodded. The man came back with some more wine. ''Ere you are, Luv,' he said adding teasingly, ''Ere you, put 'er down. You don't know where she's been.'

Lennard felt Amélie stiffen beside him. 'Idiot,' he mumbled crossly as the man moved away. He could see the confusion and pain in her eyes. 'I'm sorry,' he whispered.

'There's no need for you to be sorry.'

A bit later on, the same man was telling everyone a joke. The room was filled with raucous laughter. Lennard glanced anxiously at Amélie. He'd missed the joke but it was something about a tart. Did she think it was aimed at her? 'Take no notice of him,' he said.

She smiled and laid her hand on his. 'Has Uncle Jim told you about me?'

'He said you'd asked him to,' he said uncertainly.

267

They sat in silence then he said, 'Amélie, what happened to you as a kid wasn't your fault. As far as I'm concerned, it's all in the past.' She looked away and he could have bitten his tongue off. 'No, no, I didn't mean it like that,' he flustered. 'Of course it was utterly terrible, it's just that . . . Oh God, I'm so sorry.'

She leaned into his shoulder again and before he could stop himself he lifted her hand and put it to his lips. Lowering her hand back into her lap, he gently stroked her fingers. Then to his immense surprise, she suddenly reached up and pecked his cheek. Dizzy with delight and desire, he gave her a shy smile.

'You are a very kind man.'

'Come on, Len,' Ginger shouted breaking the spell. He was putting his glass on the lid of the piano before taking over from Christine. She got up and Ginger sat on the stool. Running his fingers over the keys, he picked out the refrain from the song 'I'll Be Seeing You'. 'You've got a good voice. Come on, mate, give us a song.'

The buzz of conversation all around them drifted away as everyone looked in their direction and Lennard was greeted with a chorus of, 'Yeah, come on Lennard. Sing us a song.'

He was happy to give them what they wanted but he stayed where he was on the stairs, and still holding her hand, he sang his heart out . . . just for her.

It was late by the time Bob reached Worthing. He'd had to walk from Lancing but he was glad of the exercise after being cooped up in that lorry. He had no money, nowhere to stay and was starving hungry. He hung around a couple of fish and chip shops along the seafront and thought about snatching somebody's parcel as they came out of the shop, but it was too risky. He didn't want to get caught because if he was, he'd be back in the jail faster than you could say, 'escaped prisoner.' After a while, he noticed a couple sitting on a wall to eat their meal. When they'd finished, he watched them screw up the newspaper covering and throw it into the bin. Much to his shame, Bob waited a while and then went to the bin to retrieve it. There were lean pickings left inside but very welcome all the same and he was lucky enough to be able to repeat the exercise a few more times before the evening was out.

After an uncomfortable night sleeping in a shop doorway, he made his way to Worthing hospital in the morning. His timing was perfect. The porter's room was empty. His work colleagues were already dispersed throughout the hospital so he had free range. Someone had obligingly left his sandwich lunch on the bench in the corner. Bob made short work of that and the flask of tea beside it. Next, he looked in the lost property box for a change of clothes. Quite often there were a few good quality items in it, usually stuff left behind when a patient was discharged or died and nobody bothered to claim it. Bob was in luck. He found a clean-ish shirt and some trousers as well as a comb and a couple of wash bags. There was also a jumper but he was picky. He didn't like the colour. There was still nobody about when he came across a wallet in a jacket hanging on the coat rack. Not much in it but he was pleased to find a neatly folded ten-bob note in a hidden pocket inside. Obviously somebody's emergency fund. Well, he had an emergency right now so it would come in handy, thank you very much.

After a good wash in the gents', he used his finger to clean his teeth rather than risk using the toothbrush in the wash bag. You never knew what the patient had died of. The trousers were a bit short barely reaching to the top of his shoes but hopefully no one would notice. Besides, he had no other choice. With his hair looking tidier, Bob helped himself to a porter's brown coat in case he needed it. Hearing voices, he had only just nipped out of the room before a couple of men came in to have a cup of tea and a bit of a break.

Bob knew the nurses were moved around the hospital, so he had no idea which ward Amélie would be working on. When he had befriended her all that time ago, she'd been in men's surgical. It was pot luck as to where she would be now. He walked around the building peering into windows but when a nurse on the children's ward spotted him, he realised that was a bad idea. He desperately needed another place where he could safely watch out for her. That was when he remembered the tea bar run by the WVS was not far from the staff canteen. Amélie was sure to go there in her lunch break. It was time to change his tactics.

He bought a newspaper and with a cup of tea in front of him, he positioned himself so that he could keep an eye on the girls as they came to the canteen for their lunch break. In the quiet moments when nobody was about, he read the newspaper. He was a bit alarmed to see that the accident and the prison break had already reached the Stop Press column.

Two guards and young offender killed in prison van crash. Prisoner and guard injured. Five escape. Police appeal for witnesses.

Bob breathed a sigh of relief. There must be a God in heaven. Although it was in the paper, there were no pictures and no names.

Chapter 33

As it turned out, the next day, Lennard had to attend a church parade in Christ Church, Grafton Road. The church, famed for the Fishermen's Gallery, was the preferred option because it seated nine hundred people. The place was packed but after the service itself, Lennard marched out into the autumn sunshine with the rest of his comrades to be dismissed.

Amélie had attended the same service and joined him in Crescent Road.

'My car is around the corner,' he said.

She slipped her arm through his and he walked proudly towards it.

Parts of the south coast were banned to anyone but those living there and even the people going to work in Lancing had to have special permits. The troops gathering all along the whole of the south coast of England had to number in the thousands by now and it seemed that the whole country was awaiting the call to liberate France. It couldn't be long now, surely. For that reason, it seemed expedient to go up country for the day.

'I'd like you to meet my family,' he told her. 'They live

in Petworth. If you like, we could drive over there and have a game of tennis.'

'Oh I wish you had told me,' she complained mildly. 'I'd have brought my racket.'

Lennard grinned. 'I'm sure they can find you one.'

She had done her best to take it all in her stride but in truth she was suddenly nervous. Was he serious about her? She liked him a lot but the thought of what her step-father had done hung over her like a heavy black cloak.

He suddenly reached over and squeezed her hands in her lap. 'It'll be fine.'

The drive was wonderful. His car had a soft top which was wound down. With the sun on her shoulders and the wind in her hair, it had been a long time since Amélie felt so happy, so free. At times they passed army vehicles, but for the most part it was only rolling hills and the Sussex weald, grazing sheep and the sight of groups of volunteers from the agricultural camps banking up row upon row of potatoes. The camps were proving to be very popular. It was an ideal way to have a holiday and earn some money. Men could earn a shilling an hour, women ten pence. The camp itself cost four shillings a day, and all they had to bring was a cup, plate, a towel and a pillow case. Everything else was provided. If she hadn't been working so hard in the hospital and helping out in Norah's market garden in her off duty, Amélie would have been sorely tempted to join them.

They arrived by a pair of empty gate pillars in a small lane and Lennard turned the wheel. After going a fair distance down a driveway overshadowed by tall rhododendrons, they burst into a bright gravel driveway leading to a beautiful country house. It was small by country house standards but Amélie loved it straight away. Lennard circumvented a lily pond and pulled up. Jumping over the driver's door onto the gravel, he strode to the front door and pulled an ornate handle fixed to the wall. The jangle of the bell was enough to waken the dead.

A few moments later, the door opened and a grey-haired woman cried out, 'Lennard, darling! What a lovely surprise.'

She hugged him tightly. Amélie watched them with a slight tinge of longing to see Mireille again and of course, Linnet. Oh to have such a greeting.

'Mother,' she heard him say as they linked arms and walked back to the car, 'I want you to meet a very special person. This is Amélie.'

Amélie stepped out onto the gravel path, her hand extended for a formal handshake.

'How lovely,' said Lennard's mother, and ignoring Amélie's hand, she embraced her, kissing both cheeks. 'Amélie . . .' she said, threading her arm through hers, 'That's French, isn't it?'

Bewildered but happy, Amélie nodded.

'How marvellous,' the older woman cried. 'My grand-mother was French.'

The day had been tedious. Bob had made his tea last for ages. Eventually the WVS woman came up to him. 'Are you going to have something to eat, dear?' she said picking up his empty cup. 'Only I'm closing at three.'

Bob hesitated before admitting, 'Actually, I'm waiting for someone.'

'Oh,' said the woman. 'And who's that?'

Bob chewed on his bottom lip.

'If you tell me her name, dear,' said the woman, 'perhaps I can help.'

'Amélie Osborne,' he said. 'She's my cousin.'

'Your cousin,' the woman said uncertainly.

Under the table, Bob clenched his fists. 'Yes,' he went

on, dropping his accent for a less educated one. 'We ain't seen each ovver for ages and I'm on leave, see? I fought I'd surprise her.'

The woman frowned. 'I can't say as I know her, dear.'

Bob shook his head sadly. 'Shame,' he murmured. 'I was 'oping to catch up. I'm off abroad, see. Far East. Should 'ave liked to have seen 'er afore I go.'

'What a shame.' The woman was full of sympathy and as a group of nurses, all laughing and talking, walked by she called out, 'Here girls, you don't know where Emily Osborne is do you? Only her long lost cousin 'ere wants to find her.'

Bob kept his head down in case one of the girls recognised him.

'You mean Amélie?' said one. 'She's off duty today.'

Bob frowned.

'You don't know where she's gone do you?' said the woman.

The girl shrugged. 'Home, I suppose.'

'Do you know the address, dear?'

The girl shook her head. 'Somewhere near Worthing station, I think.'

They went on their way and rising to his feet, Bob said, 'Fanks,' to the WVS woman.

'Sorry I wasn't much help, Luv.'

'Oh believe me you were,' said Bob.

'You mean you know where she lives?'

Bob touched his forelock in a mock salute. 'I knows exactly where she lives.'

Lennard's mother was a delightful-looking woman. Tall and elegant, she wore a lightweight dress in pale violet with a wrap-over neckline and short sleeves. Although not formally dressed she did have a two-string pearl necklace at her throat and she wore white court shoes. A delicious scent of English lavender wafted around her as she led the way into the house.

Lennard's sister Nanette was in the kitchen making sandwiches for lunch. Tall like her mother, Nanette was wearing a WAAF uniform. The familiar blue gave Amélie a jolt as she remembered Mireille but it also meant that, once they'd been introduced, the two girls had a common experience. Nan, as everyone called her, had her dark hair swept back off her face.

'I'm so glad to meet you,' she told Amélie. 'It's an absolute fluke that I'm here this afternoon.'

Amélie discovered that she was stationed at RAF Coolham near Billingshurst but even though they were in the same service, Nan had never met her sister.

It wasn't long before Lennard's mother had them all sitting in the garden among the apple trees with a pot of tea and the hastily prepared sandwiches. Amélie loved it here straight away. The flower borders were filled with old-fashioned English blooms although many of them hadn't fully blossomed yet. Mrs Carruthers chatted amiably about this and that; the WI raising funds for the war effort (she was chairwoman of the local group), the new vicar who was rather fusty and Lennard's brother who was now in Burma. Nan had been busy helping to set up the station at Coolham which was now fully commissioned. She was interested to hear that Amélie was a nurse.

'Do you think you might go abroad?'

'I can't go anywhere until I'm fully trained,' Amélie said with a smile. 'I should have almost finished by now but my term was interrupted by illness.'

'Oh?' said Nan. 'Nothing serious, I hope?'

With a quick glance in Lennard's direction, Amélie shook her head. 'Everything's fine now.'

Lennard could tell that his sister was dying for the details so he interrupted the conversation. 'I forgot to tell you, Mother. They've put me in the Royal Army Pay Corps,' he said. 'I'm to be a paymaster with the rank of captain but once I've settled in, it looks as if I shall shortly become a staff paymaster.'

Mrs Carruthers looked slightly bemused but Amélie understood perfectly. The day they'd had lunch at the Stanhoe, Lennard had explained that unable to shoot a gun because of his hand injury, he'd been given the choice of leaving the army or settling for a non-combatant post. Until the powers-that-be could decide where he was best suited, he'd been put in charge of rounding up deserters and men who had gone AWOL. The RAPC was a much better posting, one which meant Lennard's career in the armed forces wasn't over – not by a long chalk.

The conversation died as everyone relaxed. 'I thought we might have a game of tennis,' Lennard said, after they'd enjoyed a time in the sunshine.

'Rather,' Nan enthused. 'Shall I ask Roddy Brooks to come over and then we could have a foursome?'

'Brilliant,' said Lennard and turning to his mother he added, 'Could Amélie borrow some tennis shoes?'

'Of course,' said Mrs Carruthers. 'And perhaps you'd like to change into something more comfortable, my dear?'

They took Amélie indoors and Nan made a dash for the telephone. 'I think we may be roughly the same size,' said Mrs Carruthers as she and Amélie headed up the stairs to her bedroom, before adding tactfully, 'although perhaps I am a little bigger.'

Amélie accepted the white tennis culottes and the white blouse she offered and changed behind the wardrobe door. Lennard's mother sat on her bed with her back to her and waited. 'Have you known Lennard long?'

'A few months, that's all.'

'So you didn't know him before his accident.'

'No.'

'How did you meet?' She paused before adding, 'He never tells me anything.'

'My sister and I came to Worthing with the evacuees,' Amélie said. 'We went to live with Norah and Uncle Jim and I met him there. He and Uncle Jim are great friends.'

'Uncle Jim being the policeman?'

'Yes, that's right.'

'You're very young.'

'I'm nearly eighteen,' she added, stretching the truth a little.

Amélie emerged from behind the door.

Mrs Carruthers looked her up and down approvingly. 'Ah, tennis shoes!' she cried. The next minute she was rummaging in the back of a cupboard to look for them. Amélie accepted them gratefully.

'There,' she said when she was ready. 'Will I do?'

'You're a very attractive girl,' said Lennard's mother. 'I can quite understand why he's smitten with you.'

Amélie could feel her face heating up.

Mrs Carruthers sighed. 'You know, once upon a time Lennard was such a good-looking boy.' Amélie could hear the sadness in his mother's voice as she spoke. There was a pause and then she added, 'You don't seem to mind?'

Amélie was confused. 'Mind what?'

'That ugly scar,' said his mother. 'The way he looks now.'

Amélie gave her a puzzled look. 'Why should I mind? Lennard is a lovely person. He's been so kind to me. He makes me feel safe.'

'Safe?' said Mrs Carruthers. 'That's a strange word.'

Amélie looked away, feeling slightly awkward. She wished she hadn't said it and she didn't want this conversation either. 'I know your son has a war wound, Mrs Carruthers,' she said in a more measured tone, 'but I honestly don't think about it. Lennard is Lennard and I'm just happy to have his friendship.'

Back outside and on the tennis court, Amélie and Lennard played against Roddy and Nan, beating them in straight sets which was hardly surprising because, far from the dashing young pilot Amélie imagined was coming, Roddy turned out to be at least fifty and very unfit.

Deep in the French countryside, Mireille had been helping with banking up the potato crop. It was back breaking and boring work but very necessary. If the nation was to survive the winter, the farm had to do all it could. All else had been temporarily halted. For some reason, the Germans had increased their patrols and spot checks had become more common, probably because everybody was expecting the Allies to make an attempt at invasion. Mireille could only spend seconds on the wireless because to linger any longer was too dangerous. Three groups had been rounded up in the past couple of weeks and Mireille's group were particularly jittery. They were hiding an English RAF pilot.

'I want you to spend the afternoon with Lieutenant Dixon,' Claude told her. 'He's been passed on from Lavender but he gives me a bad feeling right here in my gut.' He pressed his fist over his stomach. 'You know what I mean?'

Mireille nodded.

'See what you can find out about him.'

Mireille played the part of *bon ami* in the barn for the whole of one afternoon. They kept watch for the German patrol which was in the habit of coming around every second Tuesday. If it turned up, the pilot would have to be hidden under the trap door beneath some bales of hay.

Lieutenant Dixon – *do call me Nigel* – said he was

stationed at Tangmere but from the way he said it, it was obvious that he hadn't expected Mireille to have even heard of it. She was thrilled to be able to talk to him about somewhere so familiar.

'Before the war,' she told him as she opened the box of games they kept there in case their 'guests' got bored, 'my sister and I used to stay in Littlehampton with my aunt.'

'Ah yes,' said Nigel. 'Littlehampton.'

'Haven't you been there?' Mireille said as she got the draughts board out. 'It's less than ten miles from Tangmere.'

'Of course,' he said. 'I know it well.'

While she set up the draughts board, they chatted amiably about the English love of cricket and playing tennis. Nigel told her his father was a doctor and his mother came from a wealthy family. As a boy, he explained, he had been a pupil at Christ's Hospital in Horsham.

'Very impressive,' said Mireille turning the corners of her mouth down. 'I guess that's why you plumped for a Sussex airfield for your service.'

'Nothing beats Sussex,' he said, taking one of her pieces.

'Why the RAF?' she asked. 'Why not the army?'

'Every chap wants to fly,' he said decisively. 'How long were you in England? What's your favourite memory?'

'Only a couple of weeks and my favourite was when Uncle Edward used to take us fishing off Littlehampton pier,' she said, her eyes lighting up. 'He was quite old and after lunch he always fell asleep. As soon as he started dozing, we used to slope off and have a ride on one of the end of the pier amusements. I especially liked the American dodgem cars.'

'How funny,' Nigel agreed as he tapped his counter right across the board taking with it five of her draught pieces. 'That was what I always enjoyed as a child.'

'Well spotted,' Mireille sighed. 'You're so much better at this than I am. Can you play piquet or backgammon?'

Nigel pulled a face. 'I've never been much of a one for board games.'

'Tell me,' she began again as they got the playing cards out, 'did you ever go to that lovely café in the twitten?'

Nigel shook his head. 'What, in Littlehampton?'

'No, silly,' Mireille chuckled. 'The one opposite the airfield.'

'Oh, that one,' he said. 'No I haven't tried it out yet.'

'When you get back home, you really should try it,' said Mireille, dealing out seven cards each. 'Of course everything may have changed what with the war and everything, but they do the most delicious bread pudding.'

The German patrol didn't pass by the farm that day and later in the evening, she told Claude the reason why. 'He's no RAF pilot,' she said, 'and he's certainly never been to Tangmere. There's no pier in Littlehampton and if he'd lived in Sussex he'd know that a twitten is a Sussex word for the alleyway between two houses.'

She never asked Claude what happened to Lieutenant Dixon – *do call me Nigel* – but she never saw him again. The German patrols recommenced a few days later.

Chapter 34

Ivan was tired. It had been a long day and there was so much to do in the market garden. He loved being out of doors, but he was beginning to feel his age. He just didn't have the stamina he'd had when he was thirty. Back then he could do a full day's work and tend his garden all evening. He and Ada often took a walk along the seafront, getting home late, but back then he could get up first thing in the morning and start all over again. These days he needed a rest between jobs.

He drove the spade into soft earth by the shed. It needed a clean. 'A workman is only as good as his tools.' He'd had that drummed into him as a lad so it was always his habit to clean his spade or fork or trowel when he'd finished for the day but he'd have a bit of a smoke first. He took out his roll-ups and settled into the clapped-out old armchair in the shed. He might even have a bit of a doze until tea time.

He'd finished his cigarette and was thinking of getting up when he became aware that he wasn't alone. Someone was outside. People often called round to buy stuff but this didn't feel right. The hairs on the back of his neck began to rise. Suddenly wide awake, he sat up and peered through the tattered curtain at the window.

The sun had cast a long shadow on the ground by the wall. Someone was just around the corner. He had pressed himself against the brickwork and was watching the back door. Ivan could hear the sound of the dogs barking from somewhere inside the house. He frowned. 'What the devil . . . ?'

He pulled himself wearily up and opened the shed door as quietly as he could but the door creaked on its hinges. As the person in shadow turned to look at him, Ivan gasped. 'Good God! What the hell are you doing here?'

Their time in Petworth ended all too soon. Amélie had enjoyed herself as never before. As they took their leave of Mrs Carruthers and Nan, the women all embraced as if they had known each other for years. Lennard kissed his mother and sister and climbed into the car alongside Amélie. With a toot of his horn, they both waved and he drove back onto the main road.

'They are such lovely people,' Amélie sighed.

Lennard chuckled. 'They were certainly taken with you,' he said. 'My mother especially.'

'Oh?' Amélie said innocently.

'She's probably only thinking I could do with a personal nurse on the cheap,' he said teasingly.

Amélie shook her head. 'Bad idea,' she said. 'I'd give you castor oil every night.'

'Oh spare me, spare me,' he cried and they both laughed.

They'd only gone a few miles when Lennard pulled the car over and stopped. A second or two later he turned to face her. 'Amélie, I know we haven't known each other all that long,' he began what was obviously a well-rehearsed speech, 'but you've become very special to me.'

She smiled shyly.

'I'm no oil painting—'

'Don't say that,' she interrupted.

They held each other's gaze and then she added, 'I have scars too. The only difference between us is that you can't see mine. Yours are visible and it hurts me to know the pain you've suffered, but when I look at you, I see you Lennard. Not the scars.' She reached up and gently touched his face. 'Since I started my training again, I feel much stronger although I confess that I'm a bit worried that my scars may be more difficult to overcome. But when I'm with you I'm not afraid like I was with my step-father.'

'I would never ask you to do something you didn't want to,' he said.

'I know.' She smiled again. 'Thank you.'

'I-I think it best if we take things slowly,' he went on, 'but I wanted you know that I'm serious about us.'

She nodded and he turned to start the car again. 'It doesn't have to be that slowly,' she said suddenly emboldened.

He hesitated. No words passed between them as he turned the ignition off again and leaned towards her. As she lifted her face, he lowered his head and his lips found hers once more.

'Where is she?'

Bob Kane walked across the yard towards him. For a man who prided himself on his appearance, Ivan thought he looked distinctly odd. His trouser bottoms were above his ankles and the shirt he was wearing looked more like a workman's. Even his shoes looked a size too big. 'What are you doing here?' Ivan said. 'I thought you were in jail.'

Bob poked him with his finger. 'I asked you a question,

old man,' he said, his plummy voice sounding even more menacing than usual. 'Where is she?'

Ivan frowned as he tried to make sense of what was happening and then it dawned on him. 'That prison van,' he said cautiously. 'It said in my paper that three people were killed and the prisoners had escaped. They caught three of them pretty soon after but one is still at large.' He took in his breath. 'That's you, isn't it?'

'Too right it's me,' said Bob, his face inches away, 'and I've come back for Amélie, so where is she?'

'She's not here,' said Ivan leaning back. 'She must be on the ward.'

Bob's hand went straight to Ivan's throat. 'Well, she isn't at the hospital because I went there. They told me she'd gone home, so where is she?'

Ivan struggled to get Bob's hand away but he was already choking him. 'I told you,' he spluttered. 'I don't know but she's not here.'

Bob let go. 'She wouldn't go out on her own because I told her not to,' he said. 'Is she with that Norah?'

'Look lad,' Ivan said in a more measured tone as he tried to calm the situation. 'You got yourself into a bit of trouble but everything's moved on. Give yourself up; do your bird and then you can start over.'

'What do you mean, everything's moved on?'

Ivan sighed. 'Amélie's got herself a new beau now.'

The minute the words were out of his mouth, Ivan regretted them. He saw something flash in Bob's eyes and the grimace on his face became even more terrifying. He lashed out with his fist, hitting the old man on the jaw and Ivan staggered backwards. Before he could regain his balance, Bob grabbed the spade Ivan had left in the ground and swung it back.

'No, no,' Ivan cried, but the spade hit him with such

284

force that he was propelled into the shed door. There was an almighty bang as it slammed shut and Ivan crumpled to the ground. Winded and in pain, Ivan was only slightly aware of the spade being dropped and his assailant running away from the house. As he tried to move, Ivan winced. He could hear the dogs barking frantically to be let out but something was happening to him. It was as if his mind was losing its sharpness, becoming woolly. His head hurt where he'd hit the door but more than that, he couldn't focus his eyes properly. He tried to lift his left arm but it felt like a dead weight and he couldn't do it. When he pushed himself up to stand, he couldn't do that either. There was something wrong with his leg.

The back door opened and the dogs rushed out. They looked around in bewilderment before dashing towards the road. Then out of the fog surrounding him, Ivan heard a voice – Christine's.

'Ivan! Oh my goodness, what's happened? Are you all right?'

He tried to answer but the words came out all wrong. He'd meant to say, 'I feel a bit queer,' but instead, he heard himself saying something that sounded like. 'Pot – face – driver.' What was all that about? And why was his mouth all floppy? He didn't like this. His heart began to beat faster.

'Numbly.' Now he was overwhelmingly frightened. 'Numbly. Hay car fline,' he said his voice louder but even more slurry.

'Norah,' Christine yelled in panic. 'Ring for an ambulance. I think my Ivan's had a stroke.'

Lennard thought it expedient to take Amélie straight back to the hospital. She had made him deliriously happy with her kisses and they'd lingered longer than he had intended. He'd had a wonderful day. As he drove back to Worthing,

285

he kept glancing in her direction and then he'd smile to himself. *How lucky can you be?* He'd got a beautiful woman who was self-possessed and strong; she was every man's dream. He could understand her reticence when it came to intimacy but he was determined to take that one step at a time. He guessed that when he held her close to him in the car, she was thinking of what that bloody swine had done to her. He'd done his best to soothe her fears away. It wouldn't be easy for either of them. After all, he was battling with his own natural urges. His skin had tingled, his heart had thumped and he'd burned with desire as they'd kissed, but he'd held himself in check. Not that easy when she was such a terrific girl! Even thinking about it now made him want to hold her all over again. He concentrated on the road and forced himself to think of something else.

'When is your next day off?' he asked as she opened the car door outside the nurses' home.

'Not for two weeks,' she said glumly. 'I'm on night duty tomorrow.'

'I'll take you out when it's over. Don't take any other bookings,' he joked.

'I won't.' She smiled. 'Thank you for such a lovely day.'

He pressed her hand to his lips and kissed her fingers. 'The pleasure was all mine.'

A man with his hands in his pockets turned his head as he walked past but he didn't speak. Lennard waited until she had opened the door of the nurses' home. She turned and waved before closing the door. Lennard gave her a mock salute and drove off.

At eight o'clock the next morning there was a knock on Amélie's door. When she opened it, Home Sister was standing there. 'Matron wants to see you in her office,

Nurse Osborne,' she said curtly. 'I suggest you get dressed quickly.'

Amélie was puzzled. 'Is something wrong?'

'No time for questions, girl,' Home Sister snapped. 'It doesn't do to keep Matron waiting.'

After a hasty wash and a change of uniform apron, Amélie was ready. To her surprise, Home Sister was still in the corridor waiting for her. The two of them hurried to the main building together.

Matron was behind her desk when Amélie was called in. When she motioned for her to sit down, Amélie's mouth went dry. Nobody ever sat down in Matron's office. You stood by the desk and looked straight ahead as if you were a naughty school girl. She lowered herself into the chair. Something dreadful had happened, hadn't it? Immediately her mind went into a tailspin. Who was it? Mireille? Norah? Uncle Jim? Lennard? Oh please don't tell me something's happened to Lennard.

Matron's expression didn't change. 'I've been asked to inform you that your foster grandfather is on Men's Medical.'

Immediately Amélie was on her feet. 'Ivan?'

Matron nodded gravely. 'I'm sad to say that he appears to have had a stroke.'

'A stroke!' Amélie gasped in horror. 'Oh no! May I go to him now, Matron?'

Matron nodded and by the time she'd picked up the internal telephone to tell Sister Warren that Nurse Osborne was on her way to the ward, Amélie had already left the office.

When she got to Men's Medical, there was a screen around the bed. Amélie pulled it back and Christine rose to her feet. Her eyes were puffy from crying and she was very pale.

287

'Oh Mémé,' Amélie blurted out. She held her arms open and Christine went to her.

'He's quieter now,' she whispered tearfully after they'd hugged each other. 'I don't know how it happened. He seemed perfectly all right yesterday afternoon. He went out for his ciggy and to clean his spade and then we heard this terrific bang. I went to see what had happened and he was sitting on the ground with his back to the shed door.'

Amélie moved towards the bed. Ivan looked peaceful, but it was obvious that he'd lost control of the left side of his face. The skin was droopy and his mouth lax. There was a bruise on his jaw and he was drooling. She sighed. Poor Ivan. If it was a stroke, he'd probably lost the use of his arm and maybe even his leg as well.

'I'm so sorry, Mémé.'

At the sound of her voice, Ivan opened his eyes and became very agitated. He was trying to tell them something but his speech was slurry and he wasn't making sense.

'It's all right, Ivan,' Amélie said as she patted his arm. 'Don't upset yourself. I know everything feels strange at the moment, but you need to rest.'

'Lob,' he cried earnestly. 'Lob.'

They both jumped as the screen was pulled back and the ward sister came in with a kidney dish and syringe. 'Now, now Mr Steele,' she said curtly. 'We mustn't get so het up, must we? You're disturbing the other patients. Now hold still. I'm going to give you something to help you sleep.'

They watched as she injected him and gradually he became quieter.

'I suggest you go home and get some sleep, Mrs Steele,' said the ward sister. 'After that injection he'll be knocked out for a while and the sleep will do him good. Visiting is from five-thirty to seven tonight.'

Ivan was unaware that the two women were leaving. And as Amélie watched poor Mémé's hunched and sad figure heading for the bus stop, she could feel her own eyes pricking with tears. Ivan was in the best place; he was having the best care but it didn't look good.

Chapter 35

The day was overcast but it wasn't raining. There were few people about in Homefield Park. The children were back at school after the half term spring break so the only strollers were the elderly or those, like herself, waiting to be allowed into the hospital.

Norah had badly wanted to see Ivan but of course Christine took precedence. He had been on the ward for almost a week now but there was no sign of improvement. At times he seemed to be aware that someone was with him. When Christine chatted about family things, he would become very emotional, but his lines of communication were limited. At times he seemed frustrated, as if he was trying to tell them something important but the right words just wouldn't come. At other times there was a look of despair on his face which was hardly surprising because he had lost the use of his left side and was doubly incontinent. It was all very distressing for her mother-in-law which was why Norah had suggested that they take Terry for a walk in the park. They had pushed the pram from Clifton Road, then Norah had done a circuit while Christine went to the ward. The idea was that Christine would come out just before visiting time was over and look after the baby while Norah went in to see Ivan for the last ten minutes. Terry would be a welcome distraction, giving Christine the opportunity to come to terms with whatever the situation was before they made their way back home.

'Victor, Victor, come here.'

Norah froze. She recognised his mother's voice at once. A little boy threw himself at her legs and hugged her skirts. Norah looked down to see Victor . . . and her hand automatically ruffled his hair.

'Hello sweetheart,' she said, bending to his level. As she gave him a hug, Norah was aware of Penny's shoes coming up beside him.

She rose to her feet. 'Sorry,' she said, her face heating with embarrassment, 'I had no idea you'd be here.'

'We usually play on the green,' Penny said, 'but I've arranged to meet someone.'

The two women exchanged an awkward smile.

'Is that . . . ?' Penny began.

Norah nodded. 'We've called him Terry.'

Penny stretched her neck but didn't go any nearer to the pram.

'You can look at him if you want,' said Norah, adding, 'if it's not too painful.'

Penny hesitated but then Victor said, 'Me see baba, Mummy.'

Penny gave her a helpless look.

'I'll walk away if you prefer,' Norah said quietly.

'Me see baba, Mummy,' the little boy insisted.

Penny sucked in her lips. 'No,' she said to Norah. 'It's all right. They're going to grow up in the same town, aren't they? It would be better if everything was as natural as possible, wouldn't it?'

Norah nodded and at the same time she gave Penny's

forearm a friendly grip. Penny reached down and picked up her firstborn son then the two of them leaned over the pram to admire the baby who was his half-brother, something he would never know.

'Baba,' Victor said, and at the same moment, Terry opened his eyes. He gazed intently at Victor hovering in his mother's arms just above him and eventually gave him a gummy smile. Then Victor wriggled to get down.

As she let him go, Penny's eyes were red-rimmed. On impulse, Norah put her arms around her old friend and gave her a hug. 'Thank you,' she whispered into Penny's hair. 'I'll always be grateful for what you've done.'

As they parted, Penny looked round and saw that her son was heading for the lake. There was no time for goodbyes.

'No, Victor,' Penny shouted as she ran after him. 'No. Come away from there.'

Much to Norah's relief, Penny caught his arm when he was about six feet from the water's edge. From there she looked up and gave Norah a friendly wave. As Norah returned the wave, it all felt rather surreal, but at the same time, she was glad that there hadn't been any awkwardness. Not that Penny could do anything about changing the status quo anyway. The papers were all signed. Terry was her baby in every sense of the word. Hers and Jim's.

'Was that Penny?' said Christine, coming up behind her.

'Yes,' said Norah. 'She and Victor came over to look at the baby.'

'Funny we never seem to see her these days, do we?'

'Umm,' said Norah, handing over the pram.

'She all right?' said Christine.

'Fine,' said Norah. Her mother-in-law was giving her a sceptical look. 'You know how it is when you've got an under five,' Norah continued. 'She's busy, that's all.'

*

Ivan looked peaceful when Norah got there. She lowered herself onto the chair beside the bed and reached for his hand. It was as cold as ice. She sat stroking it for the ten minutes she had left before the ward sister rang the bell to signify that visiting time was over. As she stood to go, Ivan opened his eyes.

She was alarmed to see a look of bewilderment, confusion, or was it fear, flitting across his face? He grasped Norah's fingers with his right hand and said something completely unintelligible.

'I have to go now, Ivan,' she said quietly. 'Sister has rung the bell but we'll be here to see you tomorrow, okay?'

'Porter,' he said with a sudden clarity but she still couldn't understand. He tried again mumbling something, something then 'zeer.' She frowned. 'Portson zeer.' She still didn't get it and now he was beginning to sound desperate. 'Lob.' When she only smiled he shouted louder. 'Lob.'

The sister came over.

'He's upset about something,' Norah said apologetically, 'but I'm afraid I don't understand.'

'It happens a lot with stroke victims,' she said. 'Don't worry. He's being well looked after.'

Ivan sank back down onto the pillows and let her hand slip from his fingers. Norah reached over and kissed his forehead. 'Try not to worry, Ivan,' she said gently. 'We'll come back tomorrow.'

He turned his head away and Norah felt awful. Something was deeply troubling him. If only she knew what it was.

Worthing police station was always busy. Jim had spent all morning dealing with the drunk and disorderly from the night before. Some had to appear before the magistrates because they'd caused a lot of damage in their inebriated state and others had to be signed over to the custody of the military police. It was all paperwork and moving people around.

It was hardly surprising that the town was in the grip of a minor crime wave. There were a lot of disgruntled and bored military personnel in the surrounding areas and at night time they would drift into the Worthing pubs and bars to drown their sorrows. For the last three months everybody had been preparing for the so called 'big push' but so far it hadn't happened. The men were resentful because they felt that they had travelled halfway around the world, leaving home and family and all that was dear to them, just to sit around in their tents or to play war games on the Downs. All they wanted was to 'just get on with it'.

Relationships with the locals were deteriorating as well. The punch-ups between Worthing lads and the soldiers had become more vicious and there was resentment when the girls they'd grown up with ditched their old boyfriends and took up with the Canadians. It all seemed rather trivial when compared with what was happening on the mainland of Europe but it meant a lot of careful diplomacy between the army and civic leaders with Jim more often than not acting as piggy-in-the-middle.

The memo, when it appeared on his desk was a welcome distraction. He'd seen a report about the accident in his newspaper. A prison van on its way to Lewes prison had hit a bomb crater, veered off the road and down a steep embankment, coming to rest against the upright of a railway bridge. The driver and passenger were killed outright, as was a young lad inside the van. One of the guards inside the van had a broken leg and four prisoners had escaped. Three had been recaptured by police the following day but one man was still at large. The one bit of information that wasn't in his newspaper was the name of the absconder. Robert Kane.

Jim's blood ran cold. If Bob came back to Worthing,

Amélie could be in danger. He knew Bob had no family ties in Worthing so he might go back to . . . Shropshire, wasn't it? Or maybe it was Ruislip. The man was such a pathological liar it was hard to know the truth. On reflection, Jim couldn't risk it. He had to find out if the man was in Worthing and the only way to do that was to go to the hospital.

Jim took a young constable with him. PC Bromley was as keen as mustard and had the makings of a first-class copper. Having seen Matron and got her permission, they made their way to the porter's room.

It didn't take long to discover that no one in the hospital had seen Kane and none of them were in touch with him.

'I doubt he'd come here anyway,' said Mr Mallard, the senior porter.

'Oh and why's that?' asked Jim.

'Nobody liked him much,' said Stan who appeared to be the spokesman for the rest. 'Cocky bastard.'

Jim blew out his cheeks. It was obvious there was nothing to be gained here. 'Well if you do come across him,' he said, 'get in touch with the station.'

'There is one thing,' said Stan. He glanced at his fellow workers. 'We don't know who, but a couple of days ago, somebody helped themselves to Mick's sandwiches.'

PC Bromley couldn't help himself. He scoffed. Jim looked more thoughtful. 'Sandwiches?'

'Come on, Stan,' someone else said. 'It was probably some dotty patient going walkabout.'

'And you are?' Jim asked.

'Cyril Docket.'

'So tell me,' said Jim. 'Where were these sandwiches?'

'I left them on the bench,' another man said, presumably Mick. 'I was late in, see, so instead of putting them in me locker, I left them there.'

Jim nodded. 'And not many people know where this room is,' he observed.

The men nodded their heads in agreement.

'Was anything else disturbed?' asked Jim.

'The lost property box had been moved.'

'Yeah,' said Stan. 'That's right. We normally leave it round the corner by the pillar but it was on the table. I know because me and Mr Mallard had words about it.'

'He's right,' said Mallard. 'I thought he'd left it there. I like a tidy workplace.'

'Percy said he thought somebody had been burning clothes,' said Cyril.

'Yeah,' someone else piped up. 'That's right.'

'Percy?' said Jim.

'Percy Cooper,' said Mr Mallard. 'The boiler man.'

Jim thanked them for their co-operation then he and Bromley left.

It was beginning to come together. Most likely Kane had been here, but where was he now? Outside in the corridor, Jim sent PC Bromley back to Matron's office.

'I want you to talk to Nurse Osborne,' he said. 'We've got no proof, but my gut tells me that she's the reason why Kane could have been here. He used to work here; she used to go out with him. The man's a nutter. That's why she packed him in but he could be sniffing around because he wants her back.'

Bromley nodded.

'I'll go and have a word with Percy Cooper,' Jim went on, 'but she needs to be warned.'

'Do you think she could be hiding him, sir?'

'Absolutely not,' said Jim. 'I want you to tell her there's every possibility he's been in the hospital. She needs to be on her guard. She could be in danger.'

'I understand, sir.'

'Go easy on the girl,' Jim cautioned. 'She's the innocent in all this.'

'Yes, sir,' said Bromley. 'Right you are, sir.'

'I'd do it myself,' said Jim, 'but it would be better coming from you. I have a vested interest.'

PC Bromley raised his eyebrows.

'I am Nurse Osborne's legal guardian.'

Chapter 36

'I don't want you to alarm yourself, Nurse,' Matron began, 'but this policeman has some rather disturbing news.'

Amélie felt her legs giving way. She had been making her own bed when Home Sister had knocked on her door and told her to go to Matron's office immediately. Her first reaction was – *what, again? What now?* The last time she'd been summoned to see Matron, it was to tell her that Ivan was in Men's Medical following a stroke. Had something happened to Ivan? Most girls only ever went to see Matron once in a lifetime and here she was, going twice in one week. When she'd walked through the door, she'd been shocked to see a police constable was with her.

'I think you'd better sit down, Miss,' said the policeman.

'Yes, yes,' Matron agreed. 'Sit down, Nurse.'

Amélie lowered herself into the chair in front of the desk and put her hands into her lap. It was a struggle not to cry out, *What's happened? Please, just tell me,* but she knew Matron was a stickler for protocol and a panicking nurse was not a good nurse.

'As you may have heard,' the policeman began, 'several prisoners have escaped from a prison van. We have now discovered that one of them was Robert Kane, the man we believe to be your ex-boyfriend.'

Amélie almost stopped breathing. It had been months since she'd seen him and it had taken all that time to come to terms with the fact that he wasn't the hero she had first thought, but a manipulative and coercive bully. Having met someone as wonderful as Lennard, the last thing she ever wanted was to come into contact with Bob again.

'He was in the process of being sent to Lewes prison,' the constable continued his well-rehearsed speech, 'to await trial on several other charges.'

'PC Bromley believes that he may try and make contact with you,' Matron interrupted. 'Now we don't want to frighten you, but yesterday Mrs Marshall, the lady in charge of the WVS tea bar, told me that a man was asking about you. He said he was your cousin.'

'I don't have any cousins,' Amélie said with a frown. 'My only blood relatives are my two sisters.'

Matron and the police officer exchanged an anxious look.

'Well, there's no point in hiding away,' said PC Bromley, 'just be careful. And if—'

'I'll ask one of your colleagues to keep an eye on you and don't go anywhere on your own,' Matron interrupted again, 'especially at night.'

'I'm on night duty for two weeks, Matron.'

'Even better,' said Matron. 'Which ward?'

'Children's.'

'I'll have a word with Night Sister.' She looked up at Bromley. 'Is that all, Constable?'

'I think so, Matron.' He glanced back at Amélie. 'If you should see Kane, ring the station immediately. Don't approach him. We believe he's a dangerous and unpredictable man.'

Amélie nodded and rose to her feet.

'Thank you, Constable,' Matron said dismissively. 'Good afternoon, Nurse.'

Percy Cooper, the boiler man, had been most helpful. Yes, somebody had been burning material but he couldn't say what it was. He'd noticed it when he'd come to fill up the boiler although the smell gave the game away long before he'd opened the hatch.

Just as Jim was about to leave, he asked if Jim had spoken to Mrs Marshall.

'Is there any reason why I should?'

'It's probably nothing,' Percy conceded, 'but a few days ago she spoke to some bloke who was asking after one of the nurses. Funny-looking chap, he was, so she said. Smart trousers that were way too short and a workman's shirt. Said he was her cousin, but when she'd thought about it, it didn't seem kosher, if you know what I mean.'

'Did Mrs Marshall tell you the name of this nurse?'

'She may have done,' said Percy, 'but I can't recall.'

'And where is Mrs Marshall?'

'She only mans the WVS stall on Thursday and Friday,' said Percy. He sighed. 'Pity really. I'd like to see more of her. She's got a nice pair of legs.'

Jim suppressed a smile and turned to leave.

'Osborne,' said Percy as he suddenly recalled the name. 'That was it. Nurse Osborne.'

Jim thanked him. So it must have been Kane. He'd come to find Amélie the day she was out with Lennard. Thank God for that. Because he knew PC Bromley was with Amélie right now, Jim decided not to seek her out. He didn't want her frightened any more than she needed to be and Bromley's cautious warning should suffice for now. While he was in the hospital he decided he may as well visit Ivan. Lord knows when he'd get another opportunity and what with everything else going on, he hadn't had time to see him yet.

His mother was sitting next to the bed when Jim poked his head around the screens. Ivan seemed calm and when he saw Jim he tried to speak but he could only make guttural sounds. Jim shook his good hand and drew up a chair. Hospital visits were always awkward because he could never think of what to say.

As his mother prattled on, Jim was looking intently at Ivan. 'It looks as if someone has given him a sock in the jaw, Mother,' he said absentmindedly.

'I thought that too,' said Christine, 'but there was nobody with him outside. You went out for your ciggy, didn't you Luv.'

Ivan became agitated.

'Has he got any other injuries?' said Jim.

Christine pulled down the bedclothes and opened Ivan's pyjamas top. There on his chest was a large oddly square shaped bruise. 'The nurse asked me how he got it,' said Christine, 'but I don't know.' She buttoned up the jacket. 'Perhaps when he fell?'

Ivan was making noises again and . . . and was he trying to shake his head? Jim couldn't be sure. He moved his chair closer to the bed. 'I think you can understand what I'm saying, can't you old chap?'

Ivan's eyes widened.

'I'm going to hold your good hand,' said Jim, 'and I want you to squeeze mine once for "yes" and twice for "no". Got it?'

Ivan squeezed Jim's hand once.

'Now do a "no".'

Ivan's tremulous fingers squeezed his twice.

'Was someone with you when you had the stroke?'

'I already told you, Jim,' Christine interrupted. 'He was on his own.'

Jim turned to her. 'Mother, I need you to be quiet. I want to hear what Ivan has to say, all right?'

Irritated, Christine pursed her lips.

Her son repeated his question. 'When you had your stroke, were you alone?'

Two squeezes.

'Did that person hit you?'

One squeeze.

'Punched you on the jaw?'

It took a few seconds but there it was: one squeeze.

'And did he hit you with an implement?'

No reply this time. Jim decided it was the word he'd used. He rephrased the question. 'Did he have something in his hand when he hit you?'

One squeeze.

'Do I know that person?'

'Lob,' said Ivan. 'Awwrrass Lob.'

Jim glanced at his mother. 'He keeps saying that,' she said with an exasperated shake of her head. 'It doesn't mean anything.'

'Oh I think it does, Mother,' said Jim. 'Ivan was it Bob Kane who hit you?'

One solid squeeze told him all he wanted to know.

They had all gathered in the Lilacs, everyone in sombre clothes and black ties, to say their goodbyes to Ivan. Elsie had come down to look after Terry for Norah and Jim and in a few minutes they'd all walk to St Matthew's behind the funeral cortege.

The end, when it came, had been peaceful. Christine had been beside him, holding his hand when he'd opened his eyes for the first time in almost a week.

'Hello, Luv,' she'd said moving closer. She'd had high hopes that he would start to pull through now but then he'd let out a long sigh and his head lolled. Her first reaction was to shout for the nurse but of course as soon as she came running, Christine wished she'd waited a minute or two to collect her thoughts. She was shooed away while they checked her husband, something she already knew was a lost cause. Ivan was gone.

It was a bitter blow. They'd only had four years together; four very happy years. The best four years of her whole life. She had thought they would grow old together but it wasn't to be. Everybody was very kind but her greatest surprise was to come on the day of the funeral. So many people turned up to say their goodbyes. Friends and neighbours, people from the school where he'd been a caretaker for over twenty years, fellow market stall holders and customers alike, members of the police force, folks from the church and people he had helped in those first dark weeks of the war. They lined Clifton Road and they were all along Tarring Road almost as far as St Matthew's. 'He was much loved,' might be a tired cliché but in Ivan's case it was true.

After the service, the cortege went up to Durrington cemetery where Ivan was laid to rest near an ash tree halfway up the hill. He would have liked that. It was almost like being in the countryside.

Back at the Lilacs, when friends and neighbours stopped by for sandwiches and a cup of tea, there was a bit of a wait for a cup and saucer until Val Boon next door ran home to fetch some of her crockery. Amélie had time off from the hospital and Ginger came from Tangmere to play some of Ivan's favourites on the piano. Lennard was there too and it pleased her to see how happy he made Amélie. The girl was like a granddaughter to her and she deserved

303

a little happiness after all that business with that blighter. Christine sighed. She wished he would get caught. Ivan as good as said he was the reason why he'd ended up as he did. If only she could lay her hands on that Bob creature, he wouldn't hurt anyone else, that was for sure.

A widow for the second time, she wasn't sure what the future held for her but she wouldn't allow herself to become bitter again. Ivan had shown her a better way and she wasn't about to go back. When she felt more up to it, she would go to the WI, and the crafty ladies. She couldn't manage the market stall on her own, but she could take a turn in the market garden shop.

Amélie slipped onto the arm of the chair beside her. 'All right, Mémé?'

Christine nodded. 'So many people.'

'Everybody loved Ivan,' said Amélie. 'Even my sister!'

They laughed and then someone called Amélie into the kitchen. After giving her a hug and planting a kiss on the top of Christine's head, she hurried away to help with the teas. Christine watched her go with a small tug of love. Amélie hardly ever mentioned Mireille these days. Where on earth could she be and what was she doing? She was supposed to have gone to France but surely she wouldn't have been there all this time? Christine shivered. There was no knowing if she was dead or alive.

The last time Christine had gone to the pictures, which was not long before Ivan died, Gaumont British News showed a film of the Allies bombing German installations and factories in France, but with no idea where Mireille was there was little point in worrying about her.

Only she did worry about her – for Amélie's sake.

Chapter 37

Mireille was exhausted. If the average lifetime of an agent was six weeks, she'd done well. She'd been in France for almost six months but during most of that time she had been living under the most enormous strain. She had begun her sojourn by reporting to HQ and helping the local resistance with raids and sabotage but now her duties had changed. Walter Mitchel (code name Zeus) had been captured a few weeks after the rail disaster, betrayed everybody thought, by someone in the village. Never a popular man (he had a bad reputation as far as the ladies were concerned) he had been taken to Gestapo HQ where he would presumably be tortured. Yveline had been quite upset about it, refusing to talk about him. She and Zeus had been walking out together and she'd told Mireille that she'd hoped they would marry after the war. But that was before she found out that he was also seeing Pierre Latout's wife. Even though he was a bit of a rogue, everyone was concerned because they knew from past experience that there was every possibility they'd never see him again. As soon as word got around, steps were taken to move vulnerable agents and sympathisers alike. It wouldn't be long before the Germans came to round them up. Sure enough two weeks later, while Mireille was taking a message to another village, Yveline and her brother were arrested by the Gestapo. When she got back to the farm and realised what had happened, Mireille was devastated. She and Yveline had become great friends. They'd shared not only their hopes and dreams for the future but their secrets as well. Of course, Mireille never spoke of SOE or of the whereabouts of any of Mother Hen's other chicks, but she had trusted Yveline with things she'd never shared with others. The thought of what awaited her friend after her capture, gave Mireille sleepless nights. Sometime later, when the news filtered through that Yveline had been shot, Mireille took some time to recover from the shock and her mood wasn't helped by news that others were being taken too, including Mari, a girl from the neighbouring farm and the local doctor. There was talk of a traitor in the midst but nothing was proved.

Mireille had had a few narrow escapes herself. One was when she was delivering a quantity of money to the local resistance. She had to go to a barber's shop in a village fifteen miles away and while she was there, a German jeep drew up outside. There were three officers inside, one well decorated. It was common knowledge that the Germans had to buy their own uniforms so they were always a good fit and looked smart. This one, even more so because he had used the services of a bespoke tailor. His jacket was made of a high-quality wool gabardine and had pleated pockets. It also had the new style green scalloped collar worn with a neck tie.

Outside in the small kitchen area, Mireille and the barber shared a couple of minutes of blind panic while he stuffed the money behind an old tea caddy under the sink, then she whispered in French, 'What do I do?'

'You're my daughter,' he said giving her an encouraging smile. 'Act naturally.' The three officers sauntered in and the more senior one sat down in the barber's chair.

'Good afternoon, gentlemen,' said the barber beaming from ear to ear. 'What can I do for you?'

'A shave,' said the German in the chair. He removed his *schirmmütze* from his head and laid it on his lap.

When Mireille emerged from the kitchen, the barber turned to her and said, 'Run along home now, my dear. Tell your mother I may be home late today.' He kissed her on both cheeks as Mireille murmured, 'Yes Papa. See you later.'

She slid past the customer's two companions and went out onto the street. Aware that one of the Germans was following her with his eyes, she forced herself not to look his way. Picking up her bike from where she'd left it leaning against the wall, she mounted it carefully so that none of them would know the terror she felt. As she biked past the open door she heard the soldier say to her 'father', 'Pretty girl.'

The barber waved his finger in a circular movement around the side of his head and the last thing she caught sight of was the sympathetic looks on all their faces. As she left the village for the open road, Mireille chuckled to herself. *Thanks Papa, that's one way of keeping me safe I suppose!*

For several weeks at a time, nothing much happened. There were toy (code word for guns, explosives and ammunition) drops on moonlit nights but the weather was pretty awful for the time of year so everything had slowed down. Sometimes she was asked to escort agents or British personnel who had either escaped from custody (or had been left behind after some kind of Allied action) to a place of safety. Everyone was always careful when someone turned up wanting help to get back to Britain. It was well known that the Germans infiltrated the resistance hoping to discover their safe house and escape routes.

Over the past few months, she'd been involved in several incidents but the strain was beginning to tell. Her latest one had been laying detonators in a factory making spare parts for the war effort and that was to prove to be her undoing.

It had taken careful planning. Mother Hen had arranged for several drops to get the much-needed explosives, detonators and equipment to carry out the raid they were calling the Christmas present. Because it was a massive target, it involved men from three different resistance groups. The bombing of the factory was to coincide with a raid on the nearby town to create maximum chaos and hopefully limit German reprisals on the local population. Luckily there had been few arguments in the planning stage and the groups seemed watertight.

They set off in the dead of night. Stealth and speed were of the essence. They made good use of the countryside, crossing a small ford over the river and hiding in the undergrowth until it was time. Having gained access to the factory through the perimeter fence they dealt with two of the guards. The men went in first, then Mireille and another Brit, code name Hermes, followed on, after which they began setting detonators and explosives where they would do the most damage. For the first time, Mireille was part of the same team. Now at last, all the training she'd received at Wanborough Manor was put to good use. She'd been allowed to set a few devices before, but the men had always taken the lion's share. This time she was on a par with the others and in her element.

They had almost finished when Mireille spotted a man creeping up behind Hermes. Puzzled she stopped moving and watched. Was he one of the resistance or a factory worker? Even more alarming, was he a guard? In the half-light she suddenly realised that he was carrying some sort of iron bar. She caught her breath silently and her training kicked in. It was imperative that the man didn't sound the alarm and even more necessary that he didn't interrupt Hermes with what he was doing. One mistake now and they'd all go up in smoke. She would have to kill him – silently. Above her head, she could hear the distinctive sounds of aircraft engines. The RAF were on their way.

Keeping as close as she could, as she saw him begin to raise the bar with his right hand, she tapped him on his left shoulder. As he instinctively turned his head, she aimed her knife at the carotid artery on the right side of his head and he went down like a ton of bricks.

He made no sound but there was so much blood. She hadn't expected that.

'Thank God you were here,' Hermes whispered. 'We're done now. Let's get out while we can.'

But Mireille was frozen to the spot.

Afterwards she didn't remember how she ended up outside again. She had a vague awareness of someone pulling on her elbow and she remembered scrambling through hole in the fence. The rest was a blur except the moment when she'd stopped to wash her sticky hands in the cool river water as they'd hurried back over the ford.

When they reached the field, there was an almighty explosion and the sky became livid red. Everyone congratulated her, kissed her, hugged her and told her it never would have happened if she hadn't ensured that Hermes had been able to make that last connection, but Mireille felt numb. There was no way she could respond to this accolade. Didn't they understand? She had killed a man – actually ended his life. Someone with a wife or a mother;

someone's father, or uncle, or brother. She was a murderer. This wasn't to be celebrated. War was a bloody, bloody awful thing.

In the days that followed, several things troubled her. She couldn't get her hands clean. Mireille would wash them over and over again until her skin was red and sore but they still felt warm and sticky. For the whole time she'd been with them, everyone had admired the fact that she'd integrated so well into the French way of life but now she'd lost her impeccable concentration. Every now and then, an English word would creep out as she spoke; it was usually an expletive but nevertheless just as dangerous because you never knew who was listening.

Mireille was sent to live with Sylvie who ran a baker's shop which meant she could combine delivering bread on her bicycle with taking messages and money to the rest of the group. The trouble was, on a personal level, it didn't help her very much. Mireille did her best but the hand washing became more frenetic. She had dark circles under her eyes. She had also become a liability because she was having bad dreams and sometimes she cried out in her sleep – in English. It didn't seem to matter how many times they told her it had been necessary to kill the German and that by her stealth she had saved many more lives. Mireille didn't seem to be able to take it in.

'She needs to cry,' Sylvie told Claude, 'but these English, they hold everything in so tight, so tight.'

But it was more than just that. It was becoming obvious to everybody that Mireille was tired – so very tired. Even when Mother Hen sent instructions they couldn't be sure she was getting it right. Finally, everyone agreed, Mireille was no use to them. She had to go back. She didn't argue when Claude told her, which was unusual in itself but they had to wait for some decent weather. It had been awful of late, gusty winds, driving rain and cold. The usual fields were becoming soggy and the plane could easily get bogged down in the mud.

Which was why, in desperation, Claude decided to send her to a convent.

Chapter 38

It had been a while since Bob had been to the home but the staff were pleased to see him. Everyone was sorry to hear that he'd been in hospital and hoped that he was fully recovered. He thanked them and told them that since his recovery, he'd managed to get himself a job as a porter in Cranleigh village hospital in Surrey just to be nearer his mother. The real reason was that it was the perfect hiding place. The attractive timber framed cottage built by St Nicolas Church in the fifteenth century was small, but it suited his purpose completely. He could live in and as long as he kept himself to himself, no one would know he was there. He'd saved what he could, grown a moustache and with the help of a little petty thieving had smartened himself up again.

'Your mother is in the garden room,' said the nurse as he walked through the door. 'I'm sure she'll be delighted to see you again.'

'How is she?' Bob asked, a look of concern and worry on his face.

'As well as can be expected,' said the nurse. 'She never has been what you would call robust, but she enjoys life as best as she can.'

Bob shook his head sadly. 'I only wish I could take her back with me and look after her myself.' He coughed into his hand and let out a slight wheeze as he struggled to catch his breath.

'Tell you what,' said the nurse. 'Why don't we put her in a wheelchair and you can take her for a spin around the gardens.'

Bob's face lit up. 'Could I really?'

Perfect. If she was alone with him, she might open up a bit more about his father.

She was looking at an old photograph album when he walked into the garden room. 'Bring it with you, Mother,' he suggested. 'You can show me the pictures.'

To begin with, because he knew the nurse would be watching them, he trundled around the flower beds and across the lawn, making small talk. Once he was sure everyone had gone back to work, happy with what he was doing, he wheeled her to a more secluded part of the grounds to an area not easily seen from the lounge.

There was a rickety garden chair nearby so he sat opposite her. 'Show me the album, Mother.'

The photographs were dull. Grainy pictures of men and women posing by a garden gate, on the beach or inside various sitting rooms. He wasn't interested in 'my mother and father,' 'your Auntie Doris' or 'the dog called Rover' but eventually they turned a page to find pictures of some sort of gathering.

'That was when we were in the Albert Hall,' she said.

'The Blackshirts?' he asked.

When she nodded, he could hardly contain his excitement. 'Who's that?'

He'd pointed to a tall, good-looking man with a rather superior expression coming through the crowds.

'That's Oswald Mosley,' she said. 'We went to all his meetings. I didn't like him much, but I loved your father.'

Bob turned the page. 'That's the same picture as you've got in the frame by your bed.' He ran his fingers over the faces of the two men staring down the camera lens and slipped the photograph from the corner pieces holding it in place. 'Can I have it?'

His mother became agitated. 'No, it's mine. It's all I have left.'

Ignoring her protest, he slipped the picture into his pocket. 'You've got the one in the silver frame.'

She tugged at his coat. 'Give it back. I want it. It's mine.'

He pushed her away and accidentally caught the side of her face. She glared at him, stunned.

'You've got the one in the silver frame, Mother,' he repeated. 'I want this one.'

Her lip curled. 'You're your father's son, all right,' she said, her voice filled with contempt. 'Fancy hitting an old woman.'

'Don't be so dramatic,' he scoffed. 'It was an accident.'

She turned her head away. 'He used to hit me. That's why I got ill. In the end it got so's I couldn't think straight so they put me away.'

Bob frowned. 'Then you must have done something really bad,' he said stiffly. 'My father was a gentleman.'

'A gentleman!' She snorted. 'I don't think so.'

Bob took the picture from his pocket and looked at it again. 'He looks like a proper gent,' he said. 'Distinguished, well educated . . .' As he spoke he was drawing himself into the same pose as the man in the picture – an aristocrat, tall and good-looking, standing proudly next to his chauffeur, a much shorter man with a terrible birthmark on his face.

His mother began to laugh.

'What?' Bob demanded. 'Why are you laughing?'

'You fool,' she said contemptuously. 'You think Ffox-

314

Webster was your father. Well, let me tell you, I wouldn't have touched that slimy pig with a ten-foot barge pole.'

Bob blinked in shocked surprise.

'Your father is the man standing next to him. Nelson Robert Hedges. The love of my life, he was. That's why I named you after him.'

Bob stared down at the photograph. This was his father? The man with the birthmark?

'He was a good person until he got in with Ffox-Webster,' his mother was saying. 'There was a time when he loved me.'

He stared at her in disbelief. The red mist was coming back. She was lying. This couldn't be right. His father was a hero, not some stupid scar-faced chauffeur.

'Shuddup,' he shouted. 'It's not true, you witch. Shuddup, shuddup!'

He'd hit her over the head then ripped the photo album to shreds. The next moment he was running as fast as his legs could carry him. He had to get out of this place and away from her and her twisted lies. He kept running until the anger left him and by that time he was miles away from the home. They'd find her eventually, tipped out of her wheelchair and lying next to the compost heap. Best place for her.

The phone was ringing at the Lilacs. Norah put Terry's bottle onto the kitchen table and lifted him onto her shoulder. He made a milky sigh but no protest.

'Hello?'

'He's here,' said an excited voice. 'Our son. Peter.'

It was Dan. Norah caught her breath.

'Ten days late,' her brother-in-law went on. 'He was supposed to be born in July but he's fine. Ten pounds three ounces. A bloomin' whopper!'

'Oh Dan,' Norah cried, 'How wonderful. And Rene? How is she?'

'Exhausted but very happy,' said Dan. 'Tell Jim we'll get together some time to wet the baby's head. I've gotta go. I have to tell me ma.'

'Okay, okay,' Norah said, the laughter already in her voice. 'I'm so happy for her . . . er, for you both. Give her my love . . .' But he was already gone.

She put the telephone receiver down and laid Terry in her arms. 'Well my darling, it looks like you've got a little cousin to play with.'

He regarded her with a slightly puzzled expression and then burped.

Chapter 39

Mireille was feeling a lot better. She had no idea how long she'd been in the convent but winter had turned to spring.

When Claude left her there, he promised that as soon as he was able, he would make sure she would be taken back to England but the weather, the lack of personnel because cells had been betrayed or broken up and more importantly, the danger posed by the German strangle hold on the French countryside, prevented a speedy result. In a sense, when she arrived, she wasn't unduly concerned about it. Her mind was still in a fog and she couldn't focus on anything more than the immediate moment. Her thoughts just wouldn't let go of the man she had killed.

The convent was quiet. Sometimes, the only sound was that of the grandfather clock in the entrance which chimed on the quarter. The nuns did their work without frivolous chatter although, contrary to her first assumption, they hadn't taken a vow of silence. There was no talking at meal times either because each day, one sister was chosen to read from the Bible as they ate, and as Mother Superior explained, 'To talk when someone is reading from the Holy Scriptures is disrespectful to Our Lord.' Mireille had never bothered to read much from the Bible so she was surprised when she found the words soothing and helpful. In time, she looked forward to meal times simply to hear the words being read aloud.

Her days weren't idle. Although nobody made demands of her, Mireille tidied the quadrangle garden and cleaned in the house. When it got too cold to work outside, she took her turn to do the laundry, polish the parquet floor in the hallway or to help cook the meal in the kitchen. When the nuns said their prayers in the chapel, she declined to go in but over time, she gradually moved from the corridor outside, to hanging around the doorway and eventually she sat on one of the chairs on the back row. She grew to love their singing as well, their high-pitched soprano voices ringing out in a way which sent shivers down Mireille's spine. She wasn't sure why but perhaps it was because nuns had been singing these lovely hymns and anthems for centuries. Sometimes, when she closed her eyes or looked up at the beautiful stained-glass windows, she imagined she could hear the long dead nuns joining in.

For her own safety, Mother Superior had insisted that Mireille wear a novice's garb. 'The Germans sometimes come to the convent,' she told her. 'If they see a young girl in peasant's clothing, they are bound to ask questions. If you are here as a novice, they will respect you.'

Mireille didn't argue; after all, these women were risking their lives by harbouring an English agent so it followed that if the Germans knew she was partly English, they would all be in trouble.

She did a lot of thinking as well. What was she going to do if she survived this war? The obvious answer was to marry Ginger and settle down but whenever she toyed with that idea, all the old feelings of insecurity came back. He loved her; he'd told her that, and he'd always treated her with respect, so why did she want to run away from him? Slowly it dawned on her. She loved him as a dear friend but that was all. She never wanted to lose him, but she didn't – couldn't – love him in that way. Maybe she would never love any man enough to be his wife. It was a bit scary. The accepted norm was to meet someone, fall in love, get married and live happily ever after, but Mireille didn't want that – not yet anyway. So why was she hanging on to Ginger? Was it because she didn't want to be alone? Or did she just want to be the same as everybody else? Mireille struggled to answer that question and although she couldn't pin-point the day she finally understood what she'd been doing, the sense of release was palpable. She didn't need a man to define her. She was her own person. Ffox-Webster had used and abused her, but he hadn't broken her spirit. She had no idea what the future held. Maybe she'd never get out of France alive, but if she did, she was determined that the one thing people would remember about her was that Mireille Osborne was the kind of woman to break the mould.

And what of the man she'd killed? She was thinking more rationally now. The other members of the cell had been right. It was a question of kill or be killed and she had, after all, saved Hermes' life if nobody else's. She told herself that the fact that she was so upset by what she had done, proved that she wasn't a killer by nature. Would she do it again? The answer had to be 'yes'. This was what she had signed up to. She was a trained member of SOE. The country was at war and as unpalatable as it was, she had to stop the enemy at all costs.

As spring approached, Mireille was restless so she was relieved when Claude came back for her.

Chapter 40

At the beginning of June 1944, Matron had asked for all the student nurses to gather in the canteen, Amélie included. As they waited, there was a lot of guesswork as to why they had been summoned. Were they in trouble for something?

It hadn't gone unnoticed that there had been an awful lot of troop activity over the past two days. The whole town was bathed in an air of expectancy as the tanks and armoured vehicles which had been holed up in the quiet side streets for months on end, suddenly emerged and rumbled along Warwick Street and up Chapel Road. There had been no official announcement, but that didn't stop the speculation. For several days there had been calls for volunteers to give blood and the railway stations had posters warning that trains may be cancelled at a moment's notice. Perhaps they were going to be asked to donate their blood or maybe it was simply to announce that all leave was cancelled.

A hub of conversation died as Matron walked into the room.

'I know that some of you would dearly like to be part of the war effort,' she began. 'Well, now you have an opportunity.'

Every girl stared at her with bated breath.

'The army is looking for nurses to accompany wounded personnel to hospital.'

She stopped for effect and there was a small murmur of excitement.

'If you would like to be part of the team, it means that you will have to go to Portsmouth or Southampton,' she continued. 'There is no time limit as to how long you'll be away and I must warn you that you may see some harrowing things, but I am confident that any nurse from this hospital will conduct herself in a very professional manner.'

Amélie leaned forward eagerly. Was this it? The moment everyone had been waiting for? Was the Allied invasion of France about to begin at last?

'This is extremely hush-hush,' Matron continued, 'but I'm sure that you are aware of a lot of troop movement in the town at the moment. I know we had a similar experience last year but this time it appears that an invasion of France may be imminent. For any girl wishing to be selected for escort duties, come to my office at six this evening.'

She swept from the room leaving behind a buzz of excitement and trepidation. Amélie could see several of her friends shaking their heads. 'My mother would never allow me to go.' 'I can't go now. I take my exam next week.' 'I'll go, if you go.'

Even though she trembled at the thought of it, there was no question in Amélie's heart. If Mireille could go abroad and risk her life for France, could she do any less? How could she hold back? So despite her fears, Amélie was waiting outside Matron's office door just before six. By half past six, she had scribbled a quick note to Mémé to tell her that although she didn't know where she was being posted, she was all right. She also asked her to pass a short note on to Lennard the next time he came to the house. After that, she packed a small case. This was the only time Amélie had ever been allowed to wear her uniform outside of the wards and it was a proud moment as she and her fellow nurses marched to the station. As they passed early morning shoppers, a few people clapped and called out good luck wishes.

When they arrived at the railway station, the plans had been changed. Apparently, because of other troop move- ment, they were unable to go by train after all so they would be transported by the army. The moment she climbed into the army truck and sat on the bench running along the side, Amélie felt both excited and a little scared. There were nine of them in all from the hospital. Some newly qualified, some with plenty of nursing experience and three nurses still in training like herself. Nobody spoke but pulling their cloaks around their bodies, they waited for the army officer to tell the driver to move off.

Bob Kane was feeling very pleased with himself. Once again he'd been pretty clever. It had taken quite a while to get over his mother's revelation and during that time he'd gone through a gamut of emotions. To begin with he'd been angry, so angry. He'd been proud of the thought that he was Ffox-Webster's son. The man in the photograph was tall and handsome, just the same as he was. He'd had the same eyes and when Bob stood to one side in the same pose, there was a definite resemblance. He'd been confused as well. Why had his mother led him to believe Ffox-Webster was his father? He recalled their few serious conversations and the more he thought about it, the more convinced he was that she had done it deliberately. Damn the woman! The other man in the photograph, the one she said was his father, looked so mediocre compared to Ffox-Webster. Bob decided he wasn't that bad looking apart from the birthmark, but he didn't look aristocratic!

It took some considerable time to move on from his rage and disappointment but then Bob began to think about his next step. He'd admired Ffox-Webster. The man was a hero and they'd hung him for it. Like so many others, he was looking for a new world order, one which would begin with a cleansing of the human race. Amélie was spent, used, contaminated, a whore, but her younger sister . . . she was the cherry, ripe for the picking. All he had to do was get Amélie to tell him where she was and he would do whatever was necessary to find out.

Going back to Worthing was risky, especially as her foster father was in the police, but all members of secret societies took risks, didn't they? As a precaution, he dyed his hair and stuck a theatrical moustache on his top lip to make his own moustache look bigger and he'd added a small goatee beard.

He had planned to go down to Worthing at the weekend, but in the pub last night he'd heard some soldiers talking about the coming of 'the big push'. Pricking his ears up, it didn't take long to discover that everything was being sent south. All leave was cancelled from the beginning of the week, so something was afoot. However it wasn't all bad. With a lot of troop movement, there was a better chance of getting around without being spotted. Bob left the pub immediately and packed his case.

He'd been lucky enough to catch the morning milk train to Worthing. It was a frustrating ride because the train stopped at unscheduled stations and there were long delays. He kept his head and didn't make a fuss because he couldn't risk being chucked off altogether and eventually, two hours late, the train rumbled into Worthing central where the station staff announced that the rest of the journey had been terminated. It was with a feeling of relief and elation that Bob clambered out onto the platform.

As he emerged into the morning light, Station Approach was a hive of activity. Army lorries waiting in queues were moving out in convoy, jostling for position with a fleet of buses picking up passengers and putting them down. It looked like organised chaos. He waited on the steps for a few minutes to allow some of the traffic to pass before crossing the road. His eye followed a couple of lorries moving towards Teville Gate and then he saw her. Amélie. She was in full nurse's uniform, sitting in the back of the truck with a whole lot of other nurses. His heart almost stopped. Where was she going? He had to talk to her. He couldn't let her slip through his fingers. Not now. He shouted, 'Hey, Amélie! Amélie.' But she couldn't hear him above the sound of a dozen or more idling engines.

The lorry lurched to a stop and he saw her bend down as if to tie her shoe or something. Bob waved his arm frantically. 'Amélie, Amélie.' She didn't look his way but one of the other nurses obviously heard him and he saw her tap Amélie on her shoulder. As the lorry began to move again, Amélie sat up and looked in the direction of the other girl's pointing finger but she couldn't seem to see him. Damn it, his disguise was better than he thought. He'd have to run to catch up with the lorry before it set off again. Without a second thought he raced down the steps. He was still shouting her name as the convoy began to pick up speed. As he threw himself into the road, the one thing he didn't notice was the speeding bus coming up behind him.

*

324

At the Lilacs, the day began a little differently. Norah called Jim and he came running downstairs in his pyjamas. He had a day off today and they'd planned to go for a walk later on. Christine turned the knobs on the radio and all three of them lowered themselves down onto the chairs. Nobody spoke. As they sat in silence, the only sound was the ticking of the clock.

It had been an awful night and Norah wasn't the only one in the house to have had little sleep. As darkness fell, the endless movement of army vehicles which had rumbled through the streets of Worthing for the past two days showed no sign of abating but by two or two-thirty in the morning, the roads were quiet once more. Norah had stood by the bedroom window for ages but there was nothing to see. However, after the military stagnation of the past four years, it seemed that the troops who had filled the town for the whole of that period, were on the move at last. It was the air of expectation which made it difficult to sleep. Could it be . . . ? Was this it? And if it was the beginning of the end, peace would surely follow. Peace . . . what would that look like? For so long, Norah had refused to think of the halcyon days before the war when they could go where they liked, when they liked. Days when you didn't dread the appearance of the telegram boy; careless days of frolicking on the beach and eating ice cream; summers of afternoon teas in the garden and picnics on Highdown; times of cosy Christmases and singing carols under the street lamps. The memory of such times was too painful and made it hard to cope with what they had now. Better to do what everybody else was doing. Leave the past behind and just get on with it.

Then at around five in the morning, wave after wave after wave of aircraft had filled the skies. According to Jim, who stood by the window next to her, they were pulling gliders full of troops.

The weather wasn't kind for the time of year. The day before it had rained with a cold and blustery north-east wind. 'Hardly the weather for June,' Christine had remarked sourly. Today was cloudy with the promise of bright intervals.

The wireless crackled into life and they heard the voice of John Snagge.

'D-Day has come. Early this morning the Allies began the assault on the north-western face of Hitler's European fortress. Supreme Headquarters of the Allied Expeditionary Force said: "Under the command of General Eisenhower, Allied naval forces, supported by strong air forces, began landing Allied armies this morning on the northern coast of France."'

They looked at each other hardly daring to breathe, then Christine grinned. 'Is this it then?'

'I rather think it might be,' said Jim. 'We've probably got a long way to go, but it looks like we're going to give Hitler a bloody nose at last.'

Christine reached for the sherry bottle and three glasses.

'Mother,' Jim scolded. 'It's not even eight o'clock in the morning.'

'Who cares,' she said brashly. 'I feel like celebrating!'

Chapter 41

Since she'd passed the message on, Mireille and her circuit had been busy. As soon as she left the convent, Mireille had slipped back into her role seamlessly. Just a few days before, she had tuned the radio knobs until she'd found the BBC. Someone was reading a poem. *'Les sanglots long des violons de l'automme . . .'* For a nano-second she froze. Paul Verlaine's poem. She caught her breath. This was it! This was the code they'd all been waiting for.

'The Long Sighs of the Violins of Autumn' was the code to prepare the way for the Allied invasion by sabotaging the railways. Although her breakdown meant that Mireille was no longer allowed to position their bombs and detonators, she was once again very much part of the team. They posted her as look-out or they sent her out into the countryside on her bicycle with messages for other resistance groups. Everyone was aware that they probably only had a few days to pave the way before the Allies arrived so it certainly focused the mind.

When the news finally filtered through that they had landed in Normandy, everyone was elated. But if they had thought their troubles would soon be over, they were in for a shock. True, the Germans were being pushed back but not without some fierce fighting. Not only that, but because of the ferocity against the Allied advance, the French people became the meat in the sandwich. Reprisals by the retreating Nazi army were vicious and terrible. Men, women and children were shot for no apparent reason. Whole villages were destroyed, along with animals and crops alike. The resistance prevented troop reinforcements from reaching the battle lines by keeping the Germans pinned down but everything was achieved at a terrible cost. Fighting in the fields and ditches was intense.

Amélie and her nursing comrades had reached Portsmouth. At first the numbers of wounded being brought back to England from Normandy was only a trickle, but it didn't take long for that trickle to become a flood. Matron was right; it was good experience but she saw some terrible sights. For every man with a broken arm or a superficial bullet wound on the leg there was another with half his face shot away or with agonising burns on his body. The army medics had patched them up on the boat coming back and she knew that whichever hospital they were going to, whether it was St Mary's, St James', Haslar Royal Naval Hospital or the QA, they would be well treated and nursed back to health.

'Your job is to comfort frightened or dying men as they are transported to their place of care,' the staff nurse in charge told them as they waited by the quayside for the first of the wounded. 'In my experience, some will be quite stoic but others will weep for their mothers or their sweetheart. You must not judge them as cowardly. They have seen things which will haunt them for the rest of their lives.'

Amélie's first casualty was John. She waited for him as

328

one of the navy boys helped him down the gangplank because his eyes were completely covered in bandage. Amélie took his hands in hers and gave him an encouraging squeeze. 'Hello John,' she said softly. 'You're back home now and I'm going to take you to hospital. Careful, there's one more slight step down.'

He hung onto her for dear life as she walked him to the ambulance then she climbed in after him.

'Does it look bad?' he asked her as they felt the engine start and they moved off.

She cried out, 'No, no,' but he'd already pulled the bandage away. She could see at once that one eye was missing and the other was swollen and opaque. 'I can't see at the moment,' he went on, 'but they can patch me up right?' His filthy fingers were already reaching out to touch the wound.

Amélie caught his hand and forced herself to take control of her queasy stomach. 'I'm no expert, John,' she said softly, 'but I think it's better if you don't touch your eyes. Now that you've taken this bandage off, I'm going to put a clean one on.'

She covered the gaping wound as best she could.

'Thanks, Nurse,' he said. 'Only I'm a bit worried about my job, see? Once this bloody war is over, I want to go back to it.'

'What do you do?' In asking the question, Amélie was hoping to lighten the moment. It had the opposite effect.

'I'm a watch maker.'

The silence between them grew heavy.

'It's bad, isn't it?' he said.

'I'm no expert,' she repeated.

'But you are a nurse . . .'

'I'm not yet qualified,' Amélie blurted out.

The ambulance swung into the hospital grounds.

'We've arrived,' she said, fighting her tears.

She escorted him from the ambulance into the Accident and Emergency and from there to a cubicle.

'I have to go now, John.' He put out his hand and she shook it.

'Thanks, Nurse,' he said, 'and I'm sorry I put you on the spot.'

The doctor pulled back the curtain and as Amélie turned to leave she whispered, 'Good luck, John.'

The girls themselves were put up in a village hall. They had camp beds and were each given a towel and some soap. There was nowhere to hang their things except on the dado rail which went right around the hall but at the end of their shift, the WVS had prepared them a substantial meal. It had been a tiring day and for some, they would have to stay up for a night shift as well.

'We shall only need you girls for a few days,' said the QA nurse in charge. 'As soon as they can, the lads across the water will build a field hospital and our boys can go there for as long as they need it.'

'Are you going to take us to France then?' asked Green Jenny (so called because whenever their lecturer called her name in class she invariably stumbled over it by saying her surname first).

'We only have fully trained nurses in the field,' was the rather cutting and dismissive reply.

Amélie giggled as Green Jenny stuck her tongue out at her receding back.

At the Lilacs, everyone spent their time glued to the radio. People came into the farm shop to chat about their hopes and fears in a way they hadn't done since Dunkirk so Christine kept the kettle boiled and the tea flowing. Playing with Terry in his playpen became a delightful distraction and of course he lapped up all the attention. The dogs lay beside him, grateful for a pat and a kind word.

Anxious to keep herself occupied, Norah divided her time between working in the nursery and serving in the shop. As for Jim, he was taken up with a fatality after Station Approach when some foreign-looking chap had run out into the road in front of the number nine bus. The driver, Cyril Lumley was in a profound state of shock.

'Poor old Cyril hadn't a cat's chance in hell of avoiding him,' said one witness.

'The stupid idiot just ran down the steps and straight out into the road,' said another.

The victim had been rushed to Worthing hospital but there was nothing anybody could do. The doctor wrote on the patient's notes DOA (dead on arrival). All that remained was to identify the body. Jim went to the morgue to see it for himself.

The body was on the cold slab covered by a sheet.

The mortuary assistant, a man he'd met scores of times over the years, greeted Jim with a wry smile. 'Well, this is a turn up for the books, isn't it?'

Jim frowned, puzzled. 'What do you mean?'

With a practised flourish the mortuary assistant pulled back the sheet and Jim gasped. The victim had extensive injuries. The back of his head had been damaged as had his chest and one arm, but his face was still recognisable. A false moustache hung loosely above his top lip and there was what looked like some theatrical glue stuck to his chin, but there was no doubt in Jim's mind. This was no foreigner. This was Bob Kane.

'I don't mind telling you,' Jim told Norah and his mother later that evening, 'I'm relieved he's gone.'

They were sitting at the dinner table eating some boned

and stuffed pig's trotters with new potatoes and carrot, celery and onion which had been slow baked for three hours. Terry was already in bed.

'Do you think we should say something to Amélie?' said Christine.

'We must,' said Norah. 'After all that happened with Mireille, I promised myself none of this family should keep secrets from each other.'

Jim nodded. 'But no need to go into details.'

'What was he doing here?' asked Christine.

Jim shrugged. 'Your guess is as good as mine but the man hadn't changed. He was wanted because he'd gone on the run from that prison van and Surrey police wanted him for an assault on his mother.'

'His mother?' Christine squeaked.

'Tipped her out of her wheelchair and left her under a tree,' said Jim.

'Horrible man,' said Norah. 'Was she all right?'

Jim nodded. 'Shaken up a bit obviously.' He paused. 'There is one other thing. It's a bit odd but it turns out that Bob Kane was the son of Ffox-Webster's chauffeur.'

'What, Hedges?' Christine cried.

'Good Heavens!' cried Norah.

'But it's not even the same name,' said Christine.

'His parents weren't married,' said Jim, 'but it's him all right.'

Norah seemed puzzled. 'Was that why he wanted to have Amélie . . . because of the connection with his father and her step-father?'

'No idea,' said Jim, 'but he was obviously a pretty bad lot.'

'And the apple doesn't fall far from the tree,' his mother said sagely.

*

'There's a general strike in Paris,' Claude said. 'People are putting up the barricades.'

It was August. The fighting had been going on for ten weeks and although progress was slow, the resistance hadn't let up. Victory was within their grasp and they weren't about to relax their guard. Not yet. Everyone was tired but it didn't matter.

'Then we must go to help our comrades,' said Pierre. And so it was decided. The group moved first to the suburbs and then into Paris itself. Now Mireille was faced with street fighting and German snipers but she could cope with that. If she couldn't 'see' her target, she was as good as the next man. It was only hand-to-hand fighting or killing by stealth that she couldn't cope with.

Claude teamed them up with a resistance group near the centre of the city and the stories they had to tell, rekindled her longing to go back to England. Food rationing was very strict, much more so than in England but the Germans helped themselves to anything that took their fancy. There were stories of wine cellars being emptied, children being pushed to the floor for the shopping they held and young girls selling themselves for a chocolate bar. Most Parisians were slim to the point of being thin and they were lucky if they managed to eat a thousand calories a day. The only luxuries they enjoyed were brought in from the countryside by friends and relatives and if the Germans stopped them at a check point, as likely as not, everything would be confiscated. In addition to the usual privations, the Maquis were adding to their problems. To frustrate the Germans, power plants were blown up but of course that had a knock-on effect for the people. They took it with stoic resolution but it did make life a lot harder.

Paris was a dangerous place. Now that the Allies were advancing and the end was in sight, some settled old scores.

Armed men roamed the streets sniping at any soldier and gun battles had people dashing across the streets to get away from the fighting. It wasn't long before Mireille found herself caught up in just such a situation.

She had been sent with a message for Xavier. Xavier, code name for Alphonse, was head of a group of men working in Paris itself. They had had limited success but nobody could doubt their courage. Three of their members had been betrayed to the Gestapo and after a period of torture, they had been sent to concentration camps. The group itself had changed its name to *Les diables* and metamorphosed into a ruthless and deadly cell, which the locals held in awe and fear in equal proportions.

Biking through the streets of Paris, Mireille heard something she hadn't heard for years. Church bells. It began with one church but in no time at all it seemed that every bell ringer in Paris was pulling the ropes. It filled her heart with joy but when she took a turn into a side street, everything suddenly changed into hell on earth as a group of German soldiers on one side began firing pot-shots at some members of the resistance on the other. People were running in all directions. Women screamed and children cried. Trapped in the open with nowhere to hide, Mireille pedalled as fast as she could to get to the end of the street. Her heart was thumping wildly and when a man riding a bicycle just in front of her was hit, he went down like a ton of bricks. Mireille swerved violently to avoid crashing into him. With bullets flying in all directions, it was far too dangerous to stay in the road and sitting high up on the bicycle she was clearly a sitting duck. Rolling from the saddle onto the ground and keeping as low as possible, she scrambled for a doorway. The one she chose had a recess but it was not very deep so there was little shelter. Mireille flung herself down and prayed for the shooting to stop but when a stray bullet ricocheted off a dustbin at the entrance and hit the opposite wall, she knew she had to take another risk and try to get off the street altogether. Her only hope of survival was to find a doorway with a deeper recess.

When another crowd of people hurtled en masse down the road, she followed them. They were all running away from the shooting. After another burst of gunfire, she saw the recess with two doors together. Mireille hurtled towards them, her whole body shaking. Shouting and crying in panic, she hammered on the wood. After a few agonising seconds, she heard a bolt slide on the other side of the door. Someone opened it just a crack but now she was too terrified to stand up. Mireille curled herself up into a ball, sobbing and almost wetting herself with fear.

The door opened wider and bright sunlight flooded the entryway. At the same time, Mireille felt a strong, vice-like grip on her upper arm and someone pulled her to her feet then pushed her with great force towards the light. She tripped and stumbled beyond the door then fell onto cobble stones. She heard the door slam behind her. Shaking and terrified, she lifted her head to find herself in a tiny court-yard with a cluster of three or four other doors. She sat back on her haunches, tears and snot on her face; her wild hair making her look like a scarecrow. Her heart was pounding in her chest and she could hardly breathe. She looked up at her rescuer, then in utter amazement, Mireille took in her breath.

'Yveline! Is that really you?' she gasped. 'I don't believe it. I thought you were dead!'

Chapter 42

Amélie had spent almost two months in Portsmouth and already she felt like a very different person. As a nurse she had been challenged and stretched. She'd had to deal with some heart-breaking incidents; young men like her first patient John, whose lives had been radically altered. There were wives and sweethearts, who on the one hand were relieved to have their loved one safely back home again, but now had to cope with all the privations and difficulties that lay ahead because now they had become totally dependent. She'd coped with comforting the relatives of those who hadn't made it out of the operating theatres and trying to help bewildered children understand why their mothers were beside themselves with grief because they would never see their father/ uncle/ older brother again.

Portsmouth had been an eye opener for them all. 'When I left Worthing I was young and foolish and completely out of my depth,' Green Jenny confided in her. 'I've done a lot of growing up since then.'

Amélie nodded her head vigorously. 'You and me both.'

And it was true. Portsmouth had changed her whole

outlook on so many things. Having seen how people dealt with really harsh realities, Amélie realised, perhaps for the first time, that life was far too short to drift through it holding on to a pocket full of 'if only's'.

For far too long she had held on to the stubborn belief that *if only* she could find Linnet, or *if only* Mireille would write, everything would be hunky-dory. Talking with Green Jenny in the dormitory, she began to feel that her blinkered way of thinking had begun long before that. How often had she told herself that life would be so much better *if only* her mother hadn't died or *if only* her step-father hadn't done what he did . . .

It was true of course, but she'd allowed something which could never be changed to dominate all her decisions and her relationships in the here and now. Maybe, she told herself sternly, she never would find Linnet. Perhaps Mireille wouldn't even come back from France. Both scenarios were too painful to contemplate, but her sisters had every right to live their lives as they wanted, just the same as she did. She had brooded far too much on what might never be. As ridiculous as it was, she had begun to see that the pain of her past had for some weird reason been comfortable and familiar. Hadn't she been grateful for the sympathetic glances people gave her now and then?

'You never come to the hospital dances,' Green Jenny said one evening as they shared a heart-to-heart over a fish and chips supper wrapped in newspaper.

'Because half the time I never know they're happening,' Amélie said huffily. 'Nobody ever mentions them to me. If the person organising them wanted me to come they'd ask me, wouldn't they?'

Green Jenny turned her head away.

Amélie frowned. 'What?'

'She never asks you because you always refuse,' she said.

337

She paused then added, 'I don't want to be rude, but some-times you come across as a bit stand-offish.'

'You're joking!' Amélie spluttered. 'Whoever said that?'

'Amélie, nobody wants to make you feel awkward.'

Amélie stared at her in disbelief. Stand-offish? That was ridiculous.

But as she lay in her bed that night chewing things over she had to admit that she'd never told them anything about herself, not even Green Jenny. If she was feeling miserable she preferred to wallow in her own pity party rather than ask for help. Some would say she had every right to do that, but having seen how some of those stoic soldiers and their families dealt with the knocks they'd just received, Amélie was beginning to understand that she was only making herself the martyr, left behind, left out and forgotten.

Yes, what Ffox-Webster had done to her was inexcusable. It never should have happened but from now on she was going to grab hold of life with both hands. If she didn't let go of the past, she would be doomed to carry the memory of that dreadful man on her back for the rest of her life. It wouldn't be easy but she was determined to stop being bitter and resentful. If she didn't, it would only destroy her and he would have won. So that night she made up her mind that he was not going to dominate her thoughts anymore.

'When is the next hospital dance?' Amélie asked her friend the next morning. They were on their way to the jeeps which would take them back to the waterfront.

Green Jenny grinned. 'It'll be the last one here in Portsmouth before we go back home, but if you want to come I'll make sure Helen tells you.'

'Helen?'

'She's the girl who organises everything,' said Green

Jenny. 'If we left it to Home Sister we'd end up with a rubbish band and no men.'

The day was a little brighter than it had been of late. As they waited by the jetty for the last time, Ffox-Webster drifted into her thoughts once again. Amélie shivered involuntarily.

'You all right?' asked Green Jenny.

'Never felt better,' said Amélie and in her mind she said to her step-father, 'And you can go back to hell where you belong.'

Fixing her eyes on the incoming boat she told herself that she would pick up the pieces despite him. She'd make something of her life. To Lennard she would be as chaste as a virgin. She didn't need to lie to him. He knew her past and he'd already told her he was content to leave it there. She had never willingly given herself to her step-father but she would for Lennard if he still wanted her. She shivered again but this time it was with excitement.

Lennard was taken by surprise by the enthusiasm of her welcome when they met up at the Lilacs at the end of August. Calling out a 'hello,' as he came around the back, he found her alone in the kitchen standing at the sink and washing a couple of Terry's cardigans for Norah. As the dogs yapped and danced around their feet, jumping up at their legs, to his absolute delight, Amélie, her hands still covered in soap suds, threw herself into his arms and showered him with kisses.

'Hey, hey,' he called out, laughing, 'what's all this?'

'Oh Lennard, I've missed you,' she said breathlessly. 'I've missed you so much. I don't ever want to be parted from you again.'

With a look of bewildered surprise, he held her face and gazed into her eyes. 'Then marry me, darling,' he moaned as his lips found hers, 'Please.'

'Oh yes, Lennard,' she said as they came up for air. 'A thousand times yes.'

Mireille was deliriously happy to see Yveline again but her friend seemed a little more reserved. As they stood by the door, she rolled her eyes to the left. 'Don't say anything,' she cautioned quietly. 'Just come with me.'

Mireille glanced over Yveline's shoulder and the woman in the apartment opposite dropped her curtain. Without saying another word, Mireille followed her friend through a blue door and up some stairs.

She found herself in a beautifully decorated flat. The 'L' shaped living cum dining room had been decorated a delicate yellow and green. The sofa was floral and flanked by two plain yellow bucket style chairs. In front of the sofa stood a green coffee table. The dining table was the same colour. The walls were a creamy yellow although one wall had brown wallpaper with large yellow roses on it. The whole place looked like something from a posh magazine. How on earth could Yveline afford to live in a place like this?

Mireille's old friend closed the door behind them.

'Have you been here all this time?' Mireille blurted out. 'Why didn't you get in touch? When we heard you were taken by the Gestapo, we were all terrified. How on earth did you escape? And how did you get here?' Mireille couldn't stop the questions tumbling from her mouth.

'Stop, stop.' Yveline laughed as she put up her hand. 'You're making my head spin.' She paused. 'First things first. Would you like a drink?'

Mireille nodded and followed her into the sumptuous kitchen. This time the decor was yellow with pale grey. The white units had open shelves where Yveline had stacked her beautifully matching tins and plates. The room itself was semi-circular and the floor tiles were pale grey with wider dark grey bands around the edges. It was more of a show room than a cosy kitchen.

'Is this your flat?' Mireille asked cautiously.

To her great relief, Yveline shook her head. 'I work for the people who live here,' she said.

Mireille made herself comfortable on a chair while Yveline turned her attention to the coffee percolator. Mireille reflected on how much she would miss a cup of French coffee when she got back home. With the stringent rationing rules it was becoming more difficult to get it but back home Norah only bought Camp coffee and although Mireille liked it, it really wasn't the same as freshly made ground coffee. She decided she really must try to take some back to Worthing. It would be a nice present for the family.

'This is certainly a lovely flat,' Mireille remarked. 'You keep the place looking immaculate. Are they good employers?'

'Oh yes,' said Yveline turning only slightly.

'And you don't mind the occupation forces being all around?' Mireille probed.

'They don't bother us if we don't bother them.'

Mireille frowned. She had changed. Yveline had always been so fiercely patriotic before but there was an air of resignation about her now.

'When Mari and Zeus were betrayed,' Yveline said reaching for a small tin of cream, 'I knew I'd had enough of the resistance. It was too nerve-wracking.'

'But how on earth did you escape from the Gestapo?'

'You know what they told us,' Yveline said with a nervous laugh. 'Look for an opportune moment.' And judging by the expression on her face, she wasn't going to elaborate. It was a bit unsettling.

'But what of your brother?' Mireille hardly dared to ask.

Again Yveline shook her head and turned back to making the coffee. She had her back to Mireille but everything she was doing was reflected, albeit slightly distorted, in the shining mirror tiles over the hob. Eventually she gave the two coffees a stir and turned towards Mireille. 'Anyway, enough about me; what are you doing in Paris?'

'The Allies are so close now,' Mireille said with a shrug, 'and I want to go home.'

Yveline pushed the two cups of coffee onto the table.

Mireille smiled. 'Thank you. I'm looking forward to this. Do you have any sugar?' As Yveline turned to get it she asked, 'By the way, how did you know it was me at the door?'

'I didn't,' said Yveline placing the sugar bowl in front of her. 'I heard the shooting and then you slumped against the door. It was simply good timing.'

They sipped their coffee. 'Umm, delicious,' said Mireille. She looked up at her friend. 'You haven't asked me about the farm.'

'I try not to think about it,' said Yveline. 'I know the people in the village will hate me for running out on them but I just couldn't do it anymore.'

'Monsieur Lavigne has it now,' Mireille said. 'Because we all thought you were dead, le Maire decided to rent it out to him until your brother is able to return home.'

Yveline nodded. 'Fair enough,' she said bleakly.

'Do you want me to tell them I've seen you?'

'No!' The tone of her voice was so sharp that now they were both a little embarrassed.

Mireille fanned her face with her hand. 'Phew. Is it me or is it hot in here?'

'Drink the rest of your coffee,' said Yveline. 'It'll make you feel better.'

Yveline's cup was already empty by the time Mireille had drained hers. She ran her hand over her forehead. 'Oh dear.'

Conversation had become a little awkward. There were so many questions Mireille wanted to ask but she knew Yveline was as cautious as she was. Her friend's cheeks had a high colour as she leaned back in her chair and opened the drawer under the table. Mireille caught her breath as she saw Yveline put her hand inside and draw out a gun.

Chapter 43

The gun wobbled in Yveline's hand. Mireille's eyes grew wide and she took a deep breath.

'Don't try anything,' Yveline said.

With a horrified look on her face, Mireille made a small sound as she put her own hand to her mouth. 'Oh Yveline, what have you done?'

'You won't die,' she said, blinking hard. 'I put a sedative in your coffee, that's all. In a minute, you'll feel a bit drowsy, so it would be better if you lay on the bed.'

Mireille shook her head slowly. 'I can't believe this,' she said quietly. 'I thought we were friends. I thought you were loyal to France. What happened? Why are you doing this?'

Yveline was rocking herself backwards and forwards. She held the gun unsteadily as she put a shaky hand onto her forehead. Mireille could see beads of perspiration on her top lip. 'I don't need a lecture from you,' she snapped. 'And just because the Allies are here it doesn't mean you've won. France belongs to Germany and there's nothing we can do about it.' She made a small sound as if in pain. 'Now, I'm not telling you again, get up and go to the bedroom.' She attempted to stand herself but sank back down into the chair. 'What's happening to me?'

'You won't die,' said Mireille, repeating Yveline's own words, 'but you will feel drowsy.'

Her ex-friend looked up sharply. 'What?'

'I'm afraid that you drank the coffee you intended for me,' said Mireille.

'But how . . . ?'

'It's a good job you're so house proud, Yveline. There's not a speck of dust anywhere.' Mireille paused. 'You put some powder, presumably the sedative, into my coffee so when you got up to fetch me the sugar, I swapped cups.'

Yveline stared at her with a puzzled expression.

'I saw your reflection on the kettle and the tiles.' Mireille smiled. 'Or should I say, mirror tiles?'

With a small cry Yveline lifted the gun with both hands until it was level with Mireille's chest. She did her best to aim, but she was already having trouble trying to keep her eyes in focus. Her gun was wavering all over the place. In the end she didn't raise an objection as Mireille simply took it from her hand.

'Do you want me to help you into the bedroom?' Mireille said. But at the same moment, with a helpless groan, Yveline fell forward, her head hitting the table with a smack. She was out cold.

Mireille glanced up at the clock. There was still time to deliver her message but she'd better go as quickly as she could. She had no idea if Yveline had managed to tell a third party she was here before she'd opened that door. Stuffing the gun into her pocket, Mireille flew downstairs and across the little courtyard. As she closed the street door behind her that same nosey neighbour was dropping her curtain again.

The streets were quiet now. A couple of bodies lay motionless in the road near where the shooting had started, including the man on the bicycle who had been shot so close to her. His bicycle lay underneath him but Mireille's bicycle was gone. As far as she could see, there was nobody else about but she didn't dare stop to look for it. The church was only about half a mile in the opposite direction.

Slipping a scarf over her head when she arrived on the church steps, Mireille pushed open the big oak doors and went in. It was cool and peaceful inside. After a second or two to collect her thoughts, she walked into the aisle and knelt briefly out of respect for the Sanctuary. As she stood, she looked around but the church appeared to be empty. Oh dear. Was she late . . . too late? Even if she was, she decided to carry out the plan regardless. Walking briskly towards the candle stand, she crossed herself. Then using the flame of one candle, she lit another one but instead of putting it into one of the empty holders, she placed it as far to the right as she could and left it on the stand. Behind her she thought she heard the slightest rustle coming from the confessional box. She didn't look round but a second or two later, she heard the big oak doors open and close.

Mireille sighed. The message (she had no idea what it was) had been delivered and someone in the resistance was on their way to put a plan into action. She sat in the stillness of the church for a while collecting her thoughts. Maybe it wouldn't be long before she could go home again. She had a deep gnawing in her chest; a longing to see her sister and possibly Ginger. It had been so long since she'd seen him. Would it still be the same between them? Would he still want her friendship or would he want more? People met, fell in love and got married; that was the norm, wasn't it? Everybody said how nice he was but she still couldn't think of him in that way. She felt a tear trickle down her cheek and lighting another candle, offered up a prayer.

Her prayer finished, Mireille sat on the nearest pew and

gazed up at the stained-glass windows. She would have to tell someone about Yveline. Her own guess was that her old friend had been the traitor. Zeus had been taken while Yveline was still around, but Mari and the doctor had been arrested long after she'd gone. Was it possible that Yveline had betrayed them to the Germans? Anyway, who'd ever heard of anyone escaping from the Gestapo? Everyone knew the windows on their interrogation rooms were sealed and they were usually on the third or fourth floor of a building so that anyone throwing themselves through the glass would only succeed in falling to their death. It stuck in her throat to think how they'd all been so horribly deceived by Yveline. How could she? How could she?

Mireille could hear the sounds of a crowd gathering outside but this time instead of shots being fired, there were cheers and cries of 'Hourra,' and 'Welcome.' She took in her breath. They were here at last! The Americans and the British! She stood up and turning for a quick kneel, hurried outside. Already hundreds of people were lining the streets. Some waved flags or scarves; some threw flowers into the road; some clapped, their hands high in the air and everybody was cheering as a long line of military vehicles trundled along the Paris streets. The parade began not with the British as she had expected but with members of General Philippe Leclerc's second armoured division of the Free French Army. Every now and then a woman ran from the crowd to give a soldier a flower or a kiss. There was a huge shout of joy as half a dozen German soldiers emerged from a building with their hands in the air. People surged forward to jostle them, spitting on the cobbles in front of them or hurling verbal abuse. After suffering four years of occupation, privation and insult, the Free French Army soldiers who held them captive now struggled to keep angry Parisians at bay.

Mireille set off towards the Hôtel de Ville, which Claude had explained would become the HQ of the National Council of Resistance as soon as the Allies arrived. The crowds were becoming so dense it was hard to push her way through. Everywhere she looked, people had impaled pictures of Hitler and Göring on the railings. Young men and boys were climbing up the lamp posts with the French flag. As she approached the area where Yveline lived there was a sudden commotion. A lone voice, shrill and ireful, shouted so loudly above the cheering all around them that a silence fell. 'That's her. There she is.'

Instinctively Mireille stopped. As she turned towards the voice, she saw the woman who had spied on her as she entered the courtyard with Yveline, the same woman who was watching her when she'd left the building. To Mireille's horror, she was pointing directly at her. 'She's one of them. I saw her. I saw her.'

All at once, Mireille became aware of rough hands and someone propelled her forward. 'You've got this all wrong,' she protested. 'I don't know that woman.'

'Dirty German whore,' screamed the woman and a man standing nearby slapped Mireille's face. The blow was so painful it brought an immediate tear to her eye.

'No, no,' Mireille protested as she struggled to free herself. 'I'm not who you think I am. I love my country. *Vive la France*.'

But nobody was listening. Ducking to avoid other blows, she was unceremoniously bundled through a shop door where several other women, their eyes downcast, sat dejectedly on chairs. Some had their heads shaved, others had cuts and bruises on their bodies. A small child sitting on his mother's lap was sobbing. It was only then that Mireille realised that she was in a barber's shop.

For a moment or two she was stunned, and then it

dawned on her. These women had been fraternising with the Germans. While the rest of their countrymen and women struggled to manage on meagre rations, they had lived well. Although the population of Paris wasn't exactly starving, just about everyone was underweight. Their meagre diet was monotonous and uninspiring so the only way to be able to enjoy a few luxuries was to barter with the enemy and if they didn't have anything worth having, they went without. Childhood illnesses had increased and the tuberculosis rates soared. On the other hand, every dejected-looking woman in the room was well-nourished and well-heeled. The baby was most likely the son of some Nazi soldier.

'I'm not one of them!' Mireille cried desperately. 'Listen to me. You've got this all wrong!'

A woman with a gaunt face and holding a rifle stepped in front of her. 'You can have your hair shaved or have your head blown off,' she said coldly. 'The choice is yours.'

'But I am in the resistance,' Mireille said gulping down a sob.

The woman raised the gun.

Mireille put her hand up in a feeble attempt to protect herself. 'No, no!'

She was suddenly shoved from behind as a man carrying a bulky camera on a tripod pushed his way into the shop. 'Listen Bud,' he said in a pronounced American drawl. 'I'm from Movietone News. The rest of the world will want to see this. Put these gals outside where I can get a decent camera shot.'

The woman already in the barber's chair, her lovely golden hair almost gone, was unceremoniously dragged outside and onto the street. They pulled a bench onto the cobbles and stood a chair on the top of it then she was told to climb up and sit. The man with the camera set it up in front of her and a crowd quickly gathered. One lock of curls hung below her left ear, and the top of her head was covered in scratches where the barber hadn't been too kind. Mireille watched, horrified, as the barber snipped it off and then began to use some clippers.

When it was done, the crowd clapped and cheered. The woman was told to get down from the bench and stand on another chair. She did as she was told, keeping her head down and her eyes lowered. They spat in her face and jeered until another girl, defiant and angry, was hauled onto the bench and made to sit on the chair. The Movietone camera man whirled away, getting shot after shot. The barber; his shears; the victim; the other women, including Mireille, awaiting their fate; the jeering crowd; the children standing around, their mouths open in horror.

As the defiant woman climbed down, she tossed her head and smiled for the camera, incensing those around her. Like a pack of wild animals, the women pounced on her, tearing at her clothes and beating her with their fists.

When it was her turn, Mireille was still trying to make them understand she wasn't a collaborator.

'Please,' she cried helplessly. 'You can't do this to me.'

'Shut your mouth whore,' shouted her accuser. 'Don't deny it. I saw you with that other bitch.'

'Yes, but . . .' Mireille began but then the woman with the gun snarled in her ear. 'Your choice. Hair off or head off.'

And in that moment Mireille knew she had no choice.

Chapter 44

Hugh Slater, always affectionately known as Ginger, had had a very busy couple of months. He'd known D-Day was coming and when it finally got underway, it meant long hours and a lot of hard work for the ground crew in RAF Tangmere. When he finally got a forty-eight-hour pass the first weekend in September, it was too far to travel to his home in Yorkshire so he made his way to Worthing and Norah and Jim's place. Norah had given him an open invitation so he had no qualms about dropping in whenever he could.

They were delighted to see him and of course made him very welcome. As luck would have it, Lennard and Amélie were also around for the same weekend and as soon as Ginger heard that they were engaged, they all decided to make an occasion of it.

'Have you heard from M . . . ?' Lennard began but Amélie touched his arm and shook her head so nothing more was said.

Little Terry was already crawling around the furniture and he took to Ginger straight away. His favourite game became sitting on Ginger's foot and being tossed up high.

Mrs Steele looked a little more frail but she joined in the fun like the trouper she was.

On the Friday evening, they went to the Richard Cobden (all except Norah of course who was babysitting her son) for a few drinks and then they came back to play cards and swapped their D-Day stories. They began with a game of Rummy.

'I was surprised to hear that you went to Portsmouth,' Ginger told Amélie. 'I didn't have you down as the adventurous type.'

'I think I surprised myself,' she said dealing everybody seven cards, 'but I gained such a lot from the experience.' She glanced up at Lennard and gave him a shy smile. 'Some of those boys have a long road ahead.'

Ginger nodded. 'And what about you Lennard? Busy?'

'As a matter of fact I am,' said Lennard. 'It gets a little difficult when you have to keep a check on men who are in the battlefield. Most of their pay goes straight into the post office but things can change moment by moment and the army doesn't want me banking a soldier's pay only to have to claw it back because he was killed a month ago. It certainly keeps us on our toes.' He smiled at his friend. 'What about you? Busy, busy, busy?'

'We had an interesting start to the invasion,' Ginger said matter-of-factly. 'The control tower got taken.'

The card game paused in mid-air and everybody stared at Ginger who was arranging and re-arranging his cards with a passive expression on his face. They all knew him well enough to know there was a pretty good story coming up . . . or maybe it was only a yarn. You could never tell when Ginger was concerned.

'Got taken?' Jim said eventually. 'You mean by the enemy?'

Ginger nodded. 'We were pretty busy,' he went on, 'but once the main group had gone, I was watching the planes going over. Bloody hundreds of them.' He paused for effect. 'Then all at once we saw a group of about six or eight soldiers with Bren guns rush inside the control tower. When they burst in, they were yelling their heads off. Terrifying, I can tell you.'

Everyone waited with bated breath. Was he talking about a German invasion on British soil? There had been nothing of this in the papers, nor on the radio.

'So what happened next?' Norah gasped.

Ginger kept his eyes down and ran his tongue over his lips. He was clearly enjoying the re-telling of the tale. 'Well, they demanded that the Brigadier surrender in the name of the King.'

The rest of the family looked from one to the other with puzzled expressions.

'Surrender in the name of the King?' said Christine laying down a card. 'What king?'

'Ours,' Ginger said mysteriously.

'You're pulling our legs,' Lennard said picking up the Jack of hearts.

'Oh no I'm not, squire,' said Ginger. 'Our boys had all gone over in gliders to attack the Germans from the rear but there was a wind change see, and the pilot slipped them too soon. So when they landed the glider, they all thought they were in France, and when somebody spotted the control tower, they captured it.'

There was a moment of silence then everyone burst out laughing. 'You're joking,' said Jim.

'Nope,' said Ginger emphatically. 'It's as true as I'm sitting here. Anyway, it all turned out okay, although the CO was so scared he burst into tears.'

'I don't blame him,' said Norah, laying down a card. 'Just imagine how awful it would have been if they'd gone in with all guns blazing.'

It was Amélie's turn and she took a card from the pack before laying it straight back down again. 'Are they going to get into trouble?' she asked.

'That'll be one for the history books,' said Jim, re-arranging the cards in his hand.

Ginger shook his head. 'I doubt it. It'll be all hushed up. You mark my words.'

Christine wiped her eyes. 'What happened to the soldiers, once they all realised their mistake, I mean?'

'We loaded them back into the gliders,' said Ginger, 'and as soon as somebody was available, we shipped them back over to France. There you are,' he added, revealing his hand. 'Rummy. Three sixes and the ten, Jack, Queen and King of diamonds.'

The next day, they had planned a picnic but the weather was not kind. It was blustery with an overcast sky and the threat of rain, so after a short walk in the morning pushing Terry in his pram, they all met at the dinner table to enjoy some vegetable turnovers Norah had made. Having cleared up the kitchen for her, while Christine went into her room for a rest and Jim settled down with his paper, Lennard, Amélie and Ginger decided to catch the afternoon show at the pictures. Norah preferred to be with Jim so the others set off at two o'clock. *Double Indemnity* was showing at the Gaumont. It starred Barbara Stanwyck, Fred MacMurray and Edward G. Robinson and the girls at the hospital had said it was a terrific film. They were a bit late because the 'B' movie, a British made comedy called *The Way Ahead,* staring David Niven and Stanley Holloway, was already underway. When it finished and the lights went up, a pretty girl dressed in a short pink and white checked skirt and apron stood in front of the screen with a tray of ice creams. Lennard got to his feet to buy one and while he queued, Amélie nipped to the ladies'. The ice cream was lovely and very welcome because the auditorium was hazy with blue cigarette smoke and her throat was dry.

Before the main feature, there were some advertisements, then came the Fox Movietone News. Pictures of the liberation of Paris dominated the coverage. They smiled as they saw deliriously happy people cheering the troops along Les Champs-Élysées. Women were throwing flowers onto the armoured cars and climbing aboard the tanks to kiss the American soldiers. Men climbed the lamp posts and hauled the French flag to the top. It was such a happy occasion but then came a darker side. The camera man had filmed a group of women who had fraternised with the enemy and the commentator explained that they had been the prostitutes and mistresses of the German elite. Humiliated and exposed, the French people were taking their revenge by shaving their heads. As the excited crowds gathered, one woman was made to climb onto a chair placed on a table. At the same moment, Ginger dropped his ice cream onto his trouser leg and Lennard was distracted as well. While the two men set about mopping up the ice cream, Amélie's eyes were still fixed on the screen.

As the accused woman turned to sit on the chair and meekly face her accusers, Amélie took in a loud breath. 'That's my sister!' she said in a strangled whisper. 'That's Mireille.'

Lennard looked up but already the picture had changed. 'Where?'

'That was her,' said Amélie, her eyes bright with unshed tears. 'Didn't you see her? She was on that chair.'

Now Ginger had turned his attention back to the screen. 'What's up?'

'My sister. Mireille. She was there.'

The woman in front of them turned around angrily. 'Shhh!'

Lennard apologised and the three of them continued watching the screen but the commentator had already turned to another subject. The Canadians were mass producing a wonder drug called penicillin which had already saved the lives of countless injured soldiers, sailors and airmen and the fact that the British public had moved from the blackout to dim-out. People would still have to be careful but from now on, there would be a few street lights at night time.

As the Movietone News finished, Amélie leaned forward. 'Did you see her, Ginger?'

Ginger shook his head. 'It might have looked like her but it wasn't,' he whispered. 'It couldn't have been. She's not like that.'

'I know she isn't,' Amélie retorted, 'but it was her. I know it was.'

'Darling,' Lennard said softly, 'those women were traitors to France. Surely you don't think . . .'

'Of course I don't think Mireille is a traitor but it was her, I tell you!'

The woman in front of them turned right around. 'If you lot don't shut up,' she snapped, 'I shall ask the manager to chuck you out.'

Once again Lennard apologised and the woman turned back huffily. Amélie waited for a moment or two then jumped to her feet and left the auditorium. The two men followed. Outside in the foyer, she had burst into tears.

As Lennard comforted her, the manager came up to them. 'Is there something wrong, Miss?' he asked, giving Lennard a suspicious stare.

'She's upset because she thought she saw her sister on the screen,' Ginger said.

'I did!' Amélie cried. 'It was her. Don't you think I know my own sister?'

The manager offered them a free cup of tea in the tea rooms downstairs and although the men weren't too keen, Amélie accepted.

Having accompanied them to the tea rooms, the manager explained to the waitress that 'the lady had been upset by something on the screen, so she didn't have to pay.' As they sat at a table, Ginger suggested going home but Amélie was having none of it. 'We have to see the news again,' she said doggedly. 'Don't you see? You keep telling me I'm wrong so I have to make sure.'

'That seems like a sensible idea,' the manager agreed. 'It'll put your mind at rest.'

'Well, I've never met her,' Lennard reminded them. 'All I've seen is that one photograph you have.'

'And I wasn't looking properly,' said Ginger. 'I dropped my ice cream on my trousers.'

As soon as the manager left, Ginger turned to Amélie. 'I can't believe you're doing this.'

'Well, I'm not making it up,' Amélie insisted.

'I'm not saying you are,' said Ginger, 'but I just don't believe Mireille went all that way to France just to sleep with a German.'

Amélie hung her head. Put like that, Ginger was right, but it was Mireille . . . It was . . . It was her . . . wasn't it?

The next couple of hours were unbearable. They went back into the theatre just before the end of the 'B' feature, the manager giving them seats near the side fire door exit, in a spot which was not very popular with audiences.

When the Movietone News began again, they all sat with their eyes locked to the screen. As the story about penicillin rounded off for a second time, the three of them made their way outside.

Amélie was very quiet. Ginger seemed to be in a state of shock.

'Well?' said the manager.

'It seems I owe the lady an apology,' Ginger said dejectedly. 'That woman was her sister.'

Chapter 45

The past few days had been very traumatic for Mireille. She was cold, her clothes were damp and her feet were sore. Her treatment at the hands of the mob had been very upsetting. No one would listen to her protestations of innocence. In fact the more she tried to tell them, the more aggressive they became so in the end she just gave up.

She and the other women in the barber's shop had been paraded through the streets of Paris for most of the afternoon. They'd been jostled, pushed, pinched, punched and spat on. Mireille's head was sore because the barber was none too careful with his razor and like the others, her clothes were torn. At one point, someone relieved her of her shoes so now she was barefoot.

When the crowd finally let them all go, the other women went off, leaving Mireille alone. It was only as night fell that she realised how desperate her plight was. She had nowhere to go. She knew no one in the city. Her handbag had been in the basket of her now missing bicycle. It had contained all her papers and her money but of course everything was gone so she had no proof of who she was, albeit with the code name of Françoise. She had no food and the Parisians made it very clear that they had no intension of sharing their precious rations with a bald-headed collaborator. She had nowhere to sleep except a doorway and even then the police moved her on every few hours. Her only covering was a piece of discarded sacking she'd found near the market. Even in her sorry state, men propositioned her. She managed to resist or fight them off but every time it happened she collected another bruise or two.

Mireille found the Hôtel de Ville which Claude had told her would become the headquarters of the French Resistance once the Germans had gone. The building itself was iconic. Once the headquarters of the French Revolution, the fourteenth-century building had been the backdrop to public executions by guillotine during the Reign of Terror. A hundred years later, it was the meeting place of the Paris Commune, and then in 1940, it went under the Nazi jackboot.

There was no way she could just waltz in as she was, but something told her to hang around for a bit. Why not? She had nowhere else to go. If only she could simply walk up to the door and announce that a member of SOE was here, but of course, it was well guarded and she couldn't even get close. By now she was in a bad way. Desperately hungry, stinking to high heaven and feeling quite ill, she spent the day watching the people who went inside. Her only hope, and it was a very slim chance, was to see someone she recognised.

But late that afternoon, her luck changed. A car drew up by the door and a man climbed out. Although he was a hundred yards or so away from her, Mireille recognised him immediately. It was Parker, the man who had interviewed her in London and he was with Major de Wesselow. She rose to her feet and staggered towards them but a British soldier barred her way.

'Clear off,' he said roughly. 'No place for you here.'

Desperately trying to see over the soldier's bulk, she shouted his name, 'Parker! Major de Wesselow, help me.'

Parker stopped and turned around but it was obvious he was having trouble in sourcing where the voice was coming from. Summoning every ounce of strength she had left, Mireille tried to move the soldier but only succeeded in landing on the pavement as he shoved her away.

'No, no,' she cried in English. 'I must see him. Major de Wesselow!'

The soldier was stunned to hear his own tongue but did nothing to help her. Major de Wesselow must have heard her shout but he'd dropped some papers and was busily trying to pick them up. Parker had disappeared into the hotel foyer. Mireille tried to stand but in her weakened state, she couldn't do it. A small sob of frustration fell from her lips and in that moment she knew she was lost. She wouldn't last more than a couple of more days without help and already she was feeling dizzy and sick. She was going to die here, wasn't she? She was so close to going home but it may as well have been a million miles away.

Her head was muzzy but as she closed her eyes in surrender, she felt a firm hand on her shoulder. Then just before everything went black, she heard the sweetest words she ever heard in her whole life. 'Mireille Osborne, is that you?'

Chapter 46

Mireille leaned back in her deck chair and adjusted her sunhat so that she could rest her head. The sun was warm and apart from the occasional car, it was quiet. As she closed her eyes she could hear the cry of the gulls and the sound of willow on wood. A cricket match. She smiled to herself. How quintessentially English.

After the wartime success of the football match, the summer cricket match between the Bobbys and Tommys had become an annual event although there was every possibility that this could be the last one. Now that peace had come to Europe, the vast majority of the service forces were being disbanded and people were returning to their roots or moving on to the far flung places they called home. It was time to put the past six years behind them and think of the future. Before long, she was going to have to make the same kind of decision for herself.

When Major de Wesselow had spotted her outside the Hôtel de Ville, he had undoubtedly saved her life. She had come round long enough to see the alarm on the faces of the hotel staff when he had helped her through the doors and she had since discovered that the man she'd only known

362

as Parker was in fact Selwyn Jepson, an actor turned author who ran the London office of SOE.

When the major explained to the hotel staff that she too was a member of SOE, she had been given the star treatment. He'd seen to it that she had a bath and someone ferreted around for some clothes because her own things were only fit for the boiler. She was given a light meal; she hadn't eaten for at least four days and anything more was likely to make her ill. After that, Parker summoned a doctor who insisted she go to hospital because the razor wounds on her head were infected and there was a very real danger of blood poisoning. Mireille was taken to a private clinic where she was given bed rest for ten days and a course of a new wonder drug called penicillin.

Once recovered she had gone back to the Hôtel de Ville to give her employer a briefing. It upset her deeply to talk about Yveline but it had to be done. It turned out that her old friend had been responsible for the deaths of several agents and now she was passing herself off as a champion of the resistance.

'There's going to be a war crimes tribunal,' Parker told her, 'where the Germans will be brought to book but I am pushing for the civil courts to deal with other traitors. People like Yveline mustn't be allowed to get away with what they've done, but we cannot leave them to the rule of the mob. That will lead to anarchy and then we shall be no better than they.'

Yveline had been arrested and was being held in a Paris prison. Over the next few days, Mireille and Claude made sworn affidavits but Yveline never did have her day in court. One morning when the guards unlocked her cell, they found her hanging from the bars on the window. The incident was never properly investigated – lack of staff, the police tied up with other duties, so they said. Mireille was left to wonder if Yveline had planned her own death or if some French patriot had given her a 'helping hand', but she would never know for sure.

When she came back home in October 1944, Mireille was more than a little anxious about meeting her sister and the others. She was ashamed to have treated them so badly and had even gone as far as rehearsing a speech to that effect.

Everything looked just the same when she walked up Clifton Road from the station. For a moment or two it was almost as if she'd never been away. When she got to the Lilacs, she went round the back. Empty boxes were scattered around the yard and the washing was flapping on the line. A little flaxen-haired boy was playing with a toy train by the back door. She turned towards the shed expecting to see Ivan sitting in the dilapidated old armchair having a ciggy but the chair was empty. Max came out of the kitchen door with a short bark which immediately turned into a hysterical whine. He rushed at her jumping up and twisting his body this way and that as she came towards him. Sausage followed and was just as pleased to see her. The little boy stood to his feet and stared with a quizzical expression. When she heard the commotion outside, Norah came to the door wiping her hands on her apron.

'Mireille!' she cried. 'Oh darling, you're home.'

She swept Mireille into her arms and began to call for Amélie. A moment later the two sisters were in each other's arms, laughing and crying at the same time. Christine soon joined them, hugging Mireille so hard she thought she would suffocate. All Mireille's apologies were swept aside and it brought a lump to her throat to realise that they were all genuinely delighted to see her.

As things settled down, Mireille was upset to hear that

poor Ivan had died but she loved Jim and Norah's little Terry from the moment she saw him. Although shy at first, he was soon following Auntie 'Meyall' everywhere she went. As for Linnet, it was obvious that despite all their efforts, neither of the girls had managed to track her down. Mireille had even written to Maurice Buckmaster the controller of SOE. She knew he had many influential friends in high places and so it wasn't such a long shot that he might know someone who could help. The friend Lennard had spoken about turned out to be his cousin Selwyn Jepson, Parker to Mireille, but even he drew a blank. Linnet would never know her sisters were alive and pining for her.

Mireille had to be frugal with what she told the family about her time in France because, of course, she was still subject to the Official Secrets Act but she did go so far as to explain that being classed as a collaborator was a case of mistaken identity and that Major de Wesselow had told her that she would be in line for some sort of medal for what she had done for France.

It was obvious that the whole family was so proud of what she had done. After a couple of weeks' recuperation at the Lilacs, Mireille reported for duty back at Tangmere. Dizzy-the-Lizard had gone, sacked for embezzling some funds if you please, so Mireille was invited to step into her shoes as Group Officer for the duration.

At Christmas, and back home on leave, she had a lot of catching up to do. Amélie was engaged, not to Bob as Mireille had supposed, but to Lennard. He was a lovely man who clearly adored her sister. Amélie had finished her training and was now a fully-fledged State Registered Nurse but sadly, once she married, she wouldn't be allowed to continue with her nursing in hospital. It didn't matter too much anyway. Lennard was exploring a plan to buy a house with some inheritance money and set up a home for wayward boys. Thus, Amélie's skills would be needed, although perhaps to a lesser extent, when their babies came along.

And now that they'd reached July 1945, their wedding was only a few weeks away now and she couldn't wait to be Amélie's chief bridesmaid.

As for Mireille herself, her much-anticipated meeting with Ginger turned out to be far less awkward than she'd feared.

'I felt as sick as a pig when I saw you on the Movietone News,' he told her. 'It's such a relief to know than you're all right.'

They had met in the pub a few days before Christmas and Mireille was absentmindedly running her finger around the edge of her sherry glass. 'I can't tell you what I was doing in Paris,' she explained, 'but I can promise you that I was never a Nazi mistress.'

'I never for one moment thought you were,' said Ginger, glancing up at her hair. 'What they did to you, it was barbaric.'

She now wore her hair in a bob, which was very chic. Mireille nodded and they fell silent. 'Ginger,' she began again. 'About us . . .'

'It's okay,' he interrupted. 'I know what you're going to say.'

She looked up at him and their eyes met. 'You're a great guy,' she began again, 'but . . .'

'I'm not the one you want.' He finished the sentence for her. 'I think I knew that all along. I just didn't want to admit it, that's all.'

'It's my fault,' she said, hating herself for sounding so pathetic, 'not yours.'

He reached out and touched her hand. 'I know and I appreciate that. Really, I do.'

'I hope you find the girl of your dreams,' she added. 'I'm sure you will and I want to thank you for being the best friend a girl could ever have.'

They'd parted as friends and although she knew she would most likely never see him again, in the spring of 1945, she heard on the grapevine that he was getting married to a girl called Thelma.

On VE Day Mireille found herself alone in Worthing. Norah and Christine were getting everything ready for a bit of a bash later that afternoon but from eleven o'clock, Mireille would be on parade for the last time by the town hall.

The excitement had begun the night before when she and Amélie had been part of the impromptu crowd which had gathered near the pier. As the news came through that the war in Europe was finally at an end, people poured out of their houses and onto the streets. It was easy to find street hawkers hanging around the town centre with bunting and flags to buy and all the shops were decorated in red, white and blue. As the numbers of people swelled, the singing began. People cheered, slapped each other on the back and drank to the health of Mr Churchill. The noise from the revellers lasted far into the night although the two sisters didn't stay long. Amélie was on duty the next day and she didn't have a late pass.

Mireille woke up to a dull day weather-wise but the party mood lingered. The new Town Hall was the focal point for the day where a purple and gold dais had been set up for local dignitaries. She marched with other uniformed servicemen and women and stood to attention. At eleven a trumpeter sounded a fanfare which was followed by a speech from the mayor, Councillor Shalders. With the official stuff done, it was time for the party to get underway. There was little point in going back home because she had to march again at two so she joined the crowds in South Street and Montague Place where servicemen and civilians were dancing. Army trucks, packed to the gunnels with party goers drove around the town gathering more people to the focal point near the pier.

Mireille joined the rest of the service personnel at one forty-five and they marched around the streets finishing up back at the new Town Hall at the junction of Chapel Road and South Street. At three o'clock, people clustered around the loudspeakers to hear Winston Churchill's speech. As he finished, a great cheer went up then the buglers of the Scots Guards sounded the Cease Fire.

Mireille was dismissed but she hung around until late afternoon, walking along the prom and finally sitting in a deck chair by Victoria Park, before she made her way back to the Lilacs. When she walked into the kitchen, the whole family was gathered, including her sister and every eye was on her.

Puzzled, she looked around. 'What?'

Lennard smiled. 'Can you sit at the table?'

'Why?' she said. 'What's happened?'

'We have a surprise for you,' said Norah and Mireille saw Jim nudge her arm sharply.

'What sort of surprise?' Mireille repeated, but nobody answered.

Lennard motioned her to sit next to Amélie but when Mireille looked at her for some sort of explanation, her sister only shrugged her shoulders. It seemed she was as much in the dark as she was.

'Is it something to do with our grandparents?' asked Amélie. 'Have you found them?'

Lennard shook his head. 'I'm still working on that one,' he said, 'but I'm hopeful that I can find your English family.'

As Mireille lowered herself onto the kitchen chair next to Amélie, Lennard leaned over and placed an envelope in front of them. The two girls looked down. It was addressed to the both of them, an air mail letter, light as a feather and covered with foreign-looking stamps. Amélie frowned.

'They're South African stamps,' Mireille mused.

Her sister took in her breath sharply. 'Linnet?' she whispered.

Mireille turned the envelope over and they stared at the address on the back.

'"From Miss L. Osborne."' Amélie took in her breath again. 'It *is* from Linnet.'

Mireille looked up at Lennard. 'You've found our sister!' she said incredulously.

Lennard smiled and nodded. 'With the help of Major de Wesselow.'

Mireille's shoulders were shaking. Amélie reached for a table knife and slid it under the flap. When she opened the envelope, she pulled out a single sheet of paper, her hand trembling as she unfolded it. There was a single word on the page. 'Hello.'

The two sisters glanced at each other, totally confused. When they looked up at the family again, Lennard and Jim were standing shoulder to shoulder and everybody was smiling.

'What's this about?' Amélie asked.

The two men stepped to one side to reveal someone standing behind them. A small young woman, aged sixteen, beautifully bronzed with honey-coloured hair and a brilliant smile emerged. 'Hello,' she said. 'I'm Lillian.'

Amélie covered her mouth with her hand and let out a small sob while Mireille jumped to her feet, knocking her chair backwards with a bang.

For a second or two, everyone in the room froze, then the three sisters who had been parted one from the other for more than a decade, fell sobbing with joy into each other's arms.

Acknowledgements

I am so grateful to the Avon team for their encouragement and help to make this book the best it could be, especially my editor Cara Chimirri. A big, big thank you to my agent Juliet Burton who is absolutely brill and I would never have managed it without the love and support of my long-suffering husband who is still waiting for his tea!

Two sisters. One secret.
A daring wartime journey . . .

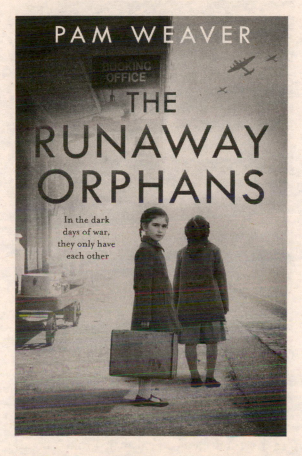

PAM WEAVER

THE
RUNAWAY
ORPHANS

In the dark
days of war,
they only have
each other

Will they find the strength to confront what they have
been running from, when their past finally catches up
with them?

Can she be brave enough to follow her heart?

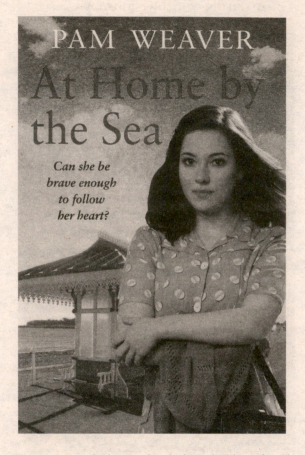

PAM WEAVER

At Home by the Sea

Can she be brave enough to follow her heart?

Can a second chance heal their broken family?

Can love find a way to overcome hate?

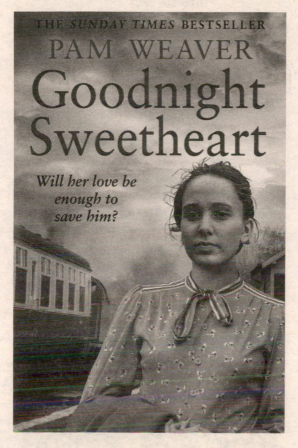

THE *SUNDAY TIMES* BESTSELLER

PAM WEAVER

Goodnight Sweetheart

*Will her love be
enough to
save him?*

A moving, thought-provoking story, perfect for fans of
Katie Flynn and Maureen Lee.

An unexpected letter will change her
life forever . . .

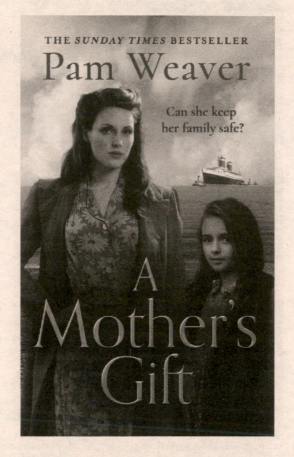

THE *SUNDAY TIMES* BESTSELLER

Pam Weaver

Can she keep
her family safe?

A
Mother's
Gift

A dramatic story filled with family, scandal and
friendships that bring hope in the darkness.

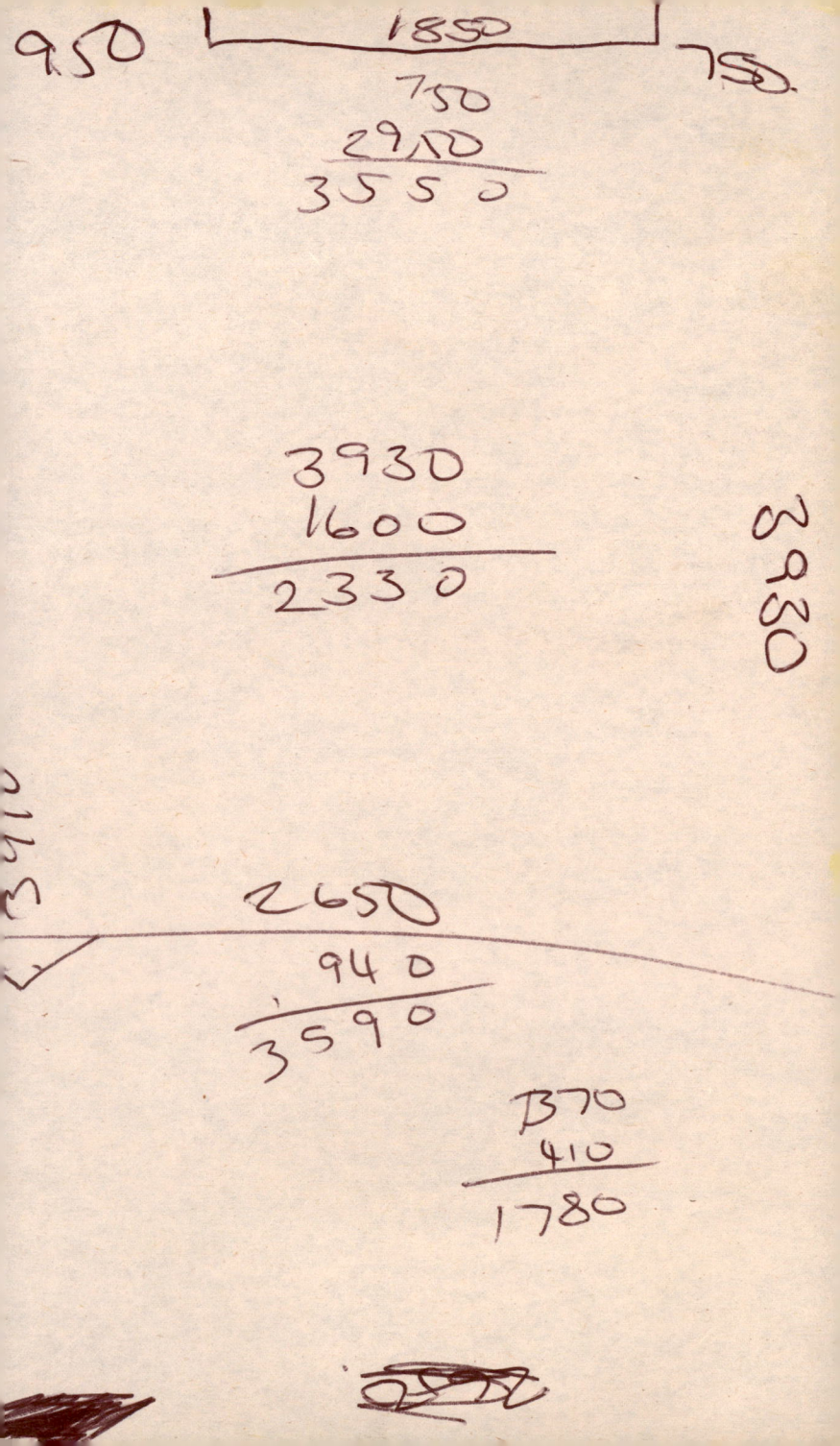